Praise for Faith O'Shea

Faith O'Shea is a contemporary women's literature writer who loves writing about romance, magic, conviction, and loyalty, with strong women and the friendships they build. She has created many series of stories to make us laugh, cry and feel empowered and writes in a voice that speaks to women of all ages. Faith believed there were subjects and life that needed to be written about. ~ Loyce M.

I truly love the Everyday Goddess series. The strong, leading women characters, in this day and age, are inspiring to me and keep me coming back for more! The books are light, fun, extremely relatable and I can't put them down! ~ Kathryn B.

I just finished the Fire and Ice series. It had romance, strong friendships between the women characters and complex stories that were clearly very well researched. Loved all of them and looking forward to the goddess series next! ~ Gail N.

Oh wow! I just finished reading the *Magic Bean Café* and I must say that I was hooked from the first chapter and loved every page. The characters were full and believable. The child, Willow, had my heart with her wild imagination, gift of laughter, and the way she melted Aisin's heart and helped him to realize that you can love a child that wasn't yours. Thank you for gifting me this awesome read. ~ Your newest fan, Carol F. ❤

Magic Bean Café is a fantastic book of compassion for others with realistic characters. Plus a generous millionaire to help fulfill dreams. ~ Belinda

Books by Faith O'Shea

The Greenliner Series
Four baseball players, one team on the rise

Thrown for a Curve
League of Her Own
Clutch Hit
Out in Left Field

The Scalera Family Series
Five boisterous Italian siblings, five ways to find love

Cold Sweat
Edge of Forever
Thin Blue Line
Coming Home to You
Finding Joy

Scalera Family

Five boisterous Italian siblings, five ways to find love

Cold Sweat

Johnny's the oldest, drummer for the heavy metal band Raging Thunder. The man knows how to rock and roll and thinks he's just the one who can teach Letitia Jones, a classically trained pianist, everything there is to know about life but when the tables are turned, he runs scared. Will he come to realize that settling down, isn't the worse thing in life that can happen?

Edge of Forever

Rissa's sketches of Luca Caroli, bassist for her brother's band, are uncovering edges, and revealing things meant to stay hidden. He's not what he seems and she's beginning to think he might be her forever. Problem is, he's stuck in the past. What can she do to align the stars in her favor?

Thin Blue Line

Lana, the youngest, never got over her father's death, and swore she'd never marry a cop. Her mother had paid the ultimate price for loving such a man. So how did she find herself married to Zachary Taylor, a cop, who's more than willing to put his life on the line every second of every day? If she sacrifices him now, will it save her grief in the end?

Coming Home to You

Tony is his father's son, with a badge and a gun, but he's not going to leave a widow behind like his father did. When he takes Tansy McPhail under his wing, and gives her shelter, he thinks he's just doing some community service. How long will it take for him to see, that his place isn't a home, without her?

Finding Joy

Dennis has been married before and has no plans on walking that aisle again so when he meets the sexy diva Artemis, under protest, he has no illusions. But as he works to produce her new record, he finds she's more than the tabloids have led the public to believe. She's warm and funny and down-to-earth, but she's still Artemis to him, not Joy Munroe. Does he have what it would take, to win her love?

COLD SWEAT

Scalera Family
Book 1

FAITH O'SHEA

Cover Design By Jaycee DeLorenzo at Sweet 'N Spicy Designs
Formatting and Interior Design by Woven Red Authors Services, www.wovenRed.ca

Cold Sweat/Faith O'Shea—1st Edition
ISBN: 978-0-9987229-1-7

www.faithoshea.com

Printed in U.S.A.

To My Readers

Thank you so much for choosing *Cold Sweat* to spend your time with. I love curling up with a good book, and have read my fair share of romance novels and love the way they make me feel.

I have finally given the characters living in my head a chance to speak out, tell me who they are, what they want and what they need. I loved working with Tish and Johnny and I hope you enjoyed their journey as much as I did.

My second book is at the editor and I hope to have it out before the end of the year. Rissa Scalera is the one at loose ends and will be joining Raging Thunder for their summer tour. She's not looking for love out on the road but when she follows her urges, she just might find it.

Please feel free to contact me at website www.faithoshea.com and follow me on Facebook and Twitter.

Faith

CHAPTER ONE

As soon as the elevator doors opened Letitia Jones ran as if the hounds of hell were at her heels. She brushed her hair back, her eyes darted to every corner of the deserted hallway, as the dread mounted. She knuckled her tears away for lack of a tissue before putting trembling fingers to the task of opening the door. She was taking more time than she would have liked and her head snapped around as she re-checked the elegant hallway making sure there were no witnesses to her break-in, the shaking making it almost impossible to align the key with the hole. Finally gaining entrance to the well-appointed condo, she pushed the door closed with both hands, throwing the dead bolt to the left. Her pulse raced and her limbs wobbled as she leaned her head against the ingrained wood.

Then she sank to the floor.

She had escaped.

She was safe.

For now.

She hadn't felt that way in a long time and as much as she wanted to breathe it in, she couldn't get past the lump in her throat. Pressing at the blinding ache at her temple, she tried to relax her quaking body, but the madness that consumed her didn't allow that luxury.

Up at dawn, unable to sleep, after hours of staring at her bedroom ceiling, she had moved through her mother's condo with the quiet footsteps only the disheartened could accomplish. The routine her mother set for her never deviated so Letitia knew the exact time she would become a slave to the piano.

After hours of mind numbing play, she heard the distinct click of heels and the critique of the sonata she was still trying to reassemble in her mind.

"Not your finest, Letitia. Mozart must be rolling over in his grave."

Her mother stood at the baby grand, dressed in a Just Cavalli sheath that didn't quite fit with her age or body type. Letitia knew better than to offer her opinion.

Weary, she replied, "I know Mother. I'm doing the best I can."

Veins pulsed in Madeleine's rigid neck.

"I disagree. You are doing this on purpose, although I don't understand why."

Letitia rested her hands in her lap, her fingers laced together. "I'm not Mother. I'll keep working on it."

Leaning down to be at eye level with her daughter, missing the despair Letitia couldn't keep from her face, her mother admonished, "That would be smart. Your tour starts in September and you're nowhere near ready."

Unable to meet those steely hazel eyes, the goldish tinge adding depth, Letitia answered, "I'm not sure—"

"I think you need help. I know one of the board specialists at Mass Mental. How about I have you committed? How does that sound?"

Her eyes shot up.

"I don't need psychiatric services, Mother."

"Then what do you need, Letitia? You have everything you want right in your hands but you're throwing away our chance at greatness. That's crazy, don't you think? It just proves you need some type of help."

Letitia rubbed circles into throbbing temples. "I need some sleep. And a break from the migraines."

"I'm sure Mass Mental could accommodate you."

Pushing her arms through the sleeves of her three-quarter jacket, Madeleine Jones looked at her daughter and said, "I expect that sonata to sound like Mozart intended when I return. If not, I'm making that call."

"Yes, Mother."

With that Madeleine slipped out into the hallway, heading for the elevator and the limo that would take her to her luncheon engagement.

With the final click of the door, Letitia allowed the tears to fall.

Why was it always about what her mother wanted?

Just once, she'd like to be listened to, acknowledged, maybe even hugged.

But her feelings never mattered.

In her demeaning tone, her mother stated that they shouldn't have any bearing on her abilities.

"You've been playing since you were a child. Precision should be instinctual by now."

Madeleine thought Letitia was merely refusing to cooperate and blamed it on the stubborn streak she'd inherited from her father. Disdain dripped from her voice as she explained that Oscar Jones found out soon enough that it didn't work. Madeleine had told both father and daughter they'd be nothing without her. If they didn't put her on the pedestal she deserved, they paid for it.

Since her father's death, Letitia had become invisible, shrinking into a nonentity in Madeleine's quest for glory. Her mother had the uncanny ability of pushing the right buttons of guilt, fear, and shame before bulldozing over her daughter to achieve her objective. The result hadn't been what Madeleine wanted.

Instead, Letitia had lost her music and her soul.

She had to get away.

Her life depended on it.

There were two ways to go, one she refused to consider.

Now all but hidden in the overstuffed chair in her agent's study, Letitia chewed her thumb nail and waited. It had only been a few hours since she'd liberated herself from the confines of her mother's residence. She didn't know how much longer she'd be able to sit frozen. Her insides swirled in agitation. The solitude had been needed but the threat of her mother banging on the door grew with each passing minute. Her whole life was an anchor around her neck, drowning her in the depths of hopelessness. Letitia had hoped to feel safe at Diana's but fear had followed in right behind her.

She needed to sleep, to dream, strength winning out over weakness, clarity over blurriness, peace over chaos.

Her mother's words came back to her. Those that taunted and those that praised. Letitia never knew which she was going to get.

The compliments raised her hopes that she was interpreting the music correctly.

"You are so talented, my dear girl, one of the most talented pianists the world has ever known."

But then the cutting criticisms would slice through her, bringing her to the depths of despair.

"You are my worst failure by far, Letitia Marie. How could you be so selfish, so irresponsible? You are certainly not the daughter I deserve."

The slurs came much more often lately and although Letitia had tried to rectify the opinion with every keystroke, she had only ended up magnifying the truth of her mother's statement.

"We could be the highlight of the concert series if you would just be a good girl and do what you're told. When will you learn I only want what's best for you? You need to practice getting it right. Why can't you ever get it right?"

The words echoed in her head.

A multitude of harsh critics lived and breathed there too, picking up where Madeleine left off, pointing out where Letitia failed and how she wasn't up to the task of virtuoso extraordinaire.

Her mother's disapproval hovered like a merciless raincloud, threatening, dark, never giving way to light. Letitia drowned in the outburst, rawness seeping into her marrow, chilling her bones.

The toxic verbal assault would begin as soon as her mother found her here at Diana's. With ruthless abandon, her mother would continue to excavate for a talent that had been stripped away.

Or, maybe, she'd get the cold shoulder, instead, the steel curtain that ostracized her in silent disdain.

She wasn't sure which was worse. When the silence came, the inner critic would take over, disparage her performance, her lack of grace, her inability to think. It was more destructive in its assessment than Madeleine Jones was.

There was no way to get away from her mother if Madeleine lived in her head. And she was always there in form, thought, opinion.

Letitia had fought against the disparaging remarks, but she was empty now, unable to fill the gaping hole that had once been overflowing with her music. Without it, she had no fire with which to fight, no means of expressing who she was. This lost sense of self was the one debilitating outcome of her mother's vindictiveness that Letitia couldn't overcome.

She had become trapped in a life of dead ends.

Tears streamed down her face, her arms too cumbersome to move, her fingers too sore to bend. Moisture tickled her ear and slipped down her neck. The drops were cool and familiar, sliding down the tracks that had become embedded over the years. She gave in to the release.

The drip of the faucet from the kitchen, the gentle hum of the air conditioner did nothing to soothe.

Where was Diana?

With the click of the door as it was unlocked and the thump of the carry-on wheels in the foyer, Letitia's heart hammered a staccato beat.

It wasn't Diana's entrance that unnerved her.

Who she was talking to was much more significant.

"I don't know Madeleine. I'm just walking in the door this minute. I've been out of town."

Letitia heard the door close, a bag drop to the floor, footsteps coming in her direction.

Then a light was flipped on and Letitia squinted against the harsh glow, which illuminated the surprise on Diana's face.

"Look, let me get my bearings and I'll call you back."

Diana's finger went to her lips, but Letitia didn't need Diana's cue to remain silent.

"I'm sure that's true, Madeleine. But I don't know what to tell you."

Kicking off her shoes, Diana dropped onto the overstuffed couch.

"Give me twenty minutes and then I'll get back to you."

Diana slid the phone onto the glass-top coffee table, rubbed her hands over her face. "What the hell happened?"

"I had nowhere else to go."

Her voice sounded pitiful even to herself.

Diana tempered her tone.

"Sorry. I'm spending my anger in the wrong place. You know you're always welcome here. It's why I gave you a key. What's going on?"

"Mother said she's going to send me to a mental facility for evaluation."

Diana's breath came out in a whoosh as she flopped back against the cushion.

Her agent had to know the reason her mother had threatened her. Diana had been the one to cancel the last few concerts, the panic attacks becoming so severe Letitia refused to even approach the stage. Since then, her mother had been worse than ever, more demanding, more insulting, more demeaning, repeating a years-long caring-cruel, passive-aggressive cycle. Diana had always intervened when possible but Letitia hadn't told her agent the extent of the most recent barrages. After she'd reassured Diana she could deal with the conflict, that her mother's admonishments were a trivial inconvenience, Diana had to be caught off guard by her appearance in her living room.

Today the cost of dealing with it alone had become much too high a price to pay.

"Oh, Letitia. I'm sorry. You're not the one who needs it."

"It doesn't matter. Mother's in control."

Her voice was fragile and strained.

"I'm not insane, Diana."

"Of course, you're not. She's just blowing steam, you know that. Last time I talked to her, she told me everything was wonderful."

Letitia could hear the singsong quality of that word. Everything was *wonderful* when Madeleine didn't want people to know the truth.

"That's what she wanted you to think. I overheard her tell you that I was sleeping. I haven't slept in weeks."

Letitia passed a sodden tissue under her eyes. "I can't deal with the insomnia anymore and I'm not living with the threat of the psych ward over my head."

She had come to see her mother as the devil in designer clothing. Short, matron-like with dark hair, she spent all kinds of money on procedures for her neck, her eyebrows, her face. The infamous fountain of youth hadn't done Madeleine any good. The plastic surgery had only made her look queer and artificial. She looked nothing like the woman Letitia had grown up with.

Leaning closer, Diana patted her leg. "I don't blame you sweetie."

"Will you help me?"

As she asked, Letitia felt guilt eating away at her.

Why would Diana want this kind of aggravation?

When Diana said, "Any way I can," Letitia breathed a sigh of relief.

The musical ring of Diana's cell phone sounded but in a second it was muted, buried deep within the confines of her oversized purse.

She ignored it.

After changing into sweats and a chunky sweater, Diana made them both a cup of tea and settled into the corner of the couch. Curled up on the opposite corner of the couch, Letitia said softly, "I appreciate your willingness to help but I don't even know what kind of help I need. Maybe just some peace, time away from her."

"You need more than that and you know it. Your mother has controlled the agenda and she's made a mess of things. You need to recognize that Madeleine is the problem, not you."

"I'm beginning to...I think."

"That's a good first step. You finally took the initiative to leave and I'm going to do everything I can to make sure you never have to go back."

"How?"

"I called Annie before I changed, and we came up with something that might work. Let's call it a field trip, with Annie as chaperone. A three-month field trip that will cover a big part of the country. After that, we'll see."

A three-month field trip?

The answer did not make her feel safe.

The only up-side was that Annie would be with her, and according to Diana, it was Annie who had come up with the plan to get her out of Boston.

Letitia shuddered when Diana asked, "How did you get away?"

Needing to warm fingers that had lost all feeling, Letitia gripped the teacup with both hands.

"I called Ned."

Letitia's driver had become her friend and when she'd called him, told him that she needed to escape her mother's place, he'd rushed over to pick her up. Transporting her across town, refusing to take any money for the fare, he'd dropped her off at the address Letitia had given him.

Diana's eyebrows arched in surprise.

Letitia gave her a wan smile.

"I know. Where did I get the nerve?"

It had taken everything in her to make that call, the deep-seated fear of reprisal almost crippling her.

Diana took a sip of tea and admitted, "It's not something I expected from you."

Pulling at her fingers as she rocked back and forth Letitia admitted, "Walking over to the landline was like walking to the gallows."

There was a long pause before Diana asked, "What made you give in and do it?"

Fearful images invaded her mind, stark hallways, white jackets, cups full of pills.

"I already had the noose around my neck. Mother tightened the hold with her threat and all I wanted was to breathe again."

"What did Bruno say?"

Bruno was what Letitia called the man Madeleine had hired to keep her imprisoned in the condo and all potential visitors out.

"I told him Mother had changed her mind about my practice hours, said I needed a break, and wanted me to join her for lunch. My mother might have a strict regimen for me, but her attitudes *about* me shift like the wind. It wasn't hard to convince him my mother was being magnanimous."

Diana mused aloud, "Seems your mother's mood swings paid off this time."

Letitia's stomach dropped in dread before she jumped up from her seat, her hands covering her cheeks.

"Do you think they'll both get fired?"

Beginning to pace, she didn't need Diana to answer that. Panic assaulted her and she felt her heart racing again. "Of course, they will. I didn't even think of that. My God, I'm ruining everyone's life."

Diana didn't waste any time contacting Ned, the grad student who'd been driving Letitia's for over a year, offering him compensation for delivering Letitia to her place.

Letitia listened closely to Diana's part of the conversation, wishing she'd put it on speaker so she could follow the entire thread.

"But you have to know..."

As if Diana read her mind, she did just that, so Letitia heard Ned's response.

"I hoped I'd get that call one day. I quit the service the minute I dropped her off. No way was I going to continue working for Madeleine and I already got another job working for the competition. Don't worry I'm fine."

"If you ever need a reference, you've got it."

"Thanks, Diana. Take care of her."

When Diana disconnected the call, she swiped across her cell phone screen then grimaced.

"Well. Madeleine's already at it. I have two more missed calls and a few waiting texts. I'm going to have to get back to her soon or she'll be banging down the door. I'd like to put that off for as long as possible."

With a hitching breath, Letitia sank back into the cushioned couch, trying to forget about the cataclysm that might be around the corner. Diana moved and slid next to her on the couch.

"Ned's fine. You'd be surprised at how many people want to see you sever your ties with Madeleine."

"Why do I have to sever them? Why can't she just give me some peace?"

"You know what Annie thinks."

With an advanced degree in counseling, Diana's sister treated a variety of clients with mental, behavioral or emotional problems. It was Annie who had long ago pointed out Madeleine's narcissistic and borderline personality disorders.

"I know what you told me."

"You shouldn't have to earn her love, Letitia."

"If I could just—"

Diana reached over and patted Letitia's knee.

"Sweetie, it's futile. She doesn't have enough room in her heart for anyone but herself."

"I thought I was managing her. I've tried Annie's suggestions. They don't work."

Never knowing who Madeleine was on any given day, charismatic, calculating or in one of her rages, it was almost impossible to know which strategy to use. Letitia had learned over the years that drama only fueled the mood swings. She'd all but given up the fight and her mother was still intent on crushing her.

Diana nodded her head in understanding.

"I've tried a few myself. Sometimes I lost more traction than I gained."

Diana handed Letitia the box of tissues that sat on the end table as the tears continued to fall.

"Annie's going to be here soon, and we'll discuss our next step."

"We have a step?"

"We do. With your approval, I'll deal with the repercussions. Madeleine's going to find out that her threat had the opposite effect of what she'd thought. Instead of caving, you've finally set some boundaries. You've taken back control of your life."

"I don't know about that. I don't feel like I'm in control, but I can't go on living this way."

Determination coursed through her. "I'm scared Diana, but I have to do this."

Letitia massaged her temples as her jumbled thoughts raced.

She was so submerged in her fear, that the chime of the doorbell gave her a jolt. She jumped up out of her seat for a second time and looked for someplace to hide.

Diana proceeded to the door, taking small steps. "Wait here until I see who it is."

Nodding, Letitia felt her heart constrict, her breathing becoming labored. Diana tried to reassure her, "I'm sure it's Annie."

When the door was opened and Annie rushed in, Letitia exhaled in relief.

Annie was dressed in professional attire as if she'd been pulled away from a meeting. She was taller than Diana, and the family resemblance was evident in the color hair and shape of the face, but her glasses gave her a more scholarly appearance. She was a sight for tired, red-rimmed eyes.

Empathetically Annie offered, "Oh, Letitia, I'm sorry. I should have texted to let you know I was here. I wasn't even thinking when I rang the buzzer."

Letitia felt Annie's arms go around her and fought off another round of tears. She rarely cried, had learned early on tears made matters worse. Only when her back was against the wall, and she felt cornered, did they fall.

"I'm so sorry I'm causing—"

"Don't you dare," Annie admonished. "There is nothing to be sorry for."

"But my mother is going to create mayhem the likes of which you've never seen. I don't want you in the middle."

"The middle is my favorite place. And Diana is always looking for someone to make her day. She'd love nothing better than to take your mother apart."

Letitia's voice wavered. "I don't know what I was thinking. This is so bad. I *have* lost my mind. Maybe Mother was right, and I belong—"

Annie grasped Letitia's shoulders, giving them a little shake. "You've walked away from the landmines. Doesn't it feel good to be here?"

Letitia admitted, if only to herself, it felt wonderful, if she didn't think about her mother's anger or hear Madeleine's jarring voice screaming in her head.

Terror choked off speech, so she nodded her head in response.

Taking Letitia's hand, Annie led her to the couch and they both sat down. "We've come up with a possible solution."

Letitia had regained use of her voice, but she could hear the warble as she asked, "What is it?"

Diana interjected, "Keep an open mind."

Time fell away as she looked into her agent's eyes. She was twelve again, and Diana had taken her on as a client. Oscar Jones had wanted someone to protect his prodigy daughter's interests and it seemed like she still needed Diana's guidance, maybe even more so today. She'd been so happy then, filled with her father's love, her music an intrinsic part of who she was, satisfying her soul. Her father's heart attack and death within a year of hiring Diana's firm. The LoScola Agency, had changed her life. Once he was gone, so was the unconditional love he'd given her making her feel valued, visible. Love was no longer free. It had to be earned. Over the years she had to grapple with her feelings of loss, fight against her mother's domination, her muses vaporizing into nothingness and it had sapped the joy out of playing. For the past eight years, she'd battled for her soul, her form of expression, her magic and it appeared, in the end, she'd lost the war.

With a vacant stare, she asked the sisters, "Where am I going?"

Without hesitation Annie announced, "On tour with Raging Thunder."

CHAPTER TWO

Johnny Scalera sat slumped in the worn sofa that had come with the airplane hangar. Wanting a different sound for their next album, Raging Thunder's record producer had decided to get away from the routine of the studio. But it wasn't working.

The place was huge, the tin ceiling and walls great for amplification. Or so they had thought.

In Johnny's estimation, the music wasn't responding well due to the physical dimensions of the place. There were no isolation booths, no drier rooms for vocals, the background noise distorted the purity. If you could call heavy metal pure. The instruments sounded as tinny as the frame of the building. The big wigs at the recording label had rented it, informing them that this time they wanted to hear the words, not just the jarring electric beat they had always been known for. Yet they had neglected to outfit the hangar with what the band needed. There were a couple of well-known recording studios that had been legendary, producing some amazing tracks, but they'd been equipped for that specific purpose. This was just one huge building, cold and devoid of creative space. Proving to Johnny that the head of the new label knew nothing about them or their sound. Tim had jumped labels last year, at the end of their contract, and Johnny had been livid. The front man hadn't made the decision without him, but he'd been outvoted and since then he'd been disinclined to use his voice on any important issue.

Tapping his drumsticks against his leg, impatient for take...ten, the song just not inspiring, he watched Tim, his bandmate and one-time best friend going over some changes to the score.

Johnny's voice issued a snarl of words.

"You do know this isn't working."

Tim threw down the pencil stub he was using to scribble notes. "Then you figure it out."

He regretted opening his mouth.

There was no way he could make the song better. It was dull and without the feral beat that he could have worked with. He wasn't going to waste his time or energy trying.

"I say let's go with the next song on the list. This is like beating a dead horse."

"You've said that several times now. We still haven't recorded one song you're happy with."

Johnny knew Tim was right, but he didn't care.

He was tired.

And they didn't have a vacation coming for months.

Within a couple of days, they would be back on tour, the second leg of a cross-country gig, and all he wanted was warm sun, soft sand and an ocean breeze. Sitting on the beach for endless days, not thinking of the new album, the lack of fresh material, the breach that had split the four-member band into two factions. It had been fun once, and the women who came out for the concerts still made it worthwhile, but Johnny could find them anywhere.

What made matters worse was that the band's accountant had downgraded their accommodations this time out, using buses instead of planes, staying in three-star hotels instead of five, if they ever left the bus at all.

It was a rude awakening.

One he hadn't seen coming.

Raging Thunder had been so successful over the last few years, producing hit after chart topping hit, Johnny had gotten used to the perks of his trade and he wasn't ready for the fall.

"Let's quit while we're ahead. We can pick it back up after the tour ends. Try again. Maybe in a different location. Like the studio we're used to."

"Look, this is what the label wants. I think we've got to at least give it a chance," Tim replied.

"We have. For two weeks we've been working our asses off to get some semblance of a song recorded. It's obvious that the experiment failed. Time to move on."

"Johnny..."

"When are you going to admit this was a big mistake?"

He clutched his drumsticks tighter as he tried to keep control of his temper. He still couldn't believe his opinion about the label had been ignored, or that the other members of the band sided with Tim on the issue. There was a time his word had been law, when he'd pretty much run the show, and they had done pretty, damn well. Seemed Tim didn't have the kind of perspective it took to make savvy decisions regarding their sound. If only...

Tim interrupted his musings

"I don't have time for looking back. We've got to have this wrapped if we want it ready for Christmas," Tim reminded him. "The tour doesn't end until August. That doesn't give us much time."

"Unless we find our groove, this is useless."

"Groove? We haven't hit that in months, Johnny. Maybe longer."

Tim was scowling at him and he felt his jaw clench in return.

"Recording shitty songs in a shitty building isn't going to help us find it again."

There was a rise in volume as Tim bit out, "This used to be a two-man writing team. It's now on me so if you don't like what I'm doing, feel free to contribute."

"Sorry. Got nothing for you."

"I've noticed."

Johnny felt the rumblings of a fight coming on and he wasn't in the mood for it.

"I've got to get out of here."

Sticks in hand, Johnny headed towards the hangar door, but Tim snagged his arm before he could get far.

"I've got to talk to you about something before you go. Annie called and she asked me for a favor."

Annie was Tim's wife and another of Johnny's best friends since childhood.

"I'm not in the right frame of mind for decisions. Do what you want."

"But—"

"Tim, unless you're quitting, disbanding or dying, I don't care."

Sticks in hand, Johnny hurried out leaving the rest of the band no recourse but to put the session off indefinitely.

He drove to his place on Commonwealth Avenue in Boston, the one place he could relax. The old brownstone was one of the perks of his wealth and fame. He'd bought the entire building, which had consisted of several condos, and renovated it so that it was once again a single-family home. Built in the 1920's, it was three stories and almost ten thousand square feet of living space. Real estate in the Back Bay didn't come cheap. Neither had converting it into a primary residence but he loved the period details and location. He was close to everything Boston had to offer. It also gave him privacy. He could pound away at his skins when in the mood and it was big enough that the band could hold jam sessions on the third floor. He'd knocked down one of the walls to create a large space for the instruments and soundproofed the room, so his neighbors didn't hear the brunt of his late nights. Wearing a tool belt himself during some of the reconstruction had been kind of meditative. Stripping paint, re-sanding the old wood floors, refinishing the woodwork had been a hard, back-breaking experience but it had made him appreciate the results more than he might have. There was still some work to do in what the listing sheet called the marble music room. He thought of it as a grand ballroom and although he didn't know what he was going to do with the place, he'd wanted to update it, get rid of the gold and glitz. A grand piano would feel quite at home in the rotunda-like room, but he didn't play so it didn't make sense. He'd make the decision when the time came.

As he entered, he dropped his keys on the mirrored console in the entryway foyer, the Persian rug he'd purchased a true hand knotted one from what the salesman had told him. He had taken him at his word. He knew nothing about that, he'd just liked the colors. This was not the house anyone expected him to buy.

When he'd shown up for the appointment to see the house, in jeans and tee shirt, the listing agent had taken one look at him and gotten belligerent.

"Do you know what this house costs?"

"Yeah."

"I don't like my time wasted...Mr....Scalera."

The broker had to check his Blackberry to refresh his memory on the name of the man standing in front of him.

"I don't like wasting mine, either. Are you going to show it to me or not? I can get another agent if you don't want to work with me."

"I'm going to have to have written verification that you have the funds to purchase it before we go further."

"Fine."

Johnny had called his accountant who'd taken care of it within a matter of minutes. It'd the broker catering to his every whim, all while eating crow.

That had been four years ago, and it was still a work in progress.

After retrieving a cold beer from the refrigerator, he climbed the three flights of stairs and entered his music room.

This was home.

Not like the studio that Tim had built on his property, all up-scale equipment, shiny and new, but worn, like a comfortable pair of jeans. This drum kit was his favorite, one of his original custom made, familiar, with Sabian cymbals, maple snare, double-braced chromed stand which took his heavy hits with ease, solid and consistent.

He should have packed these up and taken them to the hangar. Maybe the sound would have been more to his liking. The first kit they'd brought in had been electric and he'd hated it. The only thing it had going for it was a better stick bounce. It sounded fake, it required extra amplification which prevented him from achieving optimum acoustic sound. It had no soul and he'd refused to play until another kit had been brought in. Even that one had lacked the quality he was used to although it allowed him to move across the spectrum from quiet to loud and finesse the sensitivity of touch he was known for.

Before long, his drums beckoned, and he answered their call. For hours, he pounded the skins, needing to exorcise the disappointments, the anger that still surged in his chest.

He wiped his forehead with his shirtsleeve, sweat pouring out of him as it always did after a good workout. Taking the last swig of now tepid beer, feeling a bit more like himself, he picked up his sticks. It was time to head to Tim's house.

Tim had been his best friend for what seemed like forever. They were losing their connection and Johnny didn't know what to do about it.

The music of late was second rate and though he didn't want to acknowledge it, he knew he was part of the problem. Leaving the songwriting on Tim's shoulders, he didn't have the right to complain. He had tried picking up a pen when he was alone but nothing meaningful came out of it. There was nothing to draw on anymore. On top of that, the tour wasn't the success they had anticipated. Ticket sales were down, and the venues weren't selling out, critics were less than kind.

The last review he'd read after their concert in Philadelphia was a brutal attack on their weak sound, placing the blame squarely on his shoulders.

Where once Raging Thunder held the world in their hand, they have become a less than stellar example of true heavy metal. The drums, sticks held by once legendary Johnny Scalera, have sounded a different kind of beat...one with less intensity and less attitude.

When had he lost his edge?

He still played with ferocity. The primal beat that pounded in his chest was as forceful as ever.

He gave it everything he had night after night

It couldn't be all his fault, could it?

CHAPTER THREE

Heading west on Route 2, the car reverberating with the strains of classical music streaming from the iPod, Letitia fiddled with her ever-errant hair, her breathing still a bit labored. She was about to walk into the unknown and the fear was becoming a knot in her belly.

What had she agreed to?

Squinting into the late-afternoon glare, she noticed the thoughtful expression on Annie's face. Needing to shore up her confidence, she thought a little knowledge about Raging Thunder might be in order.

She knew they were a famous metal band, had risen into legendary status during their first few years. It was intimidating and she needed some idea of who they were as people to calm her racing heart.

"What are the guys in the band like?"

Annie glanced over at her, as if measuring her mood, or perhaps her fear quotient. Letitia hadn't been overcome by excitement at the prospect of being thrown into a frightening adventure, had almost balked as she was led out to the vehicle in which she'd make her escape. Annie knew her social interactions had been limited and this would be a change of shattering proportions.

Annie flicked her bangs off her forehead and pushed her glasses up higher on her nose. Shifting her hands on the steering wheel, she began the brief description of the men they'd be on tour with.

"Terry Flynn is the lead guitarist. Married. Wife Marci. Kind of laid back, a bit under his wife's thumb. Luca Caroli, known as Reject, a name he picked up when we were in high school, is the bassist. Johnny Scalera is the drummer and has been one of my best friends since we were kids. You've met my husband, Tim. He's the rhythm guitarist and a great guy- if I may say so."

"I've heard some of your stories about Tim and Johnny. Tim's nice but Johnny sounds scary."

"He's changed a lot since we were younger. He's become more of a showboat. Not sure I like his attitude, but my memories and our bond run deep so I overlook it."

The ring of the phone interrupted the conversation.

Letitia tensed as Annie hit the answer button on the Blue-tooth.

Before speaking directly to the caller, Annie said to reassure her, it's Diana."

"Hi. You're on speaker."

Diana's voice boomed into the interior of the car, cutting right to the chase. "You guys left just in time."

Annie asked, "Should you be calling on your own line? We don't want anyone to connect me to Letitia, do we? I thought we were going to use disposable phones, at least for a while."

"Just calling my dear sister, whom I am very close to, to let her know that we have a runaway pianist."

"That makes sense. What happened?"

"Police just left my humble home."

There was such a vicious roll in Letitia's stomach, she thought she'd be sick.

When Diana added, "Madeleine's raising holy hell," she opened the window hoping the fresh air would stop the heaving motion.

Annie stroked Letitia's back while admitting, "No surprise there."

"I just got the third degree by Boston's finest. Madeleine filled out a missing person report."

As Letitia listened, she was amazed at how calm and in control Diana sounded. Madeleine could be a nightmare. It evened out the roll a bit.

Annie asked, "Don't they have to wait twenty-four hours or something?"

"Not anymore. The police move on it right away. They came knocking because Madeleine suggested I might have caused Letitia harm. Convinced them I was a threat to her well-being."

Sheer terror shivered through Letitia. "Oh, God, this is not good at all."

Her breath now trapped in her lungs, she felt the signs of a panic attack, the symptoms making a steady run for full tilt. Gasping for air, the flutter of her heart in hummingbird mode, she heard Annie suggest, "Take a deep breath. Diana's got this. Everything's going to be fine."

Pulling at her fingers as if she were trying to twist them off, she tried to stem the tide of the feelings rushing her.

"Listen to Diana. Listen to how much in control she is."

As if on cue, Diana said, "It's not all bad. The police were cool. It didn't take long for Madeleine to piss them off with her ranting and raving. One of them told me he didn't blame you Letitia for running away. That you're twenty-one isn't helping Madeleine's case."

The pit of anxiety was shrinking, her breathing becoming more regulated, as Diana's voice had a calming effect on her jagged nerves.

Letitia asked, her tone strained, "So, are they going to leave us alone?'

"For now. It didn't take them long to determine I wasn't out to hurt you, so they backed off. My poker face worked like a charm, but I'll have to keep it handy. Madeleine informed me on her fifteenth call that she'd hired a private investigator and I'd probably have another visitor before the day was out."

"Did they talk to Ned and Bruno?"

"Yes. Bruno relayed that Letitia told him she was meeting her mother for lunch. Ned was more creative. He came up with a story that he dropped Letitia off at a restaurant. He told them he had no idea that it wasn't where her mother was dining."

"So they backed her."

"They did but Madeleine still isn't satisfied. It isn't computing that her daughter is of legal age and can go anywhere and do anything she wants. The law might recognize that fact, but Madeleine makes her own rules. All she knows is that her golden goose flew the coop. She'll do anything to get her back."

"There are security cameras at your place," Annie added. "If they check, they'll know you were lying."

"There's nothing outside my condo itself, only at the front entrance. They might prove she came by, but they can't prove she got in. I was away, remember? She'd already been gone a good couple of hours by then."

"How about cameras at the restaurant?"

"She got out of the car and took off. She was alive and healthy when she left both Bruno and Ned. The police shouldn't expect foul play."

Taking a breath, Diana went on, "Madeleine said some money was missing, Letitia. Did you take it or is she lying?"

Madeleine was known to twist the truth when it suited her purposes.

Letitia stammered, "I didn't steal it. Not really. Some of it has to be mine."

"All of it is yours, sweetie," Diana confirmed. "Your mother forgets that sometimes. But where did you get it? I can't see her leaving it out in the open. I also can't see her filling out a report for theft. Your disappearance isn't news she'd like to see in the tabloids.

"I was in her room looking for my passport. I thought I might need some kind of identification."

Riffling through her mother's things had given Letitia the willies. She had never been allowed in there but had gladly scoured every inch of it with shaking fingers until she found what she was looking for, with a bonus.

"There was a box with bills wrapped in elastics. I took one before I left with Ned. I wanted to be able to pay him for the ride, but he refused to take anything. There were ten one-hundred-dollar bills all rolled up. I still have it."

There was suspicion in Diana's voice as she said, "So your mother keeps a stash of money at her disposal. Interesting. I'd love to know where it came from and whether she has a right to it."

Letitia didn't grasp the implication.

"What do you mean?"

There was a short pause before Diana said, "I was just thinking out loud. Don't worry about it. I've got to go but I'll keep in touch."

When the Blue-tooth signed off, soothing music soon filled the car again. Letitia rested her head against the seat.

"I can't believe this. I've involved so many people in this...and they don't seem to mind. Some of them are even covering for me."

She heard Annie swear under her breath.

"Letitia, you've been brainwashed into thinking no one cares about you Your mother made you believe she was all you had. It's a lie. There are a lot of us who want to help you. So, let us."

She had become good at numbing her emotions, of denying them rather than letting herself feel them. It was time to take back her life and, in doing so, move through the pain caused by the unrealistic expectations concerning her mother. Madeleine had brainwashed her in other ways as well. She was angry, she was sad, but surprisingly she was relieved. She couldn't believe she'd had the courage to walk away. And she was going to take the offer of help.

Giving Annie a tentative smile, she asked, "I'm really free?"

"Yup. And we're going to make sure you get to keep that freedom. And help you learn to stand on your own."

"Standing on my own won't mean anything unless I get my music back."

"I see them as interchangeable. You might want to think about playing keyboard for the band instead of just hanging around with me for the summer."

"What? Where did this come from?"

"I was talking to Tim and it just kind of hit me. It might be a way for you to inch your way back."

Letitia's stomach churned at the thought. She had a hard time expressing music she knew on an instrument that was as familiar as her own name. Play keyboard with a heavy metal band? Was Annie out of her mind?

Giving her head a vigorous shake, she let Annie know without words that wasn't going to happen.

⌒

The fears that had stalked the confines of Letitia's mind during the drive began to jog. There were half a dozen cars parked ahead of them in front of the house. Annie maneuvered around them and slid into the garage. A chaotic mix of emotions swirled through Letitia, snaking around her neck as if to strangle her, squeezing the air out of her lungs.

Annie and Tim's stone house was massive. Almost palatial with curved shapes and jetties, pointed rooflines and dormers, all playing together to create a symmetrical showpiece. She'd visited once before and seeing it for the first time then had been shocking. She'd spent a couple of nights here although her mother had thought she was with Diana. It was one of the few times she'd been given a reprieve from the tiny condo she called home. Not that her mother would have cared. When Madeleine was enthralled with a man, as she'd been back then, she threw her whole being into him. Her cruise down the Rhine would have blocked out anything else, her daughter's whereabouts included.

Her appreciation for the house hadn't changed. It was still stunning.

The interior was just as impressive with floor-to-ceiling windows that let light spill into the rooms, making the enormous space warm and inviting. She had marveled at the gleaming wood floors, the chef's kitchen, the extraordinary family room that could fit half her mother's condo, with room to spare. The fireplace was the focal point and there were several couches and chairs arranged around it that could accommodate a small army.

Judging by the cars parked in the driveway, it looked like it was already here.

On trembling legs, she became Annie's shadow, following at a snail's pace as she entered the mudroom and her new life.

She had grave misgivings about this plan.

The same misgivings she'd felt in the wings of the concert halls that had held her captive: the audience restless with her delay, the stage fright that incapacitated her to the point of uselessness, no memory, no movement, no soul. All frozen someplace outside her body.

Irretrievable.

Dogs came running, paws sliding on the entry tiles, tails wagging in greeting. The building pain in her head made it difficult to move. As Annie had suggested last time, she allowed the dogs their sniffing time without crumbling. The cats were more palatable, curling their bodies around her calves. Her breath was shallow, her heartbeat erratic and a rapid pulse throbbed at her temple. She took in her surroundings, knew what was just out of sight. The animals were less dangerous than what she'd find beyond the doorway, the voices, thick with camaraderie and laughter coming from down the hall telling her she'd be face-to-face with them soon.

She started to shake, first her knees, then up to her churning stomach and her now sweating palms. She willed it all to stop.

Hesitant, she followed Annie. "Do they already know why I'm here?"

"I'm not sure."

"What do you mean?"

"Tim was going to talk to them, but he hasn't had the chance yet."

And then Tim was there, flashing a dazzling smile.

"Hey, Letitia. It's nice to see you. Are you ready to rock and roll?"

He was as friendly as she remembered, his eyes twinkling in welcome. She never had a real chance to get to know him, he'd been in and out so much during the short time she was visiting but his warmth was all encompassing. Like her father's.

A name from her past flashed into her head, the name her father had given her when she was just a toddler. It was a name that brought back love coated memories and she decided that if she was going to have a new life, she wanted a name to go with it.

With trembling lips, she asked, "Can you call me Tish from now on?"

When Tim nodded and opened his arms, she walked right into them and hung on for dear life.

There was another impressive thing about this house. Love lived here.

"Who do we have here?"

The deep, raspy voice echoed in the foyer.

Her nerve endings tingled as chocolate raked over her. The dark brown eyes were predatory, and Tish felt Tim's grip tighten before releasing her.

Her hard-won courage deflated into nothingness.

The man before her was tall and ripcord lean. Well-defined muscles extended from his sleeveless vest, and a crown-of-thorns tattoo circled his upper right bicep. One hand tucked a lock of long brown hair behind an ear, displaying a gold hoop earring, while the other clutched a pair of drumsticks. Above a dark, stubbled chin she couldn't help but notice the heat of his smile. His black jeans and calf-high, black boots did nothing to ease her nervousness. This man was dangerous, and she had a sinking suspicion she had just come face-to-face with Johnny Scalera. Annie had told her stories of how he'd jump into the frenzied audience, strip down to next to nothing on stage on very hot nights and encouraged a hands-on approach to the women who milled around after the show.

Tish had never seen anyone like him.

The people she knew came from a very different world, formal, cultured, conservative. Here was a man whose essence was primitive, with the markings of pure animal-male to prove it. A shiver ran up her spine. She hoped she wasn't staring with hopeless longing. His strength drew her in, and she felt a strange connection, as if he were someone she could cling to. He could also entrap her in a fate worse than the one she was dealing with.

She shuddered at the thought as Tim made the introduction.

"This is...Tish. She's the new keyboard player."

Johnny took in the ethereal beauty in front of him and his brain sizzled.

The shock of her was a punch to the gut. And his groin.

She was dangerous but he couldn't fathom why. She was nothing like the women he was drawn to. Maybe five-four thin, with wispy blonde hair parted on the side and pulled back, loose curls framing her oval face. Freckles dusted the area under her eyes, eyes the most potent shade of turquoise. They burned into him with the intensity of a brand.

Irritated with Tim's announcement, he was ready to talk Tim out of the far-fetched scheme, but when his eyes slid over her again, he asked instead, "Do we need one?"

He heard the huskiness in his voice and arched an eyebrow in query to see if Tim noticed it, too.

As soon as he saw the protective stance, he had his answer.

"I want to try it as back-up. I think the keys would give a couple of our songs some depth."

Tim's voice chilled. "If there's no new stuff, maybe we can improve the old."

The drumsticks kept a hidden beat against his leg, and his voice held a tinge of steel.

"Why didn't you talk to us about it first?"

"I tried but if you remember, you told me you weren't in the frame of mind for making decisions."

Johnny couldn't argue, knowing that was, word-for-word what he'd said, but this was an overreach of Tim's authority. Glancing back at the blonde, he decided to save his objections for now. He wasn't sure she'd even cut it in the band, so why fight an unnecessary battle?

"Right. You're the boss."

Johnny noticed the gritted teeth, the hard look on his friend's face when Tim said, "One of these days we're addressing that."

Johnny shrugged his shoulders in response.

When they'd formed Raging Thunder ten years ago, the share of duties had been balanced between them. Over the last year, he'd let his portion slide onto Tim's shoulders. He didn't want the responsibility and he was much too busy with the women. Yes, he felt no small amount of guilt that the songwriting was no longer a joint venture, nor was the producing and he had dumped the lion's share of work on Tim. But he figured Tim was married, settled, and had all the time in the world to deal with the business end.

His contribution was promoting their brand.

And he did a damn fine job of it.

His eyes remained on Tish while Tim introduced her to the rest of the guys, some band members, some members of their entourage.

His first impression had been that she was intoxicating but as she hovered close to Tim's side, he amended that. She looked fragile, like a bird that had fallen out of its nest and had broken a wing. He took a step closer to her.

"A keyboard player, huh? Might be interesting."

He gave her a predatory smile when she retreated a step.

Then Tim's hands were on his chest and he was pushed back out of the room.

"She's not up for grabs. Leave her alone."

Johnny whistled under his breath. "Who is she?"

"A friend of a friend," was all Tim gave him in response.

Johnny's last glimpse of her included Annie, who was whispering feverishly in her ear, and he had an inkling it was a warning. About him.

CHAPTER FOUR

Diana had agreed to meet the private investigator at her condo, her mental list of what she would give away made and filed.

She had composed herself enough to return Madeleine's calls. It had taken effort to become detached from the emotional fit she was in, but she needed to get the call over with before the PI's inquisition later that afternoon. Picking up her cell, she punched in the number not on speed dial.

In no time Madeleine was shrieking in her ear.

"Diana, I demand you tell me where Letitia is."

Struggling to keep her tone even, she explained, "And like I told you earlier, I've been away and have no idea where she went."

"She doesn't have many places to run to, so don't give me that."

Diana bit her tongue, wanting to say, "You made sure of that, you biddy," but instead, stated with as little emotion as she could muster, "You said she has money."

"She stole money. My money."

The anger simmered but Diana fought it down and kept her voice monotone.

"I didn't know you had a job. It must feel good knowing you can provide for yourself."

"I get a monthly stipend for being her guardian and you know it."

"You earn money being your daughter's mother? How sweet that must be. Most mothers give everything they can to their children, not take it from them."

"Don't you dare talk to me like that. I've taken very good care of her. I know what's best for her, what she needs."

"You mean, what you need. What's best for Letitia isn't the same thing."

"If she doesn't fulfill her obligations, Diana, we have a lot to lose. Both of us."

Diana couldn't hold back the fierceness in her voice.

"Don't you dare lump us together. You might have something to lose, but Letitia has already lost what's important."

"Her mind. I know. I was going to set up an appointment at Mass Mental so we can get to the bottom of this foolishness. The doctors there should be able to cure her panic attacks and then we can get back to making money."

"No Madeleine, Letitia hasn't lost her mind. She's lost her spirit, her music. It's gone and getting it back should be your priority."

"Bull. She owes me. Look what I've done for her. She's one of the most respected pianists in the world."

"Once maybe but not anymore. Doing it your way hasn't gotten very good results."

"She'd be nothing without me. Will be nothing if she gets her own way."

"Don't delude yourself, Madeleine. She can be even more without you. I'm glad she got away from you."

"She's my daughter and I have a right to know where she is."

Snorting, Diana stated what was, to her, the obvious.

"She's twenty-one. If she wants to stay AWOL, she has the legal standing to do so."

Ignoring that fact, Madeleine railed, "She'll come crawling back when she's out of money."

Diana was pacing now, reining in her temper. Madeleine had made Letitia an emotional hostage, demolishing her self-confidence in the process. Leaving had taken courage, and the young woman seemed determined to stem the tide of her emotional burnout. Letitia had an indefatigable spirit and would never crawl back.

And as her agent and her friend, she wouldn't allow it.

Moderating her tone, Diana said, "Deluding yourself again. If anyone does the crawling, it will be you. She's the one with the talent, the gift, the heart. You are nothing without her."

"Bitch. I'll be watching you like a hawk. If she comes within miles of you, I'll know it."

"Again, she's of age. What will you do? Kidnap her? Chain her to her bed? She won't earn you any money from there."

"I have a contract. The one that gives me full control of her career until she's twenty-two."

"Oscar would not be pleased with the way you've handled her career."

"That man never had any balls. He never would have brought her to the pinnacle of success like I did. He wanted his precious daughter to have what she needed, and I supplied it."

"You may have a right to her earnings, but not her life. But then again, that's what her life means to you. She's just dollar signs."

"Of course, she isn't. But I've sacrificed my life to get her this far and I think I should be able to reap some of the benefits."

That she had sacrificed nothing but played the role of vampire to Letitia's spirit was obvious to everyone but Madeleine. It was useless arguing with her about it.

"There's nothing in her contract that implicitly states she has to tour, only that you get a percentage of her earnings if she does. I believe if it comes down to it, she could take the next year off to rest. When the contract expires, we don't even have to rewrite it. But I'll let our lawyer figure out how to make sure Letitia's needs are met when the time comes, not yours."

"This is ridiculous. People would forget about her and she'd have to start all over."

That Madeleine couldn't see that Letitia was already in that position and needed to start over already, was maddening.

"As her agent I won't allow that to happen. Whether she plays or not, you'll still get the money from her recording sales, but I'd start saving up for retirement because it's coming sooner than you realize."

"We'll see about that. Oh, and Diana, you're fired."

Diana exhaled a sigh of relief when she heard the disconnect, steeped in contentment. She had kept her cool even though it would have been easy to let Madeleine have it.

Calm, detached, forceful.

Annie would have been proud.

CHAPTER FIVE

Still standing in the marble-tiled foyer at the edge of the kitchen, Tish stared down the empty hallway where Johnny had disappeared, letting her eyes linger. His personality had filled the space and now…

"So, what did she say?"

Shifting her attention, her ears pricked up, and she strained to fill in the spaces of the one-sided conversation.

Diana had spoken to her mother.

Madeleine was determined to find her, and she'd fired the agent.

That should have been cause for concern but the knot forming in her stomach was the result of something even more terrifying.

The face of the infamous drummer was imprinted on her brain.

That meant danger ahead if Johnny Scalera didn't back off. She didn't know a lot about the mechanics of a come-on but what she had seen in his dark eyes was a slow burning heat that even she could read.

Annie's concern was evident when she closed the distance between them and asked, "Are you okay? You know your mother can't really fire Diana, right?"

Annie's question brought Tish's attention back. She nodded her head.

"Well, it's handled for now. Come on, let me show you to your room."

She followed Annie to the guest bedroom on the other side of the house, her voice hushed in awe. "That was Johnny."

With those three words, she let Annie know her mind wasn't on Madeleine and Annie's expression held a flicker of apprehension.

"Yeah, that's him."

"He's...he's..."

"Not for you."

"Oh, I know that. I'm sure I'm not his type at all. But the way he looked at me..."

Her heart had lurched at his intent gaze, and something had burned low in her belly. It was a feeling she'd never experienced before, an invitation to something new. Dangerous. She should be running long and hard from the passionate challenge, but the simmering heat was hard to resist.

"Just stay away from him and he'll leave you alone."

"Will he?"

"I'll talk to him, I promise. There are plenty of ready, willing and able women out there and Johnny still has thousands to go before he's finished."

Thoughts of the drummer brought a tingle, a sensation she couldn't define. It was disturbing and she knew it had to do with all that sexual heat emanating from him. There was strength there, too, a power source she'd give anything to draw on, but she knew in her heart that she'd be much too afraid to get near it.

Tish looked back to find Annie's face etched in annoyance.

"Is something wrong?"

Flustered, Annie sputtered, "Everything. My God, Johnny...then Tim putting you on the spot like that. This is not going the way I'd anticipated. I'm sorry."

Knowing that Annie was referring to the smoldering look Johnny had given her, Tish glanced out the door of the bedroom, listening to the click of a door closing somewhere. For as daunting as the look Johnny had given her was, she couldn't even imagine a man like him bothering with someone like her.

"He's everything you said he was."

She heard the flicker of awe in her own voice.

Getting the jumble of emotions under control, Tish assured Annie, "Don't look so worried. I'm sure as soon as he gets to know me, all interest will vanish."

Annie snorted.

"That will be because you're inexperienced. He won't come within miles."

Swallowing past the lump in her throat that had grown with talk of the drummer, Tish asked, "You grew up with him, right?"

"Yup. I told you a couple of stories that time you stayed with me, didn't I?"

"Yes, I loved hearing about the concerts, the cities you toured. I wish I could have seen the sights when I travelled but..."

Her mother had made sure Letitia had been confined to the hotel, her room, to the piano.

"They band has done some crazy, insane things. Tim says Johnny's still acting pretty outrageous. The man's a few years shy of thirty. You'd think he would've outgrown the shenanigans by now."

"That bothers you. Why?"

"We used to be close, and I get sentimental about the old days. He really is a great guy beneath all that...image. He used to be a big pussycat. I don't know what happened. Maybe ego...maybe restlessness or boredom."

Annie was giving the room a visual check.

"You were comfortable here before, right?"

Tish scanned the room. Nothing had changed. Calming, pastel colors, huge bed, an overstuffed chair and an antique looking bureau.

Tish pulled at her fingers.

"Is anyone else going to be sleeping in this part of the house?"

She didn't want to worry about bumping into anyone in the middle of the night. Anyone by the name of Johnny Scalera anyway.

"No," Annie assured her. "This suite will give you the privacy you want. I got around to decorating the loggia so there's furniture out there if you want to get some fresh air. As you know, the library is next door. I'm running out to pick you up some clothes. I didn't see a bag, so I assume you escaped with what you have on your back."

Tish had thought about it. Stood in her room, eyeing the closet, the highboy, before deciding to take anything would give her away.

"I didn't want Bruno suspecting the truth."

"It's not a problem. I'd wait but we're not the same size. Anything special you want?"

"I don't know. My mother always did my shopping."

She would come home to find her bed covered with dresses, shoes, shawls, slips that her mother would preen over. If they fit, they were transferred to her closet, if they didn't, they were returned to the store. It never mattered if she liked them or not and that argument was not one, she was willing to have.

"It's time for a new look. Your own Tish look. Do you trust me?"

"I guess."

What was a Tish look? And how did Annie know what that was when she didn't have a clue?

"Okay. Make yourself at home. I shouldn't be long."

"But..."

"You'll be fine. The guys are out in the studio, getting things organized. You won't even know they're there."

Tish watched as Annie left the room, heard the outer door open and close. She peered out the window as the car eased back out of the garage and down the drive. Finding her way to the comfy chair, she sat, almost frozen in place, straining to hear voices that never materialized.

Annie wouldn't be long, would she? The guys would stay busy until she got back, wouldn't they?

The minutes ticked away, the hands on the clock slowly marking time as she sat and waited, her mind numb.

Through the fog, she thought about her mother, shivers accompanying the thoughts that swirled through her restless mind. On a regular day, right about now, with practice wrapped up for the day, they'd sit together going over various recordings. Madeleine would be pointing out the nuances she thought important, those that Tish could incorporate into her own interpretation. It had once been an everyday exercise she'd shared privately with Arturo.

Arturo Schenbal, master that he was, had brilliant interpretive insight and a profound musical understanding. Her mother had neither. Where Arturo would contrast stylistic differences, an inherent understanding of what would work best for Tish's personality, Madeleine did not. After her beloved teacher had been fired for inciting Tish to grow and expand as a pianist, Madeleine had taken over the regimen. Madeleine's opinion changed every day, or at least often enough that Tish had never been sure which methods to use and which ones to let slide through her memory.

The result was today she could no longer differentiate between Bach, Brahms, Rachmaninoff and Ravel. Could no longer tell the ordinary from the enlightening, could no longer play with riveting power.

The depth of the loss sent her racing from the room, wanting to flee the images of an orchestra ready and waiting for her arrival on stage, her mother's verbal attacks that knew no bounds, and the shunning that resulted, the absolute rejection she could no longer endure.

After she entered the library, her eyes were drawn to the baby grand sitting in the front of the bay window. She let her emotions bubble and boil, hoping one would spark her old passion for the majestic instrument. Bereft at the lack of desire to sit at it, to sort through her mind for a piece to play or conjure up the magic that used to burn within, she feared she'd need to exorcise the piano from her life as much as sever her interaction with her mother.

What did that leave her?

She was feeling cornered again, frustrated, and the tears that had threatened to surface since leaving Diana's finally broke through. She dropped to the floor, all resistance to hold them back gone, and she let them flow, until sobs racked her body as she begged someone, somewhere for a way out.

"Please. I don't want to do this anymore, don't want to feel this way," she cried out, her body doubled over, her arms braced against the carpet.

"It...hurts...so...much."

A voice intruded, one she trusted. Annie's arms were around her, pulling her against her body, embracing her in a hug.

"Oh, sweetie. I'm so sorry."

"I don't know what to do. I'm so scared."

"I know. But you've decided to change your life. You can't do that without some growing pains."

"I feel like I've lived with pain my whole life. When will it end?"

"I don't know where you found the courage, but you've walked away from the source of your pain. It will get easier from here, I promise."

"I feel like I did when my father died."

The excruciating loss had changed her life and not for the better.

"In a way, it's the same thing. This time it's your music that's died. It's been a critical component to your happiness. Your mother's insensitivity to both events made the losses worse."

"I've tried so hard to do what she wants."

"That won't get you what *you* want, sweetie."

"What do I want?"

She couldn't get that untangled any better than the variegated symphonies in her head.

"Love, respect, acknowledgment."

Tish sat back on her haunches, true understanding of the situation becoming clear.

"I need to get my mother out of my life."

"Yes, you do. Experts don't usually recommend that except in extreme cases of toxicity. Whether you like it or not, that's where yours falls. The only way for you to have a healthy relationship with Madeleine is to have no inter-action."

Tish was hurt and disheartened that her mother couldn't be what she needed. Had never been.

Her throat aching, she cried out, "Why can't she love me?"

Annie moved out of the hug and sat with her legs crossed, still holding on to Tish's hands to retain physical contact.

"It's part of the disorder, Tish. It's her failing not yours. Love involves empathy, caring, connectedness. She is unable to feel any of those things."

Tish had done all she could to please her mother, and in spite of it, she'd never received the love she had craved. It was one-sided, distorted. What would a real picture look like? Her mother's image was exaggerated, taking up the whole frame. She wasn't even visible. What would it be like to erase Madeleine from the photo?

"Without her, there's nothing. She's all the family I have left."

"You've got me and Diana. The band. We could be your family if you let us."

Tish's legs tightened as if getting ready to run, but she forced herself to stay in place.

"I don't know who I am without her. Without my music."

"I know. Part of the pervasive disorders involve absorbing you into her force field. You've fought your way out and now the healing can begin. I'll help you find your own voice, help you express your thoughts, help you uncover who you are without her. Then you can stand on your own."

"Can you do that?"

"Yes. Here you have no limits, no forced confinement, free self-expression. You can play or not play. You can isolate yourself or form connections. It's your choice. Yours."

Nodding to the piano, Tish hiccupped. "I don't want to play that anymore, but I need to connect with something or someone."

"You can start with me."

"And maybe the keyboard."

Tish's labored breathing returned. She didn't know where that thought came from and she wasn't sure she liked it. The thought of playing keyboard in front of a live audience sent her into a whirling funnel of panic. But another thought fought for precedence. The tall, dark, dangerous man who had her heart beating in quarter time. She couldn't bear the idea of Johnny Scalera seeing her reduced to a quivering mass of jelly.

As if Annie could read between the lines, she said, "Only if it feels right. You've taken the first step. Now you need to take another in whichever direction you want to go."

"Tim won't force me to play or practice with the band?"

"No. You're safe here. You can say and do what you feel, and it will be valued."

"By you maybe."

She wasn't sure about the rest of the band yet.

Or the voice of her mother that still judged her harshly even from a distance.

"You're going to have to become your own mother. We all have to at some point. You're just getting a leg up."

Without a role model to follow, Tish didn't know what that would entail.

"How do I do that? I feel empty. I have nothing to give...myself."

"Your music is still inside of you. We need to find a way to unlock it."

She would give anything to find that lost key. Music was her life, and she wanted it to be as much a part of her physiology as her brain, lungs, and heart again. It fulfilled a need, a craving that couldn't be satisfied any other way.

"I'm not sure you're right. I feel like I have a hole inside, you know, where the music used to be."

"You think that your mother's acceptance can fill some of the emptiness. It can't. You have to do that yourself by accepting who you are at the core of your being. You have the false belief that you're nothing without your mother's approval. We're going to change that perception while we're on tour. You should have talked to a grief counselor after your father died, gone into therapy when your panic attacks started but your mother's outright refusal made any kind of remedy impossible. Her solution is a mental institution, not the slow process of maturation and growth."

Annie cupped her hand and explained, "My palms are full of the aspects of who you are. There's courage, curiosity, intelligence, and heart, along with a brilliant talent for the piano which adds feeling, emotion, and vulnerability. These are the things that will fill that hole when you own them."

"That's not how my mother sees me."

"That's because your mother looks at you and sees her reflection. Not who you are as an individual."

"How will I get her out of my head?"

"I'll help you. And when you can embrace a more positive belief about yourself, you can take over."

"I need a place to start."

"You're already there."

Hugging Annie, Tish felt a layer of guilt melt away. She was determined to take this opportunity and make something out of it. She didn't want to let Annie down, but she was beginning to realize she didn't want to let herself down either.

Annie clutched the bags sitting next to her on the floor and raised them up in a ta-da gesture.

"There's nothing like new clothes to make you feel better about things. I didn't have time to go to the mall, but I picked up a few goodies at one of my favorite stores close by. Why don't you try them on and see how you feel in them?"

With a slight smile, Tish said, "That's something my mother would say. If it looks good on the outside, all's right with the world."

"Oh, sorry. Put like that I guess I shouldn't be so excited, but you have to get out of that dress. It is so not you."

Tish glanced down at the Liz Claiborne A-line.

"Why not?"

"Your mother bought it for you, am I correct?'

"Yes."

"It looks like a dress a forty-year-old would wear."

"And your choices would be better because..."

"They'll at least let you look your age. Besides, you can't dress like that on tour. Once we're on the road, we'll go shopping and you can pick out your own stuff, develop a personal style."

Tish thought about that as she followed Annie into the bedroom.

Closing herself in the en-suite bathroom, she inspected every garment Annie had purchased. Every piece was different than what she was used to wearing. Her whole wardrobe consisted of conservative dresses and low-heeled shoes. Even her slacks were tailored, her sweaters cashmere, her blouses silk. Her mother had insisted she dress the part of success even when it began to fade.

Unzipping her dress, she let it fall to the floor as she picked up a pair of jeans that bore a Rock and Republic tag and stepped into them. They sat low-rise on her hip bones and she yanked the edge up without success. Exhaling in exasperation, she ripped the tags off a turquoise tee shirt and pulled it over her head, letting it settle just over the top of the jeans. She did a double take in the mirror. Awkwardness made her second guess the choice, the pants snug and unfamiliar, but she loved the colors. She leaned in for a closer look. Her eyes were darker, more vivid and her complexion appeared healthier. So, used to the neutral tones her mother purchased, she felt a giddy rush of adventure awaiting her. Maybe she could find a style all her own. A flutter of excitement skirted through her. Using the bathroom as a dressing room, she tried on several more articles of clothing, some form-fitting, that outlined her butt. She studied the curves she'd never been allowed to display before. Folding the rest up in a neat pile, she settled on the outfit she felt the most comfortable in. If she could call it that.

Annie's impatient yell, "Come on, I'm dying here to know what you think," prompted her to open the door a crack and slip out.

"I've never worn clothes like these before."

Uneasy in the new mode of dress, she felt her cheeks flush.

Annie insisted, "Turn around. Let me see."

Tish did a slow rotation, showing off the fit of the low-rise skinnies and the off-the-shoulder peasant top.

Annie all but squealed, "You look great. Killer body. Who knew?"

"I feel...exposed."

"Well, you can't keep dressing like a...classical pianist."

Tish felt an acute sense of loss. Given that she couldn't even play a hint of a prelude at the moment, she couldn't call herself that anymore. So, what was she?

An even more important question?

Who was she without her gift?

Annie broke into her philosophical musing.

"Does everything fit?"

"I guess."

Some of the shorts were a bit...short, and a couple of the tops were more revealing than she was used to, but she didn't dislike the idea of wearing them, especially the ones that were bright and bold. The clothes weren't high-end like she was used to, but they weren't stuffy. She liked that about them. They were the kind of clothes she could wear hanging out with friends, at least the imagined ones she practiced with in her mind.

"There's a traveling bag in the closet. You can use that to pack your stuff in."

Tish looked down at her feet, the cork-bottom wedge sandals a strange sight.

Glancing up, she asked Annie, "Can I paint my toenails?"

She'd often seen women at her concerts wearing sandals and colorful nail polish that matched. It was one of those things she dreamed of doing, but her mother thought polish looked garish, and it hadn't been allowed. It might be small and inconsequential but was important to her for some reason.

"Of course. I'll let you go through my polish collection and you can pick out whatever color you want. Out on the road we'll get pedicures as often as you want. There's nothing like having your feet pampered to feel girlie."

"I don't think I can afford that."

"It'll be my treat. Friend to friend."

"I've never had one before."

"A pedicure?"

"No. A friend. I don't really know what's involved."

It was a humiliating admission, but one Tish almost felt safe sharing with Annie. The friendship was still new, but Annie offered the kind of acceptance that made it easy.

"Just be yourself."

Tish didn't know who that was yet, but she was more than willing to do some digging to find out.

Annie began to scrunch up the bags, glancing around to make sure Tish had what she needed and when she was satisfied, she said, "We had Chinese food delivered and the gang is already eating."

"Who's here?"

"The guys in the band, Ron and his wife Melanie, Joe, Rambler and Chappy. Some of the crew who'll be on the buses tomorrow."

"What do they all do?"

"Ron Farnham's the tour manager. Makes sure our life on the road runs smoothly. Melanie picked up the accounting piece and draws up the budget and makes sure the bills are paid. They've been part of this circus since the beginning. Rambler, Joe and Chappy are the roadies. Their job is to take an empty stage and create an audio-visual masterpiece. They're some of the best in the business, making the sounds and lights come alive during the performance."

The safety Tish had felt only moments ago was evaporating like water in a boiling tea kettle. Madeleine had always done the talking, leaving her to her piano and skill. She had no idea how to behave in a group setting, always just standing to the side as her mother took center stage.

Maybe it was time she learned.

Not really interested in food but knowing she'd have to get used to the pandemonium, she said, "Sure. I guess."

She had to annihilate her demons and overcome her fear of people judging her. Or better yet, get to a place where it didn't matter if they did.

"Give me a minute, will you?"

"Sure. Come on out when you're ready."

"No. Please wait. I'll only be a few seconds."

Returning to the bathroom mirror, she studied the figure standing there. There was an Olympic-sized mental exercise going on in her head. She'd never been given the chance to be herself before. She'd always been isolated in a sterile environment, and there had been no one to talk to. Now she was being given the gift of connection and she didn't know how to unwrap it. Or what she'd find once she'd opened herself up to it. Annie had suggested she become her own mother but there she found only impatience and the stinging slap of ridicule. Tilting her head, she thought of her father. Maybe she could emulate his behavior instead.

Using his words, she whispered to the girl in the mirror, "You are loved to the moon and back. And you can do whatever you set your mind to. Go get 'em, my girl."

Love flooded through her.

Squaring her shoulders, she exited the room and headed out to the kitchen, Annie by her side, towards the discordant laughter, her father's words still echoing in her head, while the knot in her stomach continued to grow.

The kitchen and dining room offered enough seating for the whole group, although to Tish it seemed that they were broken into factions, each comfortable within their own group but somewhat fractious with each other. There was joking and teasing at the individual tables but an undercurrent of something she couldn't define. She watched, observed facial expressions, measured comments, studied interplay, and it seemed to her there was tension between Johnny and Tim in the way they spoke to each other from opposite sides of the room. Mesmerized by the aura of one-particular man, her eyes were invariably drawn to him. Sparks skittered through her veins. He both frightened her and interested her far more than was reasonable, and her fingers fluttered, before tracing the braided twine she wore around her wrist.

Johnny noticed the way her compelling turquoise eyes grazed on him from time to time.

It was deeply disturbing as if the very air around her was electrified.

What he didn't like was that his system was feeding off it.

She sat with the marrieds, but he had a clear view of her from his position at the dining room table. Toying with his food, he watched her as she made repeated attempts to join the conversation, but she couldn't keep up. Then she withdrew altogether.

He couldn't help himself, and his eyes sought her out again and again, studying her with intensity. There was an awakening fantasy here, but he'd already decided to stay as far away as space allowed, and the caution lights were flashing furiously. If she was this awkward at social interaction, he knew for a fact she'd have zero experience in the sex department. He didn't introduce anyone to the art of love. That had been written in stone a very long time ago.

How in the world did Tim know her?

He'd said a friend of a friend, but he knew them all. So, who was the friend?

And why had Tim agreed to take her on as keyboard player? They both knew dozens of musicians they could've hired who would have worked just as well, or, as he was beginning to think, much better. The way she disassembled when Ron tried to pull her into the conversation led him to the undeniable fact that Tish didn't have the right stuff for a performer.

So why her?

Tim had deflected every question he had thrown at him earlier. In the dark, Johnny began obsessing about it

She hadn't come to the studio for their earlier practice, so there was a sneaking suspicion as to whether she could even play the instrument. He was determined to solve the mystery.

His attention remained on her as she helped with the clean-up. He became perplexed at how skittish she was as they walked downstairs to the media room, the pull as much of a mystery as the woman.

Quickening his steps, he was soon following close behind her.

"So, Tish, where are you from?"

She took a step closer to Annie, shy as a mouse around a tomcat.

"Um, around."

Totally inept at social discourse.

Annie tucked her hand in the crook of Tish's arm and pulled her forward, giving him a look that said, "*beat it.*"

Slight as a sparrow.

Why in the world was he so intrigued? And so damn attracted.

She was an enigma and once he'd figured her out, all would be good again.

He pushed his hand through his hair, the thought of watching a movie not really grabbing his interest. He had to admit the media room was state-of-the-art, with a theater size screen and reclining chairs that sat in rows. From time to time, he'd agreed to join them in the past, but it was too mundane for his taste. Any short break was enough to cause boredom and being idle was not something he did well.

As he debated whether or not to take a seat, Reject asked, "So what are we doing tonight?"

Reject's booted foot tapped as he waited for a response.

Johnny took a step into the room. "I'm sticking around."

Reject's voice held a note of exasperation.

"What the hell for?"

With a casual air, he replied, "I want to save my energy for Richmond."

"Yeah, right."

Johnny didn't miss the sarcasm and knew what his bandmate was implying. Tish looked fragile and broken, and what he was doing didn't make any sense.

As he took a seat, Reject asked, "You've gotta be kidding, right?"

"I'm staying in. You're on your own."

"Fine. I'll be in Allston if you change your mind."

Johnny heard Reject's booted heels clicking on the wooden treads as he moved in the direction of the front door and driveway.

Losing himself in his thoughts, Johnny conjured up images of a waif-like creature with eyes that were shining bits of turquoise, mesmerizing, brilliant, metallic. Almond-shaped with eyebrows that framed them perfectly. The jeans she had on looked new, as if she'd never worn them before, as if she didn't like the way they felt. But the blue-and-white-peasant top fit her very nice figure to a tee, showing off a long, graceful neck and her peaches-and-cream shoulders. Like a porcelain doll, without the spots of color rubbed into her cheeks.

He shot a glance over to where Tim sat beside Chappy to see him laughing along with the movie. Tim seemed content with his life. He envied that at times. Most of their days and nights were spent practicing, performing, recording, touring, but Annie and Tim filled the down time with family and each other. He didn't have that anymore, letting his family slip away from him one member at a time. His sister Rissa was the only one he talked to anymore and that was more her doing than his. She was getting married in the fall and had demanded he attend the wedding. He still wasn't sure he wanted to. It would mean uncomfortable conversation with his stepfather and brothers, although he was beginning to miss...

Too many distracting thoughts floated around in his brain along with the enticing flavor wafting from the seat in front. Vanilla? Cinnamon? Baking cookie dough? It had his stomach growling, a taste he was beginning to salivate for. A taste he'd denied himself for as long as he could remember.

He refused to allow Tish or thoughts of his family disturb the life he'd designed for himself.

Edginess drove him up and out of his seat, through the door and into the night.

The bar in Allston was crowded, the drinks strong, the band was loud, the women were beautiful and attentive. His irritation with everything was irritating him.

He'd needed to escape the sensory overload at Tim's and sought out a more kinetic type of action in one of the band's regular drinking holes outside of Boston. Reject had already been immersed in a sea of women, and as soon as Johnny took a seat at the table, the swell spilled over to him as well. Reject welcomed him with a sardonic smile.

"Glad you could make it."

Johnny studied the familiar face of his band mate, who was seated between two blondes. The bassist was enjoying the one consequence of their success they both valued. Snagging a waitress so Johnny could order, Reject lifted his glass in a toast. "Here's to tonight."

He gave each woman a kiss that would determine which lucky lady would get to feast on a rock star later.

Johnny swallowed his distaste along with a sip of tequila.

Lost in his thoughts, he considered what had taken place over the last few days.

Was it apathy that had led him to hand over all decisions to Tim?

The more pressing concern, at the moment, had to do with the who rather than the why.

A tug brought him back as the woman seated next to him snagged her finger in his hair.

"Stop. That's my head."

The demand was a bark and growl.

Women were forever fiddling with strands of it, and when they pulled, it rankled.

The woman loosened her grip but didn't retreat, and she was much too close for comfort.

Her breath was heavy in his ear when she whispered, "How about we take off for your place?"

Her voice was high-pitched and shrill, so unlike the soft words that tumbled out of Tish's mouth. He didn't want to go anywhere with this woman, so he ignored her request, drumming his fingers on the scarred wooden table.

Thinking about the fiasco at the studio, anger hit his gut.

They had to shelve the recording, which didn't sit well with any of them. From the minute they had stepped into the cavernous hangar, there had been problems. They couldn't put more than three songs down with any success. Nothing was jibing. Unable to string more than two sentences of lyrics together, with the riffs uninspiring, they had thrown in the towel. Why Tim thought a break in the tour would be productive, he wasn't sure. The guitarist had thought that breaking the tour up into two parts, with a three-week hiatus in between, would give them the opportunity to get another couple of songs written, recorded, and added to the disc he had titled *A Muse*. He had to give Tim credit for working night and day to reach the objective but what none of them had counted on was the weak sound, the arguments, the inability to put life into the music. Frustrated that the creative juices had dried up, they had all decided to pick it back up after the tour was completed in the hopes, they could get their creative spark back.

Johnny knew it was a crock.

Going straight for six years, without a break of any kind, they were, as they say, running on empty. The cross-country trip would not fill their tanks.

Rebooting the conversation with Tim, right before he left the hangar earlier, his temper sparked again.

"Can you give me a couple of hours, Johnny? Maybe we can put a song together like the old days. Just you and me."

Taking his eyes off his friend, Johnny focused on something over Tim's shoulder.

"Don't have two to rub together, buddy."

"Bet you'll find time later for screwing."

Tim's caustic remark hit below the belt.

"I can always find time for that. Besides, you're the one who wanted to take the lead."

"I didn't take it. You abdicated."

"Weighs me down. Go home and see Annie. Relax. Take her to bed."

"Is that all you think about?"

"Pretty much. It makes life easier."

"Why don't you come home with me? We can hang out. We haven't done it in a long time."

He laughed out loud.

"It's bad enough I have to stay over tonight. I don't know how we let you talk us into staying at your house the night before the kickoff for a tour."

Tim and Annie lived in a small town about thirty miles west of Boston and it had very little in the way of entertainment.

"Maybe we can just jam for a while. See where it takes us."

Already heading for the exit, Johnny explained, "I'm all jammed out. Want some action."

Grabbing his arm, Tim forced Johnny to meet his eyes, imploring, "What the hell's happened to you? You used to give a shit."

Tim continued glaring at him before adding, "You do realize if there's no music your popularity won't last long."

Shaking the arm off, he dismissed the imagined threat.

"Let me worry about my popularity. I'll let you worry about the rest."

"Thanks, Johnny. Thanks for nothing."

Tim had turned his back on him and walked away.

Or had he turned his back on Tim?

His eyes scanned the cramped space, his ears ringing with a tinny beat.

He'd walked away again for a night...of this.

His fingers flicked the table, his nervous energy accelerating with each chord being played by the house band, and Johnny pushed his chair back with a shove and left the bar without a backward glance. The place was nothing more than a frat party with a cover charge, and he was beginning to think he was getting too old for this shit.

When he reached his car, he sat wondering what the hell he'd do now.

Turning the ignition, he veered out of the parking lot, and hit the highway that would take him back to Tim's.

Maybe he could spend some time in the studio, look at the songs he'd casually discarded. Maybe he'd find some kind of spark.

It had been a long time since he'd felt one.

CHAPTER SIX

Tish couldn't seem to concentrate on the movie. Fingers pulled and fiddled, clasped and unclasped, her foot tapped from restlessness as thoughts of the keyboard bounced around her mind. Her fingers itched for the feel of ivory beneath them, but her mind still stubbornly refused to bring one of her classical favorites into consciousness. She was going to have to find another way to channel her emotions and this might be the only alternative she had. Giving into the possibility, she asked Annie on the way back to their rooms, "Do you think I could look at Thunder's sheet music?"

"There's nothing written down."

Stopping short, alarm throbbing in her temple, Tish exclaimed, "There must be something on-line."

"Drums, guitar, yes, but they've never included a keyboard. I can lend you some of the CD's. You know their music. Maybe you can write an accompaniment as you go."

Her mother had anointed her as hopeless when it came to interpreting music. The thought of having to create on her own was a daunting prospect.

"I can't do that."

"Yes, you can. I've heard you play."

"I just play what's written and lately I can't even do that."

Patting Tish's back as they regained their path towards the main part of the house, Annie gave Tish a lop-sided smile.

"If I know anything, I know what kind of heart and spirit you have. You can play whatever you set your mind to. Besides, isn't that the whole idea? To play what's inside, not what's on paper?"

The hole in her stomach yawned wider, reminding Tish of how empty she was.

"But that's the point. There is nothing inside of me anymore. It's gone. I can't hear or feel a thing."

"Maybe not your concertos but this is different."

"What if I don't do it well? What if I play what's in my head and it isn't good enough?"

"Tish, Raging Thunder doesn't play Carnegie Hall. They play to screaming women who drown out most of the music."

"But I'll hear it."

"Yes, and you're a harsh critic. God, Tish, you've excelled at every piece you've tried. Been called a genius with magical interpretation. I'm sure you can interpret Thunder's music. It's just basic chords played with an inordinate amount of noise."

Biting her lip, she conceded, "I guess I could try."

Could Annie feel her racing heart?

When she glanced up, she met eyes without judgment, compassion shining through. Reaching forward, Tish wrapped her arms around Annie and mumbled her thanks before letting her return to her own life in another part of the house. Straying into her room, Tish sank to the bed.

Placing her head in her hands, the turmoil started roiling again. She knew now why people stayed with the devil they knew. It was easier than facing the unknown. And she was in such foreign territory that she began to hyperventilate. Fear was here with her. She hadn't escaped it. Her bosom buddy that followed her around like a shadow of doom. She longed for the day it would no longer hover over her.

To experiment with her own voice, to live life the way she wanted was frightening but there was also an eager anticipation that spurred her on. Face the fear and do it anyway.

She was starting now.

Pulling her breath in, she got up on rubbery legs and faced the mirror that adorned the maple bureau. There was a stranger there.

Letitia Jones had never worn jeans in her life.

Gone were the classic lines, the designer labels, the modest attire.

Licking her lips, she readjusted the image to see Tish standing there in her place.

After giving herself another pep talk, she crept out of the house through the loggia, not wanting to disturb the dogs or the sleeping household. Annie had given her the code for the studio alarm so that if she wanted to play, she would have access to the instruments. She wasn't sure what she was going to find, she wasn't sure what she was going to be able to do, but she knew she had to initiate a start. If there was a chance for survival, she had to master the art of this strange, new form. Relieved rather than inconvenienced that the rendezvous with fate would be conducted after midnight and in private, she wanted to be alone the first time she sat at the keyboard. There was still the looming possibility she couldn't cut it and she wanted to know before anyone else did.

Forewarned was forearmed.

So, with half a dozen CDs grasped in her hand, she punched in the four-digit code number, waited for the green light to appear and entered the square building that Tim had built as a recording studio. When she switched on one of the overhead lights, the fluorescent bulbs flickered, illuminating the modern facility. She stood transfixed at the sight in front of her. It hadn't seemed so...complicated when Annie had first shown her the set-up while some of the guys were still eating dinner.

On one side, the wall was made up entirely of amplifiers of all sizes, and a control panel that must be the soundboard, took up the length of another. A set of drums, with too many components for her mind to register, sat throne-like in the center of the space. Microphones stood in clusters, dozens of guitars rested against racks, speakers hung from the walls, sat in supports, faced the mics. The floor was littered with pedals of all kinds and colors, their cords zigzagging like snakes across the expansive room. A keyboard sat atop a table and was looked down upon by a computer, with another amp keeping it company. Tish's hands were sweaty although she felt a chill race through her bones as she took in the complex world that had become her own.

She wanted to run but she knew this was all she had left.

Stealthily approaching the sound system that sat in pieces on a metal shelf, she looked with trepidation at the intricate gadgetry, having no clue as to how to even switch it on.

Squinting, trying to get her bearings, she searched each toggle, each knob, hoping she'd find one that read Power. Her trembling fingers didn't make it easy.

So engrossed in what she was doing, she didn't hear the approaching footsteps.

"Who's in there?"

The CDs slipped from her fingers as she spun around, facing the man she knew belonged to the baritone growl.

"I-it-t's me, Tish."

"What the hell...?"

Johnny strode into the room, his unlaced boots making no sound on the carpeted floor that covered the entry, his face a curious mixture of irritation and gruffness.

"Annie said I could come out and practice whenever I wanted."

"It's two a.m. Don't you sleep?"

She bit her lip, not knowing what to say. What could she say?

No, as a matter of fact I don't. I'm too wired up, worried about being able to do this. Worried that my mother is going to track me down, brow beat me into going back. Worried that I won't be any better off in this new life than in my old. Worried I'll never fit in.

Instead, she gave him a small taste of the truth. "Not as much as I'd like."

She felt his eyes on her, but they snapped away as if he couldn't stand the sight of her.

"What are you trying to do?"

As if her tongue had swollen, she found it impossible to speak. Her throat muscles had contracted at first glance of the man standing not twenty-feet away. He had pulled his hair back on the sides, defining the structure of his rugged face. His eyebrows were almost sculpted, his nose striking, his eyes fierce. His black tee shirt didn't hide the biceps and the washed-out jeans were molded to his slim hips and lean legs.

Stuttering, she forced out, "Find the switch."

When he shook his head, and snarled, "You can't even turn the damn thing on?" she felt like an idiot.

Then she was crumbling.

When she performed her own genre and entered stage left, everything was always in place. She had no clue what to do with the electronics, not even with the small technicality of powering up the system. She decided to give up this stupid idea.

"I guess this isn't a good plan. Maybe I better wait until tomorrow."

She felt as if all the blood had drained from her body, and fainting was a real threat. When she looked up at him, she noticed his face had softened and his voice was almost patient.

"Here, let me help you."

He was beside her now and she could smell the conflicting aromas: whiskey, smoke, after-shave, perfume and something musky that she couldn't make out. She darted looks at his height and at the beautiful dark hair. Fighting fingers that wanted to reach out and touch, she envied him the long locks. Hers were so fine even the butterfly clip that held it up and away from her face couldn't help but slide off. She had permed it once, to give it body. At least that was the excuse she'd given her mother so she could get out of the condo for a few hours, but even that freedom had been taken away. She unconsciously removed the clip, twirled her hair and redid it, sweeping the flyaway strands off her face.

Squatting down, Johnny retrieved the CD cases that were spread out over the concrete and asked which one she wanted first.

Still not knowing what she was going to do or what to say, she mumbled out a nonsensical, "Okay."

"Well which songs did Tim want you to play backup on?"

Shrugging her shoulders, she snuck another peek and was caught in a web of dark, piercing eyes. Her heart turned over in response. Again.

"He did talk to you about what he wanted you to play, didn't he?"

Her mind fogged up and she answered as best she could.

"Um, not specifics."

"Which one were you thinking about practicing?"

"I don't know."

He was making her jittery, and her mind still hadn't cleared. Her intention had been to find a song out of the many that she could build chords around, but he was looking at her as if she should have a more definite plan in mind.

When he snorted, then glared at her in accusation, she read his suspicions and she knew another wave of anger was going to crash over her.

"Tell me the truth. Can you even play?"

Squinting her yes in the direction of the flat piano she'd never once thought of playing, she had to admit the truth if only to herself. She didn't know. So how could she answer him? There had been a time she'd played very well, like an angel, with clarity, shading, beautiful fullness, if you believed the reviews.

On a baby grand.

Today she played more like a mechanical robot, if she could play at all. But it didn't take away the fact that she'd taken lessons for years, from some of the greats, had won awards and had been entertaining people from the piano bench for what seemed like forever. She knew the basic understanding of the percussion instrument and had some sort of technique.

A new ripple of apprehension moved through her.

Standing at her full height, she crossed her arms over her chest, jutted out her chin and said with confidence, "Yes, I can play."

He crossed his arms over his chest and spit out, "Then play '*Lovin Easy*' and prove it."

No longer able to meet his gaze, the shivers racing through her system becoming incapacitating, she lowered her eyes, as doubt came calling again.

"I don't happen to know that one."

She read danger in his narrowed eyes and she gulped hard past the lump in her throat.

"Which one do you know?"

"Um, I've heard a lot of them. Annie gave me all the albums. I just don't know the names of the individual songs."

She had listened to a couple of Thunder's CDs while building up the courage to come out here.

Peeking her eyes back up to the ferocious look on his face, hoping her voice sounded conciliatory, she added, '*Layin' It On Thick*' has a great set of tracks. I like it a lot."

When she saw the semblance of a smile appear on his face, she relaxed a bit.

"That was one of our better ones. Can you sing a few bars of the one you might like to start with?"

Staring past him, she replayed the sound in her head giving her ears another shot of hearing garbled words but had no better luck in discerning them this time than last. Knowing he wouldn't like her answer, she faced him anyway.

"No. Besides, all I could make out were the drums and guitars."

The words had gotten lost in the primitive beat of the music.

"Our critics happen to agree with you, and it can be a problem."

"I didn't see a problem."

Except she still wasn't sure she could find something to add to the grinding rhythm.

The intensity of his gaze made her shift her stance.

He asked again, "You can play?"

The adrenaline that had coursed through her body the moment he arrived had left her exhausted. She wasn't sure she wanted to fence with him anymore. But his doubt in her ability to play had riled her. He was making it seem like she had made the whole thing up. Her mother thought along similar lines, and she was tired of being accused of lying.

"I told you I can play. I don't fabricate the truth."

She rethought her statement and had to admit she did on occasion. No one knew how scared she was all the time. Under her breath she added, "Often."

"What can you play?"

He mustn't have heard the last word, still focused on her admission of truth although he still wore a doubtful expression.

Biting her lip, she admitted, "I play a mean Beethoven."

With a rise in vocal pitch, he asked, "You do classical shit?"

Hesitating, the truth hovering on her lips, she reclaimed her wits. "Some."

"Any hard rock at all?"

"I can fake some Barry Manilow. And Elton John."

He rolled his eyes and looked up at the ceiling, and she could almost hear him praying to the heavens for patience.

"I'll plug in our most recent album and we'll see what you can do with it. Okay?"

Not requiring an answer, he poked a couple of black knobs, and she could hear the power, the low hum of the amplifier, surround her. When he was finished, and he faced her, hands on hips, he said, "Let's see what you've got."

She was paralyzed by his presence and by what he expected to hear.

Did she have what he was looking for inside of her?

Unsure of the answer, she stated, "I'd rather be alone."

Cocking a dark eyebrow, he gave her a sly grin.

"I'm sure you would but I'm staying."

Pulling at her fingers, a quirk she'd adapted in response to her insecurity, she realized what she was doing and stopped, letting her arms fall to her sides.

"I'm not sure I can play with you here."

"Then we'll just have to tell Tim. You see, I'll be on stage with you from Richmond on."

He was right. She'd have to get used to playing with him around. That was, of course, if she could play to begin with.

Why did Tim have to announce the plan they'd toyed with without her permission?

The thought of playing to Thunder's audiences, any audience, made her skin crawl.

What had started out as a rumination in her head came through a larynx she was sure had shut down.

"Do you like being on stage?"

She was talking to his back.

He was busy with the amp that was hooked to the keyboard.

"Sure. I wouldn't be a rock star if I didn't, now would I?"

"It doesn't sc...bother you? All those people?"

He sat on the edge of the table that held the computer. The look on his face only confirmed his words.

"I love it. Love banging away, love the way it feels. Besides, with all those beautiful women wanting a piece of me, what's not to like?"

She swallowed, assessing, understanding why women would find him mouthwatering. Because he was. He had the kind of rangy body that jeans looked good on, and he seemed so completely at ease with what he had to offer. Would she ever feel like that? Doubtful. She couldn't imagine men ever drooling over her. The type of concert she gave wasn't anything like his. People sat quite still, with very little emotion. Or maybe that was her, holding it all in.

He asked, "Have you ever been on stage before?"

There had been years of concerts. Lately, she couldn't get beyond her hotel room door. It had to do with stage fright so intense she couldn't get near the hall. That had to change, or her life was over. She couldn't tell him any of that, so she told another half-truth.

"Once upon a time. I have to get used to it again."

"Why? You could always quit."

Her eyes moved up to meet his, the hope shining in specks of gold.

"And do what?"

She needed to know if there was an alternative.

"I don't know. Get married. Stay home and have babies."

Her eyes fluttered closed.

Drawing in a single breath, she let hope out in her exhale. She had thought of it as an option, once her music had died. Up until then, her playing had been the driving force of her personality, her form of expression as a person and it was in her blood. The problem with the alternative was that she'd never find a man who would take her on. Now, more than ever. She had nothing to give.

Hadn't her mother told her often enough how selfish and shallow she was?

She almost laughed outright when she tried to imagine anyone falling in love with her.

Instead, she gave Johnny a sad smile.

"I expected something more helpful."

Glancing around as if not wanting to meet her eyes, he straightened and asked in a gruff voice, "Are you ready?"

He stood by the small keyboard, waiting for her to take her place.

Tish tried to figure out another way to stall for time, but she knew he wasn't going to give her an inch.

With tiny steps, she approached him and with each step that brought her closer, she felt smaller and smaller. He was powerful. Not only in a physical sense but his presence was explosive. He towered over her breathing fire. She pulled at her fingers before fumbling for the swivel stool, wanting to pull it towards her so she wouldn't have to take the final step. So used to grand pianos and her own bench, made to her specifications, she had a hard time balancing on the round seat. It didn't help any that he made her more nervous with every breath he took.

She looked down at the board.

It had a smaller range with less than the eighty-eight keys she was accustomed to.

Then her fingers touched the surface. The white keys felt more like plastic than what she was used to and her fingers recoiled in response.

"What's the matter?"

His voice rustled against her ear, he was sitting so close, and she recoiled from him as well.

"Nothing. Just trying to get my bearings. This is different than the one I play."

"It's an electric synthesizer. They're all the same."

"Do all drum sets sound the same?"

As if thinking about it, he had to admit, "No. They don't."

"Okay, see?"

"Look, just play what comes to you. Let me get a sense of what you can do."

How many times had her mother yelled at her for giving into her flights of fancy, when her fingers had flown over the keys, expressing the music in her own way? How many times had Madeleine yelled and scolded and scowled? How many times had she been punished with another two or three hours of practice, her back sore, her fingers aching, punching out the stilled notes on the sheet music?

Too many times to count. Now she was being asked to think for herself. She wasn't sure she could anymore, but she didn't want to fail in front of someone she wanted to impress.

Would she be able to prove she wasn't a total incompetent?

Hanging her head, she felt her hands shaking and it only got worse after he ambled over to the wall-to-wall system before saying, "Here we go."

She was jolted by the level of noise that filled the room, now flooded with pounding music, guitars screaming, the bass thumping and a drum beat that shot right through her. Trying to adjust to the ear-splitting volume took time. So did trying to figure out what key the song was in. The music took turn after turn, but she couldn't keep up.

She heard him mumble that she was inept.

Placing her fingers on the keys, she listened, wanting to grab hold of a riff, but as soon as she pressed down, attempting a chord progression, she jerked away. This was such a different sound than what she was used to. Her piano was deeply resonant. This was shallow and shrill. There wasn't a pedal to mute or sustain the sound.

He took one more step back and gave her a snide comeback.

"Well, babe, that ain't what I call playing. I think Tim should know what he got us into. If you don't prove you can do this soon, I'm going to tell him."

Exasperation with him came screeching out in a rush.

"You're making me nervous. I can do this. Let me hear the music. Play it again."

She shrank back and froze, bracing for a verbal punch.

He stared for a few moments and then blinked.

When he did, her whole body relaxed.

She had won a small victory with someone bigger and stronger.

He gave her the quiet she needed to experiment with some chords. When the studio was once again consumed by the pulsing beat, she began to talk herself through the chord sequences, committing to memory what she played as if programming some imaginary mechanism inside.

With a determined croak, she demanded, "Again."

He hit the replay button and the same song came through the speakers, keeping the beat with his sticks as she wound her way through the maze of changing tempos.

When the music faded away, she sat with her head down, not wanting to see his expression, waiting for the criticism she believed would come.

After a brief hesitation, Johnny said, "Okay. I've got to admit you know your way around the keys. But you're not feeling the music. You sound too mechanical."

Her head shot up, her pulse quickening when he pulled up another stool and sat beside her.

"You need to let the music flow through you and play as it does. When I play the drums, I can't be thinking at all. I've got to go with the way the music feels. And I set the tempo and hold the beat. Without me, it falls apart. If I did it by some book, it would sound...shitty."

Her frustration was thick in her voice as if she'd been told that a thousand times.

"I know that."

He didn't need to know she'd lost the capacity to play from her heart.

"You can't play any other way."

Her head drooped. Her chest tightened. She wanted to fade into the background so Johnny couldn't judge her and find her lacking. Becoming invisible wasn't an option right now so she had to fight the feelings of inadequacy and the ache that filled the void where her music had once burned in her soul.

Softening his voice, he encouraged her with gentle words.

"Look, I'll play along. You listen to my beat, close your eyes, put your fingers on the keys and see what happens."

She placed trembling digits where he'd directed.

His proximity was throwing her equilibrium off and he'd sweetened his tone, so she didn't know what to say or how to react. Her weakness was breaking her will, her body demanding something from his presence she didn't know how to explain. She wished he'd just go away and leave her to her own devices. He was too intense, and the effect was an erratic pulse, a suffocating sensation and the inability to know where to put her hands. Too timid to do otherwise she kept them curled over the keys and away from danger. What she really wanted to do was reach out and touch all the power and force.

As if reading her mind, he picked up her hand, his thumb caressing the long, slender fingers as if they were bone china. Her eyes shot up to see his expression, tingles shooting down her spine.

What was he doing?

And why did it feel like streak lightning was flashing through her when he did?

She was drowning in his warmth and heat, and as her whole body became infused with it, she made it her own. Unable to breathe as she felt the rough texture of his hand continue its inspection, she began to crave something more, although she had no idea what it was. He was playing a song, with the intimate touch. Not like the simple, sweet sound of love unfolding in a Handel piece, but more like the flutter trill of a Chopin nocturne. The light delicate notes played out in her body, creating layers of emotion with each stroke until she was herself a tightly strung instrument.

And then he was placing her hand back down, almost with a tenderness she didn't understand.

His voice was hoarse and graveled.

"Nice fingers."

Bereft of his touch, she didn't respond, didn't know how to.

So instead, she gritted her teeth, refocused, refusing to back down from the fear of sitting here beside him, her body trembling from his touch. Feeling his arm brush against hers sent the sparks flying again and she quaked at the contact. His muscles rippled and she lost the capacity to think.

But his voice held a hypnotic tone, reminding her to stay with him.

"Close your eyes, listen to the beat, and express what you feel."

She breathed in, stealing some of his strength to fund her power.

His hands were keeping the beat, his drumsticks clacking together, and she allowed it to fill her head. Her frigid fingers lay on the keys until the second stanza, when she let herself become the music, a skill she'd thought lost, hearing what the musicians were trying to say, and it came out in a way she never would have thought to play it. Discordant, choppy, nothing planned, in several different keys. Interspersing the remainder of the song with staccato beats, she sat there as the music wound down, knowing she had come up with an interpretation. It was a start.

She knew she would never have gotten there without Johnny's help.

Then a ragged thought sliced through her.

What if he didn't like her interpretation?

He had become quiet, even his sticks muted. She closed her eyes before finding the courage to look his way.

His mouth was ajar.

A cold knot formed in her stomach as she asked, "No?"

"Where did you come up with that?"

Her irritation was rising again as she felt the sting of criticism on his tongue.

She bit out, "I don't know. Sorry if it wasn't what you wanted."

She flew up off the stool and headed towards the door when he shouted out, "Where are you going?"

"Back to the house."

Where she should have been hours ago, without giving him any reason to belittle her.

She had spent the earlier part of the day reading it in his eyes.

"What about the other songs? You have to give them a try."

"I'm through trying. I'm sick to death of coming up short."

She was out the door before his voice could reach her.

Talking to the emptiness that now encompassed him, he asked, "Short? What are you talking about? That was unbelievable."

He stared at the door she'd exited, excitement raging through him. It was mixed with an unexpected desire to be with her, just for the sake of being.

She was incredible and he couldn't wait to hear what she'd do with some of their other stuff. Different things sounded in his head, new beats, new words, but he shook them out. He didn't want to take time to write them down. Or maybe he was just enjoying the spark that had erupted inside. It had been a long time since he'd felt it.

The night had started out in tedious routine. With the innovative energy Tish brought into the studio, he'd been filled with fresh and creative ideas. The time he'd just spent here in this room with her had been astonishing, filling him with a new sense of power. He laughed to himself as he considered her talent. It was as if she'd never touched a keyboard before, didn't even know what kind of sound it could make, and then she'd exhibited genius, the colors clear, bright, and bold. It was even more invigorating than sex.

He tried to analyze her reaction to his words.

Why had she completely misread him?

She'd run away as if he were raining insults, never giving him time to set her straight. Or reveal what else she had inside of her. He couldn't wait until tomorrow and the anticipation continued to build.

Too wired to sleep, he just stood there, by the side of the keyboard set-up, envisioning her efforts, her concentration, her fragile trust, her innocence and the intoxicating look of those eyes when she'd sought out his guidance.

Striding over to the sitting area, he threw himself on the couch, his arm slung over his forehead and stared at the ceiling, the lights dangling over him. They illuminated the huge space, but shadows seemed to lurk in every corner. From his vantage point he surveyed the equipment that was so much a part of his world. As the vortex of Raging Thunder's sound, his drums always sat front and center. Winding out around him in a concentric circle came the rest of the band, Tim to his right, Reject in front of him, and Terry to his left. Every night they formed the same pattern, every year they had become tighter, moving in and out of riffs and drum fills, with flawless harmony, a flow of tones that meshed well.

Today, the circle was broken.

His eyes swept over the space, designed by the entire band and some of their roadies.

Why had they let the new label executives rent the blasted hangar when this studio had worked so well for them in the past?

This room was the epitome of who they were, how they had grown, their handprint on every piece of equipment chosen. He knew every toggle, every amp and what it could give him. His drum kit, acoustic, with a great feel and touch. He could tune it himself, and he could squeeze out the tiny subtleties that enhanced the hard, vibrating beat of the music.

The one at the empty airplane hangar was devoid of...all of that.

He had complained vigorously since the first rehearsal but never did anything about his dissatisfaction, showing up every day, playing an instrument he owned like an automaton. It should come as no surprise that nothing was working. Every drum roll, every twang of the guitar reverberated, with an unpleasant feedback filled with static, white noise.

Had they lost their touch?

Could Tish help them get it back?

He had glimpsed moments of genius but there was still a long way to go before she was fluent in key speak.

How much time would it take to get her there?

And did he have the patience required?

Or the discipline?

He'd lost his sticking power along the way. Taken bigger and bigger steps away from all forms of responsibility. The only thing he hung on to tenaciously was his vow. The one that kept him out of the bed of virgins.

He knew for a fact Tish was in that forbidden territory, but she touched a chord in him that resonated deep inside.

And if he continued to spend time with her, she might be able to undermine his resolve like no one before.

CHAPTER SEVEN

Johnny ambled into Annie's kitchen, music flooding the room, strings, rising in crescendo with a piano speaking in a transcendent language and he fired a demand, "I hate this stuff. Can't you play something other than classical?"

Annie looked up from the task of slicing tomatoes, glanced at Tish who was sitting in the breakfast nook listening to her iPod and grumbled back, "Cranky this morning, aren't we?"

Putting her focus back on what she was doing, she reminded him, "My house. When you're here you listen to what I like."

Giving the others in attendance a brief nod, he grabbed a sub roll, helped himself to the platter of cold cuts, and made a Dogwood sandwich, lowering himself onto one of the breakfast stools at the island. He never made it up for breakfast, so lunch was his first meal of the day.

As he moved, he listened to the exchange going on between Reject and the Farnhams, who were sitting at the kitchen table.

Reject was complaining again about their mode of travel. Melanie was giving him the standard sarcastic response.

"Until Peter Pan grows up and starts doing his job again, it's the bus route. You're lucky the tour didn't get cancelled outright."

"What do you mean? Our CDs are still selling. iTunes does well."

"True but that's because of Rambler. He works miracles with your weaknesses."

"We don't have that many."

"Yeah, you do. You guys have fallen apart. It's not one for all anymore. It's every man for himself. There is no depth to your sound and it's hurting us."

Ticket sales were down.

So the band was on a pretty strict budget.

Splitting their time between sleeper buses and less expensive hotels than they were used to.

With the sandwich held in both hands, Johnny wondered.

Had the hunger dissipated, or had it gotten so routine they called it in, not bothering to fire up their passion? It annoyed him that they hadn't sold out the arenas.

What did they have to do to get their mojo back?

With a pointed look in Tish's direction, he thought she might be the match that re-ignited the band's fire.

Could Tim be right?

If she gave it some time, became fluent in their music could Tish add the depth they were missing?

Proficiency wouldn't matter if she couldn't face an audience of thousands. She'd had a problem with an audience of one. Hadn't she mentioned last night that she had an issue there? Would have to get used to it? Maybe she'd never make it out onto the stage with them.

As if his eyes had drawn hers, she glanced in his direction. He motioned for her to take out the earbuds. Although she seemed reluctant to do so, she removed them one at a time.

He nodded his head in the direction of the speakers and asked, "Is this the stuff you play?"

Tish listened for a moment and said with a slight smile of defiance, "Stuff? I think it deserves a more respectful description, don't you?"

"Okay. Maybe you're right. Is this the *genre* you play?"

She licked her lips during the pause and then said, "Sometimes. It's how every pi—piano player starts out."

With his mouth now full of food, his words were muffled.

"He's talented. But you could be better. You should give this...genre a try."

Eyes widened to saucers, she almost choked on her words.

"You've got to be kidding?"

Swallowing the bite he'd taken, he answered, "No, you could. You've got fingers made for the piano."

He almost chuckled as she snatched her hands into her lap.

It was Annie who asked, "And how would you know that?"

Johnny explained, "We practiced together last night. I couldn't help but notice."

And notice he had. They were long, slender and she was able to extend her fingers and hit chords impossible for him to play and his hands were twice the size. Her range was mind-boggling. He had traced the slender digits. Wanted to lick them was how he remembered it.

Uncomfortable with what that did to his body, he put his mind on something else and took a sip of iced tea.

Annie gave Tish a look of startled surprise. "You practiced last night? With Johnny?"

Tilting her head, as if contemplating how to respond, Tish nodded, then added, "It didn't work."

Picking at some potato chip crumbs on his plate, getting them to stick to his fingers, Johnny raised them to his mouth and mindlessly imagined they were pale and salty from sweat.

"Yeah, it did."

Heads snapped in his direction, Ron paying strict attention to the assessment.

Johnny bent his head over the plate to take another bite of his sandwich.

Annie asked, "She was able to come up with something?"

His eyes widened and he nodded. His gaze was riveted at Tish, and he couldn't help but read a momentary thrill of pleasure that passed across her face.

It was gone when she countered his critique.

"I was too stiff, and my interpretation was off."

"Your interpretation was...brilliant."

Wiping off some pickle juice that had oozed from his food down his chin, he added, "You're not stiff at all when you stop concentrating on what you play. Like him."

His head jerked in the direction of the speakers.

Now Annie was grinning, making comical faces at Tish as Johnny put another bite in his mouth.

"Just think, Tish. If you could play like *him,* you wouldn't have to play with the likes of them."

She was wiping her hands on a towel when she nodded her head in the band's direction.

Then her eyes met his, a devious glint there.

"And why, Johnny, are you assuming the pianist we're listening to is a male?"

He gave her a lopsided grin and shrugged his shoulders, embarrassed at being caught in an age-old mindset.

"I take it the pianist in question is a woman. I stand corrected. It doesn't change my assessment. It would take Tish years to reach this level. The artist playing knows how to interpret what the composer had in mind when he wrote it but in her own personal style. She isn't thinking about the music, she's become the music."

"Oh, really? And you would know this how?"

"A musician knows."

Annie continued to give him a hard time.

"Okay, Mr. Smarty Pants, who is the composer and what do you know about him?"

"I think it's Liszt, although it could be Bach. They always get me confused. Other than that, I don't know very much."

"It is Liszt. I'm impressed. How did you know?"

Johnny said in an easy tone, "My mother, remember?"

Tim laughed and said, "Classical is all she ever listened to. We'd be sitting at the kitchen table trying to come up with the lyrics to our own music with Mozart entertaining us in the background. It wasn't easy. It was the food that kept us in our seats."

Johnny noticed the smile on Tim's face at the reference to their early days. Then his friend glanced in Tish's direction and the smile broadened.

"Maybe Johnny's right and with some practice you could play this well."

Johnny made a chortled harrumph.

"Yeah, right. I'd have to be on stage with her telling her to close her eyes and feel the music. She'd never be able to pull it off."

Then a piece of music trilled, undulated like waves rolling across the expanse of the ocean. Johnny looked up and added, in awe, "This woman's an artist. She touches the soul."

The thrill that shot through Tish at Johnny's compliment ebbed out as she remembered her crumbling career. She hadn't been able to pull off a concert in months and it had left her feeling worthless.

Studying Johnny, she pondered his description of the Liszt rhapsody. Her playing had been called transcendent and mystical, but she'd never known what those words had meant. Johnny had just explained it to her. Touching the soul conveyed the meaning in simple terms and she withered inside knowing she had lost the ability to do that, had forgotten the secret language that once existed between her, the piano and the audience. Before her musical aura had been extinguished, she'd had a purpose. What Johnny didn't know was that she had played like this once and the days of practice, months of study and years of struggle had been worth it. A reason to get up, a reason to put up with the grind, her mother, the solitary existence.

She smiled.

Johnny had compared her...to her.

With a more confident tone than she felt, she said, "I bet I could play like this...one day."

"I want to be in the audience the day you reach this level of virtuoso."

"It's a deal. I'll send you a personal invitation."

"I'll probably be walking with a cane by then."

Annie's voice had a new lightness when she said, "I'm going to make sure you have pickles when you eat those words. You eat them with everything else."

Tish noticed the thoughtful look on Johnny's face when his eyes met Annie's.

What was going through his head?

When he popped the last bite of sandwich into his mouth, he cleaned up his mess, took a seat with the Farnhams and Reject, the opportunity to find out, lost.

Tish continued to listen to the recording, remembering being back in the studio during production.

The CD had been a labor of love although her mother had hated it. Complaining that the mixing team hadn't captured the true essence of the composer's work, that there was a lack of aesthetic pleasure and the dynamics, or, in other words, the sound was weak. Madeleine had done all in her power to get it scratched but the producer was adamant and kept control. He ranted about her mother's lack of musicality, and at the complete absence of any musical consciousness. It was the last time she'd been allowed to work with him, but she'd adored him. He'd encouraged her to stretch, play pieces she had never attempted before and the end result had been what the critics called ground-breaking, deemed the purest sensation of texture through sound.

It had won her a Grammy.

She had thought her mother would have been happy, but she'd been mistaken. It had only made Madeleine more determined to exert executive control over the recording engineers she allowed to work with her.

Something she didn't understand.

Sitting here, letting this memory bloom in vibrant color filled her with a dose of the courage she needed to take her life back. If she wanted to be free of Madeleine's iron will before her next birthday, when her contract expired, she was going to have to take her mother to court to get it null and void. That was going to take every ounce of fortitude in her. Facing her mother across a lawyer's conference table would take more strength than she had right now.

As soon as she got her confidence back, as soon as she could walk out onto a stage, sit at a piano and play again, even if it was a keyboard rather than the baby grand, she was accustomed to, she'd face off with Madeleine. The end goal would be to access the trust fund, minimize the percentage her mother received, and keep what was rightfully hers. Every penny she'd earned so far had gone into the Letitia Jones Family Trust, except for the monthly stipend her mother received as guardian. That was intended to provide for Letitia Jones' care and was based on every individual concert performed. There had been no money coming in from that source since Tish had balked at the stage door. It had spurred her mother's righteous indignation. Prompting threats that included a lawsuit against her for breach of contract with the promise the recording studio would follow suit. Making sure her hands were tied, there was also an iron-clad stipulation that Letitia couldn't play for any other label, or tour under anyone else's purview. That had been an addendum put into place a couple of years after her father's death when Tish had been fifteen, still too young to be included in the dialogue. Diana had gotten involved, had an ad litem assigned but they'd lost their claim. Diana had almost gotten fired in the process. It had surprised her that her mother had done nothing more than cut Diana's commission.

Nothing had changed since. Her career was still handcuffed to her mother's agenda. By leaving she had gotten the cuffs off but still wasn't free to direct her future.

She was breaking multiple clauses in the contract by becoming a member of Raging Thunder. If her mother found out, which she was bound to do, she could haul Tish into court and make this a very public humiliation.

Would the day come when she didn't care?

When she would welcome the court battle?

She hoped it would, but she wasn't there yet.

The longer she stayed underground, the more time she'd have to find the strength.

If and when she got her stage legs back, she was going to face some pretty tough choices. Her decision had been to take one step at a time. The complete break from her mother's dominance didn't seem insurmountable that way.

⌒

Sitting in the home office Annie had created for herself and her patients, Tish looked out the three-panel window, the rain splashing against the glass. It might be June, but the weather was cool and the dark and gloomy skies did nothing to lift her spirits. Seated on the symbolic couch, Tish pulled her legs under her and waited for Annie to gather her thoughts. She had agreed to sessions with her for an hour or two throughout the tour so that she could talk through whatever was on her mind. Today was the first and last conducted in this room. They'd be leaving later tonight heading towards Richmond.

There was so much for her to process she wasn't sure she'd ever get to the other side where courage was hiding. There was still guilt eating away at her for leaving home, anger at her own ineptitude. Madeleine might be difficult to deal with, but she was still her mother. And yet to heal, she had to cut the ties that bound them, deal with the painful wounding that had taken place during childhood. She was no longer compelled to sacrifice herself to her mother's demands.

There was a long list of changes that had to be made at the core of her being and the only way to accomplish it was through Annie's guidance.

She was still grappling with her inability to please her mother, no matter what she did.

"I must be able to satisfy her in some way. What am I doing wrong?"

"Is that what you want? To please her?"

"Isn't that a daughter's job?"

With finger over her lips, Annie seemed to consider the question.

"No, Tish. It isn't. Your job was to become a productive member of society. Her job was to support that. She couldn't."

Tish grimaced at how little she knew about relationships.

Annie continued, "How did your encounters with her make you feel?"

"Frustrated, humiliated...invisible."

"A mother should never make her child feel that way. Constructive criticism is valuable, destructive criticism is just that...destructive."

"She wanted me to be successful."

"That's the irony here. She needs you to shine so she can be reflected in your glory but when you do, it takes the spotlight away from her which is something she can't allow."

Annie paused before adding, "Everything in her world needs to revolve around her, like she's the sun and you're a planet. She views everything in relationship to how it makes her feel, how it impacts her life. You are not even a blip on her radar."

"I did the right thing by leaving?"

"You did the only thing you could. She's toxic and she would have made sure you were raw and bleeding until—"

"I couldn't stand it anymore. Found a way out."

"Yes."

Their eyes met as they both remembered Tish's last attempt at escape. It hadn't gone well and had caused Madeleine to put more restrictive measures in place.

"Why did I let it get to this point?"

Where she couldn't even think about sitting at the piano, wanted to rip to shreds the empty portfolio of collected work she'd learned over the course of her career.

"Fear. You were never given the tools to be on your own. Madeleine used her manipulation skills so well, with so much cunning, she never allowed you to see how competent you were. Or how successful you'd be without her."

"You're sure of that? My music is gone if you remember. I'm not convinced that you're right."

"It will all come back. It's like amnesia. Memory wiped out due to trauma. It almost always comes back, but in phases."

"What phase am I in?"

"The primary one. We'll take baby steps, like learning to play a different kind of instrument, different kind of music. It's a new challenge, one without rules."

"And getting on the stage?"

"That phase will come when you have notes at your fingertips."

With a wavering voice, Tish asked, "But Annie, what if I never get *my* music back?"

Making eye contact, Annie leaned forward and touched Tish's hand.

"It's part of you. It's just hibernating in your cells waiting for the right time to make a comeback."

"I hope you're right."

She was invited to sit in on the last practice of the day before the equipment was loaded in the trucks, a signal that the second leg of the tour was about to begin.

When Johnny took her hand in his, to lead her out to the studio, the temptation to say no burned away with the heat of his touch. A skitter of fear shot through her at the thought of failing. Even though he'd been complimentary during the wee hours this morning, she'd learned that didn't mean the same opinion would be forthcoming this afternoon. The inventory in this musical box was thin and it might stay thin no matter how much she practiced. She was afraid to find out.

Before taking his place behind the drums, he got her settled at the keyboard.

From the first strike of the sticks on the drums, Tish sat in muted silence, his body moving with the strident beat, her own quivering from chills.

Needing to get her mind off his powerful movements, she tuned into the dynamics, listened to the way the guys played, attempting to understand who played against whom, who led, and how she'd integrate the sound of the electric keyboard. But she couldn't find a leader. What she heard were four distinct sounds instead of one united front. It was going to be next to impossible to experiment when she had no one to follow.

Until Johnny stopped mid-strike as if he'd just realized she hadn't played a note.

"We'll play what we did last night."

"I'm not sure I remember how I played it."

"It doesn't have to be the same. Feel it. Go with that."

Slipping out from behind the kit, he came over to where she sat, his drumsticks clacking out a beat, his head nodding at her in tempo.

The smile was encouraging, and she felt her fingers move in response. Her trust in him was growing and she was able to keep the flow moving as he reclaimed his stool. From his perch, he led the show, and the song came alive.

Terry, Reject, and Tim integrated their sound into one perfect package. Ron was applauding, a broad smile on his face.

"This is the band I know and love. Can they come with us this time?"

CHAPTER EIGHT

She looked out the bus window, the machinery in her head grinding gears.

What had she gotten herself into?

Pure panic rushed through her like a river flooding its banks, demolishing every shred of confidence she'd found since her prison break. She wished she'd been able to test her skills for more than a twenty-four-hour stretch, but that hadn't been an option. She was now left to practice, familiarize herself with the instrument, understand the habits of the guys from the road, without the band behind her. She'd need hours of playing time to get to a place where she felt a sense of competency. Over the next few days, she'd listen to her iPod, which Annie had filled with the band's entire collection, and hope to put together some sheet music in her head. Her memory for absorbing material had always been flawless. In fact, she knew dozens of classical pieces from the eighteenth, nineteenth and twentieth centuries. And could play each piece a variety of ways. Well, she'd been able to once. Now she couldn't even play them in her head with any meaningful sequence, the notes a jumbled mass of cacophonous noise. Her brain was bursting at the seams, the artistic overflow pounding the walls of her skull, trying to get out.

As she pressed her temples with her fingers, attempting to massage away the blinding pain, her stomach roiled with nausea that came with the migraine.

"Need these?"

Annie sat next to her, two pills resting on her extended hand.

Picking them up with one hand, Tish twisted the cap off the water bottle she had and swallowed them down.

"Thanks."

Resting her head back, she closed her eyes, hoping the pills would work soon.

She hated taking them, hated being dependent on anything, hated her weakness.

"What am I doing here?"

Grasping cold, restless fingers and squeezing, Annie reminded her, "Rest and recuperation."

"Then why do I plan to spend my time learning how to play a machine with no heart?"

"I don't know. The initial plan was to just get you away from your mother's influence. I'd hoped we could spend some of our days shopping, sitting by the pool, enjoying the dog days of summer. I wanted an accomplice for doing nothing."

Annie added with a laugh, "So tell me again why you're going to spend time with a machine instead of me?"

Tish answered with a sound that was half laugh, half cry.

"Maybe I'm finding out I'm masochistic."

"I guess it could be that. Or maybe it's because you love what you're doing."

"Nope. Don't know it well enough to love it yet."

"There's always love at first sight."

"This was hate at first touch."

Jarring, shrill, no soul, no meat. Electric juice. Although it was fun listening to the programmed music and trying to follow along in pianoforte, Latino beat.

"It is helping me find some kind of musical statement even if it's not the one I want to make."

Tish felt the beginnings of a real smile tip the corners of her mouth.

"Old Mr. Keyboard isn't as much of a snob as my baby grand. He makes anyone sound good with a minimum amount of involvement."

"Right. Like you could stay minimally involved."

"I only plan on practicing four hours a day. That's part-time for me remember?"

At least it used to be. For the last couple of months, she couldn't even move her fingers. She'd sit looking at the keys, her mind a jumbled mess, trying hard to remember how to play...anything.

One piece.

Nothing came.

Except one of her headaches.

Annie picked up a book and was sitting beside her while she played the unplugged keyboard, the primal beat blaring from her iPod. Rambler had wired the board so Tish could hear what she was playing through the earbuds but so she wasn't bothering anyone else while she practiced.

Tish felt Annie's seat incline forward as a chin came to rest on the dimpled top. Tim was leaning in, so she pulled out the plugs and smiled up at him.

"You must like our music if you're willing to put so much time into it."

"I do. I've become a real big fan."

"Good. So even if you never join us on stage, you won't get bored listening."

"Oh, God, no. You never play the song the same way twice. I envy that. It always sounds so spontaneous."

He laughed.

"We have to work hard at that."

"You'd be better off keeping me on the sidelines. I'm not sure I could follow you."

He reached over the seat and took hold of her hand.

"Tish, earlier today, we ended up following you."

With that, he straightened and said to Annie, "I need a partner for whist. Are you in?"

Re-assuring Annie that her headache was just a vague patch of fog now, she leaned her body into the aisle and watched her friend make her way to the back of the bus in her husband's wake.

They'd been on the road for what seemed like ages, and it had only been a matter of hours. This was going to take some getting used to. Tish was aboard a caravan of sorts and she still couldn't believe how much equipment was being hauled around. Then there were the people. There was no way she would ever remember all the names. There had to be fifty of them, more maybe, including the roadies, soundmen, lighting people, a security force including bodyguards, a crew that sold the merchandise, and the bus drivers, a virtual sea of faces. She had forced herself to stay in place while the trucks were being loaded up with the equipment stored in the studio, the amps, the mics, the drum kit, lighting and sound boards, all kinds of marketing materials and electronic devices she didn't even know existed were placed in the rectangular bin as if it were an automated activity. Chappy, Joe, and Rambler took turns directing the roadies, helping with their own areas of expertise, and lending muscle power when necessary.

As she watched the hive-like busyness, she plotted.

Wanting to run far, far away, she studied her options from every angle.

And came to the disturbing conclusion there was nowhere to run to.

And so she had taken her first step on to the bus with trembling limbs.

This would be her home for the next couple of months, if she lasted that long. Hitting the road for a few hours after the concert was over on some nights, staying over in hotels on others.

It wasn't her regular routine, but it would help having one.

Her days, until her mind faltered, had been structured, scheduled to the minute.

Up at dawn for a couple of hours of practice, she'd eat breakfast before meeting her tutor. After a few hours of academic study, her piano teacher would arrive and the rest of the day and night would be spent on artistic pursuits, exercises, chord progressions, practicing scales, technique, composition, defining the characteristics of interpretation, repertoire. When schooling was no longer part of the equation, she was touring all over the world, chattel to her mother and her musical public. Under Arturo's tutelage, a master in his field, she had spent endless hours memorizing new works, working on presentation and concert etiquette. He was a disciplinarian, with the reputation as one of the best teachers of his time. She had respected him, cherished his praise, accepted his criticisms, and done all she could to make him proud. Arturo felt that the concerts kept up her technical work, but her mother disagreed. They would have huge fights about the numbers of hours she should practice. Madeleine insisted on far more than Arturo thought necessary. As animosity had escalated between them, the two volatile personalities clashing, Tish had seen the writing on the wall and had prepared for the worst.

But nothing could have prepared for the sheer, black fright that had seeped into her bones that day. Tish knew too well that she was at the mercy of Madeleine's frenetic need for control.

It was the beginning of the end for her heart, her mind and her soul.

Her catalog of music had begun to vanish, page by page, until there was nothing left and each time she'd taken her seat at the piano, her mind was a blank.

It was still blank although she was beginning to fill in some white space like it was a canvas, one new colorful shape at a time.

She drew in a deep, shuddering breath, the darkness of the night creating another wave of anxiety.

The bus had pulled away from Annie and Tim's at midnight, which Annie had told her was the norm on the road.

They'd sleep in late if they could or grab snatches of shut eye as they were driven from one city to the next. The band practiced afternoons at the venues if they felt they needed it, gave interviews, met with journalists, and spent the rest of the time in pursuit of pleasure. She would have been at a loss to know what to do with all those free hours if she didn't have the keyboard to keep her occupied. Sleeping at the other end of the spectrum might have been a problem if she slept, but she had stopped doing that on a regular basis, months ago. She was consumed with a fitful kind of energy that kept her unhinged. Like a tiger, pacing his cage, the pent-up nervousness becoming agitation, but unlike the powerful beast, hers was thick with fear.

She had hoped the motion of the bus would allow her to drift off, the meds giving her some relief from the pain in her head, but claustrophobia had set in and she'd found it hard to snooze, her nerves pumping too much adrenaline through an already over-wired circuitry.

Her exhaustion was overwhelming on every level.

Johnny was there every time she closed her eyes.

She couldn't seem to get him out of her mind. His looks captivated her, his smile made her forget the pounding in her head, his patience was winning her admiration. There was a way about him that made even his commanding presence seem less intimidating.

It had been at his insistence that she'd participated in their last afternoon practice.

"You need to try out a couple more songs. I want you to synchronize yourself to our sound."

For over an hour after the official practice was over, he'd sat with her, his sticks keeping the beat, his body leaning in close to hers, pulling out chords, patterns, progressions that she hadn't even known were there.

The unrelenting tempo, the pulsing beat of the sticks, combined with the unyielding strength of his presence created a whirlwind of emotion.

One she still felt at the cellular level.

Shifting in her seat, gazing out the window, she took up her vigil, watching the lights passing in the night. She had taken a seat near the front of the bus, as if giving in to the comfort of solitude. Being alone most of her life, she was unused to the flurry of activity that surrounded her.

The bus driver, Ralph, had kept a steady flow of dialogue going. At first, she had resented his intrusion into her voluntary confinement, but his voice was low, quiet, reassuring and he drew her out with amazing patience and persistence. He was from New Jersey, thirty-six, married with a couple of kids, loved what he was doing. The only down-side to the job was being away from his family. She had never been able to carry on a conversation with a stranger with such ease before and wondered if Ralph sensed how vulnerable she was feeling.

What she was, was darn right petrified of what lay ahead.

Tonight would mark Thunder's first concert on this leg of the tour, an attempt for her to re-enter the bright lights of the stage. Of course, if her heart continued to palpitate, she'd be dead before they arrived at their destination. She'd been to Richmond before, playing with the symphony orchestra there a few years back. This time she just might be able to see some sights in the surrounding area.

Swiveling in her seat, she took in the ransacked contents of their moving home, her fingers tense in her lap.

So used to her Spartan, furnished bedroom, where the few personal belongings her mother allowed were all in their places, her system was off kilter because of the chaos.

There were bunk-like quarters for sleeping and regular seats for riding. Various seats were piled high with boxes, instruments were strewn everywhere, empty Coke and orange soda cans littered small tables, where bags of chips and packages of cookies lay opened, books were scattered all over the space. She was falling fast into another black night, where her hollow existence could be crumpled in the blink of an eye. She wasn't sure she could keep up the pretense. The walls of the bus were closing in and she had no outlet for the jiggling energy. It would take another four or five hours to get to their destination, more if she counted another stop to stretch or refuel.

Johnny sat at the front of his bus getting to know the driver. It was second in line, following close on the wheels of the leader. His fellow passengers were the single men in the group, designated that way to keep the female fans far away from the wives of the married men.

This was Don's first gig with them, and Johnny wanted to spend time digging into his background, finding out what made him tick. He loved meeting new people. It was one of the few things that never got boring. It also helped when he needed something. The driver controlled the lights, emptied the toilets, changed bulbs and knew where they were, where they were going, when they were going to get there, and the places they'd stop on the way. The manager made it clear he wasn't going to be the go-between so if anyone needed something done, they had to ask the driver themselves. Don had driven for some other bands, so he knew the routine and he was single, which was why he'd been assigned to this particular bus. Being a member of this segment of the band, he'd get to see a lot, get to know some groupies who would invade the space. And share if he wanted.

Johnny swiveled his seat to stare out into the inky darkness. Don had pulled ahead of the lead bus a few miles back, so all the other vehicles were now behind them, black asphalt the only thing in front.

Their first pit stop was still over an hour away and he didn't like the edgy feeling that gnawed at him. Cramped, he didn't understand why they hadn't leased a private jet for the tour. This was so beginner track, and they had put in their dues big-time. His drumsticks in hand, he tapped at the window and then stopped. Looking around the dim interior, he noticed some of the guys napping and he had to be careful not to make too much noise.

Tilting his seat back, he thought about their last practice. Ron had been right. During the couple of songs Tish had joined in on, they had sounded like themselves instead of the inferior version they'd become. Stronger, tighter.

Was it Tish who had made the difference?

He had watched her as he played, her innocence captivating him, her concentration becoming less focused and her facial expression mirroring what she did with the music. Adding depth, she also brought a magical nuance, an otherworldliness that was mystifying. Their play had notched up an octave in both intensity and technique.

When the practice had broken up, she'd agreed to stay behind with him.

Sitting beside him, soft waves of shimmering heat radiating out, she'd drawn him in like a moth to a flame. When his gaze sought out the creamy expanse of her neck, he'd to hold himself back from tasting the sweet skin. And when she'd completely abandoned herself to the flow of notes beneath her fingers, a breathtaking essence had emanated from her.

She was beautiful.

He had thought her soft and vulnerable at first, but he'd been wrong. There was power there, a force she buried, but it was at the core of her being, nonetheless.

And it didn't sit well with him.

She made him edgy.

He'd have to make sure to stay away from all that steely vulnerability.

And yet when he ambled to his bunk at the back of the bus, the rear window giving him an expansive view of the receding highway, he could just make out her figure. Ralph had his overhead light on, and its arc widened just enough that her silhouette was clear. She hadn't moved from the spot since they boarded the bus at Tim's, over one-hundred miles ago.

Did she still look like the frightened deer he'd seen clinging to the loggia of the house, concealing herself from the mainstream of activity? He'd watched her watch the commotion that was part of their departure ritual. She had been quieter than usual, if that was possible. Seeming to be uncomfortable with conversation, she had watched, observed, and listened.

Her face had remained immobile, giving nothing away, but there had been terror in her eyes, eyes an unearthly color.

Where did it come from?

What went through her head?

The mystery was killing him.

He knew nothing about her. Not even her last name. Just the tidbits of information Tim and Annie had parted with.

She was in a tough spot, had been playing piano since childhood, had no family to speak of, had some hang-ups that Annie was helping her work through.

What he had gotten from observation was oppressive.

She had no confidence, didn't appreciate her ability, wasn't good in crowds, was much too serious for someone her age, always thought long and hard before she spoke, as if what she had to say would be criticized.

Except on those few occasions when she got her back up about something and let go, yelling at him. Then she was a sight to behold, her jaw set, her cheeks flushing in a flawless cream complexion, her eyes glimmering.

When he had pushed her during the practice, she'd balked at the tone of his directives. He had suggested a certain progression for the song *Joyride*. A set of chords she didn't like.

Her eyes had penetrated, cold and flinty, her cheeks suffused with color.

"Shut up. You're going too fast. I can't even think."

He heard the bluster in his voice, but he didn't back down.

"This isn't rocket science. Just play the damn chord."

She hadn't backed down either, although for a split second it'd looked like she would. In a calm voice, she'd stated, "I think another sequence would work better. Back off and let me try it."

And he had, floored by the one she chose, knowing it would enhance the song in a way he hadn't expected.

When she gave him a satisfied smirk, her eyes met his. Eyes that made him sweat. In a different shade every time. Florescent-tipped sea green, icicle blue, strangling ivy, flashing turquoise. Surrounded by a rim of silver that lightened a pupil sprinkled with gold specks. He had found himself getting lost on occasion, trying to fathom what she was thinking, feeling, what she was so afraid of.

He was pissed. It was the sum of the shrouded secrecy of her life added to the unanswered question, why was she here.

He'd cornered Tim before boarding the buses to get some answers.

"She has to be one of Annie's charity cases."

Tim gave a measured answer.

"I wouldn't call her that."

"Then what?"

"I told you she's a friend of a friend."

"Who's the friend?"

"That's not important, is it?"

It was but there were more urgent questions Johnny wanted answered.

"If she can play the damn piano, why does she need so much coaxing?"

"She's—"

"Scared as a rabbit. Why?"

"That's one of the things Annie's helping her with and it's not my story to tell."

"Really? Then who should I talk to, to get the details?"

"Johnny, can't you just let it go for now?"

He was more frustrated now than angry, more with himself than Tim.

"I know I gave up any rights to the decision to bring her on when I walked away that day, but come on Tim, she can't even carry her own weight."

"You're helping her get there."

The sticks in Johnny's hand began a four-quarter beat against his leg.

"I'm no wet nurse. And I'm not going to spend the next few months babysitting her."

"We're hoping it won't take that long."

"And if it takes longer than we have?"

When he got no response from Tim, he knew he didn't have an answer either and he stomped away.

Maybe he had gotten the witch to do things that the others couldn't, but he was done.

She'd have to suck it up or she was history. They didn't need to put up with someone who couldn't cut it.

Shifting to get a better view, he noticed Tish's arm working her hair into that blasted butterfly clip. He would have preferred her wearing her long blonde hair down, a style she never went with. Squinting his eyes, he sought the impossible. He wanted the chance for a closer inspection. The strands were silver blonde. Or was it spun gold? Every thread was a varying shade, with silver and gold fighting for prominence. Between the ever-changing color of her eyes and hair, she had too many looks to count. It would be like being with a different woman every day and the thought was almost appealing. Grabbing for his eyeshades, deciding it was time for some sleep, he tossed her out of his head.

He didn't want her there.

She was way out of his league. Way out. Not his type at all. Too needy. Way too fragile. Virgin territory from what Annie had felt compelled to tell him, not that he hadn't already assumed that. She must have figured out that information would help him keep his hands off and she was right. He'd secured the lock on the experience a long time ago. No way. No how.

But the vision of Tish persisted, kept him from settling in.

Tossing on his side, he closed his eyes.

But sleep wouldn't come.

When the buses pulled into the only pit stop of the drive to Richmond, he joined the others for an early morning breakfast. At least it was early for him. He didn't often see nine a.m. but the traffic was heavy going through New Jersey and the drivers decided Bordertown was a good place to hole up until it died down.

There must have been twenty of them that had settled into the benches. He'd made sure he sat in the bench behind her, so they were back-to-back, a wooden slat partition separating them, and he'd hoped he'd get the opportunity to touch her hair, to see what it felt like. Just out of curiosity, but Rambler had squeezed in beside him, pushing him to the end and he had lost whatever chance he'd had. He sent a glowering look the roadie's direction.

And got a glowering look in return.

"What's up with you? Hungry?"

Johnny's stomach growled but that wasn't the kind of hunger that ate at him.

He could only bark back, "Nothing."

Leaning his head back, he scrubbed his stubble. He hadn't shaved in a couple of days, and his cheeks were starting to itch.

Chappy told him what he already knew.

"If looks could kill, buddy, we'd all be dead."

He didn't answer but rather looked at the ceiling of the truck stop envisioning killer legs. Creamy, peach, long, slender legs. The kind that peeked out of a very short pair of blue shorts. A pair he'd had to watch while she'd played at playing during the practice session. Legs that could make a man salivate.

If he'd gotten a good look at her legs earlier when they'd been alone in the studio, he would have had a much harder time sitting there waiting for her to get the chords right. The shorts she had on when they boarded the bus left nothing to the imagination.

The groan surprised him.

Then the voice grabbed his attention.

Melodic, quivering, light and fresh.

Her scent drifted, like home baked cinnamon rolls, the aroma soft, warm, enticing, filling the air.

"Oh, they're so cute. How old is Hannah?"

"She's seven, Molly's three."

Ralph turned in his seat, putting his arm behind Tish, apologizing when he bumped into Johnny's. Instead of removing it, he managed to accommodate it.

Looking at Tish, Ralph asked, "Will you be with the guys for a while? You haven't toured with them before, have you?

"No. I'm not part of the band. Just a temporary addition. So, I'll be with them for just part of the summer."

"Then what?"

"I don't really know. It'll depend on what happens while I'm here. On tour."

"What do you mean?"

Johnny strained his ears to pick up Tish's response. The guys at the table were deep in idle chatter and a shade too loud for eavesdropping.

"If I want to have a career, I have to get over my aversion to the stage. It's an important aspect in our line of work."

Annie supplied a positive assessment. "She's going to be fine. She won't be in the limelight here, so she can just hide in the shadows, gradually build up her confidence again."

Johnny heard surprise register in Ralph's voice.

"You don't think people will notice her?"

Annie stumbled a bit when she said, "No. No one will be expecting her to be here, and she'll never be part of the band, so why would we think that?"

"She's a knock-out. I have a feeling all the boyfriends of all the females who drool over the guys will now have sweet revenge."

"Annie?"

Johnny heard the timid squeal, felt the panic stuffed into that one word right down to the toes of his boots.

He shifted to the corner, swiveled his head and spoke to her profile.

"Don't worry, Tish. There are lots of men who won't give you the time of day."

Ralph came to her defense.

"Most of the men I know would trip over themselves to get to her."

Johnny's nostrils flared at the thought of how many men would go for the fragility she emanated. And he didn't like the fact that Ralph was aware of her appeal, even if he kept telling himself it didn't do a thing for him.

"I didn't mean it like that. Most of the men come for the music. Besides there'll be too many women to cut through to get to her."

And although he hadn't figured out the why quite yet, he was determined to prevent any man making it to the rim of their inner circle.

Tim sat back and said, "I think Ralph could be right."

Johnny heard the trepidation in Tish's voice when she asked, "What am I going to do if that happens?"

Tim reassured her, "I'll keep an eye out for you. I won't let anyone get to you unless you want to be gotten to."

"No spotlights. And no solos. I don't want to be visible."

Johnny almost told her that invisibility was a fruitless endeavor. With social media what it was, every song performed would make it to YouTube.

Instead, he offered with a bite of sarcasm, "You might not mind it so much if you ever figure out how to play our stuff."

Annie huffed out an answer. "She's doing better than anyone could have expected. She's had to create sheet music for the songs she's learning, or haven't you noticed?"

He scowled in recognition of the truth and slunk back against the seat.

Ralph's voice, one too close for comfort, offered, "I'll pick up the slack, be her bodyguard. No one will get by me."

Johnny became aware of Ralph's bulk, and how it suited the role.

When Tish offered her thanks, he wondered if there was gratitude shining in those brilliant aquamarine eyes.

He grumbled all the way back to the bus.

"What's up with you?"

Reject had caught up with him at the foot of the steps.

"Nothing. Why?"

Johnny was getting bored with that question.

"You're acting very strange, my friend. You're not letting her get to you, are you?"

"Of course not. Way too innocent. You know my rule."

"Then why are you...helping her?"

Johnny stopped in his tracks and snapped out, "Because Tim and Ron are right. When she plays, she adds a piece that's been missing. We've lost our magic and she might be the key to getting it back."

"She's a fake. No way could anyone be that needy. She's just playing you."

"Oh, and the women who want a piece of our ass, aren't?"

"No. They're contributing to our pleasure quotient."

"Speak for yourself."

Johnny started up the stairs and headed toward the back of the bus, ignoring Reject's last jab.

"You better watch out, Johnny. She'll have you eating out of her hand if you don't."

Flinging himself onto his bunk, flinging Tish out of his head, Johnny cursed what was becoming a demonic obsession.

CHAPTER NINE

Tish studied her reflection in the storefront glass window.

Cargo shorts and a skimpy pink top. Bare legs and nothing-to-them sandals. Her hair knotted on top of her head.

She smiled.

If her mother could see her now, she'd be mortified.

She peered up at the deep blue sky.

How did her mother manage to sneak into her head no matter what she was doing?

Madeleine was always right there, casting glances of disapproval.

She had to shake her off, get her out.

What she wanted were the lights, the heat, the love she had for her instrument, the passion she felt while her fingers were running over the keys. She'd had it all once. But flashes of confinement, of isolation, and loneliness were part of a carousel going round and round in her mind.

Criticisms from both her mother and the press.

Technically impaired, the sound diluted.

No good. No good. No good.

She put her head in her hands, her fingers massaging her temple, attempting to bring back other memories to consciousness. There had been applause. She'd heard the appreciation. And Diana had stuck by her. Her agent must think she had quality left in her.

But where was it?'

The meaning, the interpretation?

Buried deep under layers of guilt, shame, and inadequacy.

Then a rush of loud, heavy metal flooded her, surged through her blood. Head splitting, take over, pounding music. And it filled her to overflowing. Full of images, sounds, scales, chords, and the incessant beat of Johnny's drums.

Maybe she wasn't as empty as she thought and that thought was exhilarating.

She could arrange the score anyway she wanted with invisible notes, which couldn't be memorized. She'd only be mindful of that moment in time when her fingers touched the keys.

But she hadn't been able to get on the stage yet.

Annie had stayed with her that first night in Richmond, the hotel room the prison where she'd incarcerated herself.

The incapacitating fear had taken her over, her body convulsed with fright, and Annie had helped her breathe through frozen lungs. She'd hung on to her friend for dear life, never getting a foot near the arena, never mind the stage. The next two nights were no better.

And although no one had asked outright what was going on, she heard the murmurs amongst the roadies.

Tim had asked through Annie. Reject, a bit more sarcastic, made the only direct comment.

"All that talent going to waste. Oh, wait a minute, what talent? No one's seen it yet."

Swallowing hard, she tried to ignore the sting of his criticism.

She'd been avoiding Johnny, not wanting to see the disappointment. It would hurt the most.

He thought she had something inside of her that she'd lost a long time ago and if he'd witnessed her breakdown, her anxiety, he would have found her lacking.

There were piles of broken promises behind her. Concert halls full of people who had waited for her to show up on stage, angry at her for a wasted night, bitter at the cancellation of the concert they had paid good money to attend.

Johnny didn't know any of that and she didn't know how to explain it.

How many times had she been told she was a waste of money and a waste of time?

How many thousands had her mother spent on her for teachers, clothing, recordings, her piano, transportation and international travel expenses?

What Madeleine had gotten was a very inadequate return for her dollar.

That was a side of her she didn't want Johnny to see.

And he would if she let him in.

Her fear of what he'd find out about her was almost as traumatizing as the stage itself.

She was keeping her nightly excursions into hell from everyone but Annie and Tim. They were the only witnesses to her paroxysm of weeping and shaking.

The others thought, as her mother did, that she was just being difficult.

So, she'd escaped every day, to avoid the speculative glances. Accessing the Internet on Annie's computer she had pulled up some interesting things to do with her days. And nights.

Still unsure of what she'd face when she returned to her life in Boston, she wanted memories that would help her weather the unpredictability of her future. She wanted to experience historical sites, museums, zoos, amusement parks, walking trails, blues clubs so she pushed her limits, connecting with people she met out on her side trips while the band was performing, or the guys were sleeping. If she didn't stay away from Johnny, he'd work his magic on her, get her to try things that seemed insurmountable.

Late to bed, still only able to catch a few hours of deep sleep, she rose again at dawn, got dressed and ventured out, the warm southern sun helping melt the chill in her heart.

She was always back for an hour counseling session with Annie, and they'd find a quiet spot in the hotel or some coffee shop. Yesterday it was the back of the bus, the guys off at a radio station giving an on-air interview.

"We need to discuss your panic attacks."

Pulling at her fingers, Tish countered, "You can discuss them all you want but they won't go away."

Pinching her lips together, Annie paused, then asked, "What is it out there that frightens you?"

Tish began to rub her arms, a clammy sweat covering her. Envisioning herself at the edge of the stage, peering out at the crowd waiting, the score no longer cemented in her mind, grasping to regain hold over it, her panic grew roots at her inability to do so.

"That the music won't be there. That my mind will be blank, and my fingers will feel like lead."

"But this isn't the same thing at all. The fans aren't expecting anything from you. They won't even know you're out there, so if you never play a note, they won't have missed a thing."

Confused, Tish looked up.

Annie was right. But she couldn't shake the shame of what had happened before, the material untethered in her mind, the keys striking a cacophony of sound, not the flowing string of notes she'd once had at her command. As she dug in her mind for an answer, Johnny's face appeared.

Was he the root cause of the queasiness?

Not wanting to give that illogical excuse, she chose another.

"It must be the band then."

"So you think you'll disappoint the band?"

"I know that sounds silly. I have nothing invested in them. They have nothing invested in me."

"If that's the way you feel, it's not silly. If that's the trigger, we have to figure out a way to crack its code."

"Yes, but I've mastered the art of disappointment. Just look at the last six months. An endless stream of them."

It was the faces in the audience, expectant then irate, that kept her from sleeping.

Annie couldn't argue with that out-right it would diminish what Tish felt. She wasn't dealing with an imagined slight but a real one. That it was the result of an intense emotional reaction that had to do with a who, not a what, didn't lessen the anguish Tish felt.

"Those meltdowns compromised your identity."

"Do I have one anymore? Without my music..."

"You do. You're a pianist, always will be. It's who you are. At the moment, you're feeling vulnerable in front of an audience and we need to find a way to overcome that."

"Vulnerable is a good word. My well-being is at risk."

"Your mother pointed out her perception of your deficiencies, which led you to a perpetual state of uncertainty. Wanting to avoid further humiliation your mind shut down. Your body offered you a defense mechanism to keep you safe. She isn't here anymore. What's left is what she symbolizes."

Annie placed her index finger over her lip to let a few moments pass before adding, "There are forces at work here that your mother set in motion. She helped you create the hostile environment through her criticisms and inconsistency. The stage symbolizes this. Any stage will set off the time bomb that's ticking. You've come to believe you'll fail in this setting, so you refuse the one thing that fills your soul."

"So, what you're saying is it's not the stage but what it represents?"

"Exactly. Madeleine's toxic fumes choked your creativity. Her insidious need to belittle you caused you to lose faith in yourself. You have what you need to turn this around. The band has fun out there. They make the stage come alive. They own it. You need to start doing the same thing, see it as a safe place, and experiment with it."

Annie's perspective was an interesting one.

And she'd been turning it around in her mind since they spoke. It hadn't changed last night's outcome. It was the fourth concert she'd missed.

That had to change.

Glancing up into the store window, knowing she was going to be late getting back, she walked in the direction of the hotel, needing to put distance between her and her feelings of weakness, which still clung like ivy on a trellis.

⌐

"Where is she?"

Johnny ambled into the lobby from the bank of elevators, his carry-on over his shoulder. The band was due to board the bus that would take them to Charlotte within the next five minutes to a pre-arranged practice, but all he noticed was Tish's absence. He didn't like the fact that his eyes always sought her out, but they did.

Annie paced in the corner, near the windows that overlooked the street. Pushing her hair off her face, she admitted with a sigh, "I don't know."

"What do you mean?"

"She left right after breakfast. Ralph said she packed her things on her bunk and headed out on foot."

"I thought he was supposed to be looking out for her."

Annie wrinkled her brow and then cast her eyes in his direction.

"Just around concert time."

"What good is that if she doesn't show up for them?"

"Johnny, please, don't start."

"Why did I go to all the trouble of practicing with her, why did Rambler go to all the trouble of setting up the keyboard, if she wasn't going to perform with us? That was the plan, wasn't it?"

"What does it matter to you anyhow?"

Not wanting to let on he heard the difference when she'd rehearsed with them, he said the first thing that came into his head.

"If she's here to contribute, she needs to be on stage with us to do it. And if we're going to pay her, she should earn it."

Tim looked at his band mates and said, "She hasn't taken a dime since she got here. Do you comprehend? We're not paying her."

That took the wind out of Johnny's sails, but it didn't stop him from trying to figure out what was going on.

"So, she must have money of her own."

He knew Tish couldn't be going out without some kind of pocket change. But they were shelling out for some things, like the hotel room. Annie's voice was pensive. Her answer sounded vacant. "She brought a little money with her."

"Enough to keep this up? We'll end up putting out more than she's bringing in. Do we have a history of paying people who don't show up?"

Tim had his hands on his hips. His mouth was set in a thin line.

"Since when do you give a shit about financial arrangements?"

Not expecting an answer, he went on. "If it's a problem for you, and if she needs it, I'll give her money out of my portion. I know just how little you earn. Especially with the drop in ticket sales. I'm sure it would be a hardship."

The sarcasm only increased the tension in the air.

In a gruff voice, Johnny asked, "Why is she here? I don't get why she's even here. There are dozens of musicians who would have grabbed the chance to tour with us. Why her?"

There was blatant smugness in Johnny's tone.

Annie came out of her corner swinging.

"Look, you thimble brain. She—"

"Stop it, Annie. Johnny's right. I won't take anything from the band I don't earn and I won't take any more of a handout from you and Tim."

Tish's voice had come out of nowhere. She peered over to where he stood as Annie scrambled towards her.

"But Tish—"

"No. I'll have to give it up. Admit I can't manage this. I can't make it seem safe, even in my head."

He watched her head dip, her cheeks flushed as if ashamed, her voice low, almost a whisper.

"You've been there with me every night. I'm ready. I know the music, I can replicate their style. But I can't climb those stairs, can't mount the stage. Can't even leave the hotel. I keep running away."

He was pissed. This wasn't the woman who leveled him with an indignant glare. Just a pale copy.

"I thought you had more guts than this."

She winced at the bitter edge to his voice.

When she lifted her eyes to meet his, stark pain glimmered.

"You don't know me at all if you think that."

Her eyes fluttered closed.

"Annie, if you could lend me your charge card, I'll book a flight back to Boston. I'll give you all the money I have left."

"What are you going to do once you get there?"

Her fingers fidgeting, she said, "I don't know yet."

Annie pleaded, "Please don't Tish. You need a little more time, that's all. Like you said, you've got the music down. You would really give the band a much-needed punch in the arm."

Her hands had become fists, and Johnny stepped back sure he'd be the one she'd use them on.

He watched Tish take a couple of steps forward, her arms wrapping around Annie, then step back to face her, her fingers clasped together.

"I really appreciate what you tried to do, but I can't keep going through this night after night."

Looking from one guy to the next, she said with conviction, "And the band is great without me."

Johnny stalled for time.

When Tish had put her arms around Annie, he'd felt a net of helplessness entrap her. Or was it hopelessness?

He didn't like what was going on, but he didn't know what to do.

He needed some answers.

"Where did you go?"

He had taken a step closer, his hands on his hips, his voice demanding.

Planting her feet, she stared into his eyes and asked, "When?"

When he'd asked the question, he'd expected a simple answer and then started thinking about every time his eyes would seek her out, never finding her. She'd been missing in action far more than he'd realized. His curiosity drove him, his mind sifting through all kinds of scenarios, and he focused on one that brought an even deeper scowl to his face. What if she had a drug problem and that's why she was here? That would take rehabilitation of sorts and in-depth counseling. They had been that route with one of the original band members, and they had kicked him out when his problem came out into the open. They had never gotten involved in that lifestyle although they'd be hard pressed to convince some of their critics of that fact. He didn't want anyone connected to drugs on this tour and he became resolute in finding out what she'd been up to.

His voice had turned hard.

"Since Richmond."

That was five days and four cities ago.

She bit her lip until it must have throbbed with pain.

"I went to some of the Civil War sites. Richmond has more of them than any other place in the country."

"Huh?"

He was confused.

"The White House of the Confederacy is in Richmond. It's where Jefferson Davis lived while he was president."

"I didn't know that."

There was a tinge of regret in his tone.

He noticed the excitement in the flush shining on her face.

"It was beautiful. Most of my life I was homeschooled. My tutor loved history and I picked up her enthusiasm. I walked some of the battlefields that I learned about and it brought it home. What they went through. How many died."

Johnny wavered. Tish looked crestfallen when Reject made a remark about how the South lost the war, as if her balloon had been pricked and was deflating in her hand.

"What did you do in Virginia Beach?"

Their second concert had been at an amphitheater with a sprawling lawn and huge canopy. It had changed names a couple of times over the last few years so he could never keep the current one straight.

"Annie and I went shopping. And to the beach."

"No. That night when you didn't show up for the concert. You weren't sick like Annie told us, were you?"

He'd thought he'd been successfully ignoring her, but she'd been ignoring him.

"I went to a Norfolk Tides baseball game."

"A what?"

"They're a double A team and part of the Baltimore Orioles franchise. It was great. I learned a lot about the game. People started talking to me. When they found out I was from Boston they told me stories about some curse and how one of the teams broke it."

Reject was back with a vengeance.

"No shit. Everyone from New England knows that."

"I didn't. I'd never been to a baseball game before."

Johnny's mind flashed to one of the World Series games he'd gone to with his father, brothers and Paul. Paul had gotten them tickets through a friend of his and had invited his best friend and sons to go with him. It had been a great day, although the Sox had lost. Paul knew so many stats and shared his love of the game with him. At ten years old, Johnny had been a sponge for sports trivia.

He was pulled out of the memory when Tish informed him, "My upbringing was a bit limiting."

That was something he already knew.

"Charlottesville? Raleigh?"

Concerts three and four.

There had been a keyboard on stage but no Tish.

"I spent one day at Monticello, the next at the Museum of History. It had the Wright Flyer, a plane built in Kitty Hawk. And a drugstore from the 1920's. It had..."

Johnny wasn't satisfied yet even when Reject prodded them to leave.

"Days don't count. You were MIA both nights."

Her uneasiness was written clearly enough for him to read. But he knew she was hiding something, and he was determined to get to the bottom of it.

"Last night I went to a place called Rum Runners."

"A bar? What the hell were you doing in a bar? Alone?"

"They had a dueling piano show."

He hadn't wanted to know anything more about her than he already did for a reason that lurked too close to the surface. The band had been going non-stop over the last few days between interviews with the press, radio appearances, photo-ops, autograph signing sessions, concerts.

Tish hadn't been involved in any of it. Wouldn't have been since she wasn't part of the band. Except for the concerts. She should have been present for those.

He didn't point out that she should have been participating in a concert, not attending one but it hung suspended over them in a pregnant pause, before he asked, "Get home late?"

She averted her eyes when she said, "Yeah."

Because of her hesitation, Johnny stepped too close for comfort and bit out, "Are you on drugs?"

He saw a shiver go through her, noticed her breathing was labored and waited for her answer, which she seemed hesitant to give.

"Um, not now."

Johnny's eyes shot up to Annie.

"Does she have a problem we should know about?"

"Of course not. She's on a mild sedative...a prescription for depression. And medication for migraines. She's not an addict."

He flinched as Annie's pointed response pierced him.

Then he felt the poke of a slender finger in his chest and heard a high-pitched rebuke.

"Look, I have issues but drugs aren't one of them."

He could tell by the way she glared at him in indignation he was way off base with that particular accusation. Her haughtiness was genuine, and it would have been comical, if there wasn't still a driving need to know what was going on. Returning the glare, he demanded, "Tell me just one of those issues."

She gulped, as if she was swallowing past a lump in her throat, stared, her eyes searching his for...permission?

Maybe he gave it because she answered him.

"I've lived a pretty secluded life and I want to get out, see things, do things. I've decided that I'm not going to let a day go by without doing something I've never done before. If I have to go back to Boston, I want to take memories back with me."

Pushing some strands of flyaway hair off her forehead, she added, "Last night I wanted to bear witness to piano players who could perform, on a stage, in front of people. And I really liked the music."

She made eye contact with every person standing with her before heading for the revolving doors that would push her outside.

"I'm sorry. For...everything. The wasted time and energy, the money. Maybe I can reimburse you one day. I'll get my bag off the bus."

He watched the droop in the shoulders lift into a more confident stance her purse dangling from her fingers, those long, elegant, graceful fingers that could span an entire keyboard. Johnny took off after her without even thinking about what he was doing. The look on Annie's face had almost crippled him and he knew her well enough after all these years to read her expression. Tish going back to Boston this soon was a bad thing. He had no idea what the consequences were, but it didn't matter.

If Tish couldn't go back home just yet, he was going to make damn sure she didn't.

And maybe one day he'd find out why.

The second reason was less subjective. He didn't like Tish giving into his tirades. He liked it much better when she used her stun gun of prickly heat and shooting sparks.

"Tish, wait up."

He was surprised when she stopped cold.

When he grabbed her arm to turn her to face him, he felt her tremble.

"Look, I'm sorry I started this whole thing. Stay. We'll get you out there. I know we will."

"I appreciate your willingness to help. But I can't be helped. More qualified people than you have tried."

There was an air of vulnerability that enveloped her, another facet to her personality that was far too fractured for him. And far too fascinating.

His eyes narrowed as another question for Annie slammed into his head and he added it to the growing list, which he was presenting her with as soon as he could get her alone.

Gentling his voice, he held Tish's eyes captive.

"You didn't think you could figure out our music, and you did."

He didn't understand why her pupils dilated in primal fear, but he knew he'd do anything he could to help her be free of it.

"That was a fluke."

"You know it wasn't. You need a coach. I can be that for you."

He took a giant step closer.

Her hand against his chest halted his advance.

"No. You have your own life to live. You can't be spending your time attending to me. It's not fair."

He'd gone over this himself since the first day he met her, and he'd almost been able to put his priorities in place. Almost being the operative word. Sometime during the last few minutes, he was back to his initial desire to work with her, bring her out of her shell. After he'd found her in Tim's studio, he'd coaxed her to experiment with the music, encouraged her to find the right chords. Okay, he hadn't done much since they got on the road, but he'd been too busy to take a breath never mind an interest. Ron made sure they were out in the public's eye every chance he could, in the hopes the ticket sales would pick up. There was an inherent belief that Tish's presence could catapult them back to their past success better than any interview.

The interest was back. Magnified this time in a way he couldn't explain.

"Why don't you let me worry about what to do with my time."

"Johnny, please. I'm tired of letting people down. Just let me go."

"You won't disappoint me. You can't give up on your talent."

Her eyes met his, pleading as she begged, "Please don't make me do this."

His fingers traced his jaw. Fear glittered stark and vivid in her eyes.

Her look scared him again, those glossy jade green eyes as much in turmoil as the sea awaiting a storm.

"Tish, I don't know what you're so afraid of, but do you really want to go back to Boston?"

He brushed her tears away, feeling her shiver as she gave in.

"I'll be there every step of the way."

He tucked the fine, golden strands that had strayed from the knot behind her ear, thumbing the tresses as if testing the texture.

Biting her quivering lip, she took a deep breath before agreeing.

"One more try. Tonight. Just tonight. If I can't do it, do you promise to let me go home?"

"Yes, Tish. I promise."

Stepping back and out of his reach, she noticed Annie and Tim hovering close by.

Giving them a semblance of a smile, she stated, "I guess I'll be going home tomorrow instead."

Johnny watched Annie lead Tish away like a baby lamb to board the bus.

Johnny spun around to face Tim.

"What the hell is going on?"

"I'm not at liberty to say."

Tim waited until the women had vanished into the interior of the bus before saying, "She needs a break."

Johnny still wasn't sure why he was volunteering to give her that and he refused to admit how important it had become to help her through whatever the hell this was. It would force him back into the leader role tonight and he didn't want it. Thrusting his hands in the pockets of his jeans, he strode forward but Tim stopped him with his next few words.

"If she goes back this soon, she has no future. It's kinda life and death."

Johnny reeled around and gaped at his friend.

"What?"

"She's had it rough. I'd take over for you, but you seem to be the one she trusts. Sorry, buddy. I never thought you'd be in this position."

"It would help if I knew what I was up against."

"Let's just say her mother is the wicked witch of the whole western hemisphere."

"Her mother? I thought she had no family."

"Tish has us. That's it for now."

"Us?"

His fingers started a quarter beat against his leg.

"Yup. But it could be a two-way street. We help her, she helps us."

"I'm assuming she has stage fright. So tonight..."

"She'll be a bit...nervous."

Johnny gave Tim a look of exasperation. He could be walking into a field of IEDs with no idea where they were planted.

As much as he didn't like it, he felt obliged now to see it done. He'd made a promise and he'd keep it. And he wasn't going to blame Tim because he'd waded into a pile of shit.

But he also wasn't going to make it a tour-long commitment.

"I'll help get her out there tonight but then I'm done. This is a onetime deal."

Johnny hadn't heard Annie's footsteps when she came out to join them, but she hadn't missed his qualification.

"Johnny, please. Just wait and see before making a rash judgment. You haven't seen the panic attacks. They're bad. I'm not even sure you'll be able to handle it."

Tim added, "I told Annie this was a crap shoot. You've been backing away from any and all responsibility for years, and to trust you with this...I'm not sure we should."

Annie grabbed Johnny's arm, imploring, "Getting her on stage for one night might not do any good. She's got to gain some confidence out there. She trusts you for some reason. Please don't let her down."

Johnny stared at them, knowing there was a hint of truth in what Tim had said. There was a stirring inside to prove him wrong.

"One night at a time. We'll see what happens. That's all I can promise."

And with that he turned on his heel and hopped aboard the bus that would roll them into Charlotte, North Carolina, less than three hours away.

CHAPTER TEN

"Tish, Diana's on the phone."

Annie walked up the aisle of the bus and handed her phone over.

Taking a deep breath, Tish put on a fake smile. Diana wouldn't see it, but it made her feel more in control of her mood. With the promise extracted to try to gain her piano stool later that evening, she wasn't in the right frame of mind to hear about what Madeleine was up to.

"Hi, Diana. I assume my mother's been in touch."

"I seem to be her first call every morning. I think she's sorry she never allowed you a cell phone. She has no way of reaching you."

"I wouldn't be answering her calls even if she had."

Although the knot in her stomach would have tightened at seeing the number. It would have been almost as bad as the talking.

"Does she know where I am yet?"

"Not from what I can tell. But from what Annie tells me, you haven't made the stage. Once you do, all bets are off. Thunder has a huge following and if you go on, you will be a subject of interest. It will go viral I can assure you."

"I may be going back to Boston before that happens."

"What do you mean? I don't think that's wise. Not until you've performed again in some way."

"One more attempt. Tonight. Johnny said he's going to help me."

"Scalera?"

The tone was high-pitched.

"Yes, why?"

"That's so magnanimous of him. Does he know about your attacks?"

"He knows, although he has no idea of what they do to me. He's never witnessed one."

Mere words couldn't measure the effects. One had to see for oneself to understand their power over her.

She took a gulp and added, "He will by the end of the day."

That was where all her courage was being channeled at the moment. Allowing Johnny to see her in that fugue state could be a huge mistake.

"Anything new with the contract?"

Diana had hired a lawyer, Judith French, a firebrand of an attorney, to review the financials but Madeleine was stalling.

"We might have to get a subpoena to get her to part with the bank statements."

"Why can't she just let me have some of my money so I can get on with my life? Why does she have to make everything so difficult?"

There wasn't one bank account she had access to. She had been so stupid signing away all her rights, but she'd only been fifteen and hadn't known any better. Hadn't known she had other options. Like emancipation. Diana had mentioned it, but she didn't have the nerve to buck her mother.

"Do you know how much is in your trust fund?"

As if she was being set up, Tish stated the terms of the contract she had found the day she searched for her passport.

"Sixty percent of everything I've made over the last nine years, including recordings and concerts. There won't be as much as there should be, seeing that I balked at the last couple of tours."

Diana added, "Ten percent was supposed to go to music lessons and music."

"My upkeep is expensive."

"What are you talking about? The only expense was Arturo and he's gone now. There isn't a piece of music you don't know."

That wasn't true. She had learned hundreds, but no one could learn all the composers, all the pieces in one lifetime. But she knew what Diana meant.

"That's not quite accurate anymore."

There might be music stored in her head, but she had lost the key to open the vault.

"She told me I was a waste of space, wasn't earning what she projected. I've lost her a lot of money over the last six months."

Diana's sharp intake of breath sounded to Tish like the hiss of a snake.

"Letitia. Tish. Listen to me and listen well. Madeleine has spent far more on herself than she ever spent on you. She's the one who feels she's entitled to the best of everything, entitled to what you earn. That you owe her for some reason I just can't grasp."

"If I can't perform, none of us will have very much."

"Do you know what you've earned in recordings?"

"Not really."

She had asked countless times, wanted an accounting so she could take it over when her contract ended but her mother told her it was none of her business. Her business was playing and if she did as poor a job of managing her finances as she did at that, they'd be destitute. The truth had been hard to argue with.

This was one part of the financial picture that Diana was familiar with. Her commission came out of it.

"Millions, Tish. Millions."

With a rush of breath, Tish asked, "How could that be?"

Diana explained, "You're very good. People love your expressiveness, your technique so they buy your albums."

"But I've seen some of the reviews. They weren't very flattering."

"You've only been given a small piece of the pie. The CD produced by Darnell Haskins, the guy you loved working with, the one that won the Grammy, was given five stars by every critic and according to some, it was one of the best recordings of the century. If you get to work with him again, you will generate even more money and praise. You are exceptional."

"Mother told me that you always found the most flattering critique, to boost my ego."

"I showed you dozens. They all said the same thing."

Tish waited through the moment of silence until Diana was ready to continue. "If you do decide to come back tomorrow I can find you a place to stay until we settle the dispute with your mother, but I think you need to see the tour through. You have a precious gift. I don't want to see you give up on it."

Tish thought about Diana's words.

Her love for the instrument had been a precious gift. It had always felt that the gift had chosen her, not the other way around and she'd been grateful. She loved expressing herself through the flow of chords, lost herself in it, and was able to shut out the rest of the world.

"I'm asking you to stay with Annie and the band. You have nothing to lose and everything to gain. You are perfection, in your very human way. You might have disappointed people, but it was because you didn't show up. It was never the way you played."

"If I can't give them what they deserve, I don't want to do it."

"You give them yourself. I've heard it every time you play. That, in and of itself, is your gift to them."

Tish wished she could see the value, but promised, in spite of her misgivings, "I will give it my very best shot tonight."

That would be everything she had in her. It would have to be enough. Too many people had wanted more. Or was it just one?

Diana ended the conversation with, "I'll call you tomorrow."

Tish could have amended that, but she didn't want Diana thinking that she had already given up. She hadn't. The one thing she had going for her was the promise that Johnny had made to her. He'd be there, although that brought an additional dimension to her nervousness.

Her heart thudded against her ribs. The mere thought of him incited it to play a powerful rendition of Mozart's symphony, a work of intensity, stress and agitation that begain with the first note. Johnny was as powerful, and he was taking her on the same type of journey as Mozart, a dangerous and unexpected one.

His strength might be the only chance she had of overcoming her fright. It was a gamble but one she'd have to make.

Taking one step onto the stage would be an accomplishment, and she'd be one step closer to getting her life back.

Maybe, just maybe, she could do what, up until now, had been impossible.

Booted feet thundered onto the bus, and when she glanced up, Johnny was standing there, his hand around the silver pole by the driver's seat.

"I know we were supposed to practice this afternoon, but I think we should skip it. Take Tish out, keep her from thinking about her debut tonight."

His eyes were set in Tim and Annie's direction.

Annie said, "I think that might be a good idea. Can you afford to skip a practice?"

"Probably not but I figured it would help if we kept her busy."

The woman in question was getting fidgety, her fingers pulling at each other. Johnny was talking about her like she wasn't even here.

She surprised everyone, herself included when she heard herself say, "Hey, I'm not invisible."

Johnny peered at her, his eyes darkening.

"Sorry."

Releasing his hand from the pole, he sauntered down the aisle to where she sat, towering over her. "We have a couple of hours before we have to be at the venue for set-up and I thought—"

"...it might be better if I didn't think about tonight."

She gave him a sour expression.

"I was here when you were speaking to Annie."

Little did he know that redirection would not keep her from her worry spot. But being with him might be the antidote.

Annie asked her, "Did you have a plan for this afternoon?"

Admitting that she did would imply she had no intention of joining the band later.

They all knew that anyway, so she told them, "Um, there's an arcade in town. It has pin ball machines, go carts, miniature golf, all kinds of things I've never done before."

Johnny's eyes lit up.

"Sounds like our kind of place."

Tim asked, as if picking a fight, "Since when?"

Tish noticed Johnny appraise his friend as if he was going to take up the gauntlet but instead he smiled.

"Since now."

⌒

The music blared, the people swarmed and as soon as they walked in, Tish was struck by the bustling activity going on around her. Johnny had taken her hand in his as a precaution, announcing, "You're with me. I'm making sure you don't do your disappearing act."

She hadn't even given it a thought with so many machines lining the walls and as Johnny threaded his way through the masses, her excitement grew. The laughter erupting between friends surrounding her felt good, made her feel a part of the band, a group, society.

Johnny scanned the area.

"We need tokens."

Tim pointed in the direction of a booth where a short line had formed.

"Yeah, over there."

And before she knew it, she was standing at Johnny's side as he worked the pinball machine, master of the flipper, bells clanging and lights flickering. Then he was behind her, his hand on hers as he showed her how to work the buttons. When she won an extra silver sphere, she jumped in joy, her back brushing against him. He stumbled to the side, insisting she play solo from then on. He introduced her to over a dozen games, playing beside her, giving her encouraging smiles, but keeping his distance. It was when they got to the miniature golf course that he was back at the task of helping her. Again, her back was to him as his arms came around her, showing her how to hold the putter. When he lingered on her fingers, she felt a flush of steam, and she savored his maleness, his scent and the strength. She had thought about continuing the pretense of novice, but her competitive streak kicked in and she was able to hold her own with the others.

When they finished off at the go carts, Johnny did nothing more than strap her in and wish her luck.

Above the din of the engine, she asked, "Which pedal is which? I know one is to get the car going."

"You don't drive?"

"Never been behind the wheel in my life. Which one is the brake?"

She could tell from the way he pulled at his ear he was thinking about stopping her, but before he could say a word, she figured it out and went zooming down the track, careening around corners, exhilarating tremors pulsing through her. Waving as she passed him, she laughed at the expression on his face.

She was having one of the best times of her life, and she didn't give the concert a thought.

Being with him was like nothing she'd ever felt before. Her flesh prickled at his touch, her body hummed when he looked at her, and her brain sizzled when he bestowed a smile. The shock of him was a perpetual ache, an ache she didn't know how to ease. As she completed the last lap, her hair being blown by the speed, her heart light, she decided if she ever got past the speed bump ahead of her, getting on stage, she just might try to get over the next one.

The thought of Johnny satisfying another very strong need was just beginning to sprout.

The worries that had burrowed beneath the surface for the afternoon came hurtling back up as soon as they returned to the hotel. When she was alone in her room, getting ready for the night ahead, the familiar trickle of fear slid down her spine.

She wished that she could be someone else.

Taking a deep breath, she reminded herself of what Annie had said.

"With one step today, you can change what your tomorrows are going to look like."

As the prickles rose on her skin, she reminded herself that her mother wasn't here.

Chastising herself to stop the harangue in her head, she forced shaking fingers to complete her toilette.

She gave herself one long last look in the mirror. Tightly pinched lips, sleep-worn eyes, pasty complexion. Even the blush she had applied hadn't put any real color in her cheeks. Her jean skirt was much shorter than what she was used to, and she yanked the tie-dyed crop top that swirled with greens, blues and purples down to cover her midriff. It sprung right back up and she studied her belly button, so exposed it made her feel naked.

It was one of the outfits Annie had helped her pick out on their shopping sprees in Virginia Beach and her new clothes still felt foreign. Used to the beaded gowns and high fashion dresses she wore to perform, her rock style had yet to be developed. She hoped with everything in her that tonight would be the success Johnny anticipated.

But she was facing the reality. Uncertainty was still lurking in the shadows and she knew that tonight could be her last show, not her first.

⁀

Tim and Annie got her to the arena with the promise that if she didn't go on, she'd at least get to see the band live in concert. Her meltdowns had prevented her from moving beyond the hotel room, at least until she knew it was safe to do so. Then she'd run far away from their maddening crowds, so she hadn't even seen them play yet.

The thought of that had gotten her this far.

Her eyes darted around the small room off stage that she occupied, Annie coming and going, but mostly going. She could hear the roadies setting up the equipment, and the busy bee activity that was buzzing outside the door ushered in the reality of the situation. She paced, the chest pain growing by the second, her system as juiced as the electric keyboard when the power came on. Her body ached. Her head throbbed. Her heart pounded. She would not only have to get through the next half hour before the sound check, when Johnny would come in to claim her, she'd have to brace herself for the disappointment she'd see in those dark, brown eyes she'd come to...look for, look at, drown in, care about.

This day would mark the turning point and she felt the repercussions vibrating inside her.

She had asked Annie, during one of the brief check-ins since they'd arrived, why she was wasting her time sitting here.

Annie had asked in return, "Don't you want to put this anticipation behind you?"

"What I want to do is crawl into the woodwork and disappear."

"Haven't you been invisible long enough? You do your best work in front of a crowd."

That had been true once.

It wasn't anymore.

Springing up from the chair, her nervous agitation making her jumpy, she decided to bolt, just like she'd done every night before. She'd find her way back to the bus, end the nightmare. Pausing at the threshold, she took a breath and let her fear settle over her in its usual shrouded form and walked out into the open air.

And came to a standstill.

The place they were playing was an outdoor amphitheater. She scanned the growing crowd, quaking at the number of people already filling the space. There had to be thousands of fans waiting with frenzied anticipation for Raging Thunder's entrance. Ron had said ticket sales were down, but it didn't seem that way from her vantage point.

A growing curiosity kept her from her original intent, and she lingered, observing the fans, how they were dressed, in tattered Thunder tee shirts, some with beers, others walking along the pathway holding hands.

A hazy sun sat midpoint in the sky, and she breathed in the oppressive humidity. Taking a step at a time, she merged with the throng, drinking in all the sights and smells. Hearing excited talk about the upcoming concert, complaints about the parking and the price of food, friends greeting friends, air guitar players mimicking the music blaring from the speakers, she was caught up in the atmosphere, the heavy burden she had carried out from her waiting room lifted off her shoulders.

With brazen footsteps, she moved forward, along the concourse, food stalls on either side, selling pretzels, pizza, alcohol, popcorn. Skirting around the merchandise table, not wanting to be seen by those who might know her, she stood at a distance as fans bought CD's, shirts, keychains, shot glasses, even denim jackets in spite of the sweltering heat. Moving on, she noticed lawn chairs dotting the space beyond the overhang, TV screens high overhead, the steel girders covering the pavilion, glistening light towers sitting in silence, waiting for the right time to shine.

She found the courage to chat with some people who were waiting for the concert to begin. The final sound check was in process. Members of Thunder were on stage and she was drawn to it, them, Johnny, her resistance ebbing away. Each of the guys focused on his own instrument as hoots and hollers from the assembly shot out into the atmosphere.

She was close enough to see whose magnetic field had pulled her in and realized too late that she was close enough to be seen.

Johnny jumped off his stool and made it to the edge of the stage, the fans clamoring for his attention, Jett standing guard by his side, as he called out, "What are you doing out there?"

His index finger curled, and he motioned her to him.

Her insides fluttered at the intimate gesture. His glowing eyes lured her closer and she moved to his crouched position, her reward, one of his smiles.

All speech left her, his lean frame so appealing to her senses, so she shrugged her shoulders in response.

Rising to his feet, he held out his arms and grabbed her hands, hauling her onto the stage. He was close and staring down at her. Her heart began hammering in her chest and her pulse followed suit. Fingers itched to reach and touch all that heat and as she began to lift them, the spell was broken.

His hand swept the wide-open space.

"It's great, isn't it?"

With a voice that held a mixed bag of emotion, she replied, "If you like crowds."

"We do. Come on, check out the board, see if it's set at the right height."

In stunned silence, she stared at the machine.

"I haven't played this one before."

"I know. I told you we were going to get another one. It's bigger and has a better-quality sound."

"I can't do this. I don't know the instrument."

It shouldn't have bothered her. Every concert hall she played had a different piano, each with its own temperament. No two were the same. Part of her skill set had to include the talent to make the varying nuances work for her.

She wasn't up to that tonight.

Johnny's tone held exasperation.

"Tish, it's the same number of keys, same scale sequence."

She backed away, her heart turning into an icicle, making her sweat.

"Tish, you'll be fine."

When she began to hurry across the stage, she heard his footsteps behind her. He followed her back to the room off-stage she begun the evening in, and she slammed the door shut. It was a dead end without an exit. She was unable to move, her heartbeat the only sound she heard until his sharp rap at the door.

"Tish, come out."

The deep voice carried into the room, right into her pounding brain. She couldn't answer. Her mouth was desert dry, parched and filled with a thousand cotton balls. Clearing her throat did nothing but make her throat ache. Her chest felt tight, and her breathing became labored.

She tried to get some part of her working so that she could tell him to come in, but she was lost in a maze of madness and couldn't find her way out.

The knock became insistent and louder with every knuckle rap.

"Tish, I know you're in there."

CHAPTER ELEVEN

As he looked back towards the stage, Johnny's anxiety got the best of him. He was sure she had slipped inside this room.

But where was she?

He was still trying to piece together the puzzle that was Tish, and the knowledge that he hadn't even touched the tip of the iceberg slithered up his spine.

Sweat lined his palms and his heartbeat just a little too fast for his peace of mind.

Why he was so nervous?

Maybe it was the thought of those eyes when they looked at him. They made him crazy.

Hitting the wood of the door with the heel of his hand, letting his temper get the best of him, he almost fell into the room when it opened. The small cries reminded him of a whimpering kitten.

The room was enveloped in darkness and his eyes searched every corner until he found the still figure standing not two feet away. Her chest rose and fell in short, deep gasps and her body was twitching.

His anger evaporated as a rush of pure lust shot through him.

Taking a steadying breath, he closed the door, flipping on the light, illuminating her fragility. He had to rein in the insurgent need to kiss her. Her hair was brushed to a silken glow and it curled in wisps around her face, most of it caught in one of her familiar hairdos. Flushed cheeks heightened her color, lustrous highlights gleamed, her full lips were open as she tried to inhale choppy breaths of air, the shiny lip-gloss unable to hide the blue tint. The contrast between this woman and the one he had pulled onto the stage not five minutes ago was like the difference between classical and heavy metal. It covered an entire spectrum, light to dark, harmony to dissonance.

Noticing the pale face, the trembling limbs, he rushed forward just in time to catch her as she collapsed, holding her loosely against him.

Every imprint scorched his body.

He forced his mind to the situation at hand and with a silent thanks to his body for following suit, he continued to hold her.

He had to have a very sick mind if he wanted to engage in sinful sex with someone who couldn't even stand up. What he held in his arms was a shuddering volcano.

"My God. Does this always happen?"

Keeping her head down, she nodded, the violent shaking uncontrollable now.

"What can I do?"

A small voice pleaded, "Just hold me, please."

He felt her heartbeat as it slammed against his chest. As her grip on him tightened, his hands made small stroking movements up and down her back, and he felt her hanging on to him, whispering to herself to calm down.

Her prayer-like supplications merged with his soft words of encouragement. When her eyes drifted up to meet his, there was a punch to the gut that almost doubled him over.

At a complete loss as to which of them would be able to take the first step out of here, he backed off without moving an inch. Getting her on stage was no longer a driving force. All he wanted to do was shelter her in his arms.

"I was wrong. This isn't a good idea. Why don't we forget it? We can try again tomorrow or better yet, I'll give you some money, you can hang around with Annie, anything you want, but you relax and stay off stage tonight."

He noticed a slight shift in her shoulders as her chin came up. Her voice was at odds with the determined look in her eyes.

"I have to do this, and you promised to help me. I'm not going back until I do. I just need to get out there."

With the shadow of a smile, she gave him back his own words. "I thought you had more guts than this."

He had plenty of guts, he just didn't like this responsibility, didn't like that she was depending on him. He had sworn off that kind of burden.

He also didn't want to see her like this, and he was afraid of what would happen once she reached her stool.

"I don't want to force you."

"You won't be forcing me. I'll never get there if I keep running away."

"Give yourself a couple of more days."

Maybe by then he'd be better prepared, know what to do.

He felt the "no" with a jerk of her head.

And his heart sank.

Not knowing how to proceed, he tried to clear his head.

She couldn't function at all. If he wanted to move her, he was going to have to carry her out to the platform. The thought of how she'd feel in his arms surged through him before he tamped it down to a mild rush. Her voice was quivering when she said, "Need to...do this. Please."

When those eyes met his, his heartbeat in triple time and he became incapable of thought. He stroked her hair off her face and whispered, "Babe, I didn't realize. I'm sorry. We can find something else for you to do."

One thing crashed through his head, but he erected a wall to halt visions of her wrapped in his arms, sheets bunched at the bottom of the bed, her breathing sketchy because of what he was doing to her.

Not because of blind fear but because of blind passion.

He gathered her closer within his arms, rocking her back and forth, trying to calm the trembling that he still felt quaking her body.

Her nose was in the crook of his neck and he heard her inhale sharply.

She breathed him in and felt safe.

Her mind dredged up a suggestion Annie had made once. She broke down the process her body moved through during a panic attack, so she could coax it in another direction. If she found a signal to counteract her panic, she might be able to ward off the inevitable. Breathing in Johnny's strength, she concentrated on the intoxicating aroma and implanted it deep in her psyche. He symbolized power and she had come to trust him. She hoped he didn't mind that she was going to share that power, because with every breath, she made it her own.

Her head tucked into the corner of his shoulder, her lungs working in and out in an abnormal rhythm, she whispered, "Just get me out there."

If he could get her to the stool, she'd be on the stage in performer mode.

She'd achieve one of her objectives at least.

Hugging her closer, he asked, "Are you sure?"

She thought maybe the shivers were a consequence of being in his embrace, not from what lay ahead, but she wasn't sure. Wasn't sure of anything so lost in the way she felt in his arms.

Giving him a nod, she didn't expect what he did next, but her feelings of trust multiplied threefold.

Easily, in one sweep, he lifted her in his arms, opened and closed the door, and strode onto the grandstand.

She heard him bark out, "Chappy, face the keyboard away from the audience and have it positioned in front of me."

The roadie scrambled to fulfill the demand, the start of the concert already behind schedule.

The announcer had been waiting in the wings, waiting for the drummer's appearance, the audience restless, the sound of clapping hands growing in volume as they all waited for Johnny to emerge. Tish felt the stares from every man and woman in the vicinity, compounding her feelings of insecurity She had done it again. She had made a paying audience wait for her.

She thought Reject spoke for all of them when he complained, "What a waste of time."

Tish saw the warning glare Johnny gave the bassist and it sent Reject to his spot on the platform.

A darkened hush had fallen, yet the thundering sound of feet stomping echoed through the amphitheater, the horde impatient for the concert to begin. She felt one of Johnny's arms close in on her as he let go of her legs. She slid down to her feet although he still had a good grasp as she tested the strength of her legs under her.

A little wobbly, but erect.

She felt his breath in her ear, warm and moist.

"It's time, babe. Do you think you can play to me? Like we did that first night in Tim's studio?"

The word *babe* wrapped her in a bubble of warmth, his voice a low hush.

Compressing her lips, she nodded.

Johnny's hand linked with hers in a tight grasp: giving her goose bumps.

She hadn't felt the solidity of that simple gesture since she was just a child when her father would take her hand to cross the street.

Her trust in him continued to build.

Johnny had kept his word. He was here with her and she liked the way it felt. Looking down at their conjoined hands, she like the way they looked as well. She tightened the grip and felt him reciprocate. In that instant, she thought she just might be able to do this.

"You just watch me. Okay? Stay with me."

Time came to a grinding stop. Her life was frozen in the moment and it was a moment she wanted to last forever.

She heard the announcer in the background, his voice garbled, as Johnny helped her onto the stool.

Taking his time to get her seated, he lifted her chin and repeated the command.

"Keep your eyes on me. It's just you and me out here."

His smile slid sideways, and he added, "And remember, don't think."

Her smile wobbled.

"That'll be easy. My mind's a blank."

Her eyes searched his for some hint of accusation, some indication that he thought she was beneath contempt, like Reject had. But what she saw stirred her in its intensity. Before she could define what was there, he lowered his head and gave her a brief kiss on the lips. So brief she wondered if it really happened. But the tingling remained as he took his place behind his drums, his eyes never leaving hers. Confidence lapped over her and she looked down at the keys, hoping she'd know what to do with them.

Her mind was one big empty screen.

The booming voice at the mic had begun the introduction but the noise of the gathering drowned it out. She watched his mouth moving, his arms gesticulating, his body swiveling from side to side to take in the whole pavilion and then Johnny was standing behind his kit, clacking his sticks together, counting down the seconds to the opening flourish. She could only stare at the body in motion.

His eyes were on her. He hadn't wavered.

Thunder rushed into their first song, as the force of the spotlights hit them full on, spreading the entire stage in a strobe light of colors. The beat was demanding. The steely guitar moved through her, the boom of the bass reverberating inside and out.

And the crowd went crazy.

Her breath caught again, but this time from the way Johnny's body exerted itself, the passion with which he pounded the drums, up and out of his stool, back down with force and power. She remembered the way his arms had felt while she used him as a support, his muscles rippling under her palms. She now understood where they came from.

He was giving it his all and she could do no less.

The keys felt cooler than her piano's, which were a soft faded ivory and felt warm to the touch. These weren't as welcoming, yet that distinction allowed her to stay more detached as she floundered for a chord to play. This was not a song she'd practiced with them, but it was one she'd listened to dozens of times. She closed her eyes, the tempo of the music fevered, Johnny's drum beat fluid, applied with muscular precision. She let it carry her on its wild ride, until she was able to test out a stirring of an intricate pattern, the jar of melodic resonance coursing through her.

Shaking fingers atrophied after the attempt and she was unable to get them to curl in place again.

She jumped at the *crash bang* of the bass and cymbals. Johnny guided her with his eyes and his hand signals, even as he held the beat together. She held one hand in place with the other. If she couldn't do a two-handed routine, she'd settle for one. She'd settle for anything that resembled a progression of notes strung together in some fashion. The fingers arched over the keys played a simplistic and choppy melody, a couple of her digits unable to make a sound. The movement was weak, without strength, so only a muted sound issued forth.

Forcing the touch, she went from single notes to chords, at times missing blocks of the song, but her determination grew instead of dissipated.

She refused to let Johnny down.

Glancing up to gauge his reaction, she received a smile filled with glowing pride, letting her know he was far from angry and that he was still there with her.

Not caring that Tish was unable to complement their sound, Johnny relaxed. She had scared the shit out of him. Never in his life had he seen anyone that paralyzed by fear. So incapacitated.

He hoped he'd done the right things, said the right words, and hadn't made it worse for her. He had been such a cavalier fool about her aversion to play, it sickened him. If he'd known about the terror that engulfed her, he never would have forced the issue.

But if he hadn't, she wouldn't be here. She'd be back in the waiting room or at the hotel or someplace she'd chosen at random to pass her time.

And this was where she needed to be.

Her talent, even when it was erratic, was powerful and she owned the instrument. He could just imagine what she'd do in her own style. He had a feeling she could be one of the best.

She had flubbed the first couple of songs, although in fairness, they hadn't covered them with her. Her hands had been tentative as they moved over the keys but as her confidence grew, she was almost able to match their rhythm. As they moved down the playlist, Tish claimed a part of the music for herself. And with each song, she snuck peeks at him.

Was she looking for a smile, a sign he was with her, that she wasn't facing this alone?

He wanted her to believe it was just the two of them.

He felt powerful.

As if her life depended on him. He didn't want to dwell on the implications of that.

And he knew it was Tish's own courage that had gotten her on stage and had nothing to do with him.

Her features were clear, and a spark hit him in the gut. She was no longer on the stool, her slender body standing at the keyboard, and his eyes trailed down her body and admired the crop top that emphasized her flat stomach. As she played, the material that sat on her shoulders slid down revealing smooth skin and his body buzzed at the memory of how baby, soft it was to the touch. Her skirt was short, giving glimpses of great thighs and his hand itched to feel...

He punched down the powerful urge that came over him before putting his attention back on her movements.

She had kicked off her sandals, and now she played barefoot, her toes peeking out, a silver toe ring sparkling. Feminine, still somewhat fragile, all woman. His body began a gradual arousal as his eyes skimmed from head to pink-petal toes and now he throbbed right along with the music. Her lips were turned up and the small smile quickened his pulse. The kiss he'd given her hovered.

That had been a mistake.

Her lips were perfect to the touch, soft and full and so inviting, luring him back for another taste. Slamming down on his snare, he slammed the thought right out of his head. He'd have to find someone quick after the show, because he wasn't going to allow himself a roll in the hay with Tish.

Too dependent. Too inexperienced. Too dangerous.

And he had a feeling that she was going to count on him at least for the next couple of shows to be there for her.

It hit him hard when he realized that was right where he wanted to be.

CHAPTER TWELVE

He hated waking up like this, covered in perfume so thick he couldn't stand himself. For once, he'd been glad they were traveling on the bus. It made it easy to get rid of last night's groupie although he'd still had to put a dose of rudeness into the goodbye. Minimum time and effort to pick her up, but once he'd had her where he wanted her, he didn't want her anymore. That he hadn't chosen very well hadn't surprised him. He'd been making more and more of the mistakes this tour. And the fans were getting younger and younger every year. They wanted things he didn't want to give them anymore, a piece of himself as an icon. They wanted to give him things he didn't want to feel, each woman wanting to prove she was the best, the least inhibited, and he was tired of trying to satisfy their insatiable curiosity.

That he had to sit in the stench for the time it took them to get to the next town and the inexpensive hotel they were staying at had made it impossible to grab more than an hour or two of sleep.

This routine was getting old, and he was more than ready for something new.

Maybe he'd go sightseeing.

Like Tish.

Images of her flooded his head.

Her graceful exit from the bus, the way she smiled at Annie, her good morning when she caught up with him. She was so fresh and clean in her shorts and blouse and when she took an incremental step away from him, her nose wrinkled, her face showing her distaste at the way he smelled, he felt downright sleazy.

Quickening her step away from him and towards the stairwell, she gave him a backward glance before running the rest of the way, making it even more imperative to get clean.

While taking the last hurried steps to his assigned room, he mused on what she'd be doing today.

At the beginning of their career, the band used to find things, wanting to scour every inch of the country but Johnny couldn't remember the last time they'd gone out to see the sights. Over the past year all he'd seen were concert venues and hotel rooms.

As soon as he stepped into his room, he walked with single-minded purpose into the bathroom and turned the water on full blast, anxious to get his own smell back. Gathering the washcloth from the shelf, he stepped beneath the pounding spray, peeled off the paper covering of the miniscule bar of soap and lathered it down to nothing. He wanted to get rid of every layer of evidence that last night's woman even existed. Rubbing the cloth down his neck, he thought about his dwindling stack of give-away tee shirts. He'd have to start shopping for some new ones. He gave them away in quantity but if that was what it took to be rid of the formidable females, then so be it.

Visions of a blonde witch filled his senses and his body stiffened in readiness. He didn't even need to glance down to confirm what he already knew, and he raised his arms in supplication, cursing her again.

The only thing that gave him a thrill these days was a waif-like creature who needed him much more than he wanted to be needed.

A sharp rap at the door as he stepped out of the shower necessitated wrapping a towel around his midriff, before dripping across the carpet in bare feet to answer it.

Tim stood there, a six-pack of beer in his hand, along with a couple of sandwiches.

Handing one of the white-wrapped packages over, he said, "Terry and I are going over some songs we wrote. I thought you might be hungry, so I grabbed a ham and cheese for you. Do you want it?"

"Yeah, thanks. Come in. Just let me throw on some clothes. I'll be with you in a minute."

"No need. We're meeting in his room. See you."

"Wait up. Can't I join you?"

They went too far back, and he didn't like the fact that he was being left out. Tim was his best friend. It didn't matter that they spent less and less time together. No way was Terry taking over his place.

"Sure...but why? You've told me often enough this isn't your thing anymore."

Did he mean the writing? Or the friendship?

"I thought we were partners."

He heard the belligerence in his voice as he said it, knew it wasn't Tim's fault. He had abandoned the role of co-leader and didn't understand where his hostility was coming from.

Tim glared at him, anger seething in his eyes.

"Yeah, Johnny, so did I, but you proved that to be a misconception a long time ago."

Johnny's fingers rested on the towel hanging from his hips.

"What do you mean?"

Tim's lips thinned. His whole body seemed to stiffen at the question.

"Look, why don't you just go find your playmates. I'm sure Reject and Joe are up to no good by now. Don't you have to be out scouting soon? There are a whole lot of women out there waiting for your personal invitation to the show."

Johnny's hands fell to his sides, and fisted, ready to do battle.

But was he ready to wage war over a position he'd vacated all by himself?

Did he want in or out?

He knew he couldn't have it both ways.

"Fine. See you."

And with that he slammed the door in Tim's face.

⌐

Any formulated plan he had to find his cohorts was tucked away as soon as he entered the lobby. Tish stood at the front desk, some brochures in her hand. He wanted a friend right now, not an audience and he thought Tish might fill the need. A connection had been made. He had, after all, been the one to get her on stage.

"Hey, can I join *you?*"

Clearing her throat, Tish said in a small voice, "Sounds like I'm your second choice. What happened?"

"Tim's meeting with Terry."

There was an undercurrent of irritation as he explained further. "They're collaborating."

Memories flitted back to when it had been the two of them, the basement at Tim's, in the backyard at Annie's, in school, on the bus, at practice. Writing while they played, getting better and better, reading each other, connected at some insane level, almost symbiotic. It had been gone for a while now and Johnny missed it. He was at a loss as to how to get it back.

Tish asked, "You don't write with them anymore, do you? Annie said your songs were some of Thunder's best."

Johnny stared up at the giant light fixture gleaming in the afternoon sunshine.

Something he didn't even realize popped out of his mouth in reply.

"I ran out of things to say."

Tish took it a step further. "It seems you all have."

His eyes squinted at her. His body stiffened.

"What do you mean?"

He wasn't sure if his growl had scared her off. It took a few minutes before she answered.

"From what Annie told me, you guys didn't get a lot done in the recording studio. None of the songs were working."

He hadn't thought about it like that before. Had they all gone mute?

"I've listened to some of your concerts on-line. You guys used to mesh, expressed yourselves as individuals within the framework of the whole. It's off now."

Licking her lips, she glanced up into his eyes as if to see if he was going to disagree.

Agitated he asked, "Last night? You were there. How did we sound?"

Clearing her throat, she answered, "I was too busy trying to breathe, too focused on the music in my head to give you an honest assessment. But I've noticed a lot of tension between you guys when you're together. There's an undercurrent, like you don't respect each other."

That remark was discomforting. And inaccurate.

"We just like to joke around. We don't mean anything by it."

"Sarcasm isn't funny. It's contempt wrapped up to look like a joke but it's insulting. And hurtful. Trust me, I know."

He noticed the sadness that had colored her eyes, making them a dull green.

Before he could ask how she knew, she went on.

"Annie describes it as scorn, subversive style, a survival technique for the insecure."

He wrinkled his forehead in thought.

Was she right?

His eyes darted up to meet hers, flecks of gold sparkling.

"I'm not insecure."

Tish laughed.

"No, you're not. But I'm not sure you're kidding with each other. You seem to be sidestepping some truth."

"And it's affecting the music?"

"I don't know."

Her forehead wrinkled as if a thought just struck her.

"Come to think of it, Ron said the band sounded like it used to last night. That by you helping me, you accomplished what he'd been hoping for."

"And what was that?"

"Cohesion. You held the beat for everyone, Johnny, not just me. Tim playing to Terry just doesn't work very well."

Johnny tapped his fingers against his leg, convinced he didn't want the leader role back, didn't want to be the one holding it all together. And yet that's what he'd done.

And he had to admit, it felt damn good.

Shaking his head, he looked up at Tish and asked, "So you want to go shopping? I need some new tees."

He slanted his head, asking without words if she was up to it.

When she gave a quick nod, he escorted her out into the thick southern air and hailed a cab.

Hands hanging in between his legs, he hung his attention out the window, still somewhat stung by Tim's brusqueness, letting the hum of the air conditioner soothe him but Tish's words didn't give it a chance to work its charm.

"How long have you guys been like this?"

He gave her an arched brow and said, "To be honest? I don't know."

His focus was back on the passing scenery.

"Maybe you changed the dynamics."

"Me? I've only been with you for one night. If you even count that. I wasn't a smashing success."

"We were four, now there are five. With very little practice, I might add."

"And as you pointed out to anyone who would listen, it took me five cities to make it on stage."

"How did it feel?"

Joy shined in her eyes.

"I can't believe I actually did it. I owe you a pound of gratitude."

"Only a pound?"

"When I play like I know what I'm doing, I'll raise it to a ton."

He was quiet for a minute, assessing her mood, her ease with the conversation.

He had a list of questions for Annie about Tish, but he was being given an opportunity to go directly to the source.

"So, what's going on with you?"

The taxi pulled up alongside the curb, just outside some shops geared towards tourists. Johnny pushed open the door, paid the driver and took Tish's hand to help her out. They began to amble down the street, side by side, his question still hanging in the air.

She still hadn't said a word.

"Tim told me you were a friend of a friend. Who's the friend?"

She stopped to scan the interior of one of the shops.

"Diana."

"Annie's sister? My agent?"

"Yeah."

"You know Diana?"

He watched as her lids drooped down, heard the deep breath and slow exhale.

"I'm one of her clients."

One of her clients? How could that be?

He'd been as close to that family as his own and thought he knew all of the people Diana represented.

Tish took a few steps and opened the glass door of the souvenir store.

"There are tee shirts in here. Do you want to go in?"

He nodded and followed in the wake of her footsteps, while racking his brain for some mention of a woman named Tish. He came up with nothing.

"I thought I knew all of Diana's clients."

He addressed his words more to himself than to her.

"You've already mentioned you don't like my music so I'm sure I wouldn't have been on your radar."

If he had seen her picture on any CD hanging around Annie's or Diana's, he would have done a double take at her ethereal beauty.

The air conditioning hit him full on, the cool air a nice change from the stifling humidity out on the street. The interior of the store was filled with souvenirs, knick-knacks, snow globes, Charlotte North Carolina shirts, sweatshirts, and beach towels as Tish strayed over to one of the displays.

His next question pursued her.

"Have you been with her long?"

"Longer than Thunder."

His voice held astonishment.

"What were you ten?"

"Close. I was eleven when my father brought her on."

She handed him links in the connect-the-dot game he was playing, but it was up to him to complete the picture. In constant motion, as if she could escape his questions, he kept right after her.

"You've been doing what you do since you were that young?"

"I started lessons when I was six."

"And you can't play yet? I'd kind of give it up if I were you."

She gave him a small laugh and it hit a sweet spot.

"There's no reason for you to believe this, but I was actually quite good once. You've only seen what I've become."

She stopped in front of a sale sign and pointed.

"This what you want?"

He nodded, not taking his eyes off her, some black dots still disconnected.

Fiddling with the layers of shirts in various bins, he flipped through the mishmash to find his size while rummaging through his brain to figure out why he didn't know who she was.

"Are you here on tour with the band so Diana can get you back to making her money?"

"I'm here because I asked Diana to help me."

He gave her a snort and then a yeah-right smirk.

"Tell me another one."

"You don't think I'm worth the effort?"

His head jerked up, taking her in. The look on her face was one of simple curiosity, with maybe a trace of concern.

"I didn't say that. I just know Diana always looks at the bottom line."

"How's your bottom line working for you at the moment?"

"Not as good as it could be, from what I've been told."

"So maybe she's giving us both some time to get it together."

More interested in the conversation, deciding it didn't matter what kind of tee shirts he bought because he wouldn't own them for long, he picked them out at random and paid for half-a-dozen before heading out to the street again where he resumed his interrogation.

"What did you mean when you said you haven't lived life? You've learned how to play the piano."

"It's been sort of one-dimensional. I've spent most of my time touring, practicing, all solitary pursuits. I'd like to see if I can become part of the human race."

He picked up on only one thing.

"You've toured?"

She glanced over at him, her fingers pushing strands of her hair off her face and said, "All over the world."

He stopped short and sniggered.

"You've got to be kidding me."

She peered back at him and smiled.

"Let's say the joke's on me."

Taking a step to catch up with her, he snagged her arm, pulling her to a stop.

"So, what happened?"

She linked her fingers, dipped her head and admitted, "That's not an easy question to answer."

"Start at the beginning."

Her expression clouded with sadness. Her eyes became hooded.

"I'd just as soon not. Let's start when my teacher was fired."

He wanted to know it all but would take what she gave him.

"How long ago was that?"

"Almost a year."

There was a children's store, stuffed animals scattered over a picnic blanket, a rocking chair comforting dolls of various sizes and colors, and she placed her hand on the glass front as if in longing.

"What happened then?"

Taking a deep breath, then blowing it out in a whoosh, she began to tell him her story as they walked along the sidewalk.

"My mother took over my training. My repertoire was pretty much set by then so it should have been an easy transition, but she insisted I learn some new pieces, difficult, challenging pieces. And, like the good girl I was, I memorized them. But it's like traveling down the Amazon, and without a guide, the twists and turns can get kind of...scary."

She peeked up at him to see if he was listening.

"Should I go on? Your eyes haven't glazed over yet."

"Of course, I want you to go on. I want to understand last night's meltdown. The why behind it."

Pursing her lips as if measuring her thoughts, she said, "She had no idea what she was doing. Without Arturo's direction, I didn't know how to interpret the technical aspects, the composer's phrasing. I just went with my intuition. She'd listen to what I had come up with, tell me how wonderful it sounded. But if the critics found fault, she was all over me for getting it wrong and demanded I learn it another way. Then she began to want alternate versions of the pieces I already had mastered, under my teacher's tutelage. Same thing would happen. I had put to memory so many different renditions of so many compositions that I couldn't keep anything straight, everything such a jumbled mess in my head."

His heart beat like thunder as anger surged through him. Her mother sounded demented. Keeping his temper to himself, he asked, "Is that when the panic attacks started?"

"Yes. The last couple of concert series had to be cancelled, the symptoms became so invasive."

He flinched, his mouth a tight line as if a whip had cracked, piercing his skin with its lash. With startling clarity, he felt her anguish, felt her loss down to his soul.

He took her by the shoulders and turned her, so she faced him.

"You've lost your music."

It was a musician's worst nightmare.

With a faint tremor, she admitted, "I have."

There was a fine mist of perspiration covering her forehead and when he kissed her temple, he tasted the saltiness, felt her heartbeat when he pulled her close.

"I'm sorry. I don't know what I would do if I...couldn't play."

Leaning his forehead against hers, he felt not only his heart ache for her but his body as well.

His fingers traced her jaw as he said, "That's the reason you didn't want to interpret our music. You were afraid you'd get it wrong."

He felt another quiver before she stepped away, her eyes glittering in the hazy sunshine, a serious expression on her face.

"Still afraid."

They began walking again but this time with their hands linked.

"So, your mother is the only family you have?"

"She's it."

"What happened to your father?"

"He died when I was twelve. How about you? Family?"

Adrenaline shot through him when he thought about the tight-knit group.

"Lots. Brothers, sister, uncles, aunts, cousins...and a stepfather. An extended family that could populate a small town."

"You're lucky."

He barked out a laugh.

"I wouldn't call it that. I don't even talk to them anymore."

There was a rise in her pitch when she asked, "Why not?"

Needing to think of an answer, he pointed to another store that had the word *souvenir* flashing in the window and they entered the cool little shop. She went straight for the sunglasses while Johnny fingered the shirts at the round swivel clothes rack. When Tish moved towards him, the electricity amped up and he let it streak through him before backing away.

Hoping he could avert the question, he posed one of his own. "What's your last name?"

Studying her as she put on the glasses, her eyes disappearing behind the darkened lenses, he got the answer he'd been waiting for.

"Jones."

The dot-to-dot had come full circle and there was an overwhelming surge of pride for some reason.

"You're Letitia Jones?"

He thought back to the way Annie and Tim had reacted when he'd complimented the artist in the kitchen one morning. Had he compared her...to her? Admitting she'd been good once, that didn't come close to describing the way she played. She touched the soul.

Her voice pulled him back.

"You know who that is?"

He had heard mention of her from time to time, Annie giving them updates on Diana's schedule, which included tour dates with the classical performer. The music flooding through Annie's house all these years must have been...Tish. He'd just never investigated the who, preferring their own brand to the baroque and traditional composers.

He stared at her and asked for confirmation.

"Is it you?"

"In the flesh but without any of the perks that go with it."

He could have amended that. She had all the perks that came with her flesh and when he felt the familiar pull, he pushed back.

At the counter, he laid five shirts down, extracted some bills from his front pocket and paid the clerk. Waiting for Tish to pay for the sunglasses, he ruminated over which question to ask next, now that he knew who she was, but once they were back out in the sunlight, heading back to the hotel, she beat him to it.

"So why don't you talk to your family?"

"Long story."

She pressed him in retaliation, his exact words coming back at him.

"Start at the beginning."

"Let's start with my father's death."

"Okay."

"No, let's start with my mother's remarriage."

She waited for him to continue, not saying anything.

"He was my father's best friend and tried to take over my life. I refused to let him. He threw me out one night. I never went back. One by one my brothers and sister sided with him, so I didn't speak to them either. My sister Marissa is the only one I still have contact with. She knows not to broach the subject of Paul. The day she does, she's off my phone list."

"That's so sad."

"Don't go feeling sorry for me. I've been fine on my own."

"How long ago did all this happen?"

"Eight years ago, this coming Saturday."

"You remember to the day?"

"Second anniversary of my father's death."

Her hand slipped into his, linking fingers. He liked the way it felt.

"You haven't spoken to your mother since?"

"I call her on her birthday, Mother's Day. Say what I need to say and then hang up."

"Was she a good mother?"

He focused inward but said out loud, "One of the best."

"And you were still able to cut her off?"

Heaviness settled on his chest.

"Yeah."

It hadn't been as easy to do as he made everyone think. He missed them. All of them.

The hotel loomed in the distance, and they ambled on, silence settling between them as he became lost in his thoughts.

Christmas was the holiday he missed the most.

The first year after his father's death, his mother had wanted to skip the big event. No *Vigilia*, no Midnight Mass, no big show with presents, no end-of-the-year culinary feast. Paul was the one who insisted Salvatore Scalera would want them to celebrate though he'd only been gone a little over six months. He had loved his kids too much to have them go without.

He wasn't the only one who had loved all five kids.

Paul had, too, and he'd made sure Christmas that year was a special one with lots of presents and...love. He had taken over where his father had left off. The six of them had become Paul's life, too.

He shook off that thought. Paul had gotten rid of him, so that left five.

He'd have to decide how to spend the upcoming holidays. Maybe somewhere different this year, maybe with Annie and Tim. Spend it with someone he was connected to, not just meeting for the first time on a deserted beach on a faraway island.

⁓

Once they had returned to the hotel, he dropped Tish off at her room, contemplating what he had discovered so far.

She was a classical pianist, just as he'd thought, a lot more famous than he would have guessed. There were too many layers to her talent not to notice. She borrowed from her style and injected it into his music. Her technique was flawless. That came from practice.

Booting up his laptop, he Googled Letitia Jones and pages and pages of entries appeared. Letitia Jones at Carnegie Hall, Letitia Jones at the summer festival in Albany, in Greece, in Vienna, in Prague. He found the top ten

Letitia Jones profiles-LinkedIn, Facebook, Snapchat, images of her in various poses, at the piano, standing beside it, at different ages, the latest a shot of her in an evening gown that did little to enhance her body. An article, "Why you shouldn't miss a Letitia Jones concert." *Talent...varied interpretation to match the innate characteristics of the composer...passionate with great magnetism...powerful mastery...depth of feeling...vulnerable...mystical.*

Watching some of the YouTube videos, he had to agree with all of it.

Her playing touched the soul.

He didn't skip the entries that had offered the opinion that she had lost her magic. The articles that rushed to judgment about her failures, her weak sound, her inability to show her face were scathing. They were not a true testament to her talent. They lacked any understanding of what had brought about her fall from grace, her recent missteps, her fear, her vulnerability.

What her mother had done was almost criminal.

CHAPTER THIRTEEN

A sense of foreboding covered Tish in a fine mist of perspiration as the bus pulled up to the front of a glass-walled structure. A memory floated through her. She was twelve, a prodigy everyone wanted a piece of, but Diana was still booking smaller venues to get her comfortable with the prospect of performing for thousands. Her agent was a believer in starting out cautiously, that public appearances were important, but more important was Letitia's physical and mental maturity. The argument between mother and agent over differing philosophies remained pungent in the air but her father had stood with Diana and they had gotten their way. Her father had still been a part of her life back then, such a calming presence but his death a few months later had taken away the stalwart of reason.

Glancing again at the giant window, Tish let the picture unfold in her mind, saw herself at the baby grand, her fingers featherlike over the keys, her love of the music she played evident to everyone listening. This concert had been successful, and the critics had been positive and self-assuring. The write-up that her father had shown her had used words like *strong individuality, proper phrasing, and phenomenal use of the pedal.* He had been proud of her, had taken her away for a few days to celebrate her virtuosity. After Oscar's death, she'd floundered with a revolving door of teachers until Arturo was hired.

"Hey, is something wrong?"

Annie came up behind her as Tim and Terry bounded off the bus to be swept inside the back doors surrounded by bodyguards assigned to protect them, from their enthusiastic fans.

"Just thinking back. I played here once a long time ago."

Her heart squeezed at the thought of her father's pride in her performance.

Annie asked, "Good...or bad?"

Tish looked at eyes filled with concern.

"It went very well. I forgot there were good ones. Once."

Annie dropped into the seat beside her.

"And there will be again. I can feel it."

"I don't want to just play again, Annie. I want to love playing again. That was the sweetest part of it."

She had been able to put her heart into the flowing score of notes and phrases, felt the power of the pieces right down to her soul. One day that all changed. The sound was flat, the notes mechanical rather than resonant.

"You've been practicing a lot. I know you didn't like how it sounded before, but how are you feeling about it now?"

"I'm..."

Johnny appeared on the steps of the bus looking a bit frazzled.

Jett, his bodyguard, was still barking at him.

"Are you trying to get yourself killed?"

Johnny waved him off and sought Tish's eyes.

"Something wrong? Why didn't you get off yet?"

Contrite, Tish explained, "Just talking. Sorry."

"I thought...you know...that you didn't...want to get off."

Annie scooted down the aisle and down the steps.

Tish watched her go before answering.

"I'm still a little shaky but my legs aren't jelly yet. I've played here before. It kind of all came back to me."

He was gazing at the building that resembled a lighthouse, all glass and gleaming metal, the lush forests of the Smoky Mountains of North Carolina in the distance.

"It's a smaller venue than usual, only about fifteen hundred seats but the acoustics are great, and we put it on the schedule every year. Does it bother you?"

He had dropped into the seat opposite.

She took him in, worry still etched on his face. Drawing in a breath and some of his power, she said, "Less people means more attention to each instrument."

"I know you can handle it. And we promised no spotlights and we keep our promises, ma'am."

She sizzled at the way he looked at her but there was humor in his eyes, so she put some southern hospitality into her reply.

"Why thank you, kind sir."

She fluttered her eyelashes at him.

He quirked a smile and leaned forward, took her chin in his hand.

"Got something in your eye? Here, let me take a look."

A sensuous light passed between them, holding them captive in each other's gaze.

She was lost in time, the air dissolved into nothing, and her lips parted in breathlessness.

When he yanked his hand back and jumped up from his seat, he was all business.

She lowered her head and closed her eyes, not wanting him to see the disappointment there. He had been so close, but then in a flash, he was several feet away, his hands hidden in his back pockets.

"Chappy's putting the keyboard in the same place as last night. You'll be playing to me again."

Taking a moment for her breathing to return to normal, she asked, "Can I look at the play list? I've been working on some of the other songs, and I'd like to know if you'll be using any of them."

"Yeah, sure. I'll have Chappy hang it on the mic and put it near the keys. Which songs were you thinking?"

"'Mistakes', 'Down on Love', and 'Powerbroker'."

"They're some of our newer ones, so yeah, they'll be on the list."

She pulled herself up, crossing in front of him, brushing against his chest as she exited their home on wheels. Throwing her bag over her shoulder, she dismounted while Jett and Ralph protected the threesome from the fans screaming for attention.

Jett shook his head when he warned, "I swear, Johnny, you're going to regret being so careless one day. You can't just come and go as you please."

Johnny laughed. "Just making sure you're earning your keep."

Jett grumbled as they entered the glass doors and made their way to the dressing room.

Annie walked over to Johnny and pulled his shirt out to read the inscription.

"New?"

"Yeah, like it?"

"Not really. Kind of offensive."

"Talk to Tish. She was there when I bought it."

He walked over to where she stood but kept his distance.

"So, Glinda, ready to rock?"

She peered at him. "I am not a witch."

"You know who that is?"

"I watched a lot of movies when I was younger."

"You have witchy eyes."

"I do not."

"Do, too. They change all the time."

Annie giggled and said, "She's like a mood ring."

"She is. What color are they right now?"

Annie drew closer to Tish and smiled.

"I'd say a raging thunder blue."

"Appropriate. Now that we had the eye check, time for the sound check. Ready?"

Tish wasn't sure.

She felt the constricting band around her chest and all sensation pooled in her gut. It's where the seed of anxiety planted itself, growing into palpitations and shallow breathing.

Johnny moved right in, as if he could read the signs now, his fingers stroking her back, his gentle assurances whispered in her ear.

She let him lead her from the back room out to the stage, where the roadies had constructed the background of a dark sky and where the instruments waited to be checked for sound and feedback levels. Working at the keyboard, her back to the vacant seats, she fumbled through the routine, brown eyes checking in from time to time, quick smiles creating the warmth she needed to keep the cold fear at bay.

Drinking him in, his solid form, the gleam in his eye, his hair pulled back, she felt foolish being so enamored, but it gave her the dose of courage she needed. When it was time to change for the main event, she retreated to the dressing room with firmer footing.

His parting words were, "You can do this."

Those words had been prophetic, because she had, with a more confident keystroke and a more Thunder like flourish.

She was almost ready to believe what she wanted more than anything was possible.

⌒

Still unable to sleep for long stretches of time, Tish was up early and prowling the lobby. Sitting in one of the chairs that overlooked the front of the hotel, her head resting back, she thought about the concert last night. It had been another step in her evolution, and she'd been pleased with the results. The only notes occupying her brain belonged to Thunder. Their music was flowing out with spontaneity as soon as her fingers touched the keys. Johnny's thoughtfulness in facing the keyboard towards him had helped, but it was also distracting her. She had yet to immerse herself, become one with the music because of the feelings his movements evoked. He'd led them all into a night of high energy. Watching him was like watching an earthquake, the ground shaking beneath her feet, trembling vibrations, and the ripples increased as they spread out to the other members of the band. The magnitude of the change from their rehearsals to these past two nights was numbing. When she'd heard them play together during her first practice session, Terry had played to Tim, Tim played to an invisible audience, Reject had done an almost solo routine. It was obvious to her that Johnny was the true leader, the one with the energy to make things happen. Annie had told her he could play anything on drums, and she'd become witness to his many styles and levels, his ingenuous arrangements.

When he'd told her to stay with him, follow his lead, she had almost made the mistake of asking if she could, later, in his room. Grateful that she'd refrained, she knew she would have been humiliated when he turned her down.

There was no if about it.

"Hello, early bird."

Raising her head, she saw Annie awake but yawning. They hadn't gotten to Charleston until the very wee hours of the morning, but Annie had wanted to meet for breakfast before anyone else had gotten up.

Arranging a plate of fruit, eggs and yogurt with a large dose of coffee, they sat at one of the tables in the dining room, the sun a muted glow in the sky.

Taking a bite of her toast, Annie said, "You were terrific last night."

"No, Johnny was terrific. I just followed his lead."

"Everyone did. It was a refreshing change. What are you feeling about the rest of the tour?"

"Hopeful. Still scared although I'm not breaking out in uncontrollable shakes, just a cold sweat. That's progress, I guess."

"How are the headaches?"

"They're better. Not so explosive. I think it's being able to get the music out. There's light-headedness instead of tight pounding."

"Johnny's right, you know. When you feel the music, you're great."

Tish's answering smile needed some work.

"Right. Don't think. You have to understand my mother went ballistic when I didn't concentrate on my technique. Feeling and interpreting got me into major trouble. I'm still playing as if her disapproval will cost me."

Tish took a sip of her coffee. "Will I ever stop worrying about that?"

"Time. It will take time."

"I can hear the sarcastic remarks she'll make when she finds out what I'm doing."

The day of reckoning was coming soon. Her mother might not be a computer geek, but she was sure one of Madeleine's friends would drop the bomb if she ever got to YouTube.

In a voice intended to mimic Madeleine, Tish put her nose in the air and stressed her words.

"Letitia, how could you stoop to this level? You know there are three types of music: brass, crass and class. You've chosen crass over class and I won't abide it."

She felt her facial muscles tighten as her mood shifted from shame to annoyance.

"What's worrisome is that I'm still looking over my shoulder but now it's to see if I have Johnny's approval."

"He's the one helping you. I don't think you look for his approval so much as support. There's a difference."

"He can't punish me if he doesn't like what I'm doing. Is that it?"

"Yes."

He had treated her with respect, empathy, the exact opposite of how Madeleine had, and it made it even more important to play well.

After taking a bite of her eggs, washing it down with a sip of orange juice, Tish asked, "What's it like being married to an idol?"

Annie answered with her gentle laughter.

"Not easy. Sometimes I walk down to the lobby and find him surrounded by all these beautiful and aggressive women. It's hard to watch strange hands fondle what's supposed to be mine."

"What's sex like?"

Annie coughed up the coffee she'd been about to swallow.

Wiping her mouth with a finger, she took a moment before responding.

"Mm-hm. I might not be the right one to ask. Johnny has more experience that I do. I've only had sex with Tim."

"I think I'll pass having this conversation with him."

He was the reason behind the question, behind the curiosity. The way he made her shiver at just a touch, his eyes seductive, his body enticing. But she had no idea what it all meant although in her imagination she would guess it led to a very satisfying resolution.

It was his face that flashed in her mind whenever she thought she might like to taste the more physical pleasures in someone's bed. With such a vivid picture, she couldn't even dream of bringing it up without falling into his arms, with the hope he'd get the idea.

She asked Annie, again, "What does it feel like?"

"With Tim, very, very, very good."

Annie scooted her chair back and leaned against the window.

"What are you thinking?"

"That's one of your favorite questions."

"I guess it's the only way for me to gauge what's going on in there."

Annie leaned forward and tapped the side of Tish's head.

"You excel at keeping things hidden."

"I've had to."

Their eyes connected.

"So why the interest?"

"I have all these feelings. And I don't know what to do with them."

Annie peered at her before she asked the one-million-dollar question.

"Johnny?"

"Am I that easy to read?"

"Johnny's the one you've come to depend on. Are you sure you're not confusing what you feel?"

"He makes me feel all wobbly. Makes my heart beat harder. Makes me want something I don't even know how to describe or articulate."

"Ti-i-i-sh, you've got to be careful with this."

"Oh, I know. He's got so many other women to choose from. You've said he goes through them as if he's about to run out. I wouldn't even think about approaching him. But I want to know what the whole thing feels like. From beginning to end."

She closed her eyes as a vivid image flashed into her mind. Broad shoulders and rippling muscle.

"What's gotten into you?"

"I'm sick and tired of observing life. I watch the guys; I watch the women and the way they taste and touch things I've always wanted to taste and touch. Human touch. I want to experience it."

"Once you get back to Boston, once your life is on a more even keel, you'll find someone. It's so much more satisfying with someone you can build a future with, and Tish, that isn't Johnny. Why don't you wait?"

"Because, even though it seems like I'm making progress, I can't be sure what I'm going to find when I get back. You never know with my mother. She's still looking for ways to lure me back. First the investigator, now the lawyers. Who knows whether the attorney Diana hired will be able to outwit her? I'm grabbing everything I can with both hands just in case. To be honest I'd give anything for Johnny to be my first."

Tish saw a prickle of fear skitter across Annie's face.

"Don't worry. He's too experienced and way too intense. But maybe, after, who knows?"

"After what?"

"After I get the initiation over with."

Annie had told her about his rule. And convinced her that he wouldn't break it. For anyone.

"I'm not sure that's a good idea, either."

"I'll be careful. I'm not going to jump into bed with the first man I see. I can't even return a smile yet. It might take forever to get to a comfort level with that. I'll have to start going out with them. Then I can watch and learn."

Maybe if she picked up some pointers from the women Johnny bedded, she'd have a better perspective of what to do to get him there herself, when the time was right.

When the V-edict no long applied.

$\curvearrowright$

Tish glanced at her clock as the bus pulled into the parking lot, the sun trying to break through the visor over her window. They had arrived in Georgia, another of those hot, hazy, humid states where the nights were as sticky as the days. The bunk felt good, the air temperature comfortable and she was tempted to lie here awhile longer.

Ever since her first night on stage in Charlotte, all the way through North and South Carolina, her days had been a whirlwind and she had never felt so happy. Her stage fright still reared its head right before the concerts but once she was playing, she forgot about everything but the music and the man who still commanded her attention.

On and off the stage.

She'd shopped with Annie, becoming more adept at spotting what she liked the minute she stepped into a store, getting bolder in her wardrobe choices, filling her make-shift closet in a way she'd never been allowed before. Ron was giving her cash for spending after each concert, compensation for being Thunder's keyboard player and she spent it with abandon.

The Greenville Zoo had been great, and she'd attended her first movie in a theater. They were the highlights so far. Johnny had never been more than a few feet away.

She had also begun to accompany the guys out at night, after a concert. Her flirting skills were improving, although she hadn't been able to take it a step further. It wasn't only that she lacked the courage to get close to a man. Johnny always pulled her back to their table, chasing men away with a sour face before taking her back to the hotel. He hadn't given any of the women around him the time of day which meant she couldn't tell what worked with him and what didn't. Some nights she'd hoped his surliness meant he wanted her, but he never made a move, and her hope was buried in a pile of regret.

Before her mind could conjure up what additional ammunition she could use to have her way with him, Ralph announced, "Up and at-'em. I can't park out front of the hotel for long so let's get a move on."

As the members of the entourage disembarked, Ralph reminded them all, "You only have a couple of hours before we leave for the Dome. Be on time, please."

CHAPTER FOURTEEN

"Hello Atlanta."

Johnny felt the love. The band was already half way through their playlist, the crowd was on its feet and it felt great. The fans were creating the kind of feedback rockers thrived on and it was all because of the improved sound they were putting out. High-octane energy.

The critics had been generous with their praise as well and ticket sales had skyrocketed.

Looking out over the stadium, one that held fifty-thousand seats, he was amazed at how they'd been able to turn themselves around in such a short time.

It was Tish who had made the difference. And it wasn't only on stage.

When she walked out of the dressing room before the show, he had felt a flicker of desire.

Nope.

Not a flicker but a friggin flame.

Those eyes had burned into him, his whole body coming awake with it.

After wiping his wet palms against the legs of his jeans, he fiddled with his hair, rubbed his stubble, paced.

What he felt was not good on any level.

He had a rule and he was sticking to it even if it killed him.

It had been right after his first time that he'd made the promise to himself.

He'd been too large, the girl had been too tight.

Neither of them had gotten what they wanted out of the experience.

He went with seasoned women now, those who could accommodate him.

He'd learned over the years how to use it, but he still wasn't willing to knock on virginity's door again.

Not going there.

Not in a million years.

Never.

Yet, he hadn't moved from the spot since she'd left him to change, waiting for her to emerge and join him. What he saw was a true southern belle, cowboy style. The dress she wore had a cami top attached to a skirt with ruffles. The thick, brown belt sat on her hips and matched the brown cowboy boots she had bought in Greenville. She looked too tempting by far.

She was more the fair maiden than the witch and he forced himself not to step forward for a kiss. The one he'd given her days ago, as light as it had been, still spent sparks through his system.

And he wanted another.

His eyes had traveled the length of her. She always looked so fresh...and so sexy.

The thought made him glance down.

His tee shirt was new and clean, but his jeans had seen better days. Boots were a mainstay although he was starting to think about picking up a pair of Vans so he'd be cooler in the sticky southern humidity. His eyes went to Tim. He had on a long sleeve silk shirt, tucked into pressed black jeans, his dress boots hiding under the hem of his pants. Terry was put together, as well. Reject had on a sleeveless vest, ripped jeans and looked no better than he did. No analysis needed to know who hung out with whom. He'd gotten sloppy as if his fans accepted him just the way he was so there was no need to impress, no need to give a shit about what he wore.

The soft feminine voice prompted him to take her hand before leading her to her stool.

He'd told Tim his getting her on stage was a onetime deal but he'd reneged on his promise. It had become a nightly ritual that he looked forward to.

"You good?"

"I'm still standing."

The tremor was visible and her lips had a blue tinge beneath the shiny lip gloss.

A spurt of admiration for her courage shot through him.

"Just stay with me."

"Don't know how to do it any other way."

He'd noticed. She stayed with him night after night, bringing more creative harmony to each gig, a chaordic assault on the senses that was the perfect backdrop for the guitars.

Glancing over, checking in as he did throughout the show, he felt the quickening, the fire she stoked in him. During the few songs she didn't mix with, he felt the blazing sensation in the pit of his stomach that stayed with him right up until the last drum stroke.

At the end of the last set, she sashayed out from the platform, her feet free of the boots she'd started the night with, and walked over to where Annie stood, a cat-like smile on her face.

When she slipped him another look, those witchy eyes held a fire he couldn't ignore. With eyes narrowed and nostrils flaring, he went plowing by her, grabbing her hand as he moved, and took her scrambling in his wake.

He felt the tug of resistance as she tried to wrench her hand free, the mule-like refusal to follow him, then the hopping up and down as if she'd stubbed a toe as he continued to drag her along.

He maneuvered around the obstacle course of feedback amps, guitar pedals, wires, speaker jackets and scattered boxes of strings and picks. When he spun her around, her back was pressed against the wall of the backstage room, his hands on her shoulders to keep her in place.

Instead of the fear he thought he'd see, her eyes beckoned him on.

He had to get himself back in control but God, no one had ever watched him play like that before. Her eyes had burned through him at every level, and his blood boiled to the point he thought he'd explode. She had crept under his skin, gotten inside his head, become one with him. He'd felt like she was breathing with him and it had nearly driven him insane. No, what had been insane was the way he'd started playing in response. Demonic possession.

When his eyes had met hers, she'd held his gaze, and there he'd read what every downward stroke of the sticks did to her. He'd played with wild abandon, dominating her with each spiral, compelling her to feel each and every beat, sweating for her, giving everything he had and taking everything she had to give. It was the most incredible joining he had ever had, physical, mental, emotional, almost spiritual and his body was so inflamed by the end of the set, he'd struggled to prevent it from devouring him.

And she was still doing it.

Snarling, he fell into her eyes and made another short trip into hell.

"Don't ever do that again."

"Do what?"

"You know what. Don't do it."

"Don't look at you?"

"Don't look at me like *that*."

"Like what?"

"Like...I'm chocolate cake with whipped cream frosting and you need a sugar fix."

"I like whipped cream."

It was the tongue sliding across pink lips that did him in and he took the one step he shouldn't have, becoming part of her skin.

His body plastered hers to the wall, elbows bracketing her head between them, his palms trying to hold the wall in place, because it kept shifting on him. He stared at those now moist lips he had thought about incessantly since the last time he'd brushed them with his. Feeling the fusion of lips together, his body nestled into all the right spots.

The attack on her lips grew fevered, his tongue pressing its case, wanting to touch and savor the moist interior of her mouth. When he felt her hands on him, felt her adjust to where he could slip inside but for the clothes they wore, he lost all control. His hands molded to her bodice, the soft mounds searing him, the nipples puckered in pleading, and the alarm sounded, a clanging bell that jarred him back.

He pushed away from her, panting, unable to draw in breath, his lungs refusing to participate in the involuntary function.

This was not going to happen.

He heard Tim's bellow, the web ensnaring him broken, and he glared at her, muttering the word *witch*, before backing up and heading for the stage and their encore.

⁓

Johnny joined Tim at a local bar after the concert and ordered a beer.

"What was that thing you did earlier?"

"What thing?"

"Your tongue, her throat."

The sigh was long and hard.

"You noticed."

"Everyone noticed."

"Bad move, I agree."

Dropping down to the barstool, Johnny took a hearty swig.

Running his hands through his hair, wishing he had something to tie it back with, he said, "The witch drove me to it."

Before he could think more in depth of what had happened, Chappy announced, "Hey, Annie and Tish are here."

Needing time away from her, Johnny had been relieved when the women declined the invite out, with the excuse that they were tired and were sticking close to the hotel.

He didn't want Tish around, afraid she'd cast another spell, draw him in again. He had wanted to get his bearings, figure out what the hell was going on between them. Relax and not have to work at resisting the irresistible. He'd have to erect his shield, the one that didn't seem to be effective anymore. At least not with Tish.

He groaned.

"I thought they were in for the night."

Chappy shrugged. "Guess they changed their minds."

Tim slid off the stool but Johnny stayed rooted to the spot.

After his earlier transgression, he was intent on holding himself in check. And he could only do that from a distance.

But Tim wasn't accommodating him.

He walked, his arm circling his wife's waist, towards the bar and against his better judgment Johnny made eye contact with the blonde at their side who explained their presence.

"We got bored and I needed a drink."

Looking to the bartender, who'd traveled to this end of the long counter, she ordered.

"Sex on the beach, please."

Johnny's eyebrows shot up so high they almost left his head.

What the hell was she planning?

He hadn't seen her drink anything stronger than a glass of wine. Tonight of all nights she had to go bold?

Then he noticed her scan the room, sipping from the glass in her hand.

His eyes followed hers.

It wasn't a huge place but it was full. Laughter echoed from several positions taken up by a couple of roadies, while Terry and his wife were shooting pool.

"Hm. There's someone leaving. I'm going over to grab the table. Let you men get back to what you were doing."

What men?

It was just him and Tim and Tim was now preoccupied with Annie.

And what did she think he'd been doing?'

It wasn't that no women had approached him, they had, but he wasn't in the mood to act the part of interested.

His interest had since picked up.

A good-looking guy, maybe mid-twenties, stopped by Tish's table to talk to her.

The way Tish's eyelashes were fluttering, those eyes, glittering bits of turquoise, speaking a language he knew too well was making him...

When he felt his hands curl into fists and he felt his feet moving in her direction he swore under his breath.

Arriving just as the guy was about to sit down, he planted himself.

"'Scuse me buddy, but this seat is taken."

"Oh, sorry. Didn't know."

He hesitated as he looked at Tish before moving away.

Crossing her arms, she seemed to be pouting.

"What are you doing?"

"Saving you from yourself."

"I don't need saving."

"Oh, really? Then what have I been doing since I promised to get you on stage?"

She took another slow sip of her drink, her eyes drifting to another part of the bar.

"That's different."

"How?"

She seemed agitated, as if she didn't want to be having this conversation with him.

"It just is."

Leaning in towards her, he placed his hand on her arm to get her attention.

"Do you know what most guys want?"

The touch was like the strike of a match and he lifted it up and dropped it back on the table.

When she replied, "Some of you make it obvious," their eyes met and held.

The ember he'd been trying hard to tamp out, flared up again.

"You're not ready for that yet."

"And how would you know?"

"I just do."

"You don't know anything. If I want to pick up a guy, that's my business. Not yours."

Her eyes were hard metallic bits and they were burning into his.

"You think so? Time to go."

"I'm not going anywhere."

"Then neither am I."

He was as good as his word.

How could she learn what he wanted if he stayed with her all night?'

Her goal tonight was to watch how women came on to him, with maybe a little flirting of her own for practice.

She was being schooled in *that*. It didn't seem to matter that he was sitting with someone else. The women who knew of his celebrity, blatant in their attempt, were working their attributes, overtime.

The problem was, he wasn't responding to any of them.

He just sat stone-faced, sipping his drink, tapping his fingers on the table.

She didn't understand him at all.

He was known for his womanizing, so what was he doing ignoring the women who fawned over him? And why did he seem intent on standing guard as if to keep her virtue safe her from marauding males?

Did he want her?

He had all but consumed her with that kiss earlier.

Okay, maybe she had watched him with ravenous hunger. Mesmerized by his provoking performance, she'd sat speechless through a couple songs, just watching his powerful body move. Consumed by its potency, his solid thighs pumping up and down, the bass pedal working her heart beat. Arms, corded muscles pulsing, striking with bullet-like precision, not only his drums but every nerve cell in her system, his hands beating a primal path to her womanhood, searing the skins of both instruments, once percussion, one human. He had taken her over, and she'd lost herself in him, sinking deeper and deeper into a trance where he was the one single object in her world.

It seemed to have gone two ways.

The way he had dragged her off stage had to mean something.

Her breath held again at the way he'd looked, standing there, his long fingers on both hips, his stance doing nothing to ease the ache that throbbed inside her.

His jeans, almost white from wear, fit like a second skin, and her eyes had been drawn to the material that had started to fray to the right of the zipper. She brought her eyes up to his heaving chest and the tee shirt was streaked with sweat, the royal blue darker under his arms and down his sides. It was one of the shirts she'd talked Annie into buying for him. The words *Grab all you can* stared at her in bold white script. She knew the back finished the sentiment with *Cause I'm giving it away.* She wished she could do what the shirt dictated.

Then she'd been plastered against him, her desire fulfilled without having to say a word. Her heart had hammered against the solid wall of his chest, and she'd let the invasion of her mouth go undefended, giving in to the tantalizing taste of him.

A shiver ran up her spine as she remembered how he'd felt, when she'd been pressed against him, the brutal kiss.

She could no longer deny her need for him.

She wanted him with every fiber of her being. No one else. Just Johnny.

Wanted to feel his hands on her again, wanted to watch his hands caress her body, the way they had earlier. She wanted him to be the one to take her to where she'd never been before.

That wouldn't be possible as long as his V-edict was in place and she was too inexperienced to know how to change his mind.

And yet, there was something in the way he'd kissed her that told a different story.

He might not like it, but he wanted her.

Even she could read the signs.

She just had to figure out how to follow them.

Trying a different line of attack, taking a sip of her drink, she cleared her throat and asked as nonchalantly as she could, "So, no one interests you?"

As if jerked out of a trance, he muttered, "Huh?"

"There have been quite a few women who've flirted with you tonight."

"You call that flirting? I call it a shark attack."

Turning that over in her head, she asked, "So you don't like shark attacks?"

"No. Too cold-blooded. And I'm not a piece of meat."

She felt her cheeks flush.

She saw him in exactly, the same way.

A delectable piece of fine sirloin.

Should she tell him what she thought, knowing he wouldn't like her assessment?

Tilting her head, her fingers drawing an invisible pattern on the table, she said, "That's what you advertise."

Crossing his arms over his chest, his eyes narrowed. "What are you talking about?"

"The way you observe the people that come on to you. It's like you're looking to fill a job and you're reviewing the applicants."

His eyes widened.

"I do not."

"Maybe not tonight, but I've seen the way you check out different women, assessing their viability. What do you look for?"

"You're crazy. I don't do that. I don't have to."

"I'm not crazy. You publicize yourself, although maybe not intentionally."

"Like you're doing tonight?"

He was changing the direction of the conversation as if he didn't want to talk about what she'd said.

And she let him.

"I just want to meet some new people. Learn how to flirt..."

She gave him a meaningful smile. "Without being some kind of bottom feeder of course."

He was almost surly and spit out, "Don't bother. You do fine."

She lost patience with his irascibility.

"Why are you so angry? And why are you sitting with me? I don't need a bodyguard and you're not what I'd call stimulating company."

"I'm not angry and I'm sitting here because...because..."

"Yes?"

"You're a good excuse not to have to wade into the pool."

"Of sharks?"

"Yeah, I'm not in the mood tonight."

"Well, I'm not in the mood for your...petulance. So why don't you just go away."

"Good idea."

She watched him take the last swig of beer, and then felt his hand take hers, almost jerking her out of the chair.

"It's time to get back. It's getting late and all good children should be in bed."

"I'm not a child."

"You're innocent enough to be one."

"Which is something I'm trying to change. You're not helping."

"That's not the kind of help you're going to get from me. Now let's go Glinda. The clock's going to strike midnight soon. Wouldn't want you to turn into a pumpkin."

"Maybe I can wave my magic wand and turn you into a toad. Oh, wait a minute. Someone already did."

Johnny spun her around to face him, his eyes dark and dangerous.

He whispered close to her ear, sending shivers down her spine, "And what will it take to turn me back? I think it was a kiss, wasn't it?"

She quaked at his nearness, his breath warm against her cheek.

But his lips were a thin line, and there was no welcome in them. It didn't seem to matter. As she began to lean in, the magnetic force pulling her towards him, he backed off again and all but dragged her out of the club.

After he deposited her at her room with a brusque good night, she watched him hurry down the hall to his own, her body still vibrating from the kiss. It took a long, hot bath to relax her enough to climb into bed.

But sleep was a long time in coming.

CHAPTER FIFTEEN

Johnny entered the darkened lounge of the hotel they were staying at, searching the dim interior to see if Tim was here. In a better mood than he'd been in last night, less...*petulant—,* he'd woken up at a loss as to what to do with himself, so he'd gone in search of his friend. He had already stopped by Tim's room, scoured the lobby, checked the bus. When he saw movement at the table in the back, he headed in that direction. Papers littered the square wooden table and Tim's head was back, his eyes closed.

"Here you are. I've been looking everywhere."

The head snapped up and Tim rubbed his face with his hands.

"Yeah, just trying to put some music together."

Pulling out a chair, Johnny dropped his long form down and handed Tim a scrap that had been crumpled and then hand-pressed.

"I don't know how good it is, and it's very raw. Like, so raw it might bleed all over you."

Tim's eyes met his, then he snatched the paper in impatience. Tim missed the calculated squint because he was busy reading the note progression. The snort introduced a short laugh.

"I spend hours scribbling away and I come up with graffiti. You push the pencil and have the makings of a great song. You so piss me off."

"Seems I do that a lot lately."

"Seems I've gotten fed up with doing all the work."

"Seems plausible."

Tim's look was sharp, pointed.

When Johnny asked, "Want to try for a couple more?" he stared for a moment before nodding his head.

"Where is this coming from?"

Johnny's fingers unfolded one of the scraps on the table. "The song or the fact I wrote it?"

"The fact you wrote it."

The words had come simmering out of him this morning while he was lying in bed. With no woman to fight off, no smell to erase, he'd woken with a full melody banging in his head and when he'd grabbed the hotel notepad, he'd jotted down the lyrics that spilled from the pen. It was a spontaneous impulse, one he hadn't felt in...a long time. The rush of energy that came with it was an unexpected pleasure, and his first thought had been to share it with his best friend. Like he used to.

Johnny's voice held a tinge of nostalgia.

"I kind of miss the old times."

His fingers began tapping on the table top, ending with a what could have been a drum roll. He gave Tim a broad grin.

"I finally found something to say."

Tim was silent, then pressed a flat smile out. "Should we start calling you 'Jay' again?"

The old nickname threw Johnny off base. Tim had called him that back in high school, at his own request. He'd hated the name Johnny. The way it sounded on his mother's lips made him seem like a kid, so he had asked Tim to come up with something that was more adult. Jay had stuck for a while but he had become Johnny again with the fame. The press had stuck him with it; the fans screamed it out night after night from their seats in the audience. He had come to accept it as the price of success. Maybe he shouldn't have.

"Another era. But thanks for the thought. Why don't we try...I don't know? Maybe John?"

"Sorry but you're Johnny. Always will be. That's why the Jay thing didn't stick."

Tim waved the wrinkled paper like a white flag.

"Where do you want to go with this?"

"I thought we could maybe get the band together and go over to the arena and see how it works. We have some practice time set up, don't we?"

"Yeah. We haven't been taking advantage of it."

Pausing Johnny added, "We can look over what you and Terry came up with, tighten it up, if you want?"

"Terry and I came up with shit. He's a great guy but he has no talent for writing. At all."

Johnny smiled. He was glad that Tim needed him at some level.

"It all starts out digestible."

"That's not what you told me at the hangar."

"Yeah, well, I'm in a different place," Johnny admitted. "Writing this felt good."

Tim gathered up his scraps of paper, carried them over to the bar and threw them in the garbage receptacle just inside the half door.

"It's good to have you back buddy."

"Hold that thought because we do need to talk about the piss-poor label we're tied to."

Johnny already had his phone in hand, punching out texts to the band, pulling them in for a practice session.

Tim slunk back, his hands in his pockets. "You were right about that. At least about the hangar slash shitty recording studio."

Johnny kept glancing down at his phone as each member of the band got back to him.

"It could make a pretty good studio if we wanted to put some time and money into it. If we partitioned it off, put in some isolation booths, we might be able to get a good sound. And it's off property, a good mid-way point for all of us. I know there have been some successful remodels of airplane hangars in the last couple of years."

Tim's brow creased.

"What are you saying?"

Having heard back from the band, Johnny slipped the phone in his back pocket, looked up at Tim and explained, "It might be a good investment if we bought it and did what we wanted with it."

"Together?"

"That's the thought."

"But it would never be ready in time for the CD deadline."

"I know. Maybe we can renegotiate the deal, put the album off a year, work out of your place for this one."

"The label was pretty adamant…"

Reject and Terry had entered the hotel lounge and were heading towards them, smiles on their faces. It reinforced Johnny's belief that they had turned the corner and were a team again.

There might be more than one perk from it.

"If we stand our ground, keep a united front, they might back down. We're playing well again. Maybe we've gotten our clout back. Better yet, why don't we get out of that contract and start our own label? We'd have Diana's clients...hell we know a lot of bands that might want to record with us. They'd be knocking down our door if we make it state-of-the-art, create a production company to make videos. That way the bands could make their videos where they record. One-stop shopping I think they call it."

The look on Tim's face suggested he didn't know what to say. Maybe the trust was gone. Maybe the respect. He'd have to earn it back, if Tim was willing to give him the time to do it.

Then Tim admitted, "It's a great idea."

Smiling, Johnny said, "When you guys listened to me things worked out."

Tim pointed out what Johnny already knew.

"You stopped talking."

Sticks began tapping a quarter-time beat against Johnny's leg. Tim was right. He had. He didn't know whether his silence had caused the rut or was the result of it. Whatever it was, his passion for their music had resurfaced and he loved how it felt, loved the flow of creativity that had come so easily this morning.

Was this what Tish felt, only on a bigger scale? Something lost, regained.

"I guess I've started again."

It felt damn good.

"It's about flipping time. Now shut up and let's go."

Johnny slapped Tim on the back, hoping they had regained a foothold on their long-standing friendship. Reject and Terry brought an excited buzz with them that he couldn't help but feel.

He'd missed this.

The foursome tight, energized.

They'd have new material. Good new material, creative juices percolating, each instrument coming up with an individual sound and then meshing into one harmonious whole. They had lost their edge in the last year and it had taken Tish to get them out of it. And he couldn't deny she was the muse for the song that had come unfiltered into his head in the early-morning hours.

Images, one clicking into another, along with bulleted words, phrases that came in waves, rushing his mind. Notes were aligned with a heartbeat, one that shuddered, sobbed, throbbed on the page. It was the kind of song that struck at the heart of the matter.

Then she walked in, stood at the edge of the room, the sunlight as backdrop, spotlighted by the glow, and he swallowed hard. Something sensuous passed between them and it spelled danger. The waters he was wading in were treacherous and if he wasn't careful, he'd go under.

He still felt as if he were drowning, but it didn't stop him from moving forward. Once Tish had arrived at their meeting place, they took the bus over to the venue so they could try on the new song, see how it fit. In Atlanta for one more night, they still had access to the stage. It was a smaller venue than they were used to but ticket sales hadn't warranted anything bigger. They had opted for a two-night series, hoping there were enough fans to fill the seats and they'd been rewarded for their optimism.

Once the band was ready, Johnny gave them all the basic key and chord progressions, tapped out the beat with his foot. Terry went right into an introduction, his guitar wailing, as he came up with some riffs and twangs that both Reject and Tim followed. Then he jumped behind the drums, pummeling the skins with a new energy. Then everyone was pulled in to his fevered beat. After several attempts at getting what they wanted, they added the lyrics.

Johnny made sure there was clarity and he could hear the resonance in his voice. Critics wouldn't be able to complain about garbled words like they had in the past.

He sang to what he had found that night he'd coaxed Tish onto the stage. Her fears and her physical disabilities were made manifest in the words, her psyche bared for all to see, the icy thunder of her heartbeat, the chills, and the trembling lips, all combining to make way for cold sweat and hot need.

His voice reverberated out into the dimly lit interior of the theater.

Surging desire
a body on fire, witchy eyes
and the thrill of surprise.

The refrain ended with the phrase,

By the end of the night, you'll be mine.

The next stanza raised the stakes, as he filled her,

During the silver lightning
the pounding thunder, burning with fever, shaking with need
feel him split her asunder
going where he'd lead.
By the end of the night, you'll be mine.

With the flourish of the drum and cymbals crashing, his sticks raised in victory, he looked around to see if everyone else was feeling the fire, although he didn't need to. He had felt the music down to his soul. The band had come together in a ball of energy. It sounded better than he'd anticipated.

Then he looked at Tish.

He hadn't heard any attempt on her part to bring the keyboard into play and he now knew why.

Her cheeks were flaming red. Wariness consumed those delicious eyes, diluted pupils, asking him what it was she was feeling.

There was humiliation written there with a steaming shot of desire.

He didn't know which one had him on edge.

Right.

He couldn't fool himself any longer.

The song had come flush from his...not heart. He didn't feel that kind of emotion for her. It was much more primal.

A carnality that she evoked in him with a shot of silver in a sea of turquoise.

Swallowing hard, he cursed himself.

She had seen it. And so had he, reflected back in her eyes, the same driving need.

He couldn't move, so he just sat there. It was like the air had been sucked out of him and he was hollow but his heart told him with its erratic beat that he was full of something forbidden.

She jumped up off the stool, shoving bare feet into flip-flops, off-balance, and his eyes followed her trim figure as she staggered out, racing down the aisle towards the exit.

And he didn't know what he was going to do about it.

CHAPTER SIXTEEN

Ignoring the look of concern on Ralph's face, Tish threw herself on one of the bus bunks waiting for the thrumming in her body to subside. It was as if Johnny had stripped her naked, exposing her to the world, flaws and all.

She couldn't have anticipated it, never saw it coming.

Thinking the new song would be similar to the others on their set list, she'd sat at the keyboard listening to the first run-through, putting together an accompaniment in her head, but when she glanced up at Johnny, she was spellbound. His motion was animal sleek, his foot stomping on the pedal and she sat mesmerized wishing she had that kind of rhythm.

Then the lyrics had broken through the hypnotic spell he had her under.

And confusion had set in.

Forcing her eyes away from the erotic picture he made, she'd focused on the small audience of roadies, wondering if anyone else picked up on the connection, but they were all into the energy coming from the band's heated beat. Her body had shriveled as Johnny articulated what she had felt, all the emotions she'd laid bare to him that night.

Her eyes had slid to take him in again. His strength was what had held her through the entire song.

She wanted to feel all that power inside of her.

Her breath had caught and she'd fumbled through the next few breaths she'd tried to take.

When his eyes met hers, she saw something there that made her want to writhe on the stool. The throbbing sensation consumed her and she asked deep dark eyes what it was she was feeling. The flare of nostrils, the diluted pupils gave an answer that further inflamed her. Her breathing had become ragged, so she'd broken contact to concentrate on getting her lungs to work.

It hadn't worked.

She jumped up, raced, off-balance out, of the hall to get away from all the raging emotions, the last two verses searing her brain.

He bombarded her senses
an inferno commences
And by the end of the night, you'll be mine.

The phrases repeated over and over in her mind, but she didn't know what they meant, who they were for, or how she was ever going to face him.

When she heard his voice, she covered her head with her arms.

"Hey."

That was it.

One word.

Conveying nothing.

"Tish?"

She continued to lie there, hiding from his eyes, from all she felt.

The bunk tilted when he sat next to her, pulling her arm away from her face.

She peeked out, saw a blank expression on his face.

"Tish, talk to me."

The tone was modulated, as if he'd shut down all feeling, like a faucet that had been gushing and, with a flick of a wrist, it was off.

Shame spurted into anger.

"How could you have done that to me?"

She could feel her cheeks burn and she let the annoyance burn along with them.

Sliding her legs over the side of the bunk, her fingers curled tightly together, she asked, "What was that? It was about me...but you're not...you don't seem to...I don't like feeling like this."

Johnny stared at her for a minute and then admitted, "Yeah, it was and it is and I don't like feeling like this, either."

"You were feeling...that...that night?"

Unknotting her fingers, he took her hand in his, stroking the long digits and conceded, "Yes, but it won't go anywhere."

There was that thrum again, each time his finger slid down hers.

"I know. Your V-edict."

"That and a bunch of other things that go with it."

"Not enough of a turn-on?"

He smiled but it was doleful.

"You heard the song."

"Then why?"

His eyebrows gathered in as he pinched the bridge of his nose. Meeting her eyes, he explained, "I'm not ever going to settle down, Tish. I don't want a family. I don't like what they make you feel. You deserve more than a one-night stand or a three-month stand. But that's all I could give you."

She didn't care how short their time together would be. There was a sheen of sweat covering his forehead, and she could smell the mix of that and bay rum. Inhaling his musky scent, reading the lustful glint in his eye, she wanted to lean in, kiss him, give it all she had, and before she knew what she was doing, she was giving in to the powerful need.

Her lips seared his, then brushed against the soft texture, and she took her time, caressing them with her mouth.

And then he was kissing her back, his tongue slipping into her mouth and she parlayed with it, tasting the coffee he'd had earlier in the day. Then his hands were in her hair, his thumbs sliding down her cheeks.

It was like he had set off a time bomb, and there was nothing to do but let it charge the air around them, knowing the shrapnel would pierce her when it was over. She wanted more of what he could give her...no matter how much it hurt or how much it cost.

And then it was over.

He pushed her away, the groan at least giving her the satisfaction that he didn't want it to end any more than she did.

"We can't do this."

"Just one night. Let me know what it feels like."

"No."

Her mortification was complete at his rejection.

When he stood and left without another word, the "no" hung in the air until it was time to get ready for the concert.

As if Johnny wanted to make sure she understood he meant what he said, the keyboard had been moved. It no longer faced him, but now faced the audience. Chappy was her escort to her stool, and Johnny didn't appear until a minute before the lights went up. Even during the sound check, when they'd been within feet of each other, he'd never once turned her way.

He was keeping the V-edict in place, and it didn't look like that was going to change, proving that she wasn't the witch he purported her to be. There wasn't any spell.

But then again, what had she expected?

According to her mother, she fell short of her goals. This was just one more in a long line of them.

Even though Johnny's rejection had to do with him, not her, it was still highlighting her inability to be who she wanted.

Swatting her thoughts of inadequacy away like a pesky fly, she refused to bargain for his attention like she had her mother's. It was self-defeating.

And she was determined to outgrow it.

But when she glanced up, Tim in the middle of a ballad that was acoustic, without any of their flash, she met eyes that devoured her and all her symptoms of lust came rushing back.

And the driving need.

And as she sat there, her rapid heartbeat told a story, one she began to breathe life into. The notes floating in her head didn't tell a simple, sweet tale but flowed in a rise and fall of sound that clashed in rhythm and motive, an incomplete melody that she couldn't get out of her mind.

It was on the bus, a couple of days later, heading into Miami that she was finally able to get the rhythm to work for her. It was as if Johnny's absence made the impressions more vivid, the lyrics more insistent. He was still avoiding her and it was a loss that had hit her hard. And the void had brought all her feelings to the surface, as if to fill the space he'd emptied.

As she finished the final flourish of staffed black notes, her ear buds hanging around her neck, she called out, "Tim."

Taking his eyes off the magazine he was reading, he looked up and said, "Yeah?"

"I wrote down a song. It's been going round and round in my head since Atlanta. I wanted to run it by you."

Tim ambled up the aisle and sat down beside her, his leg under him, his body slanted to view what Tish held out to him. It contained both music and lyrics.

"What do you think?"

She didn't know why she was doing this. They certainly didn't need her to write for them.

"It's probably simplistic compared to what you guys do, but it won't let me go."

They had just pulled into a truck stop and as the bus whooshed to a stop, it jolted them forward. Since they'd left Atlanta mid-morning, some of the guys hadn't eaten yet, and with a few hours left to go until they reached Jacksonville, Ralph had scheduled the pit stop to satisfy the hunger.

Terry and Marci were making their way off the bus. Annie stood by waiting to do the same.

Tim's eyes brightened as he studied the page in his hand.

"It looks good Tish. Let me run it by Johnny. He's the only one who can see the big picture, put it together in his head with all the instruments."

Getting cold feet, she went to grab back the music sheet but Tim held it out of reach.

Hesitating, still unsure if it did in fact look good, wanting to give Johnny as good as he gave, wanting to fight fire with fire, she let the paper slip from her fingers.

Tish's senses went on high alert at the sound of his voice.

She'd stayed away from him since last night's concert, it being obvious that he didn't want her around. That had hurt but she'd been so let down by his actions, she didn't have the head space for stage fright and she'd probably played better than she had to date.

Noticing him avert his eyes as soon as he saw her sitting with Tim, her heart dipped even lower until Tim waved the piece of paper in his direction.

After a pause, he walked the short distance to where they sat, wariness in his eyes, his focus directed on his friend. Then, as if interested, he leaned in for a closer look and her body trembled, her anticipation of what he'd think crawling under her skin.

"New song?"

"Could be. What do *you* think?"

His eyes scanned the homemade sheet music.

Would he even be able to read it?

The lines were uneven, the notes scattered across both clefs.

She watched and waited, pulling her fingers until he said, "Interesting."

"I thought so, too."

She waited in vain for him to look up at her. He had to know she had written it.

With his head dipped, his eyes glued to the paper in his hand, he said, "I assume this is yours?"

She let the silence induce him to raise his face to hers.

The seconds ticked by but she was rewarded for her patience although his expression suggested she hadn't won anything of value.

His mouth was a tight line, and he shifted his body as if he was uncomfortable standing there.

The bark of Tim's laughter confused her. So did his question.

"What's the matter, Johnny? It's not really *hard* for you to give an opinion, is it?"

Johnny turned a funny shade of green and she could tell his mood was tipping into a dangerous zone.

The scowl he addressed her with only added another dimension to her confusion.

"I think I need a minute alone. You know, to scrutinize it better Why don't you guys go in and get a table. I'll join you in a minute."

Tim got up, slapped him on the back, with a little more force than Tish thought necessary, and led her and Annie out and into the diner.

Her eyes were trained on the door.

She had often written short piano pieces, just for the creativity. Since her own music had deserted her, her mind had been in a constant flux of blues and rock.

This one, however, had true classical underpinnings.

She hid her head in her hands, and her heart had taken to doing back flips in her chest with waves of jangling emotion.

"Do you think he hates it so much he's trying to figure out a way to tell me?"

Tim was back to chortling. "No, Tish. I don't think it's that."

Tish looked to Annie for an explanation but before she could get one, Johnny scurried into the diner.

She held her breath as he scanned the large group. The entourage had taken up several tables, which happened every time they stopped for a meal.

His eyes met hers. "Scoot over."

He was standing at the edge of the booth, waiting for her to do his bidding.

Her eyes searched to find the extra room he must have thought existed between her and Chappy. Bull Dog, a bulky roadie, was taking up most of the bench. She was unable to find more than a slice of empty space.

"Where do you want me to scoot to?"

Feeling the closeness of his body, her nervous agitation continued to assault her senses. Then his bottom nudged hers as he placed himself beside her.

Stunned by the sensation, she jerked to her right but there was no place to go and the result left her body plastered against his. When his arm went behind her, she was caught in the crook of it. His chest was hard as granite. And hot. Her whole body began to riot from her head, electric circuits going haywire, to the tips of her toes that curled from the headiness of being close to this one man.

Her hands were fisted in her lap, and when she lost patience, she asked, "So? What do you think?"

Without even glancing her way, he said, "It's got potential. What did you have in mind? This has too much depth for the keyboard. There's classical influence but we can rock this."

He raised her water glass and took a sip, his eyes still staring straight ahead.

Her voice sounded shaky when she replied, "An organ?"

He was consumed by a fit of coughing, while Annie became consumed by hysterical laughter.

Feeling her cheeks flush, wishing she had never given in to the urge to match him song for song, Tish glared at him.

"Okay. It's a stupid idea. It's a stupid song. All you had to do was say so."

Johnny continued to choke, still sputtering into his hand.

Annie tried to look serious and said, "Tish, he just swallowed wrong."

Tish immediately shifted in the miniscule space and started pounding on Johnny's back. When the fit started to recede, she stroked the hard surface with the flat of her hand, wanting to calm the straining.

He sprung up from the seat, bolted away from her and made a hasty retreat to the other table.

All she could do was watch him.

He sat there, thinking instead of eating, the banter between his tablemates not registering.

He had to congratulate himself on his initial diligence. When he'd first scanned the new song, he hadn't made the mistake of locking with brilliant gemlike eyes.

But when she'd remained mute, he'd had no choice.

And when he had, the punch had come and he was lost again, in cool, green depths.

His feelings for her were getting worse, not dissipating at all and the arousal had slammed up against his stomach as soon as their eyes met.

It wasn't just her appeal but the vulnerability so easy to read in her eyes.

He had gotten so hard it had been painful. No woman had ever affected him like this before and he hoped no one ever would again. It was agonizing. It wasn't only the physical pain but the knowledge that he couldn't do a damn thing about easing it.

When they had left him alone at his request, to hit the diner, he'd paced the aisle of the bus, coaxing himself down. Studying the notes, chords and lyrics, exhilaration had assailed his senses. She had written what could be one of their best songs. It had power, the kind of strength that came from a fusion of styles, took them outside the boundaries of the routine to a new dimension of sound.

And the lyrics.

About a…

Lost soul
who didn't know where she was going
awakening to the promise of tomorrow
would beg, steal, or borrow
to feel the magic of a stranger's kiss
Bringing her out of a sleep-induced trance
her candle in the darkness
he lit up her lonely world
where possibility swirled
If he could give in
he could be her forever
if only for one night
if only for one night.

She had written it for him, about him, about her and the magic they could make together. And he knew she was right.

He just couldn't take that step.

There was a niggling voice that had him debating his edict again, as he tuned into the conversation going on in the booth behind him.

Tim was asking if she played the instrument she'd suggested and his arousal peaked again when she said, "A little. I'm not exactly proficient but I know I can get out of it what I need."

His eyes narrowed as he considered what other instrument she could work her witchcraft on.

Loud enough for his voice to carry, he informed Tim, "I want to sing this one."

"You want to sing another one?"

"Yeah, problem?"

"Not at all. It's just been a while since you've taken the initiative."

Without hesitation, he stated, "This one's mine."

Did he mean the song or the woman?

Melanie, who'd been listening to the back-and-forth, nixed the idea of an organ.

"It's too expensive for just one song."

But Johnny pulled her aside on the way back out to the buses, and said, "Okay. I get your point. But I want you to get a piano. A baby grand. I think they have smaller versions, so get one that will fit on stage. She'll get more complexity out of it with pedals and I know she can play it, so it shouldn't be a big transition. Take it out of my share of the profits."

"That I can do. I can have it in place in the next day or two."

He loped up the steps, glad they'd have some time to fine-tune Tish's song before introducing it. He'd have to tweak it, change the *hers* to *him*, but that was it. It was a masterpiece of blended genres that would graduate them to another level of sound.

Ticket sales had skyrocketed since she'd joined them on stage, the reviews glowing, critics lauding them with praise. The keyboardist who no one ever got to see, the main attraction. Tish had forced him to find his center and the results were nothing less than stellar. Due to the buzz, the Miami venue's management team had asked for another night to be added to the schedule which meant there would be no days off during this leg of the tour.

They were climbing back to the top and it felt great to be there.

CHAPTER SEVENTEEN

Miami was wild.

Johnny couldn't believe the energy of the crowd. The seats were packed, and from what he'd heard, they would be again tomorrow. Now that the band was in demand, they had added a night.

When preparing the calendar, Ron never spread them out too thin, giving them a day off after four or five nights of performing. Those free days were going to be a thing of the past soon as more and more venues were added to their schedule. The reviews had prompted a surge in sales and they'd added a performance in Naples, another night in Chicago, Detroit and Cleveland. Curiosity about the keyboardist played no small role in their reversal of fortune. The first leg of their tour wasn't nearly as successful as this second sweep and with the energy they were expending on stage, Ron was going to have to find the right balance. Otherwise they'd be burned out before long.

Despite the exhaustion, he was pleased with the crush of bodies. It told him they were playing like they used to, that they'd gotten their mojo back. Local news reporters, music beat writers looking for a story, women by the score, local teens along with community leaders who had pulled the necessary strings to get them in, were all waiting for the opportunity to speak to the members of the band. The guy from *Rolling Stone* magazine had cornered him and Tim for an interview right after the concert.

When the microphones were directed towards him, his eyes sought out Tish like a heat seeking missile that always found its target.

She was being interviewed as well, the man standing close by her side.

His temper flared.

The guy would soon know her sweet scent, would feel the air charge around her.

Johnny had felt the heat, the steam and he had been consumed by it. No one else was going to get close enough to fall.

No one else?

Where had that come from?

Feeling as if he'd just slipped off the edge of a cliff, he shifted his stance so that both feet were flat on the ground and he was steady.

"Johnny?"

He hadn't even heard the question. He was getting to the fine line where stupidity and sense met, becoming obsessed with crossing it. All it took lately was a look. Shit, it had always taken just a look. Into those vulnerable eyes. Or the tinkling sound of her laugh.

He glanced over to see if the reporter was still too close.

He was.

He had to make this interview short and sweet. And history.

"I'm sorry. What did you ask me?"

"You seem to have calmed down a bit, become more focused on the music. Your onstage antics have been replaced by your old tightness. It sounds great. Have you taken back your leadership role?"

His body didn't tense like it might have just weeks ago. Butch, the reporter who had followed their career since day one, was referring to his on-stage presence. It had changed. He was forcing issues that he had let stagnate, picking up the demanding role of director, pulling the other members of the band into line and insisting they play to him. Glancing at Tim, who looked anxious, he chuckled, more to himself than anyone before replying, "It looks like I have Butch. It looks like I have."

"Does this mean you'll be writing again?"

Tim was the one who informed Butch, "The new songs we've introduced are his. We have a couple more lined up for later in the tour."

"The women went wild with one of them...what's the name of it...'Cold Sweat'?"

Johnny hadn't noticed. His attention had been on the woman who'd inspired it. She'd held back from full immersion, playing chords much simpler that she was capable of.

Never once had she looked at him.

It disturbed him to no end.

Which disturbed him.

He didn't like it, but he missed those nights when she'd devour him from her stool.

His eyes sought her out, an overriding temptation to fulfill the words of that song washing over him.

Tim responded with a laugh. "He did rock it."

"Will it be part of the upcoming CD?"

"Yeah. We'll be in the recording studio as soon as the tour ends."

"Johnny, what brought you back?"

A crafty witch.

His sticks drummed against his leg, a conflicting rhythm to what he felt in various parts of his body.

He knew for sure now, that she had cast a spell on him.

"A new energy, I guess."

He had to admit it felt good.

He glanced up again to find more microphones in Tish's face.

"If you'll excuse me, Butch. I'm going to check on Tish. She's not quite used to all this yet."

But before he could get away, Butch asked, "Is she part of the band, now?"

Hesitating, knowing now that she had accomplished one of her goals, getting on stage, and that her music might come back soon, he wasn't sure how to answer that. She might be gone before the end of the tour, to prepare for her own upcoming concert series.

"No. She's only here for part of the summer."

He felt a punch in the gut.

He wasn't sure what that would mean.

For the band.

For him as well.

"Gotta go. Set up some time later and we'll give you a full interview."

"Thanks, Johnny. It's great to have you back."

With a tepid smile as answer, his full focus on the woman across the stage, he threaded his way through the throng, arriving at Tish's side to hear her answering some question from the reporter from the Hispanic radio station in Spanish.

He saw a look of lust in dark, piercing eyes.

Directing the conversation her way meant the reporter would get to keep his lunch.

"When did you learn to speak Spanish?"

She didn't even look at him when she replied, "I can speak multiple languages. French, Portuguese, and a bit of German."

Raoul Santiago asked another question as if Johnny weren't even there.

"Who did you play for before Thunder?"

"No one. This is a first for me."

"You sound like you've been with them since the beginning."

Johnny's ire continued to mount, so he decided to end the line of questioning with an abrupt, "We're taking off. Say good-bye."

Now her eyes met his, her lips parted slightly, and he held himself in check, knowing he couldn't kiss her the way he wanted to. Not yet.

"Thanks, but I think I'll fly solo tonight."

Her reply really pissed him off.

A burning sensation lit Johnny's chest, followed by an elevated pulse. It pounded in drum speak.

"You can't go out alone. Not here."

"I can do anything I want."

"Sorry, witch, but you're with us."

As he grabbed her arm, she sighed, mouthing the words "*sorry*" to the reporter as she was dragged away.

Slapping at his hand, she fumed when he refused to relinquish his hold.

"I'm really getting tired of your manhandling me. I've got bruises on my bruises."

"Then start behaving yourself."

His tone was brusque, his lips set in a thin line.

"I am behaving myself just fine. It's you who needs a lesson in manners."

He felt her mulish resistance, so he jerked at her hand, propelling her forward.

She jerked back.

Bringing them to a standstill.

He frowned in exasperation at her.

"My father brought me up to take care of women."

"Seems you forgot that lesson. Or is that what you were doing with all those women you...took to bed? Just taking care of them? I've never heard it put quite that way before."

Her stance shifted and she jutted her chin out.

"Why are you bestowing all this beneficence on me? It's totally unnecessary."

He glared in answer before resuming his retreat, her in tow, out to the waiting bus. The screaming fans who had stayed late hoping to get a glimpse of their idols made the retreat more of a shoving match, elbows and shoulders pushing through the thick sea of bodies, Jett leading the way.

Once on board, she snatched her hand out of his, scurrying to a seat at the back, where Annie and Tim were sitting.

He followed closely in her wake.

The club they were going to, to unwind, have a couple of drinks, was one of the best in the city. The dance floor was huge, the light show spectacular and the sound system loud. The talent of DJ's couldn't be matched and Thunder had dropped in every time they were in the area.

It would offer Tish just what she was looking for, if he was inclined to let her find it.

⌒

When they entered the club, it was packed, bodies everywhere, some dancing, some slithering through the throng, some standing on the side-lines observing the action. Tish scanned the crowd, blinked against the lights, amazed at the surreal scene that exuded glitz and glamour. She had never witnessed anything so wild, the strobes flashing on women dressed to kill in diamond-studded heels and fingers as men swaggered towards private tables. When Annie pulled at her arm, she followed, not taking her eyes from the revelry. Reject had been dispatched to check out the VIP room and with his nod, the Thunder entourage got the green light to ascend the stairs, merging with the other very important people.

With a drink in hand, standing at the rail on the second floor, Tish became transfixed as she watched the bodies twisting and turning on the dance floor, her foot tapping to the beat, her body in need of some movement.

She asked Chappy to dance with her, and when he rewarded her with a smile, she shoved her drink at Johnny, not missing the daggers he sent the roadie as if to remind him to watch his step.

As she made her way to the dance floor, she felt Johnny's eyes on her, and felt the lethal stare as she attempted to duplicate the shimmying hips of those around her, until she forgot all about him getting lost in the reggae beat.

And it didn't stop with Chappy.

Scores of men asked her to dance and she stayed on the dance floor well into the early hours of the morning. With each drink, she became bolder, her body seductively moving to the music booming through the speakers.

When she climbed back up the stairs, her feet unsteady, she gravitated to the table the group had snagged, her cheeks flushed from the sweat and heat.

As she was about to order another mojito from a waitress who was hovering nearby, Johnny waved her off.

"That's enough for one night, Glinda."

The drinking had lowered her inhibitions and she thought she might be able to take the step to accomplish her objective. She didn't want Johnny to get in the way of those plans, so she wasn't going to let him tell her what to do.

"Enough of what? I'm enjoying myself."

"Enough to drink. Your eyes are glassy and you're overheated."

He watched her arms cross over her chest, then scan the crowd.

"I haven't found what I'm looking for yet."

His temper short fused and he growled, "And what is that?"

"I'm thinking I want to wade in to the shark pool."

"With sharks? I think maybe minnows are more your pace."

"Are you saying I can't keep up with the big girls?"

"That's what I'm saying. The difference is like night and day. You might have the honey to lure a man, but you wouldn't know how to protect yourself if he wanted to eat you alive."

She was standing close to his chair, and she inhaled his musky scent, her insides clamoring for what he could give her.

Bending to whisper in his ear, she asked, "Then teach me how to be the night."

He jerked up from the chair, almost toppling it. His eyes had a dangerous glint in them and she took a step back but he didn't let her get far. Grabbing her hands, he held them in loose bondage against his chest.

"We've had this discussion before. I'm not playing teacher."

Squirming against him, in an effort, to get away, her eyes widened. A part of him had risen to the occasion and thrust out to meet her.

She tilted her head, and whispered, "Are you sure?"

"Positive."

He punched the word out, as if it caused him some pain.

Anger surged that he was being so stubborn and she all but spit out, "Fine. I'll just find someone else who'd be willing. I don't want to be on the edge...of whatever this is...anymore."

His hand was still wrapped around her wrists and he yanked her closer, his voice a husky growl.

"Over my dead body."

Tish galled at his nerve. It seemed to be a case of *I don't want you, but I don't want anyone else having you either.* She would only be off-limits to other men if he was willing to claim her, which he wasn't.

Pulling her arms free, massaging the flesh, she answered, "I can live with that."

With haughty elegance, she walked over to where Annie and Tim stood ready to leave, then turned on her heel and trailed them out of the club.

The bus ride back to the hotel was done in silence but when she lurched into the lobby, he was right there, taking her hand and guiding her to the elevator. The humming in her body matched the tune she was humming in her throat, the song he'd written for her, and it continued all the way up to their floor, down the hallway and into her room, where he stopped short.

Then, taking the one step that had kept her from him, he placed his hands on the sides of her head and pulled her within a breath of his lips. Her whole body was vibrating, the pungent scent of him surrounding her, the vibration of her heart echoing in her ears. Time stopped as they gazed into each other's eyes. It seemed his conscience was wrestling with his libido, his body willing but his oath still holding sway. The waiting was endless as he made his decision.

Her eyes fluttered closed. Her breath was shallow, shaky as she hoped...

Stepping away, he whispered in a ragged voice, "You might get what you want because, Glinda, you're killing me."

CHAPTER EIGHTEEN

It had taken some time to wake up, a couple of aspirins to counteract the headache Tish knew came from imbibing too many of those delicious mojitos. The conversation with Johnny came back to her and she felt the heat rise to her cheeks.

Had she really told him she wanted to get laid?

Was it purely to see his reaction or was she just tired of the way he made her feel, shaky, flushed, throbbing?

She'd have to think long and hard about taking that step with someone else.

If Johnny gave her any indication he'd oblige her…need, she'd crawl right under his skin.

The sharp rap of the door echoed in her head and she laid it back down on the pillow.

"Hey, you up yet?"

Johnny.

The voice that could get her to follow without question.

But not this morning.

"Go away"

"What are your plans for the day?"

"Sleep."

She heard the chuckle through the door before he prodded, "Sorry. No sleep for the weary. You've got fifteen minutes or I'm coming in."

Covering her nakedness, she reminded herself while telling him, "It's locked. Besides you'd enter on threat of death."

She lifted the covers to confirm her lack of clothes. She had never slept naked before.

Leaning over, she took in the trail of discarded items, strappy sandals kicked off by the door, floral sundress in a heap halfway to the bed, bra and bikini panties flung across the room.

What had possessed her to strip down to nothing?

Then that voice again.

"You're really not going to go out and see the sights?"

"I'm really not. Now go away."

"I'm going to stand here and knock *very* loudly every...minute until you join us in the lobby.

"You wouldn't."

The banging started and she yanked the covers over her head, and groaned. The gesture did nothing to block out the man standing on the other side of the door.

"Okay. You win. Stop the noise. Let me take a shower and I'll be down."

"I'm waiting right here until you open up and let me in."

"What are you, the big, bad wolf?"

She heard the chuckle again before he warned, "You'll find out if you don't get a move on."

With that threat, she jumped out of bed, her nudity disconcerting, and rushed into the bathroom, turned on the hot water hoping the steam would provide cover. But she was drawn to her image in the mirror, trying to imagine it from Johnny's perspective. There was nothing that might entice him. She had all the right attributes, but nothing that stood out. Anyone could give him what she wanted to, and there were thousands who had the experience he required for a romp in the hay.

Standing under the pounding spray, she washed away remnants of last night's make-up, along with the fog that was blurring the lines.

Why was he here? Why was he insisting she join him?

He'd made it clear that she wasn't going to persuade him to break his code.

Stepping out, fumbling for some clothes she uttered loud enough for him to hear, "You are the most infuriating person I've ever met...and that's going some."

If he'd met her mother, he'd know how much of an insult that was.

She didn't want to think about *her* this morning.

Diana had been giving her constant updates but there was nothing concrete to report yet. Tish's attorney had finally gotten a subpoena for Madeleine's financial records, but Judith hadn't received them yet. It was a waiting game right now and she didn't know what was around the corner. Knowing Madeleine it could very well be a concrete wall.

After throwing on a pair of shorts and a tee, moisturizing her face, legs and arms, she slipped on her flip-flops and opened the door.

He lazed against the opposite wall.

"I had so hoped your death was imminent."

"Ah, you remember our conversation. Good to know some things are unforgettable."

Flinging herself by him, she sputtered, "Get out of my way."

Watching him with suspicion as they descended in the elevator, she stepped out to find Jett waiting for them. He was never far from his charge.

"Everyone's already on the bus. Come on, let me get you out of here."

Jett pushed his way forward through small groups clustered around the lobby, escorting the twosome out and into the blazing sun.

Tish stumbled up the steps, surprised to see almost every seat taken.

Annie was the one who told her, "Johnny has plans for us."

"He does?"

As if proud of himself, he crowed, "Who better to pick up your slack, you slacker."

"Where are we going?"

"Ralph and I found an amusement park. You said you'd never been...you won't be able to say that after today."

She groaned at the thought of the carousal's calliope music, rides that would twirl and twist, her head still hammering a warning that she needed quiet and solitude.

Ralph yelled back, "Here we go. Sit back and enjoy the ride."

Johnny took her hand and guided her to a seat in the back. The buzz in her head changed channels and decibels. Now the throbbing was causing several parts of her anatomy to ache.

The smile that set her senses spinning didn't help.

Excitement began to bubble as she felt the bus turn and tilt. Looking out the window, she saw lines of people at the front gate, others meandering along the walk as Ralph cruised down the lane designated for buses, several others ahead of him dropping off visitors at the point of debarkation at the Miami park. Then it was their turn.

Johnny grabbed her hand, pushing and shoving the others towards the door his expression matching his mood. As soon as they'd paid for their tickets, with feet barely touching asphalt, the group raced from one ride to the next, rambunctious, like kids in a candy store. Her headache was a wisp of a memory not long after they entered the gate.

She ate hot dogs, candy, popcorn, her appetite for life increasing with each bite she took.

They stopped at the muscle meter, where Johnny won hands down, the silver ball almost reaching the top of the meter board. His muscles rippled, his stance emphasizing the force of his thighs and she wiped her mouth as if her drooling at the picture was real.

She competed at games with them, throwing balls at stacked wooden milk bottles, hearing the clatter as they fell with her not-so-perfect pitch. The plastic rings, so slim and light, hit their mark once, and she preened in satisfaction.

Johnny and Tim were the big winners.

Annie was holding a stuffed gorilla, a china doll, a ceramic frog and a couple of bracelets adorned her wrist. As Johnny's trophies multiplied, he handed them off to Tish.

"Here's some things to remember us by."

After sliding the plastic lime-green ring onto her middle finger, she put the Pokeman figure in her purse and slung the white tee shirt with three monkeys, their hands raised, their bodies boogying, over her arm. It was a take on see no evil, hear no evil, say no evil that Johnny had won at the dunking booth.

She hugged them to her chest, knowing she wouldn't need the items in her arms to remember this day. Or the band. Her heart was filled with a gift even more precious.

When she balked at the roller coaster, the screams careening down on her from their perch high on the track, Johnny had convinced her to give it a try.

"I'll keep you safe."

Trusting him with her life, although not with her heart, she had climbed into the car after him and he had pulled her close.

As the car headed up the steep incline, Tish tucked her head into Johnny's shoulder, not wanting to see how high they were climbing. His fingers stroked her hair, and the rush of the ride now mixed with the heady sensation of his touch. And then she was free-falling, the exhilaration filling her with a combination of pleasure and dread. She clutched at him, and she felt his arms going around her, securing her in place. Pleasure took over completely.

As they crawled towards the off ramp, he kept her in the circle of his arms. Then his lips kissed her forehead, but it wasn't nearly enough. She looked up into his eyes, and before she could take a breath, he dipped his head and took her lips in his, caressing them.

With a tremble that came with the contact, Tish took it a step further.

She licked at his lips, the softness melting her bones. His eyes had darkened, and they were sharp and assessing. She read longing there so she extended the proffered kiss into another satisfying taste. That familiar pang deep in her belly deepened as the car came to the end of the ride.

Snapping out of the reverie, Johnny pushed the bar up and climbed out, holding his hand out to her.

She ignored it.

The man who wanted nothing to do with her was back. She could tell by the way he avoided eye contact, the stiff way he held his body.

With her heart hammering in her ears, Tish took a step out and scampered away down the ramp to the waiting laughter of her friends wanting to outdistance what he made her feel.

The shiver of wanting remained but she never let on. She never gave him a second glance as she baited the group to do everything the park had to offer.

Once back at the hotel, after the excitement of the midway, Johnny paced the confines of his room. He still had some time before leaving for the concert tonight and the room was closing in on him. It would be their second night in Miami, playing to another full house and he couldn't wait to bang his drums. Maybe then he could get the excess energy out. He looked out the window, the sand on the beach still glistening in the late-afternoon sun.

What was Tish doing?

Sleeping, watching TV, listening to music, in a state of duress like he was?

The steamy kiss he'd shared with her had done a number on him and had depleted his reserves of control. It wasn't only what she did to his body. He was beginning to like her too much.

He liked being with her and given a choice, he would choose her company over any other woman he could have.

They were a dime a dozen.

She was a gold coin, valuable and a limited edition.

He had forgotten how good it felt to be comfortable with someone, to not have the fear of disappointment hanging over him, to laugh together, to be quiet together, to be good enough being just who he was. The Johnny Scalera he hadn't been in a long time.

She was a treat for all his senses.

He could still taste the sticky, pink sugar delight she'd let him share at the amusement park. With her first taste, she'd closed her eyes, savoring the sugar-sweet taste of the fluff. When she'd stuck her tongue out after exclaiming, "It melted," he'd swallowed hard at the memory of how that tongue tasted, wishing he could help himself to another kiss. She'd smacked her lips in appreciation before letting him lick her fingers clean.

His body responded on every level, his nervous system sending signals to his brain, insisting on release, demanding fulfillment.

The discomfort had gotten so taut during the licking good time, he'd marched her over to a water cooler needing to get her fingers clean and to douse his own throbbing desire.

Picking up his acoustic guitar, he settled on the edge of the bed.

Words to a song invaded his brain as he revisited the day they'd spent together.

Flying down the roller coaster, her head tucked in the crook of his shoulder, the whip flinging them around the platform, the centrifugal force pushing her tightly against him, through the splashing waters of the log ride where she'd gotten sprayed with a fine mist, giving him a tease as to what lay beneath her tee shirt.

He shuffled phrases around, discarding, rearranging until he had some semblance of a song.

Memories were simmering up
she took his breath away
something about her eyes
could make him lose his way
he was used to the long steamy nights
pushing, driving the road to nowhere
thoughts of his past rising up
wandering along without a care

but the way she had touched him
had been a sweet surprise
so unlike the others
made him realize...

Every song that came to him now was based on his need for her.
And it had to stop.
But the only way he could imagine that happening, was if he gave in and let her fill his senses.
Maybe then he could finally find the release he wanted, breaking the spell she had cast.

CHAPTER NINETEEN

Tish was already perspiring as she exited the bus and ran to catch up with Chappy.

"Hey, can you put another stool next to the board?"

"Um, sure. Why?"

"Annie's never gotten to feel what it's like on stage. I figure she could sit next to me and..."

Tish had noticed a truck backed up to the unloading dock, a baby grand being led down the ramp.

She grabbed Chappy's arm.

"What is that for?"

"Um, why don't you talk to Johnny."

A pit of anxiety had already begun to unravel as she stomped over to where he stood, joking with some of the arena personnel and got right to the point.

"Why is there a piano being unloaded?"

He took her arm and led her to a more secluded spot, putting some distance between them and anyone within hearing.

"If we couldn't get an organ, I figured this would give us more depth, more complexity."

Her fumbling fingers pulled and twisted.

"I don't play the piano."

"Um, yeah, you do."

Fear and anger knotted inside of her. Jutting her chin out in defiance, she announced, "I'm not playing it. Is that more succinct?"

His voice was smooth when he asked, "Why?"

Fumbling for an explanation, she stammered, "I...Do you want another panic attack on your hands?"

Putting up his hands in a defensive move, he said, "Not in this lifetime."

"Well, if I have to sit at that thing, you'll have one, of major proportions."

The shakiness in her limbs had already started, it was on its way up from her toes like an elevator going up much too fast.

He took her hand, and explained, his tone calm and reasonable, "Tish, it's the same as the keyboard only with a bigger range, strings, and a pedal. We both know you can play it."

Snatching her hand back, she said, "No, we don't."

Hesitating for only a moment, he said, "You are Letitia Jones, one of the most respected pianists in the world. I've heard your recordings. I once compared you to you."

Crumbling under his words, she said, "I can't do that anymore."

"You can. I hear the classical influence every time you perform with us."

"I haven't sat at a piano in months."

"No, you've played the keyboard. Letitia Jones is multi-talented."

"She is so not."

He took her trembling chin in his fingers, his eyes demanding she listen.

"Do you remember the chord progression for 'Cold Sweat'? The Edge of Nowhere'?

Both pieces, one his, one hers, rushed into her brain, her fingers itchy with the need to express them.

She responded with petulance, "Yes, on the keyboard."

With strained patience, he said, "A "C" chord is the same on both instruments."

Her mind saw her fingers hovering over the "C" chord on the piano and all of a sudden an embellishment sprung into her head. Something sprouted inside her, and she thought, with a spike of adrenaline, that maybe she could do this.

Maybe she could transfer the music from one percussion instrument to the other.

Listening to the notes rushing into her head, she realized it wasn't filled with noise, it was filled with the exact score for each Thunder song she knew.

Tamping down her hope, she allowed, "I'll give it a try when it's set up and see how it goes. I hope you have the keyboard ready on the truck just in case."

"We do but you won't need it."

"You might be disappointed."

"Doubt it."

"I've let a lot of people down."

"You've let two people down. Your mother, who's a psychopath and doesn't count and yourself. It's time for you to have faith in who you are."

"That's easy for you to say, Mr. Popular."

He chuckled.

"That's true. But I've had years and hundreds of women telling me how wonderful I am."

"So that's all it will take? Hundreds of men telling me I live up to the hype? That might take time."

"How about one man telling you that you do? Will that suffice tonight?"

She was lost in his eyes and her breath hitched.

"Maybe."

"I'm not asking you to play Ravel. I'm asking you to play Matarrazzo/Scalera. Big difference."

"Both impressive."

"Why, thank you, but one of us is much easier to play."

There was humor there, but she saw it shift, becoming more intense when she asked, "Are we still talking piano?"

The smoldering heat in his eyes burned, and it filled her with a need she was beginning to understand.

With every touch, every kiss, every look, he fanned the embers that were ready to flame, and she was on an edge where there was no turning back.

The frown on his face told her she was still fighting a losing battle.

So did his words.

"We are."

The huskiness in the tone, the tickling sensation behind her heart made her shiver, so she closed her eyes and tried to stop the stammer.

Inhaling some of his confidence and strength, which would get her through the next few hours, her body grew heavy and warm.

"Are you ready?"

"I think so. But I'm not happy with this."

She pointed to the baby grand but thought that it also had to so with the way he made her feel.

"Figured you'd fight me on it."

"You were right."

His fingers circled her arm with gentleness, guiding her over to where the piano sat.

"This is your instrument. Own it."

He backed away, his eyes remaining on hers until she turned to stand beside the baby grand. The flu symptoms were back, the chills, aches and shivers but she didn't know whether they were due to the piano or the man.

He kept his eyes on her, trying to measure her discomfort with the piano, monitored her body movements which he tried to blot from his mind. When she had asked him if he'd be easy to play, his manhood had answered loud and clear and it was making him madder than hell. His teeth were clenched to the point his jaw ached, along with the other part of him that was one big, constant pain. He'd gotten an overdose of witch elixir and it shot through his bloodstream like a cannonball. He was in her clutches again. The look in those eyes had almost goaded him into taking her right there and then.

Yup, he was madder than hell.

Leaving her to her sound check, he strode across the stage to his drum kit, barking at the roadie,

"Get out of my way."

Chappy had been tightening the hardware on the cymbal but his mood went sour with Johnny's bluster.

"What the hell's up with you?"

"Go help someone else. I'll do this myself."

"No problem."

Johnny bent down to retighten the foot pedal, his hand stopping in mid-turn as his mind fumbled for a reason he was putting off the inevitable.

One night could be just what the doctor ordered.

For both of them.

Insanity had taken hold, and he brushed away the rationale for keeping his V-edict in place. Her round, tight ass, sexy legs that he could almost feel wrapped around him, a flat stomach that peeked out from the low-rise shorts she had on. The cap-sleeved tee, the word *Casablanca* written in big, black scrawl offered a glimpse of something he wanted to uncover, and his growl deepened.

And it only got worse.

Once her sound check was complete, she'd gone to change for the show. Every night it was a different Tish, cowgirl, peasant, cute, hot, and he never knew what to expect.

Tonight...it was vamp.

His heart slammed into his chest as she exited the dressing room. Walking towards him was a witch in every sense of the word. Encased in a red spandex racer-back dress that left nothing to the imagination, her thighs visible, her feet bare, strappy red-and-black sandals hanging from her thin fingers, her hair radiant in the soft glow of the backstage lights, she walked across the floor heading towards the baby grand with calm poise.

She had worked some magic, because she looked as if she'd been doing this all of her life.

But then again, she had.

His tongue was almost hanging out of his mouth when he uttered, "What the hell does she have on?"

Annie, who'd been hovering backstage, answered the deep snarl with laughter. "She said she liked the color."

Her response only seemed to add fuel to Johnny's fire.

"She bought that because of the color?"

"Yeah. I sure couldn't pull it off."

His eyes drank Tish in as he watched her strut her stuff.

So obsessed with her, Johnny didn't hear the announcer getting the crowd going. The noise from the audience as the words *Raging Thunder*, spiraled in volume.

It was Tim's bark, "Johnny, drums," that brought him back from his fantastical musings.

Clicking his sticks, his body already on overheated, he shook himself out of his stupor.

Lights flashed and the pulsing beat shook the rafters.

His glances throughout the night told him she was ready to get back to her instrument. The one she'd given up on.

More than ready.

Haunted by the dress, the play, the virtuosity, he had forgotten about her song. They were introducing it tonight. It was the reason she sat at the baby grand, looking the part of classical genius.

When Tim began strumming the mellow sounds of the acoustic guitar, it echoed out from the stage to the highest rafters of the arena. Then her fingers fluttered over the keys, the slow intro building into a much more powerful surge. Waiting for his cue gave him the time he needed to regain some of his control, but it was impossible to do. Her words about him would soon be offered up to the masses, remind him of what he was to her. What she begged of him.

His arm came down, striking the drum in a thunder of sound, the tempo shifting with his entrance. The beat pulsed. His voice was strong, the lyrics clear. The crowd was on their feet, the screams matching the intensity of the music.

With the last flourish of cymbals, he glanced over to where Tish sat.

She was immersed in the ending chord sequence, lost in the hypnotic spell she had cast on everyone present.

His heart swelled. He had a feeling she was back.

And she proved him right.

By the end of the night she was playing like a woman possessed.

She had raised the bar and the entire band followed her.

The music reverberated through the hall, enhancing the feral wail in Tim's voice, the guitars turning out a multitude of sounds. Johnny's playing was fevered, keeping time with his racing heartbeat, the throbbing pulse in his neck.

It hadn't slowed down since she'd walked on stage in that dress.

As soon as the concert was over, he skipped the meet and greet, returning to the hotel to shower and change. He needed time alone, to sort through his options, try to de-fuddle his brain. Tish had crammed it with sensations he wasn't used to. Her song had only added to the pandemonium, and as he stared out the window that overlooked the beach, he imagined how she'd feel under him.

Her breath would be warm, her scent intoxicating, the taste of her lips like honey.

And when he entered her?

Liquid fire.

Spinning away, he ground his teeth. To get there he'd have to break the vow that had protected him from getting caught in a trap. Avoiding that snare had been easy.

Until now.

Until Tish.

His phone pinged and he reached for it.

Where r u?

It was the third text Tim had sent asking him the same question. Johnny wasn't sure he was ready to answer but he thumbed, hotel room.

R u coming with us? We're in lobby.

Looking up and into the mirror, he stared hard at his reflection.

Was he going to risk compromising himself or find a way to break the spell?

There was only one way to find out.

B right down.

⌐

As Tish slipped out of the red dress, deciding to get more comfortable for the night ahead, she smiled to herself.

She'd done it.

She'd sat at the baby grand and played, the joy rushing her from fingers to toes at the monumental accomplishment.

Giddy and proud, she was beginning to feel like her old self. Master of her art. International virtuoso.

Though she was still unable to hold on to any of her most cherished pieces for more than a few seconds, as soon as the drums had introduced her to the music, she'd felt her back stiffen, her fingers curl, her attitude adjust.

And once mired in the passion of the song, she'd forgotten about herself completely. Diana called it her artistic trance.

She'd become Letitia Jones again.

Her "touch" was back.

Once behind closed doors, she'd done a happy dance, twirling around and around like a dervish.

Touch was the one distinguishable characteristic that made her sound different from another's. Touch produced the shading of a piece. Like a voice, it held certain vibrations, and tonal quality that made it individualistic.

Then a thought stopped her cold.

Had she been recognized?

Anyone who knew her music, anyone with a trained ear would know her voice, her touch.

Thunder's fans probably weren't up on their classical artists so she relaxed her hunched shoulders, feeling the safe anonymity she had days earlier.

But she had the sinking suspicion that someone out there, in the world of YouTube or Thunder's website, would uncover the truth she'd been hiding in plain sight.

As she studied herself in the mirror, confidence rushed through her. Steady fingers touched up her make-up, then pulled on the clothes she'd laid out for tonight.

If she was back, she wasn't going to hide anymore.

Let her mother think what she wanted.

Soon enough she'd be on a plane heading east to confront her.

As soon as the elevator opened, Johnny noticed Tish waiting near Annie, their heads together as if in serious discussion. She had transformed herself again, now dressed in a lacy tank and a denim skirt, a decorative belt that resembled a gunslingers, the loops empty. It didn't matter. She'd hit her target. Her lips were pouty, her eyes smoky. Her hair cascaded down her back in a tumble of silver and gold.

He was ready to cry uncle but he couldn't get a word out.

When he noticed a man giving her the once-over, a hint of promise in his expression, Johnny shot the innocent man a well-practiced dagger, splitting apart any atom of hope the deranged fool had for a night with Tish.

No way, no how was anyone going to put their hands on that body.

All it took was a few steps and he was at her side, his perusal taking her in from head to toe.

"Are you doing this on purpose?"

"I could ask you the same question."

"Maybe if you'd worn an even shorter skirt..."

Batting her eyelashes at him, she said, "I can always do better next time."

She was matching him glint for glint and he was becoming incensed.

Annie interjected, "Can we go now? The snark is getting a little too public for my liking."

She was goading him on purpose, using her witchy ways to get him to break. He wanted to wring her pretty little neck and put himself out of misery. With a round of silent invectives, Johnny followed with murder on his mind.

And his murderous thoughts continued to multiply as the night wore on.

They had ended up at the rooftop bar of the hotel, and he had taken up Tish-watching at the bar, sipping tequila. Country music consumed the space, and he was glad it wasn't hip-hop or salsa. It would have sounded like racket tonight and he had enough of that in his head.

The DJ was spinning all the current favorites, Urban, McGraw, Chesney, Shelton, who were crooning songs about love and loss.

He sat and watched as Tish was passed from partner to partner, turning down the many woman who attempted to get him out on the dance floor.

He didn't dance. Hadn't since they'd become celebrities. Too close, too sweaty. Too intimate. Too personal. He didn't like women wrapping themselves around him like a vine, and that's what they did. Touching was a necessity between the sheets but there was a purpose to that. And he never wallowed in it. They did it, he gave them the tee shirt and they left. No one ever stayed the night. It was the way he wanted it.

His jaw clenched as he noticed another man's arm go around Tish's waist. He had a purpose in mind, and the way it splayed around her ribcage, Johnny knew just what that purpose was. Swiping his drink from the granite surface, he swung in the direction of the table he'd sworn he wouldn't go near and snagged a seat, his eyes burning a path around the floor. He glowered at and then proceeded to ignore Annie and Tim who indulged in soft conversation as they swayed. Dancers were cheek to cheek, chest to chest, legs probing legs.

Chappy, who occupied the seat next to him was trying to get to second base with a blonde chirpy who kept glancing up, concerned at the way Johnny was scowling.

Chappy explained, "He's got a hard-on for someone he can't have."

The scowl deepened.

"Geez, I would have thought he could have anyone he wanted."

"So'd he. That's the problem."

He narrowed his eyes, shutting them both out as a slow, love song filled the air.

He continued to watch and fume.

Until he snapped.

Until the fuse had reached blow-out and the explosion in his head destroyed every shred of control he'd mustered. As hands moved down the curve of Tish's hip, pulling her close, he'd had enough.

Shoving the tumbler across the table, Johnny pushed out of his chair and walked with deliberate steps into the crowd, circling around couples embraced in each other's arms, stalking his prey.

Removing the offending arm, he slid his own around her body and plastered her against him.

"My turn."

"What are you doing?" Tish asked.

"He's not going to put another hand on you."

His hands wrapped themselves around her and any animosity to the man he'd chased away evaporated. She felt good, so soft, smelled so...her, felt so...right. And he was losing himself in the way she molded herself to his body.

"You win."

He heard the gasp right before she asked, "What do you mean?"

"I'll give you what you want."

A look of pure panic covered her face but he wasn't expecting what she said next.

"No."

Anger rushed him like a three-hundred-pound lineman, toppling his patience.

"You're not changing your mind now."

He tucked her against the curve of his body, sure she could feel his arousal that throbbed strong and insistent and he felt her melt against him.

"See how easy that was? Now be quiet and dance."

Tish's scent surrounded him, her hair felt like silk waves and she fit him so well that he couldn't avoid what the combination was doing to his senses.

He couldn't help but feel the motion.

He was dancing, moving, with a woman who brought him to his knees. Nothing in his life had been more important than getting her out of the arms of that stranger and feeling her body swaying against his.

Her nipples pressed into his shirt, hard and pebbled.

He bent his head so that he could inhale the smell of her pulse point, just behind her ear.

He would have her between the sheets soon and it would be over and done.

She'd gotten him to break his rule, the one he'd thought carved in granite.

But it would then be behind them.

He could move on and start enjoying himself again, without the worry of who'd be the first to taste her sweetness.

It would be him. End of chapter. End of story.

The anticipation of things to come was getting too much to bear.

"Let's go and get this over with."

Taking her hand in his, he led her through the maze of dancing couples, off the floor, down the three steps to the elevator, and down to his room.

All without saying a word.

And when he keyed the door open, he let her hand go, sat her down on the foot of the bed and disappeared behind the bathroom door.

⁓

Bracing his arms on the vanity, Johnny cursed himself three times a fool. What the hell had he done? How the hell was he going to do this?

She was a virgin and he was too hard and too ready to pace himself. He was going to screw the whole thing up, just like he had his first time. He'd been fifteen years old and it hadn't been the success he'd hoped. At least not for his partner. That's what had him panicking. He wanted to make it good for her, make her first time memorable, in a good way.

Taking a deep cleansing breath, he reminded himself he'd learned some things over the years. He could slow down, keep his head.

He was Johnny Scalera for God's sake, serial lover, bad boy, women's curiosity satiated every night, satisfied them all. What was he worried about? This situation could be laughable if it weren't so tragic.

He should just take her back to the bar, let it be someone else's problem.

Right.

Then he'd be in a worse predicament. He'd be facing bloody murder.

His booted feet padded against the tile floor as he bided his time, peering in the mirror, threading his hair back into a ponytail, hoping to get his erratic heart into a more moderate beat.

His ears pricked at the sound of footsteps outside the door.

Flinging open the barrier between them, he saw Tish ready to bolt, her hand on the lever, eyes filled with sadness.

"Where the hell are you going?"

His throat had closed and his voice echoed the strain.

"I'm letting you off the hook."

"What are you talking about?"

"I might not know a lot about this kind of thing, but I don't think you're first move is to hide in the bathroom."

Hide?

He hadn't been hiding. That implied weakness. No discipline, no control.

Okay, maybe he had been hiding. He had none of those things when it came to her.

He could be done by now for the length of time he'd been battling his demons.

Tapping his fingers against his leg, he began digging through his brain for some excuse, some reason, and all he could come up with was, "Well, I, um…"

"Right. I know you don't want to do this. And you don't know how to break it to me."

Her expression reminded him of her fragility.

"Not exactly."

"Then do you want to tell me what's going on?"

He met her gaze and both voices harmonized in synchronization, "Not really."

"Look, it's okay. I'm beginning to think it was a mistake, too."

He narrowed his eyes, shooting her a dark look.

"Why?"

"Let's just say it's somewhat intimidating. There's no way I can live up to all the experience in your past."

"I'm not expecting experience."

He was sure that was part of the fascination.

"I know. Which for some reason is increasing the pressure. I think it would be a good idea to forget about this."

"The whole thing?"

"Your part in it."

He wasn't going to tell her if someone's hands were going to be all over her, they were going to be his hands. He couldn't admit to himself there was some connection between them that he didn't understand at all, so how could he explain it to her.?

"I'll manage to get it done."

She stepped back as if he'd slapped her, her cheeks flaming red, her eyes filled with a deep sorrow.

"Don't do me any favors. I'm sure I can find someone who won't find it such a bother."

He gave her a tortured laugh, and his eyes shot to the ceiling as he tried to figure out how to tell her what he'd been doing. He came to a startling discovery. The truth would have to do.

"Come here."

He recognized the indecision in a misty sea of green, and he repeated his command, with more gentleness than the first time.

"Please, come here."

He reached his arms out towards her and he watched as she took a few baby steps before letting him wrap her inside his embrace.

Kissing her forehead, he took a breath before admitting, "I haven't done this in a long time, and I want to do it right."

There was a moment of silence as if she was analyzing what he had said. In a tone full of confusion and doubt, she asked, "This, as in sex? You mean you've exaggerated your...proclivity?"

His lips twitched in a smile as he caressed her head with his hand, smoothing back her hair, tilting her chin up so she could see his expression.

"No. I haven't taken a woman's virginity in a very long time."

He felt her tuck her head back in the pocket of his shoulder that seemed the perfect size for her.

"Is it much different?"

His hand fingered the silky, golden mass of hair, the loose tendrils framing her face.

"If the man is feeling like I am, then yeah, it's different."

"How?"

"I don't want to hurt you."

"But that's a given, isn't it?"

"Not if I can take my time. Not if I can pleasure you enough."

"I'm not in it for the fireworks, Johnny. Just an initiation. To know what it feels like. To get the...throbbing to go away."

He knew about the throbbing. It made it more important to get this right.

"But there should be fireworks your first time. Otherwise, anyone would do."

"Then maybe I should..."

He could hear the frustration, the insecurity. But it didn't matter. She was going to get every, single thing he could hold out for and he didn't even mind the way his insides were behaving.

"I've been working on getting myself under control so I don't hurt you, or make it too quick."

"Oh."

There was a small exclamation that came from a small voice, "You don't have to take any extra time with me."

"Yes, I do, Tish. I want you taken right. That's why we're here."

He stoked her back unable to miss the shiver than went through her with each one.

"I don't know what to do."

His insides knotted, his arousal grew in intensity and he thought just how much trouble he'd be in if she did.

"It seems all you have to do is stand here."

Sliding his hand down her back, he stopped at the curve of her buttock, pressed her close. "See?"

He felt her arms around his neck as she shimmied against him. Her fingers pressed the area just under his ponytail, her thumbs stroking the sides of his neck and he groaned. The soft contours of her body molded against him, igniting a fire he'd never felt before. There was a thudding in his ears, matching the beat of his heart, the tempo of a drum roll, and he closed his eyes, allowing it to reverberate through him.

"I think you're going to be a natural."

Her eyes met his and trust was shining in the green depths. Taking a breath, he bent his head and took possession of her lips. Those soft, creamy, full lips that he had taken before, perfect lips that could make a man grovel, make him moan. They were succulent, ripe for the taking, and he couldn't get enough of them.

He hadn't even gotten inside her mouth yet and his heartbeat pitched into a jackhammer routine at the thought of what it would feel like. When she parted her lips, invited him in, he swallowed hard before thrusting his tongue into heaven. Moist, warm, and not enough. Not nearly enough.

He plundered the recesses, stealing her tongue in his mouth, sucking, nipping in and out, wanting more than he'd ever wanted before. His hands cradled her head, the silkiness of her hair adding to his careening senses, his need for possession overwhelming in intensity.

The heat spiraled when she matched him thrust for thrust, tangled, poked, licked, and bit. It was dueling contest and each parlay induced quicker and more consuming lunges. He claimed her lips again and again, brushing her in light kisses, bruising her with demanding ones that she gave into and returned in equal measure. His hands caressed her neck, as their lips fused and parted. Her taste was like sunshine, dewy rain, and he wanted more. He wanted to kiss every part of her and he became inflamed with where that thought led.

She was like honey, molten honey and his fingers trailed down her neck, push-ing the strap down her arm to reveal one of her breasts. His palm cupped the globe, his thumb grazing the nipple that had sprung up to tempt him.

God, he wanted her.

The light from the bathroom spilled out, illuminating her body, her skin petal soft, her breasts a man's dream.

As his breathing became ragged, he caught himself, knowing he had to slow down, but for the life of him he didn't know how he was going to do it.

CHAPTER TWENTY

Tish moaned when he touched her breast. The burning multiplied when she felt his finger fondle her nipple, teasing it before bending his head and taking it into his mouth. The gentle sucking motion caused a major ripple to expand downward and pulse. The throbbing increased as his fingers removed her tank and she was exposed to his burning gaze. His hands cupped her, massaging, reshaping, molding them, guiding her to a place she demanded he take her. Her breathing came in spurts, her need overcoming her inexperience and her hands fumbled with his tee so that she could feel his skin under her probing fingers. His flesh was hot to the touch, the hair on his chest curling in dark clefts, and she combed them, brushing her palms over his nipples, finding satisfaction in his low moans.

Her heartbeat had become irregular, her hands demanding as she helped him strip her of her clothes before turning her attention to getting him out of his.

Now, fully naked, Johnny led her to the bed. Laying her down carefully, he took his place beside her, his hands once again finding their home on her body.

She couldn't quite look at him. Her nakedness revealed to him, she was afraid he'd find her lacking.

How many women had lain under him? Hundreds, thousands?

What had they felt when his dark eyes consumed them?

This kind of mindless pleasure, where no thought could be sustained for more than the time it took for him to touch her?

Her brain sizzled, right along with every nerve in her body, so she hadn't really been able to think ahead to where she'd be naked under his gaze. His hands felt so good, so right. Drawing the courage from somewhere deep inside, feeling liquid fire burning in her blood, she opened her eyes to see his brow furrowed in question, his hand exploring the surface, light feathery motions, before skimming down her shoulders, navigating the creamy exterior of her.

"You feel so good, so soft."

He moved to straddle her, his hands on his thighs, his face contorted, his breathing uneven.

With the absence of his touch came bitter agony.

What had she done wrong?

Why had he stopped?

Icy fear twisted her heart.

For as much as she wanted him to take her, she knew she was just another in a long line of faceless, nameless women. One he wouldn't even think about, except as a-means-to-an end. It looked like she'd failed to keep his interest, and the ache inside grew stronger.

"Can't you just pretend I'm someone else?"

His eyes snapped up, his voice seductive.

"Why would I do that?"

"You...you stopped. I figured you didn't like what you saw."

He took one of her hands in his own, lightly brushing her knuckles against his cheek, and breathed soft words into her body.

"Not like? I like too much. We've got to slow things down a little."

His finger trailed down her neck to her breastbone, the feather-like strokes creating waves of pleasure. Then his tongue replaced the digit, scorching a path to her sensitive nipples. He plucked them, and then his hand slid down along her belly and the pool of desire got even deeper.

She needed to touch him, feel the life that pulsed in the protruding veins. Any thought she'd had about what a man would look like, what he would feel like, was nothing compared with what she held in the palm of her hand and the overwhelming desire he provoked in her. He was magnificent. All of him. His muscles rippled as he reached for the condom, waiting and ready on his nightstand. The tendons in his thighs had stretched as he pushed himself into position to add the protective shield, and the sight had her mouth watering.

And without thought, she took the moist, flat disk and fitted it to the part of him that both intrigued and inflamed her.

He jerked, and her eyes glanced up to uncover the cause. A thrill shot through her. His eyes were hooded and dark. He seemed to burn the same way she did and she felt her stomach heave, her breath stop and her heartbeat quicken.

They were lost for endless moments, staring, touching, skin to skin. Drowning in his eyes, she writhed beneath him, passion pounding in her blood. He rolled them both back to the bed and regained his position on top of her. As if to torture her, he slowed the pace and she arched up, seeking what only he could give her. His hands stroked her skin, palms traced her shoulders, her neck, her arms, his fingertips circling the areola of her nipple, puckered to meet his kiss. He bent his head, taking the protruding nub into his mouth, treating her to a tongue bath that soothed and seared. It only increased her need, and she was still unaware where it would lead her.

He bit down, then began to nibble on her, and she arched at the jolt it caused.

A spiraling heat swirled and swirled, creating a tornado inside her, a funnel of feeling that swept her up and into another realm of existence.

Her ardor matched his own, and if she'd been experienced he'd already be inside of her. The need to plunge into the warm recess of her body pressed his to accelerate the pace, bring them to a deep and satisfying conclusion. Hungry eyes devoured him, hands fondled the tendons in his shoulders, nipples taunted his chest, her curves writhed against his body and the fire he had thought already raging, spun into an inferno. There was no fear lurking in those eyes that tore him apart, no aberration at the sight of him, only an open appreciation that almost scared him. When she had worked the condom on, he thought he'd explode. He had never felt this big, never felt this engorged. At least one of them was okay with it. He thought it would have been him.

Needing to downgrade the flame to a flicker, he did something he rarely did. It was too intimate, too personal, and he hoped it would give him the time he needed to get back the control he was lacking. Lifting her legs up over his shoulders, he opened her up to him and eased himself down for a taste.

There was a brief hesitation before the blow to his gut.

He wanted this. He wanted to taste her, breathe her in. She smelled like summer heat, moist, humid, and he wanted her the way he'd never wanted anyone before. The thought that he was the first interloper here in the fertile but unexplored territory quickened the driving need to be the first one to discover her treasures.

The only one to savor the heat.

He lifted her up so he could worship at her altar.

His blood roared in his ears as he bent his head and flicked the tasty morsel with his tongue. It was hard, like a kernel and he could feel it throbbing against him, sending him into more of a frenzy than he already was. With the tip of his tongue he licked the part of her he wanted to sink into, tasting the sweet flowing liquid and began little sucking motions, wanting as much of her as he could drink down. Unfolding her with his thumb, needing more of her nectar, he invaded, plundered until he could feel her legs contract, tightening around him, her body arching upwards, her cries in the back of her throat driving him on and on. His fingers and thumbs became part of the mission, brushing the length of her, fingers inserting themselves into a pulsing pool of desire, and he could feel the quiver of her legs, the spasms under his tongue. Her heels dug into his back, her thighs straining to reach some plateau, and he knew she was almost there.

Now?

Was it time to break through the barrier?

Or should he let her feel the shattering explosion first?

For the first time in his life, he didn't have a clue as to how to proceed.

It was his own driving need that decided it. Another first. He couldn't wait until he became a part of her.

He moved up her body, kissed the flat surface of her stomach, until his tongue was lashing her nipples, the scent of her pungent, intoxicating.

He positioned himself over her body, feeling the slick moisture, with heightened senses, no logical thought. He opened her up with his fingers and placed himself at the rim of her womanhood and pushed.

"I can't wait any longer, babe. I'm sorry."

Shimmying down to help, finding his shaft, she asked in a raspy voice, "Sorry for what?"

"For what I'm going to do. I didn't want to hurt you...but..."

The sensation of her flesh stopped all speech.

Holding on to her hips, he worked his way in, holding back the thrust that would have split her asunder, gaining entrance with slow and torturous progress.

Then he was filling her in a raw act of possession.

Perspiration beaded his forehead. His arms quivered as he tried to hold himself in check, his breathing was sporadic at the intensity of how this felt. He needed to experience whatever it was she offered.

She clenched, her body jerking in spasms.

"Babe, stop."

His body on the edge, frayed, tattered, all impulse, every nerve exposed and waiting for permission to let go. Any tiny movement would bring him down. He didn't want to give in just yet, couldn't release the urge to plunge deeply until she was ready to go with him. That had become a priority and his greedy, conniving body was going to have to wait its turn.

A sob erupted, as her hips demanded more of him and the decision was taken right out of his hands.

He felt the inner walls of her sanctum grasp on to him, clenching him tighter and tighter, as she crooned his name. The friction became too much and a rumble started somewhere around his toes and rushed like a flooding river, the eruption like a volcano and he couldn't fight it any longer.

From somewhere outside his body, he felt her bring him back, holding him inside of her, taking him into her soul's center and he was constricted in a band of soft smooth honey.

Then all thought was lost, feeling taking over, each sense alive, so powerful that it took him, shook him, carried him in deeper, so explosive that he shattered into a million pieces. That she was with him seemed to spur him on, until he had nothing left, the convulsions racking his body over and over, until he was wrung dry, his head lying limply on her chest. His breathing had never been so labored, his body never felt so drained, empty, euphoric, satiated. He couldn't move. He didn't want to. That thought itself gave him pause.

He was still lying on her. Every attempt to roll off thwarted by his lack of will.

"Please, Johnny, give me a minute."

Her voice was low and plaintive.

"Mmhm?"

"I'll need a minute. I don't think I can leave just yet."

Leave? She wanted to leave? Didn't she know what they had just done was...profound?

This had been the best sex of his life, and she wanted to get up and walk out like it was...nothing?

He wobbled to his side, his arm bringing her in to rest against him.

"You're not going anywhere."

"But I know you don't like...us...staying."

"Us?"

He forced his head up to see what she was talking about, because he couldn't understand the words. He saw her hair tangled in sweat, and the impact of how well used she was hit him hard. But her face was turned away, her teeth holding tight to her bottom lip.

"Yeah, you know...the women...you give your tee shirts to."

She had just lumped herself into a category that had no place for her. Or had she lumped him into one? Trophy status?

A flash of anger and disappointment shot through him and he asked, more roughly than he'd intended, "You want a friggin' tee shirt?"

Her eyes flashed at him as if startled by the question.

"No. Oh, no. I don't need anything to remember this by."

She lay back down and he felt her take a shuddering breath.

He buried his face in her neck, exhaling the relief. She did feel the same thing he did.

Pure and complete satisfaction. Something to take to the grave.

Something...almost spiritual...something indefinable.

He was what she had wanted. Him. Not some damn piece of clothing that she could hang on her wall, with the express purpose of telling everyone whose it was.

For all the other women, the time spent with him would have been meaningless without the reward, without the medal they could boast about. For her, it had gone deeper. It had to do with who he was, not what he was.

But she was crying. Her tears were not just streaming down her face but his as well. He slid his tongue out to taste them.

They tasted salty and bittersweet.

"I hurt you."

"When?"

He fingered a lock of her hair behind her ear and gave her a heart-melting smile. Her answering one was more fragile. He wanted nothing more than to hold her forever. His mouth became a receptacle for the drops, and he kissed the drizzles from her neck, her wet cheeks, drinking in the moisture from her eyes.

"Then why these?"

"I felt so...much. I don't know."

He did.

He had felt it, too.

"Stay with me. At least until morning."

Her eyes fluttered shut, her throat still issuing little contented sighs, her voice breathless.

"Are you sure? I know you did this out of...some sense of..."

She had yet to relax her features and she closed her eyes as if in pain.

"Ssh. Ssh."

With a gentleness that he couldn't have anticipated, he kissed her cheek, her body still vibrating beneath his hand and his heart did a strange and funny jump in his chest.

"No one made me do this. It was my choice."

He hoped she kept her eyes closed. He wasn't sure what she'd see in his own and he worried about what was written there. She thought he'd done this out of some perverse sense of...what? Friendship? Honor? To protect her from a fate worse than death?

The plain and simple truth was he couldn't bear the thought of anyone else's hands on her body, some stranger taking what, at the moment, he believed was his.

He snuggled her down under the covers, never letting go. He could tell she was already half asleep, her eyes droopy, her voice drowsy, and he was close to nodding off as well, until she murmured, "Thank you."

His chest vibrated as his heart started beating again, her song, his jackhammer special, not only because of the words, but the visions in his head. She was grateful for something he had really taken no part in, had no control over. It had been done without thought, only pure feeling.

CHAPTER TWENTY-ONE

Tish sat at the edge of the dunes, looking out at the expanse of the Atlantic Ocean. Awakening before sunrise, having promised to leave Johnny's bed before he awoke, she wanted to surround herself with the ebb and flow of waves crashing to shore, so she could remember how small she was, how inconsequential. Miami seemed sleepy this time of day. Very few beachcombers were visible.

She had witnessed the sun rising over the horizon, the changing colors and textures coming alive before her very eyes. It had been a visual replay of all she had felt last night. Johnny had been magnificent and she would be forever grateful that he had been patient and so concerned with satisfying her. Every nerve in her body had hummed, bones disintegrated, muscle lost elasticity. She'd become a puddle of emotion.

Drawing a deep breath, she let it rumble out. Never in a million years would she have known that's what it felt like.

All streaking lightning, rolling thunder, cold sweat.

He had nailed it.

In the prelude to the song and then in bed.

Any thought of letting someone else that close was gone. Since the first time Johnny had kissed her, she'd wanted him, and although she knew she'd be just another woman he'd taken to bed, to her it had been life altering.

Scriabin's Etude in C Sharp Minor flooded her mind. As so many of his works, it was filled with intricate harmonies and textures, treacherous stretches, technical challenges but she had loved playing it and it was often one of her performance pieces. She was entranced by the music, the pounding tempo. It was layered with thoughts of Johnny, an orchestral background to a swelling movement of mind and soul.

She inhaled a shaky breath and felt her heart stutter, still grateful he hadn't asked her to leave right away. She couldn't have managed it. So drained, so weak, unable to move a muscle. He had even cuddled with her in the aftermath, so cared for, not discarded.

She knew his attitude about women staying over. And yet he had wrapped himself around her, made her feel almost cherished.

Asked her to stay.

No one could have introduced her to the intricacies of lovemaking better than he had. And now she faced another dilemma.

How did she go from that experience to another she knew would pale in comparison?

And the next time, with the next man, would have to.

And there would be a next time at some point. Even if she had no desire to find it on tour, she still hoped she'd find love at some point in the future.

She smiled at her innocence and stupidity. She had thought once with Johnny would be enough. It might have been if she'd been prepared for what he offered her.

A once-in-a-lifetime offer. A let's-make-a-deal offer.

She had a feeling she'd chosen the wrong door.

Wrapping her hands around her knees, digging her toes in the warm sand, she peered up and followed the line of the horizon, wondering if he was up yet.

Johnny stirred, thoughts of Tish vivid and real, floating, swirling. He reached out, needing to make it more than a dream, expecting to find soft, silken skin, but found instead only empty air. He pried his eyes open to find himself alone. The sun strained through the sheer inner curtain, lighting the room, creating a blanket of warmth and he scanned it before climbing out of bed to check the bathroom.

When he found himself alone in the suite, scalding anger surged through him.

She was gone.

He snatched up his jeans and put them on as he took a couple of steps to retrieve his tee shirt. Tripping over the toe of his boot, he let go and kicked it across the room, then wondered why he was so upset.

Wasn't this what he wanted? No fuss, no muss.

Tish had given him the solitude he had to fight for. Now he wouldn't have to pat her on the head and send her away, which was what he'd intended to do when they woke up. Well, he had given some thought to cuddling a little and seeing where it went from there. Feeling the familiar throb that was becoming much too frequent where she was concerned, he admitted that he'd had far more in mind for the morning hours. But she had left him to his fantasies and he didn't like it. He was the one who rejected further contact, once the deed was done. He was the one that waved them off, with good riddance.

He should be content that she was gone, had ended the one-night initiation on her own.

Thoughts of her permeated his body.

He still couldn't believe he had held himself back to satisfy her, when his need had been so strong it could have sucked them both under.

But he'd waited and she had come with him.

Dropping to the edge of the bed, putting his head in his hands, he had to admit that she was the one who had done the taking and to someplace he'd never been before.

It hadn't been the other way around.

And he wanted to go there again.

An innocent had taken every shred of his control away from him. Taking a breath, he realized she was still very much with him. In fact, she was everywhere. Lifting the front of his shirt, bringing it to his nose, he inhaled her scent and it left him...wanting.

One thing that had scared the life out of him had been the possibility she would cling to him, become confused, blurring the lines between lust and...gratitude. Or something worse.

It seemed as if Tish wasn't going to have that problem. No clinging here. What should have been an out-and-out relief had lost out to irritation. She wouldn't know that what they had done last night was so out of the ordinary, that she should have clung, demanded more. Because she'd never feel those emotions, or that climax, the culmination of what their bodies found together, again.

Something in the region of his heart pinged.

He doubted he would either.

He tossed the sheets back, looking for his elastic. His hair had come undone during their journey and he could still feel his scalp tingle under her ministrations. The spot of blood on the sheet hit him like a ton of bricks.

How they had done it steam rolled over him. It hadn't been a nice easy roll in the sack, it hadn't been an act of capitulation.

It had been the most powerful mating of his life.

If he was having a hard time dealing with it, Tish had to be feeling some of the same overpowering emotions. He had to find her. Make sure she was all right. His decision had repercussions. He had a responsibility here. That was the other reason he had taken her initiation on. He didn't want her hurt in the aftermath. No matter how much he hoped she'd be okay with this on her own, he had a compelling need to make sure. Then they'd go back to being what they were before. There was a sense of vagueness about that because he couldn't quite define what that was but he let the thought drift out of his consciousness as he headed out the door.

He headed for the customer service counter in the hotel lobby. It was the only thing left he could think of. Tish often asked the concierge what the best local attractions were and maybe had done that this morning. He had already tried her room but there had been no answer of his knock, no sound whatsoever, indicating that it was empty. He'd tried the coffee shop, the restaurant, and the lobby. He had even called up to Annie and Tim's room and they had made a strong suggestion to get back to them later.

Maybe she had just needed to be alone. Well, he needed something quite different. Approaching the uniformed man behind the desk, Johnny asked, "Has a woman been by this morning? She's blonde, witch-like eyes, comes to about...here."

He had given her approximate height and it went from vertical hold to where he'd cupped her head when she was tucked against his shoulder.

A shiver of something intangible shot through him as he thought about how well she fit there.

A certain appreciation glowed in the blue eyes of the man behind the desk. "There was a woman who came through a couple of hours ago. She headed for the beach."

Johnny spun around and headed for the back entrance the concierge had indicated.

Fuming, he stalked out of the hotel, along the boardwalk, and dug his footsteps into the sand, making his way to the shoreline. Scanning the horizon, the miles and miles of endless beach, he felt the emptiness of the search and ached inside.

Voices rang out, intruding into his loneliness.

"Johnny, Johnny Scalera."

He turned to see a couple of fans approaching him, running, the sand kicking back in their excitement and he groaned. He didn't need this, this morning. Didn't want to be a celebrity, didn't want the attention.

There was a flash of irritation that he couldn't even walk a deserted beach with out having women fall over him.

He noticed the ones coming at him were young, too young to expect anything but an autograph from him, so he forced a smile, and some talk, signed his name on the napkins they handed him. As soon as he was finished he saw her from the corner of his eye. The solitary figure was just behind the dunes, holding herself in place.

Without a backward glance, he hurried to where she sat.

He caught a shimmering reflection, as she squinted in the blazing sun in his direction and forced her gaze to his, never letting go.

Not knowing what he was going to say, he tried to play it casual.

Throwing his weight down beside her, he leaned back on his elbow, the sand hot, his body hotter.

Still in the jean skirt and tank top, she looked like she had left his room and made straight for the beach.

Her hair was a bit tousled, her eyes glistening, the color an exact replica of the blue of the sea.

He wanted her again. Desperately.

He threw casual out the window.

"You left."

"I told you I would."

"I said you could stay."

"Until morning. It was morning."

He set his sights on where the sky met the ocean. It seemed as far away as she did.

"Are you all right?"

"I'm fine. You didn't need to come looking for me."

"All part of the service."

He winced when he saw her eyes flutter closed. Her hands tightened into bands around her arms as if that would hold her together.

He made it seem like this was professional courtesy, like he was some stud who made it a habit of servicing women.

Maybe that's exactly who he was and he didn't like the thought.

"Tish...I didn't..."

His finger found its way to the surface of her neck. It was slick with sweat, like it had been last night, and a bead stuck to the calloused tip. He placed it on his tongue, the saltiness a reminder of what else they'd shared.

Whatever he had meant to say got lost in is need.

"Johnny, don't..."

She twisted away from him and silence hung heavy in the air.

He closed his eyes, needing to find a way back.

"Have you made plans for the day?"

"No."

He sat up, hoping distance would diminish what he was feeling. It didn't.

"There's got to be other things to see. It's Miami."

He watched her set her chin. Her face moved a fraction as if she didn't want to see him while talking.

"I'm kind of tired. I may take a nap."

He tensed at the thought of the night behind him, the one he wanted in front of him instead. And before he even thought about what he was saying, he asked, "Can I join you?"

Now her eyes darted up to meet his, as if to read the meaning there and then they dipped down to the sand again.

"I don't think that's a good idea."

"Why? What we did last night was...good."

There was a tingle of fear.

"Wasn't it?"

What if she hadn't felt what he had? What if the urgency to experience her again was one-sided?

"Too good. You spoiled me. As it is I don't think anyone else will come close."

Grasping her by the shoulders, he forced her to face him.

"What do you mean anyone else?"

"After last night, do you really think I want to become celibate for the rest of my life?"

He didn't know what he thought.

He snorted. He hadn't thought period. He had been too busy feeling. God, had he felt her.

His brain shifted into overdrive because now he had to think. And he didn't like it. At all. She was his. He had claimed her, initiated her, satisfied her.

Bile rose in his throat as he thought of someone else tasting her, touching her, filling her.

Shit. He had too much of a conscience for this. This possessiveness would have happened with any woman he had taken for the first time. Right?

Okay, it hadn't happened the one and only time before. He'd run hard and fast away from the girl. She had meant nothing to him and he hadn't worried overmuch about what she was feeling.

He groaned and put the answer he didn't want to hear away and out of sight.

What did he think? That one night with him would last a lifetime?

It was good enough to.

For both of them.

But he didn't have plans to live on it forever so why had he expected her to? Fact was, he had planned on getting right back in the game now that his curiosity was satisfied and her initiation complete.

Leave it behind. Forget it happened.

He had just come face-to-face with a startling reality.

He'd never be able to leave it behind.

He heard giggling behind him and knew what it meant.

He needed time to think, to figure out what he was going to do. There was even less of a chance that he'd tolerate another man's hands on the little witch, now that he knew what she was like. They were going to have to come to a compromise. He couldn't discuss it rationally if there were women throwing themselves at him. With no further thought, he reached out, grabbed her hand, and bolted diagonally across the dune, heading for the water.

She fought for release. But he intertwined his fingers through hers, locking her firmly in place. As he began to jog, she asked, "Where are we going?"

"We need to talk and we were about to be interrupted."

She glanced back to see several women grouped in a semi-circle, a disgruntled look on two of the faces. The other kicked the sand and gave them the finger.

"I think you just lost some fans."

"I don't care about them right now. They think they're entitled to my time but they're not. We need to get some things settled."

"We have nothing to talk about. You did your part. I'll be forever grateful. But it's over."

His voice carried on the warm current of air.

"Not if you're planning to jump back into bed."

She glanced up at him. His mood had turned menacing.

"Johnny, you wanted this behind you. It is. You don't have to stick around."

His flesh was a temptation she couldn't seem to deny. Even more so now. They had been skin to skin. It was going to take her time to bury her emotions back beneath the surface, and she couldn't do it with him so close.

Now that they'd outdistanced the fans, he began to walk at a slower pace. Bringing them nearer to the shoreline, he removed his boots with his free hand, keeping hers clasped in his other. The water spurted in a small wave over her bare feet as he moved forward, her toes tingling as the wet sand bubbled and receded, the ocean reclaiming the ripple of foam.

With envy, she watched him shake out his hair, the wind whipping it out from his face. Her whole being seemed to be filled with wanting again.

"I forgot how much I love the beach."

His mouth curved into a smile and her heart melted.

"Tim, Annie, and I used to go to Revere Beach every free chance we had. The Atlantic at home is always freezing cold but it never seemed to stop us. We'd body-surf for hours."

As she listened to his voice, the hypnotizing effect still in play, she pulled a strand of her hair off her face.

She could imagine enjoying the sun and surf with him, their friends. Her heart skipped a beat knowing that would never happen. Their time together was almost over. He had given her what she'd asked for and now she'd give him his freedom. It seemed like a fair exchange.

His eyes were taking her in, she could feel them, like lasers and she shot him a side-glance to see a look of contentment on his face, enjoying the simple pleasure of walking along the beach.

Playfully, he began walking backwards, holding both of her hands, pulling her along.

"I haven't been up this early in a long time. It's nice this time of day. Let's just walk a bit, okay?"

Her voice deserted her, so she nodded, before giving her face up to the warm sunshine.

When he asked, "Have you ever been to the beach before?" she smiled with fond memories.

"When I was younger. My father used to rent us a cottage on Cape Cod every summer. It was just me and him."

"Your mother didn't go?"

"She came the first year but after that...the houses he rented weren't to her specifications. Too small."

"How old were you?"

"I must have been five or six."

She remembered it like it was yesterday.

"The house was old, weathered, two miniscule bedrooms, a family room and a kitchen. We didn't have a lot of money back then. Besides how expensive it was to support my craft, Daddy was just getting his business started, but he always took me away for two weeks in July. He said I deserved it for practicing so hard. It was two weeks of freedom from the piano."

And her mother's harping.

"What kind of business?"

"He was an accountant. He worked for the IRS for a while but decided to go out on his own."

"What part of the Cape?"

"Dennis."

"I've been there. It's nice."

"Daddy and I always had fun. We didn't really do very much, just sat in the sun but we enjoyed the quiet."

"You loved him."

As if that wasn't the important piece, she amended, "He loved me."

The longing was there in her voice when she added, "I really miss him."

"Was he the one who got you started on the piano?"

"No. There was an upright in one of the furnished apartments we rented. I would sit at it and bang away, driving my mother crazy. She decided to get a teacher hoping she'd hear a semblance of a song instead of the noise."

He was back at her side, their linked hands moving back and forth like a pendulum.

"When did they determine that you had the talent for it?"

"After about a year, my teacher told them he could no longer keep up with me. I needed the kind of master who could work with a virtuoso."

She laughed and it tickled the air.

"I was seven by then and they had already labeled me."

The beach was filling up, walkers passing them by, dogs splashing in the waves and they watched the activity in silence until Johnny asked, "What's it like?"

She looked up at him, a questioning gaze on her face.

"What exactly?"

Leaning into her, he bumped her shoulder in playfulness. "To be a vir-tu-oso?"

As she squinted into the sun, thinking about all the hours she had put into her craft, too young to even know it was a craft, a frown appeared on her face. Dismayed that she didn't have a childhood, couldn't go out to play with her friends, friends disappearing once she was pulled from school to be home taught. It had been a lonely life.

"Systematic training. Hours of practice. Lessons in composition, phrasing, accentuation, repertoire. Among other things."

The jesting turned somber as if he hadn't realized what all it entailed. Pulling their hands up to his chest, and giving her a squeeze he asked, "When did you begin giving concerts?"

"It started with recitals, small audiences, then bigger venues. I played Carnegie Hall when I was sixteen. It was intense, or so I thought. Then I went to Europe, home of the greatest composers and it's even more compelling."

Intimidated, she'd stood off stage, the glitz and glamor of past centuries carved into the ceilings, walls and floors.

"I sat in the same hall as Chopin, Liszt, Brahms."

"No panic attacks?"

"Not then."

"When did they start?"

Before anyone knew.

She had managed to make it to the stage, through the nausea and palpitations. It was only when the music became a jumbled mess, when sitting at the piano on stage had become a nightmare of forgotten notes and abysmal tonality.

"I'd say about six months ago. My music was becoming so mixed up in my head that I'd blank out in front of a packed house. After that, let's just say I didn't want to be humiliated again. My mother wasn't pleased."

"Does she have the background for training?"

The small laugh could have been a sob.

"*She* thought so. Said she'd been watching my teachers all those years, said she knew better than they did how to get me to reach my potential."

"It didn't go the way she planned?"

"Seems not."

There was a pause, and she waited for him to continue to mine the mother vein but was glad when he asked instead, "Who's your favorite composer?"

She embraced the question with some of her old passion.

"Oh, I have so many. Rachmaninoff, Scriabin, Bach, Chopin, Ravel...I love the scores with power. When you can do nothing but lose yourself in the music. It takes you over and you give in and follow it. They are more difficult to play but I loved the challenge."

"Are you beginning to remember any of them?"

Drawing in a breath, she released it before speaking.

"Strands. Threads."

This morning, thoughts of Johnny and the way he'd made love to her, had poked a hole in the vault and some melodies had came streaming out.

"That's good, isn't it?"

"It is. Bringing the piano on stage pierced the veil a bit. The keys feel comfortable, the acoustics familiar."

"Then I'm glad I pushed your envelope."

Looking up at him she had to agree.

"I am, too."

They continued to stroll companionably for a long stretch before Johnny made a U-turn to start back.

"Look you have to promise me something."

"What?"

"If you...want another night like we had last night, you tell me."

A hysterical laugh bubbled up. With a trembling need and a nervous catch, she said, "I don't think that will work."

Stopping in his tracks, he growled, "I just made you an offer most women would jump at. So why not?"

She flinched at the tone of his voice but she lifted her chin, meeting his icy stare head on.

"Picture this. You're already occupied for the night. Should I knock on the door, call your cell, wait outside like a puppy dog? I don't think so."

His mouth twisted.

She went on. "I have a better idea."

He squinted at her and said, "Okay. I'm listening."

"I thank you for last night. We go our separate ways from now on and do what we choose. Neither of us will know what the other's doing. That way you don't have to feel...responsible. I won't have to feel I'm rejecting an idea you think is implausible."

Cocking his head, a single eyebrow tilting he barked, "That's the worst idea I've ever heard. I...made it too good. You said so yourself. Doing it again...with someone else...trust me, it won't work."

She could feel the blush, her cheeks heating at the thought of being back in the throes of their passionate lovemaking.

"You gave me more than I expected. I'm not putting this on you again. Remember, you wanted it over and done with. It is."

He moved a step closer, his hands on her shoulders, his breath warm on her face.

His voice was husky, almost hoarse when he managed to say, "You couldn't possibly know how good last night was."

There was hope in her voice when she asked, "For you, too?"

His hands slid down her arms. His face dropped so he was no longer meeting her eyes.

"It's always good for me."

The hope burned away in a puff of smoke.

She railed against her weakness. Not wanting him to know how much she still wanted him, she began to turn away.

His hands reclaimed her as he brought his mouth down to hers, and after the startle, she gave into the kiss, her fingers in his hair, her body pressed to his.

With labored breathing, he sighed her name.

"Tish..."

Placing her hands on his chest as if to push him away, she snatched them back. She was sure it was the heat between them that had scorched her.

"No."

His fingers held her chin and he met her eyes.

"How's this? We enjoy each other's company for as long as it feels right."

Her eyes widened.

Had he really just said that?

It didn't seem possible.

"You're willing to stay monogamous?"

Lifting his eyebrows at the word, he stilled.

She waited for the reality of what she'd asked him to sink in, waited for him to take back the invitation.

When he leaned in to kiss her again, light as a breeze, it was as if he had to make sure he wasn't about to promise something he couldn't or wouldn't deliver.

She held her breath, his forehead leaning against hers, and waited.

The voice was low, the whisper soft as a breeze when he said, "For now."

It should have soothed her, but it had the opposite effect and agitation set in.

Why was he willing to do this?

He could have anyone he wanted with a mere flick of the finger.

Would the promise of another night or two with him outweigh the agony that would come when he ended it?

He must have noticed her hesitation because he asked, "What's the matter? Don't you want this?"

She admitted, "I'm not sure."

His arms slid around her, kissing her more deeply than before and she was swept under again, finding it impossible to say no.

So she agreed.

"For now."

Retracing their steps, holding hands, they found themselves in front of their hotel where they plopped down in the sand, his arm going around her and pulling her close.

The contentment was shattered as Chappy came rushing towards them with the whole crew right behind him. Water rushed their feet as they looked at each other in disappointment.

"Here you are. We've been searching everywhere."

Johnny answered for them, a look of regret on his face.

"Yup. Here we are."

Tim and Annie sat on either side of them like book ends as Tim said, "We decided it's a beach day. Glad you could join us."

Chappy held a football in his hands, Ron and Melanie held hotel beach towels. Rambler had a Coke in his hand, Marci and Terry headed down to the water. When Chappy grabbed Johnny's arm, pulling him up and away from Tish, he yelled, "Come on, let's play."

Tish's hand was a visor over her eyes as she glanced up at him. He told her without words how sorry he was that their time together was over.

CHAPTER TWENTY-TWO

Exhaustion seeped into her burning eyes but she couldn't sleep. She kept going over what had happened between her and Johnny both in bed and out.

What had she agreed to?

Her emotions had taken over her mind, which hadn't surprised her. She lost all rational thought when she was in Johnny's arms.

Another worry niggled under her skin. It had to do with her mother. Madeleine was becoming more persistent in her quest to get Tish to return, calling Diana a couple of times a day, threatening the lawsuit again. Her lawyer was still working on the financials in the search for a loophole she could squeeze through, setting her free from the contract and her mother's demands.

She swung onto her back, punching out her frustration in choppy breaths, the lethal combination of lover and mother creating a ball of anxiety in the pit of her stomach.

Her mother's relentless pursuit wasn't surprising.

But Johnny's?

She'd never seen that coming.

When she'd tiptoed out of his room before daybreak, she never imagined he'd go looking for her, or promise...what he had promised.

What did it mean?

When they had boarded the buses after midnight for the trip to Tampa, he had boarded his own. Adding the performance in Miami had gotten them off schedule, and they were traveling to the new city to make up for lost time. They guys had an interview booked for later that morning and it meant they had to drive through the night to make it. She was glad this wouldn't become the norm. The guys had refused to extend the tour and were refusing any new invitations to play. She was unsure whether it was the principle of the thing or that they were wearing themselves out the way they were playing, it didn't matter to her. She wouldn't be on the road with them for much longer.

The vibration of the wheel on her side, the hissing from the wind from the open window, murmured her aching loneliness.

She longed for his hands, his presence next to her, the way her body felt laying against the length of him. And it had only been once.

What kind of emptiness would life hold for her when he was gone?

Playing with the plastic ring Johnny had won and given her which was never out of her sight, she thought about her upcoming concert series. It was just over a month away and she had to give serious thought about getting back to Boston to prepare for it.

The fugue state was dissipating and whole phrases of musical pieces were coming back to her but she had yet to reclaim one that contained every movement. She had even gone so far as to write up a possible play list so she would know which composers she'd perform, in the hopes that one of her favorites would come crashing back into memory. It had yet to happen.

The music rumbling in her head was still heavy metal, loud and flashy. Her Thunder repertoire had expanded and as much as she loved playing it, it wasn't who she was. She had to find her way back to her roots, her soul's expression so the healing process could continue.

Annie had pushed her for a talk after their outing on the beach. She knew Annie was concerned about what was developing between her and Johnny.

In a secluded corner of the lobby, Annie had begun to review the paperwork she kept on their prior sessions and Tish watched as page after page was flipped up and over her legal pad.

"Annie, don't. Okay? Let's just have a regular conversation like friends. We do it all the time."

Placing the pad down on her lap, Annie met her eyes.

"Okay. Give me the lowdown. You two looked pretty cozy when we found you at the beach."

"I'm not sure what's going on."

"What do you mean you don't know? Did you do it or not?"

The blush scorched her cheeks and she became hot just thinking about how Johnny had made love to her.

When no words were willing to form, she just nodded her head.

As if exasperated by her unwillingness to talk, Annie asked in a wavering voice, "Can you tell me how you feel?"

Fingering the ring on her finger, reluctant to share her story, she remained mute. The intensity of the act was still too fresh, the ecstasy still palpable and confounding her. All she could do was shake her head again.

"Did it meet your expectation?"

A sob-type laugh croaked out through a smile.

"It exceeded it. I don't know how to describe it."

As if more comfortable in the friendship role, Annie sat back in the corner of the sofa, her hand relaxed in her lap.

"I remember my first time. I cried and Tim kept wondering what he'd done wrong. It's so emotional. Guys don't get it. How was Johnny when you woke up that morning?"

"I don't know. I snuck out before he woke up."

"How'd you end up on the beach together?"

"He came looking for me."

She didn't know how to interpret Annie's whoosh of breath.

"Sorry. I'm trying to be objective. That's just so not like Johnny. I don't know how to counsel you on this."

"I don't need counseling."

She needed Johnny.

"Tish, what are you feeling about all of this?"

Twisting the ring, she looked down at her keepsake, unable to speak to what she felt. It was too large, too intimate.

Instead of discussing the act itself, or the aftermath, she said in musing, "For a very long time, I woke up each morning knowing I'd be facing another nightmare of a day. I wished I could stay in bed, drift into a shadow world where I couldn't fail. As my music disappeared, it only got worse. My mother began to suffocate me with her need to control my playing. I couldn't find joy in it anymore. I found nothing more than migraines and sleeplessness."

Annie looked sad at the telling, then she held a look of concern when Tish added, "Now I love my life. It feels good. That morning was the most glorious yet."

Annie took her hand, stared at her for a moment as if she couldn't make up her mind about what to say next.

Tish knew why when her friend confirmed what she already knew. "Johnny won't make a commitment. You do know that."

He had made a commitment of sorts but she wasn't sharing that, wanted to hold it close.

Dipping her head, she gave it a quick shake, before admitting, "Do I wish it were different? Yes. Do I accept that it can't be? Yes. I'm okay with it being what it is."

She knew Annie was looking for more meaningful dialogue but she didn't want to discuss what it felt like being in Johnny's arms. Couldn't share the intimacy of the moment. And she knew she had to keep what she felt a secret. Annie would go off the wall if she knew she had fallen in love with him.

Punching her pillow, she felt the bus slowing, heard the screech of the brake as it came to a sliding stop. Leaning on her elbow, she looked at Ralph, who shrugged his shoulders and waited. Hearing the smack of a hand on the accordion door, the squeak as it unfolded and bare feet pounding up the three steps, she sat up to see Johnny striding down the aisle. He sat on the bunk opposite, stripped off his pants, whipped off his shirt and sat on the edge of her bunk, clothed only in his boxers.

"Scoot."

It all happened so fast, she didn't know if it was real or just her imagination.

"What?" she asked as she inched her way towards the wall of the bus.

As soon as he was under the sheet, he pulled her close, tucking her against his side.

"I thought you might be lonely."

She started to speak, opened her mouth and then closed it again, not knowing what to say, just staring up at him from the position of below his jaw-line.

Kissing her forehead, he whispered, "Go to sleep babe. Can't do anything with all these people around so anything more will have to wait."

Her insides quivered. At the mere suggestion that there would be a repeat of their love making, she put thoughts of yesterday away. Her eyes shifted up again to catch a glimpse of his stubble that came from a few hours away from a razor. And her stomach shifted, too. Once again she tried to say something, ask the question burning in her brain.

What was he playing at?

But then reconsidered it.

He was here, not on the other bus. He was lying beside her and she was wrapped in his arms. What could she say to make the situation any better? Not a thing. So she let his gentle caresses, the swaying motion of the bus, rock her to sleep.

He lay for a while just enjoying her body molded to his. Watching her from his back perch on his bus had been a long series of torturous moments. Reject had talked him into hanging out back stage after the concert. He'd agreed to prove to himself that nothing dramatic had changed since offering Tish his promise. He was still free to talk to the women who came to their shows. But he'd become repulsed by the way the groupies came on to him, so brazen, the way they smelled, the way they dressed. And he didn't want any part of them.

He'd taken a certain amount of shit when he'd left Reject alone with the swarming fans after the concert and hopped on the bus to sit, wait and wonder.

Once they had gotten on the road he couldn't sleep. Just kept thinking about how Tish had fit against him, how her hair tickled his chest, how her warmth cocooned him in something he couldn't define. He didn't want to dwell on how much he needed it, but the longer he'd lain there thinking about her, the worse the emptiness got.

To the point where he'd donned his clothes, told Donny to call Ralph and tell him to pull over, waiting for them to agree, ready to pull rank on them if they didn't. When Donny slowed down, following Ralph off the highway and onto the break-down lane, he alighted, racing up the tarmac, banged at the door and slipped inside, ignoring Ralph's hard stare. Most of the passengers were asleep, so he only got a shrouded look from Terry before he rolled back over on his side.

Johnny didn't care how it looked.

He knew he wasn't hooked, or about to be reeled in, it felt good for a change, and he wanted to enjoy it. He'd given in to what he wanted to do. No harm done. No big deal. He didn't want to be submerged in a memory anymore. The most incredible memory of his life. The way her lips felt, not only when he had them under his, but when they brushed against his chest, his neck. Fingers, trembling fingers, caressing his shoulder, his hips, a part of his body he hadn't expected from a novice.

In a way that was still singing in his soul.

And it wasn't enough to relive it in every cell of his body or maybe it was too much. He couldn't decide which, just knew it was burning his mind, his skin still tingling in aftershocks, eruptions in his breathing and he'd became more obsessed with having more than the wisp of a thought. He'd wanted her in his arms, feeling warm, surrounded by her scent.

He didn't grasp the significance of it until he found himself snuggling her against his side.

And then...it hit him hard.

There was a void in his life when she wasn't with him. It was an unfamiliar need, a yearning that was growing stronger every day.

He should never have given in to it but he wasn't going to lie here and berate himself for his stupidity, not while she rode his chest, her arm curled around his neck. Instead he settled into the comfort she offered.

⌒

"What the hell are you doing here?"

Johnny cracked his eyelids open at Annie's hiss. She didn't look happy in the least. In fact, the scowl was first rate.

"Good morning to you, too."

"Answer my question. What are you doing here?"

"Now that I'm awake? Talking to you."

"Why aren't you on your own bus?"

"Because I'm here."

"Johnny stop playing games."

Tish cuddled closer, tucking her head under Johnny's arm, burrowing further into the sheet.

"Shh. Don't wake her."

Peering at the figure beside him, Annie said, "She's sleeping. She doesn't get enough."

Brushing his thumb against her temple he said, "I know."

"How did you get here?"

"Didn't you hear the bus stop?"

"No. I guess I slept pretty soundly."

After a pause, she asked, "*Why* are you here?"

He'd been asking himself that right up until the time he crawled in beside her. And right up to the point he had almost convinced himself by telling Annie, "I want to make sure she's okay...with what happened between us."

"When we know for you this is purely physical."

He jerked as Tish's hand came far too close to getting a handle on the situation. Reaching under the covers, he took her recalcitrant hand in his, brought it up to his chest and away from trouble. And sighed.

"It's definitely that."

"She's not sophisticated enough for this game."

There was a spurt of anger. He knew that, but there was nothing he could do right now to alter the situation.

"Look, she wanted it as much as I did. There's no reason we can't enjoy it for the moment."

Annie dropped down on the opposite bunk, deflated.

"You can't screw around on her, Johnny. You have to make a decision here. It's her or everyone else. You can't have it both ways. I won't let you."

"I know."

At his admission, Annie's eyes widened in understanding.

"You're giving up women?"

Waiting for his mind to start screaming that wasn't possible, he surprised himself by saying, "For now."

Annie leaned in and asked in a low voice, "She's just beginning to heal and she still has some demons to face. Please don't lead her to believe this means something. Unless it does."

He nodded and contemplated Annie's warning as she worked her way back to Tim and her bunk.

He looked down at the sleeping form, needing to understand what this was because it just fell short of making another promise and committing himself to one woman.

That wasn't on his agenda.

Being tied down with kids and a family wasn't something he wanted. He'd had enough of that growing up.

It had been loud, chaotic, and he hadn't been appreciated.

And he never wanted to find himself in that situation again.

As they rode into Tallahassee, at odds as to what to do with the feelings coursing through him, he couldn't pretend they meant nothing. The stares and whispers as they disembarked made him defensive but he wasn't about to explain himself to anyone.

He couldn't have if he'd tried.

CHAPTER TWENTY-THREE

Stretching, the light struggling to stream through the hotel drapes, Tish glanced at the clock to see it was way past noon. She'd been sharing Johnny's bed for almost two weeks and the sight of him next to her when they awoke, still gave her pleasure. Filled her heart with the music from Beethoven's "Ode to Joy", the staggered rhythm, overlapping instrumentation soaring effortlessly. She refused to let it flow to the end, when it transformed into a haunted funeral dirge, refused to admit what she had with Johnny would end the same way.

Pushing that thought away, she rolled over and asked, "We're in Cincinnati, right?"

Spooning her in, he laughed.

"We are. Although it's easy to forget sometimes. Not exactly what you signed up for, is it?"

"I signed up to get on stage. I'd call that a success."

"With a capital S."

She turned in his arms, and kissed him.

Kissing her back, less intensely than she wanted, he looked disappointed.

"We can't do anything, babe. We used the last rubber around dawn."

"Can we use an old one?"

He chuckled at her ingenuity.

"Sorry but once it's used, it's gone."

"How could we have run out?"

Tugging her closer, his tone holding a tinge of surprise, he murmured against her ear, "Seems I always underestimate how many I need."

"Don't do that again, okay?"

He chuckled again, affirming, "I promise, I won't."

Tish nestled against his chest, her own regret hidden in his shoulder.

The phone set off a rendition of one of the band's earlier hits, and Tish reached out groggily to grab it and hand it over. Bunching the pillows under her head, she rolled to her side to watch him.

She studied his movements, listened to the huskiness in his morning voice, watched the way his head nodded, his fingers tapped. It wasn't healthy for her to study him so much, to wake up to him. He was addictive.

Burrowing her head in the pillow, she smiled a very satisfied smile, admitting that she had never been happier in her life. Maybe that's what drugs did and he had become her drug of choice.

"Yeah, I'll be right there."

She knew even if he left, she could lie here and enjoy the after-effects.

As he stretched across her body to drop the phone back on the nightstand, her chest tickled on contact with his. When his hand cupped her breast, and gave her nipple a tug, she arched in response. He pulled her under him and said, "I gotta go."

"I heard."

"Tim's finished another song and he wants to run it by me. Then we're going to go Riverbend and practice it, maybe introduce it during the show tonight."

She closed her eyes savoring his nearness. His fingers were brushing her cheek.

"You're coming, too, right?"

His statement aroused some old fears. She should be leaving the tour soon and it was one of the topics of conversation they stayed away from. She'd begun to outline an end date and told him she wouldn't be learning any more of their new songs. She wouldn't be around to play them.

"Johnny, I..."

Deciding to think about it tomorrow, she stopped mid-sentence, slid out of bed and padded over to her suitcase.

Pulling some clothes out, she asked, "Do I have time for a quick shower?"

He stood back up, having one leg already in his boxers, and looked at her.

"Great idea."

Flinging his boxers out of the way, he took stalking steps until he reached her. Dipping his head, he let his lips mesh with hers.

The kiss was slow and hot.

Breaking contact, she tried to remind him, "We don't have a—"

"Shh. We're going to take a shower. Nothing more. I like my water almost scalding. How do you like yours?"

Before she could say anything, he had her under the spray, his mouth on hers, then her puckered nipple, his finger sliding into her, the feeling building in intensity, her whimper driving them to do what they said they wouldn't. Lifting her up, his arms around her, he brought her down on his engorged erection and filled her in one thrust.

The water penetrated her every cell as he penetrated her core. She rode him, her muscles clenching his shaft, her legs tight around him, pulling him in deeper, her hands in his hair, her tongue in his mouth, driving them both to the edge, toppling as one.

His legs buckled, almost bringing them both down but he braced his hand on the shower wall, his head down, his breaths coming in shorter gasps than hers.

"So much for just a shower. I should have known better, witch."

The irritation with the name was buried beneath the worry that shot through her, an innocent thought countering that. They'd done it so many times maybe he'd run out of effective sperm. She tried to think back to her last period, trying to remember those science lessons that covered eggs, and cycles and when the time was ripe for fertilization but her mind couldn't fit anything more in than the sight of him.

As if he read her worried expression, he promised, "I'll buy boxes of them today, I promise. We'll leave them everywhere."

After stepping into clean boxers and jeans, he reached for a shirt that was on the floor and shrugged it on over his head.

As she finished dressing, he was half-way out the door when she'd noticed what he'd done. She called out, "Hey, that's my shirt."

"Mine, now."

Running down the hall after him, her sandals dangling from her fingers, he reached out his hand as if in relay and she grabbed on to it. She hoped he wouldn't give the shirt away.

Tish loved sitting in on the rehearsals, listening to the creative juices as they flowed in a variety of directions, loved the music and very much Thunder. Johnny and Tim were writing all the time now, and every couple of nights they introduced one of the new ones to measure which ones worked, which were the crowd favorites and they had a growing list for the upcoming CD.

Being in the venue with them took her mind off the constant phone calls about her mother. Every time she spoke with Diana, the dialogue always revolved around Madeleine and what she was up to. She knew there'd be a day of reckoning at some point and braced herself daily for the worst.

A decision would have to be made soon, an exit date from the tour, a place rented for her required practice sessions, the hole in her memory filled with her own brand of music.

The confrontation was dangling over her head like a shoe about to drop.

Johnny's voice broke through her thoughts.

"What did you think about the harmonies?"

He had come down from the stage to the front row seats where she and Annie were playing audience. She loved when he asked her advice after a long work-out session, wanting to know which rhythm worked best, whether the lyrics were good or in need of tweaking, asking what she'd do for a piano accompaniment.

"That's one of the best you guys have put together. I think it's a must for the album."

"Yeah, we do, too. What do you think we should call it?"

"I think you already have a name for it."

"Yeah, you're right. This one's called 'Enchantress'."

"Another name for—"

"You."

She was going to say witch, but she liked the way that sounded better.

He was crouching in front of her, his hands on the arm rests of her seat.

"I think you need to do a solo tonight. Right out in front, lights shining, the baby grand center stage."

"I think you're crazy."

"Nothing to lose now. Your mother's known where you are for weeks, the music is solid. Your talent needs to be worshipped."

Pointing to her temple, she argued, "*Your* music in here. Not mine."

"Well, mine is the one you'll be playing. There's no excuse."

"Johnny, please..."

Chappy's voice carried across the huge space. "Lunch is here."

"Come on, let's eat. We'll argue later."

Tish's cell phone rang just as they were packing up the leftovers, which consisted of empty boxes, utensils, and soda cans. Every morsel of food had been scarfed down and Tish grinned at the lips still being licked.

But the smile faded, her stomach knotted when she saw the caller ID.

"Hi, Diana, what's up?"

"Maybe we should talk about the weather first. Wade into the waters a step at a time."

"Okay, that tells me this has to do with my...Madeleine."

"I just got a call from your lawyer. Your mother's attorneys contacted her. You know Madeleine's been following you on YouTube and Twitter since the investigator found where you were. You're getting great reviews and your mother now believes that you duped her into thinking that you couldn't perform. She's back on the war path."

"What other path does she know?"

"This one is leading her down the path of insistence that you return and get ready for the upcoming series."

"She's been on that one since I left. What's different this time?"

"Judith thinks she's planning something retaliatory."

"Like what?"

There was a hesitation and Diana said in a low voice, "It wouldn't come as a shock if your mother showed up on tour somewhere along the line. Thunder's schedule is easy enough to find."

Now the knots were tightening and Tish thought about the possibility.

As Tish pictured what that would look like, waves of anxiety rose and swelled in her chest. Her mother ranting at her in front of her friends. Causing a scene, a barrage of harsh words that wouldn't cease until she thought Tish had given up and given in.

Yet...

"I don't think so."

"What makes you say that?"

"There'd be a certain amount of drama that she'd relish, but I can't see her walking into this. She'd never choose to associate herself with riff-raff. It would be beneath her dignity."

"You might be right, but I've learned never to underestimate her need to offend."

"I know I shouldn't either. But I'm not ready to go back yet."

"You have to start thinking about it. We have a window to cancel the series legally. Once we're on the other side of that, we could get into a contractual conflict."

Tish's thumb worked the ring on her finger, as the agitation began to build.

"I'm working on it."

She glanced around and found faces filled with concern and it filled her with a confidence she'd never felt before. Here were people who cared about her.

And she would let their strength see her through.

"She is a force of nature. We'll batten down the hatches."

Tish ended the call on that tantalizing thought and Annie asked, "Madeleine?"

Tish nodded her head.

"Diana thinks she might make time for a visit."

Johnny stepped forward, took her hand.

"Don't worry. She won't get to you unless you want to be gotten to."

"If only it were that easy."

He gave her a teasing smile as if to lighten her mood and her load.

"Hey, we're Raging Thunder. We'll throw in some lightning and she'll be toast."

"Then I have nothing to worry about."

But she did and she would.

CHAPTER TWENTY-FOUR

Tish stood spellbound as Johnny tapped his foot against the floor, watching the spectacle unfold around him. He had told her that tonight's show would be a stopper. Fans were going to be rewarded for the sell-out in a big way. The band was going to create their own fireworks in the outdoor arena and the lighting and sound people had been working diligently to make it happen.

As she watched the entire crew work as one, almost organically, each part of the whole, each a link in the chain, she knew the reaction would sizzle.

Earlier, when Johnny was trying to fast talk her into a solo in the spotlight he had explained, "The format will be different. We've planned three sets, one filled with solos. Yours will be the finale."

Each member of the band would step forward, playing individually, to highlight their talents and to showcase their instruments. He was hoping for bigger and better, louder and faster, with a mixture of celebration and reflection. The set design resembled a fractious sky with stars, clouds, shrouded in darkness that would explode with periodic thunder. When Joe had discussed it with the band that afternoon, Tish loved the picture forming in her head but wasn't sure he could duplicate it.

He was.

As he put the finishing touches on the backdrop of rust colored sunset, she could almost feel the zap of flashing sparks illuminating the stage.

Her nerves were taut, like the strings of her piano.

How had she let Johnny talk her into this?

She had told him, "Absolutely not."

"Don't you want this? We both know you can do it."

She'd seen something in his eyes that she hadn't expected.

"I'm afraid only one of us thinks I can. The other part of us, isn't sure."

"Come on, Glinda. You're going to be front and center soon. Might as well get it over with."

Was this his way of getting her to the next step? If it was, she had to admire his intention but she still quaked at the thought of it.

"I'm not part of the band. It doesn't even make any sense."

"We need some fireworks. You're just the one to give them to them."

He had stroked her hair, then cupped her skull in a fragile hold, looking all the way down to her soul.

"Trust me. You can do this. It'll be another first."

Johnny had just issued her another challenge, one she wasn't sure she was up for.

"Why do you always do this to me? You're pushing me and I don't like it."

"I'm encouraging you to see what you've got in you."

His smile could get her to agree to about anything and Tish knew he'd won another battle.

"Warlock."

His smile deepened and caused a trembling that had nothing to do with the lights, with the audience or with the premier seat she was going to occupy on center stage.

As she sat at her piano listening to Tim play, the stage shuddered and shook, before the background erupted into a visual display of sheet lightning. When Terry took over, his guitar whining and twanging, the energy crackled as the excitement of the crowd continued to grow.

Reject's solo was melancholy, imitating his own mood, his own persona. One of the best bassists out there, he could bring tears to one's eyes with his style and talent.

Johnny's drums came within a split second of Reject's last note.

And she forgot about the shakiness, the inability to breathe, completely blown away by his power and skill. Each segment was ten minutes long and she couldn't believe his stamina. When he was winding down, he was completely spent, the sweat visible from where she sat and she knew he'd need oxygen from the export of energy out to the crowd.

Before she could think any further about his condition, she was jolted forward by a pull as the piano was moved forward towards center stage.

Chappy whispered to her as he guided her stool in pursuit, "You're up in twenty seconds."

Taking a deep breath between clenched teeth, knowing Johnny had given the orders to redirect the piano's position, she sizzled and seethed. As she was transported to the pre-determined spot, just to the left of the drums, the lights were shining in her eyes. She couldn't see individual faces, just a blur of bodies up on their feet, still in the throes of Johnny's fevered play. Trying to work with his energy only made the anxiety more overwhelming, so instead, she began humming to herself, a piano concerto by Grieg. It was like a warm hand around her heart, calming her from a soft place inside. Only when there was a sensation of relief from the staccato beat of her heart, did she curl her fingers over the keys, waiting for the last stroke of Johnny's sticks.

In the moment of silence between the transition from one percussion instrument to the next, she found her muse.

As the first chord rocketed into the atmosphere, the sound ricocheting off the overhead roof, she knew Rambler had done some intricate work on the soundboard. The effects were perfectly synchronized with the visuals and it seemed like he had used all his flips and switches to make her music pulse with a thundering presence.

Given what Tish heard when her hands moved over the keys she knew the band had planned the accoutrements to be used during her solo, even before Johnny had talked to her.

The lights were lasers, silver, green, blues, reds, blinding her to the audience, giving her the courage to continue. A solo was an unwritten exercise, no notes to read, no lead to follow, for the express purpose of showing off. She had no clear direction and didn't know what the hell she was going to do, but she closed her mind of thought, gave her fingers free rein, figuring there had to be years of music inside of her. She had to be able to handle ten minutes.

When she began breathing again, her mind was teeming with different melodies, chords, beats, and as she grew in confidence, she entered a zone and became completely lost in the music.

The lights cast an eerie glow, Tish's blonde hair sparkling in luster, and Johnny watched in awe from the sidelines, having come down off his stool for a shot of oxygen and then to offer support.

Her fingers flew over the keys, and he listened to the level of sound increase in timbre as she found her way. He still had a hard time believing her brilliance. She had become quite conversant in Thunder prose and tempo and it was as if she had played with them since the beginning, was able to read where they were going as if she'd written the script herself. She filled in whatever notes were deficient, complemented their tempo and flow with a striking one of her own. Alone, she was…He couldn't come up with a term that would do it justice. He could only imagine what she could do with her own brand of music and hoped one day to see her in concert, watch her, feel the vibration of sound float through him. When he'd listened to her recordings, there was magic but he wanted to feel the mystical quality she could bring to it.

He knew it was only for the music's sake, not the woman's.

She would be out of his life by then, picking up the thread of her own. Something he knew was coming, something he knew was inevitable.

Johnny's heart wobbled and it scared the shit out of him.

He became aware of the silence beneath the play. The audience was in the same type of rapture. Spellbound by the magnificence of the moment, as if they would never hear anything quite this good again.

Savoring it appreciating the mastery of the performer.

Reject had come to stand beside him, his voice filled with awe when he admitted, "She's good."

"We're good. Letitia Jones is in another stratosphere."

Everyone in the entourage knew who Tish was now and the respect was growing among all of them, Reject included.

"How does she do it?"

"She is the music, my friend. You hear what's inside of her when she plays. She opens herself up completely and lets the essence of who she is, out. It's what makes her so vulnerable to criticism."

"People criticize this?"

Reject's face looked almost comical, so shocked by the statement.

"It's one of the reasons she stopped playing."

Johnny let himself be consumed in who she was, hearing the pain, the fear, the exuberance, the warmth. The talent was instinctive, not only learned. Each combination of notes struck, the pedal control sustaining and whimpering, only added to the melodious undercurrent that filled the space. His chest swelled with pride because he knew her, had been given the gift of her company, her…

He couldn't let himself go deeper because it would hit some nerve in the center of his being, and he still needed some distance from what she made him feel.

When the last note vibrated through the air, settling over the audience, it took time for him to come back to the reality of the moment. The applause was thunderous. The rafters shook, the floor rumbled. The stage went black. He noticed that not one member of the band could move a muscle still caught in the grip of her magic.

He approached the dais.

Bending at the knees, he crouched beside her stool. Fingering a lock of hair that was plastered to her face, his fingertip brushed her cheek.

Singed to his core, he whispered, "You are incredible."

"Thank you. But you have to suffer for this."

He could have laughed if his insides weren't scorched from her music and he decided that he wasn't going to fight what he was feeling. Not now. He was going to let it build, knowing where it would lead. The anticipation would probably kill him but the wait was always worth it where she was concerned.

One very pleasant way to die came to mind.

"Do I get to pick how?"

"I don't think so."

Her shallow breath warmed him, her trembling lips telling him what the solo had cost her.

As he slanted his face across hers, about to bring his lips down to her, he noticed Tim moving to the microphone and he backed off.

He knew the spotlight would soon be shining on her, and he wanted her to receive the accolades she deserved. Waiting for the frenzy of appreciation to subside, Tim called out, "Give it up for Tish Jones."

Every other solo fell to the wayside, which was how he'd planned it.

He watched her take a bow, give a wave, and her eyes were shining on him, the silent message easy to read.

He stepped back to his stool, but his eyes never left hers during the final phase of the concert. He could feel her melt under his gaze, felt himself liquefying right along with her, and couldn't wait until they were alone.

And she killed him softly with her song before the night was over.

⌐

Over the next couple of days, Tish spoke to Diana often. The solo had outed her completely and numerous websites were talking about her and her new gig. There were calls coming in for interviews, questions posed about the change of her focus and genre, the publicity putting her back in the spotlight, a place she didn't want to be. At least not here.

While her celebrity was discussed by the different critics along the musical spectrum, Madeleine had stopped communicating, which spelled trouble. *No news is good news* did not apply here. Tish almost picked up the phone to find out what her mother was planning. But her stomach tightened every time she thought of calling. She refused to get in a verbal fight with Madeleine because she wielded the stiletto called a tongue so well. Based on past experience, she wouldn't be able to get a word in edgewise and would end up in a screaming match, her mother twisting her words until they lost all meaning, voices getting louder with every parry. Madeleine cutting her off, determined to get the last word in. It was a perpetual dance of anger and she was always in a worsened state than when the confrontation had begun.

Letting her lawyer deal with it was frustrating but the best decision for her peace of mind.

The only thing that helped was Johnny's love making. She felt stronger, more confident, and her music was coming back in bits and pieces. In rare moments, when her defenses were down, and she longed for a future with him, when what she felt pierced her to the core, she dreamed that what they had together meant something more to him than he'd anticipated. In the light of day, when she remembered this was only temporary, she was grateful that he'd been true to his word and had stayed with her no matter how many women clamored for him from the seats.

This morning he was going to the radio station in Cleveland with the guys for an on-air interview. The DJ was introducing their newest song to the listeners and wanted to talk about the CD expected out by the end of the year.

He was shrugging into his button-down shirt and as his muscles rippled, so did something in her chest.

Pinning his hair back, he asked, "Wanna come?"

She declined.

"I have something I want to do later."

Pausing, he examined her, then asked, "What?"

Her mind was a mixture of fear and hope, and she wasn't sure she wanted to share it with him yet. But he'd been with her every step of the way and she trusted he'd understand.

Tilting her head up, meeting his eyes, she admitted, "Some of my music is breaking through. Just phrases but I thought I'd go to the pavilion and see what happens."

Before she knew it, he was sitting beside her on the edge of the bed, her hand in his, his expression wary.

"The piano's probably there but nothing's set up. You might not have the acoustics you need."

Fiddling with his fingers she admitted, "I might not have the repertoire I need, either. I won't know until I get there."

Cupping her face with his free hand, he raised it so he could see into her eyes.

"Do you want me to blow off the interview? Come with you?"

She shook her head.

"No. I need to be alone with the piano. See if we can mend fences."

He kissed her before moving towards the door, his last look long and searching.

And then he was gone and she was left with her insecurities.

Their hotel in Columbus was within walking distance of the place they'd be playing tonight so Tish walked the couple of blocks, needing to clear her mind. It was now imperative that she get to work, sit down, see what she could pull out of herself. She had called ahead to let them know she'd be going in to practice, making sure she'd have the access she'd need.

As she walked on to the stage, she called out, "Hello. Is anyone here?"

A middle-aged man, who Tish assumed was the stage manager for the venue came out, wiping his hands on a rag.

"You must be the piano player for—"

The rag no longer held his attention. He was studying her, his face a mixture of surprise and excitement.

"Letitia Jones?"

Her brow furrowed.

"Um, yes. You know who I am?"

"I do. I saw you in concert a couple of years ago. You were...sensational."

His eyes had brightened, his mood changing from disinterest to fascination and he moved towards her, his hand outstretched as if to shake hers, which he did with a firm grip and lots of pumping action.

Relieved that he'd been to one of the concerts she'd performed at rather than one she hadn't, she said humbly, "Thank you."

"When did you join a rock band?"

"I didn't join. I'm with them for the summer."

After a pause, she added, "I kind of had a meltdown and needed some time away...from classical."

"I'm sorry to hear that. You doing better now?"

"I'll know soon enough."

Shoving the rage in his back pocket, he asked, "So, the practice you asked for..."

"Is for me, so if you'll excuse me, I have a lot of drills to catch up on. I haven't played this type of music for months."

"You do whatever you need to. Take as much time as you want."

Tish knew she only had a couple of hours before the band would be back at the hotel and Johnny might come looking for her, but she thanked him for the offer.

He wandered off, leaving her alone with the baby grand.

She studied it as if she didn't know what it was even though she'd once been on intimate terms. She needed to coax her old sound out of the hammer and strings hidden within its body, a distinct contrast to the one she'd been playing.

Approaching it, she felt a familiar tingle, one she'd thought had abandoned her.

Sitting on the bench, she closed her eyes.

Okay, if truth be told, I've missed you. So could you help me out here, please? Give me whatever you got and I'll be grateful.

Brushing the warm keys with the tips of her fingers, she bent her head and began.

For the first hour, Tish played scale after scale, coaxing her hands into muscular activity, repeating the exercise of thumb over and under fingers, a technique required in every classical piece, finding the flexibility returning to her fingers that she'd need to stretch and curl. Playing classical was far different from playing the keyboard. Thunder's music was mostly short and choppy chords, whereas classical music had running scales, each detailed note in a composition needing polish, her fingers at times having to play from opposite points on the instrument, keeping the motion smooth and flowing.

Scales were an important part of her practice regiment but Arturo had scheduled minimal time to the pursuit.

"Conventional finger exercises have no soul. You are advanced enough that hours at this activity is punishment."

Her mother agreed because she would insist on four or five hours of the irritating penance if she didn't like the method of play that Tish employed while engaged in a concerto or prelude.

Tish thought it produced a stiff wooden touch but her opinion never mattered.

Today she was master of her craft so after an hour, she felt ready to get to the meat.

She could hear Arturo's advice inside her head.

"It is infinitely better to create, find your own personal interpretation, than to imitate any who came before, even those more fluent than you. Each piece is a living breathing entity and all it needs is your spark for it to flame."

Still stifling the urge to wail, terrified that she'd be unable to find her own genuine expression, she reached down into her treasure trove and pulled out one of the first pieces she'd learned.

It had been before her father's death, before Diana, before Arturo, when memorizing composer's works was a labor of love.

"Moonlight", one of several movements of *Clair de Lune,* by Debussy was light, quiet, and peaceful. Her fingers found their way through the piece although it sounded amateurish to her ears, the simplicity of the music dimmed by her awkwardness.

She stroked the ivory-like keys as if they were precious and used a soft but firm tone.

"Look, Mr. Baby Grand. I need some help here. Talk to me."

As if meditating, she sat transfixed, as if waiting for the orchestra to begin.

Taking a deep breath, needing to reclaim her identity, she was suddenly filled with a surge of memory.

Her fingers positioned themselves without any help and began the prelude, a will of their own driving them across the keyboard, expunging the pain and the vulnerability, leading her home to a port that offered sanctuary.

It all came rushing back, like a dammed-up river now free to follow its current.

Rachmaninoff's "Prelude" had taut structure, Russian intensity with strong lyrical melodies and changes in character. It crossed a spectrum from the sublime to passionate virtuosity and it poured out of her with a desperate need to escape. Her fingers flew over the keys, her body submerged in the tempo and personality, moving as if as one with the melody.

It was one of her favorite pieces, and as she felt the music flow through her, the broken chords playing in sequence, the harmonics, the left hand engaged in sweeping arpeggios that filled her soul.

When she was finished, she was drained but felt a bottomless peace and satisfaction.

She had become one with it, as if she rode the waves of tonality, the waves rushing, pushing her fingers along in their wake. She felt giddy: she felt powerful.

She had been purged.

Johnny had helped her reach this place, navigating each step with her, first to the stage, then to the baby grand. He had pulled her out of herself, had helped her reclaim who she was and she would cherish that gift for as long as she lived.

Johnny had entered the darkened hall as Tish sat at the piano. She could be a portrait, all grace and charm, sitting with regal posture at the intimidating instrument.

And he was glad he had come, leaving the interview before it was finished, a driving need to know how she was faring making the decision an easy one.

He had crept in, sat in one of the seats at the mid-way point, not wanting to intrude.

He was enthralled as the hushed melody of one of his mother's favorites by Debussy floated out, and it offered him a sense of wonder, like moonlight caressing the ocean in soft waves of sound.

It was pure magic.

Then silence.

Sitting through it was next to impossible.

What was she feeling?

Was that song the extent of her recall?

As he was about to get up, her fingers began to tantalize the senses with what he recognized as a Russian work of art and he slid back into his seat. He sat rapt, watching as her body found a home in the music, moving with each struck chord, each infusion of energy. Her slender digits went in opposite directions, complementing, demanding, precise progressions, pure creative artistry. So blown away by her talent, he could do nothing but gawk at the woman sitting there.

The power of her performance had been chilling.

His feet propelled him forward, and he jumped on the stage, taking her in his arms, lifting her up and twirling her around as if her success here was just as important to him as it was to her.

"Babe, that was incredible."

When he stopped and her feet were back on solid ground, her features became animated, her voice filled with glowing pride.

"That was me, Johnny. My mother wasn't there. It was me."

He looked into those eyes that were shattering in their intensity and his fingers traced her cheek.

"You touched my soul, Tish. I t was...transcendent."

"It all came flooding back. The prelude, the sensation, the joy."

She leaned in and kissed him as he hugged her to him. The grim reality of her achievement was bittersweet.

Her success was a blow to the gut.

The end was coming. He could already feel the tear in his heart, something that was not supposed to happen.

CHAPTER TWENTY-FIVE

Tish's feelings of victory didn't last long.

Before boarding the bus the next day, heading to Pittsburgh, she was served.

As she was joking around with Johnny, Annie and Tim, hanging in the lobby, happiness at her achievement yesterday spilling over, a short man in a suit and tie approached her.

"Letitia Jones?"

Hesitating, the name sounding foreign in her ears, she nodded.

As soon as the identification was made, the man handed her a hefty envelope and walked away without another word.

Johnny muttered, "What the hell?"

Her fingers had started shaking and the package almost fell out of her hand. That's when Johnny took it from her.

"Open it, please."

He glanced at both Tim and Annie, before sliding his finger under the seal.

Withdrawing the legal forms, he unfolded the papers inside and seemed to scan the contents.

When his eyes shot up to meet hers, she knew what was inside wasn't good.

The other shoe had just dropped and her head began to ache.

"What is it?"

"A complaint and summons."

Her stomach roiled. Her head began to pound.

Licking her parched lips, she said, "Read it, please."

When he began to read it verbatim, she amended the request.

"Just the highlights."

She watched and waited, his fingers flipping the pages so that he could complete the task before giving her a summary of what it said.

He scratched his jaw, cleared his throat and finally gave her a succinct explanation.

"She's suing you for breach of contract."

No one had to articulate who *she* was.

Tish almost fainted from the dizziness that had overtaken her.

In a small, strangled voice she asked, "What?"

"Pursuant to blah, blah, blah, for performing outside the legal boundaries of the standing contract, to regain monetary compensation withheld from trust, and conservatorship of your...life."

"Doesn't she already own my life?"

As he flipped a page, in a voice filled with disbelief, he said, "Tish...she's asking for conservatorship because of your attempted...suicide. Claims that you are not competent to direct your career and affairs due to an emotional disorder."

Shame almost smothered her and her eyes filled with raw pain.

Her one tragic mistake.

Making that one small slice on her wrist would keep coming back to haunt her.

Appalled by what she'd done, she'd run for help as the blood had squirted from the vein, never meaning to give in to that, unable to make another cut.

Her mother used it every time she wanted to gain the upper hand. And until now she'd let her. It had made her mother's attacks more damaging, the screws tighter.

Not allowed out of her prison, no one allowed in.

But there was no changing the fact that Tish had done it and had to live with the scar and all it implied.

The voice had turned gruff. "Did you do that?"

His tone was grave but without the condemnation she expected.

She felt a tear in the fabric of her soul.

When his fingers tilted up her chin, he sought her eyes, "Did you really try to extinguish the blinding light that's you?"

Afraid to see what was in his eyes, she resisted the impulse to look up.

Her voice trembled and she could feel the burn of her cheeks in remembrance.

"There was no light, only darkness. Black darkness and it was consuming me. Yes, I did in one of my weak moments. I just couldn't live like that anymore."

The pain that threatened to pierce her became a dull ache as she concentrated on the voice, the one much gentler than she'd anticipated and she hoped...

"Why didn't you ask for help?"

Bringing her eyes up, she gazed into his and questioned, "Who should I have asked?"

He winced at the implication.

"Diana? Annie? Someone?"

"Diana wasn't around. She was on the West Coast with another one of her clients and I didn't know Annie well enough back then. Arturo was gone. I have no family, Johnny."

Now the anger came but still not directed at her.

"You do, she just doesn't seem to give a damn. A glaring example of why family is useless. One of the main reasons I don't want one. They always let you down."

Tormented eyes turned on Annie.

"Did you know about this?"

"Yes. Diana told me. Madeleine made it a point of contention between them pretty much blaming Diana's influence on Tish."

Madeleine would never have taken any responsibility for the underlying cause.

Then Tish heard him ask Tim, "Is this what you meant when you said her going back to Boston could be a question of life and death?"

"Yes."

Now his voice was booming, anger laced in his words.

"So why wasn't I friggin' told? I had no idea what I was dealing with here. I could have caused...Shit."

Tish watched him push his hand through his hair, pace the tile floor of the lobby. His voice was thick with exasperation.

"This was unacceptable on so many levels. I had a right to know this, don't you think?"

Tish was the one who apologized.

"You're right you did but it's not something I like to talk about. I was so ashamed of what I'd done that I wanted to hide it. From you more than anyone."

Johnny was suffocating in the silence that settled over them until Tish took the complaint from his hand, hers still trembling.

"How long before I have to answer this?"

Rubbing his hands down the legs of his pants, he paused, then asked, "You're not going to let this—"

Knowing what he was asking, she cut in, "No. Nothing could make me do that again. I just want to know how long I have before I have to face her."

"You should email it to Diana," Annie suggested, "Get the attorney on it ASAP."

Johnny's voice was flat when he stated, "The attorney probably already has a copy. But emailing it to Diana is a good idea."

"I guess that's right. I'll call her and let her know what's going on."

Without thought, numb to her core, she let Johnny escort her onto the bus. As he placed her on her bunk, she felt his presence as she shut down, losing herself in thoughts of the upcoming confrontation.

Not knowing what else to do, Johnny took snapshots of the five-page document with his phone and sent them to Diana while Tish used hers to call the agent.

Tish seemed to have shriveled into herself.

He couldn't believe Madeleine.

Tish's own mother, her only family had filed a motion with the court to sue her only child. It wasn't something done on the spur of the moment but was a step-by-step process that took forethought and action.

He shook his head unable to understand, his insides crawling with worms at the thought of Tish all alone.

Watching her fight her demons, he knew how hard she'd worked to get to where she was and he'd strangle Madeleine with his own hands if she caused a setback.

It wouldn't be for lack of trying he thought with cynicism.

Tish needed someone she could count on, someone who could hold her hand through the next dangerous passage.

Taking a step towards her, his arms ready to wrap themselves around her, assure her he'd be there...he stopped dead in his tracks.

What was he doing?

The second thing he'd sworn he never would.

Needing distance from what he felt, he turned in the opposite direction, and made his way towards the front of the bus.

An uncertain voice reached out to him.

"Johnny, where are you going?"

He stalled, almost losing his resolve, looked back.

She was moving to where he stood, her eyes hardening as she took him in. Pulled him in.

But he stood his ground.

"I need some time, Tish. I'm going to ride the other bus today."

"Is it because..."

He was quick to reassure her it wasn't because of what she'd done.

"No. I've seen what you've gone through. I can almost understand it."

He couldn't, really, but he cared too much about her to make her think the worst.

Too much about her to stay and pretend it could be something solid and permanent.

Then her voice almost broke him.

"I told you I disappoint people."

Against his better judgment, he took a step towards her, lifted her chin so she could see what was in his eyes.

"You've never disappointed me. Not once."

For as much as he wanted to kiss her, tell her with more than words that he cared about her, he couldn't. He couldn't stay because of who she was and what she could get him to do. Swear everlasting devotion and create a family. He refused to get wrapped up in the cocoon of her love. It was too tempting and way too dangerous.

"I told you I couldn't be in this forever."

She inclined her head in acceptance.

"I've taken you as far as I can. The rest is up to you. I know you've got it in you."

She lowered her voice. "That makes one of us."

"You kick ass when you want to. Kick hers."

He turned to go, took a step down getting closer to an escape hatch, when her hand snagged his arm.

"Thank you. For all you've done. I couldn't have done any of it without you."

He nodded at her, not willing to linger, her hold on him still far too strong, and he hit the pavement, his boots making a hasty retreat to the bus he'd began the tour on.

Reject had taken his spot at the back, so he was relegated to another, at the mid-way point, so he couldn't see what was behind him or in front of him.

Reject had come to stand beside him, his hands in his pockets. "What's going on?"

Most of the band had heard the exchange in the lobby, so he knew Reject knew some of the facts, Madeleine's complaint, Tish's...indiscretion.

"I could have sworn you were standing right there."

"Tish's mother is taking her to court."

Johnny dropped down to the edge of the bunk, his head in his hands.

"Breach of contract. A contract that runs out in six months."

Reject sat on the bed opposite, his hands resting on his thighs.

"It could take that long to get it to trial."

Scrubbing at his face, Johnny looked up as if he hadn't thought of that.

"You're right. Maybe it's just a scare tactic. To get Tish back home."

Maybe it was a way to make her life a bit more miserable than she already had, as if she hadn't hurt her enough.

"Whose mother would do something like that?"

"It appears Tish's would."

His voice held resignation.

"What are you going to do about it?"

Giving Reject a hard look, Johnny's voice was gruff when he said, "Nothing. There's nothing I can do about it."

Getting to his feet, Reject barked out, "Why are you here? Shouldn't you be supporting her or something?"

"That's not my job. I did what everyone wanted me to do. It's time for us to get back to our regular lives. We have the rest of the tour to finish out. She has a concert series to prepare for."

"I thought..."

Irritated, he snapped, "I told you that wouldn't happen. Didn't you believe me?"

Towering over him, Reject's hands on his hips, he said, "But the timing isn't great, Johnny. Even you have to admit that."

"The timing is perfect. She has to know I won't be anyone's family."

Reject offered another option.

"Can't you be her friend?"

Johnny shook his head.

After what they had shared together, that was out of the question.

He was having a much harder time with this than he'd thought he would. As he lay on the bunk, the wheels of the bus spinning towards Pittsburgh, he went over and over what a mistake it had been getting involved with Tish.

The result was disastrous. His body felt like it had been disconnected from its power source.

Shit.

Punching the pillow under his head, he wished he'd never met her. The connection was too hypnotic, and it didn't align with the way he wanted to live his life. Family meant disappointment and betrayal. Love made the hurt more invasive. Deep love meant pain, and he was not going to make the mistake of going there.

He didn't need to worry about Tish.

She didn't need him.

She had made victories out of her fear, overcompensated for what she saw as her weaknesses, created music that filled the soul, opened herself up to life even though she'd been deeply scarred.

Her strength was her power and she had the means to face her mother and win.

Thoughts of her wouldn't let him go and all of a sudden a thick, liquid ice flowed through him. He was cold, soul-deep cold.

Tish sat at the edge of the bunk, her arms wrapped around her middle, the bus moving towards their next destination which was only a few hours away.

Raging Thunder would perform tonight.

She wouldn't be with them.

She was going back home, to Boston.

There was no reason to stay now.

Her music was back and Johnny was gone.

It seemed like another test, another step towards independence.

Could she get on stage, play piano, take the spotlight?

Yes.

She'd succeeded at every one so far.

Now the question was, could she survive on her own?

This test wasn't as terrifying as the others. This one was heartbreaking.

She'd made a snap decision while talking to Diana about the summons, right after Johnny had walked away.

"Do you think you could find me a place to practice? I'm ready to come back and there's a lot of work to do. I'm not going back to my mother's."

Without hesitation, Diana had responded, "You can stay with me."

"Thank you for the offer but I need to be by myself for a bit. I need to think things through, figure out what I want, and how to get it."

"If you're sure…If you change your mind…"

A streak of independence she hadn't known she had, shot through her.

Sitting up straighter, she'd announced, "I won't."

"All right. I'll call you back with the details when I've got you booked on a flight."

"Thanks, Diana. Thanks for everything."

"Oh, before I forget. I got a call from the Boston Symphony people. Georg Halberstram was scheduled to play at the end of August but has come down with a lung problem and had to cancel. They asked if you were available. Do you want a practice run before the tour?"

With a bitter laugh, Tish said, "They must have run out of options. I didn't think anyone trusted me to show up."

"Word's out that you've severed ties with Madeleine and all the publicity around the tour has been good for your reputation. There's some optimism that you'll be back on the circuit, your talent intact."

Tish couldn't quite believe so many knew her fault lay with her mother. It made it even more important for her to see her contract voided.

"You can tell them I'll be ready. And thank them for me, will you?"

It would give her some focus while she waited for the nightmare with her mother to be over, and crush any romantic notions she had concerning Johnny.

Annie had come to sit beside her, an anxious expression on her face.

"Are you going to be okay?"

"With the summons or Johnny?"

"Either. Both. You've got a lot going on."

Taking a deep, cleansing breath, Tish said, "Johnny told me right from the beginning he wouldn't do permanent."

"I know, but…"

Annie's eyes met Tish's. She didn't know how to finish the sentence.

"Look, I knew this day was coming. I think the timing is perfect. It gives me the impetus to go back. I don't think I would have as long as we were together."

The pounding in her head was starting to compete with the beat of her heart. All the beautiful colors she had felt over the last couple of days were pooling into inky blackness, a shroud she thought she had finally removed. She'd just have to make the best of it. Ironically, it was Johnny who had made her strong enough to handle the disappointment. She grasped at some of the strength that still lingered on her bunk, and smiled a tight smile.

"Believe it or not, I don't think I've ever felt stronger. My music's back and I found out I can love someone. I forgot what it felt like. Worried I wouldn't know it if it found me."

Annie sat close, and grabbed her hand.

"Just so you know, you've brought more to the band than they've given you. You tightened them up as a group of individuals who'd forgotten how much they liked each other. You give so much of yourself to everything you touch that you will always draw love to you. We're going to miss you."

Hugging her friend, Tish let the words and their meaning caress her.

Annie, now the one with tears in her eyes, said, "I'm making sure that Tim and I are at your return concert. No matter where it is."

Smiling, Tish admitted, "It would be nice to have a familiar face there."

"If you need anything, anyone of us, just call."

"I will."

As soon as the bus pulled up to the hotel, Tish grabbed the bag she'd come with, and hugged Tim and Annie.

"Break a leg tonight, Tim."

He stepped forward to enfold her in a bear hug.

"What's the band going to do without you?"

"You guys are great. You'll be fine."

Extricating herself, she walked forward, a solitary journey to the concierge where she asked for a cab, and was told a hotel van would be leaving soon for the airport.

Deciding to wait for the shuttle, she went in search of the people who had become like family, wanting to say goodbye.

What was she going to do without all of them?

CHAPTER TWENTY-SIX

Tish found them in the hotel bar. It had surprised her because Johnny never drank before a concert, only after. But he sat, glass in hand, waiting for a refill.

Three of them looked up when she entered. Johnny wasn't one of them.

His back was to her, so she knew she was going to have to walk across the space if she wanted to say what she had to say.

With baseball hat in hand, she approached only to have him turn to face her.

"We're done Glinda. I thought you understood that."

"I know—"

After he drained the second jigger of scotch, he interrupted her, "The sex was great but it's time to move on."

"I'm not—"

He threw some money on the bar and walked right past her, his eyes intent on the tile floor.

The moment he walked by her without a glance, her opportunity to say goodbye was lost, and what they'd found together evaporated into nothingness. Wishing she could lose herself in him once more in the mindless consuming madness only he could provoke, she knew wishing wouldn't make it so. He didn't feel what she did, called what they'd done having sex.

Whether he wanted to admit it or not, he'd been loved, had made love. He had given her so much but it hadn't been one way. She'd given him herself and all the love she had in her heart.

He might not want it, but he hadn't refused it either.

Sighing, the empty doorway telling her what she already knew, she turned to Joe.

"I'm heading back home so I came to say goodbye. I couldn't leave without telling you how much I appreciate your friendship. And for making me look so good under those lights."

Stepping forward, she hugged him, kissed his cheek before turning to Rambler.

"And you. You did so much for me. Fixing the keyboard so I could practice on the bus, helping me balance the sound, then making my piano sing louder and stronger than ever. I am so glad you became my friend. I'm going to miss you at my concerts. You could improve my acoustics."

He stepped forward and embraced her.

Chappy was next and this goodbye was the hardest. He had become her friend and she was going to miss him.

He asked, "Do you have to go? Johnny..."

She met his eyes.

"It's time. I have my own life to get back to. But I'll make sure I attend as many concerts as I can."

Once he'd let her go, her head dipped down as she faced Reject.

"I know you don't really like me..."

Reject had gotten up off the stool and refuted her words.

"I do, but more than that I respect your talent. Don't let anyone tell you that you can't play."

"Thanks."

Then she made eye contact.

"Take care of him, will you? He's a lot lonelier than he lets on. He misses his family but doesn't know how to change things, apologize."

She watched his eyebrows arch.

"You saw that? Only a couple of us know that about him."

She nodded.

Reject didn't need to know how much of his heart, Johnny had shared with her. It could prove foolhardy to hand Reject that secret.

They hugged awkwardly before she began to walk away, looking over her shoulder, sad smiles on their faces.

Well, she'd said goodbye to everyone that counted. Everyone except Johnny.

He'd walked away before she could.

"Would you tell him I came by to say...goodbye."

"I will."

"Thanks."

Just as she walked back out to the parking lot, the shuttle bus arrived. She lifted her bag and climbed the stairs, sat down, and watched until the hotel was no longer visible.

She stared out the terminal window as she waited for her flight to be called. The airport was bustling, the gates crowded, the seats occupied, and she felt the comfort of controlled chaos, life pulsing like it did on tour. Safety had been at the core of it, the band offering the security of friendship and acceptance and the regret at leaving weighed heavily on her. The upcoming confrontation with her mother was another weight, but it was lighter and she knew she was ready. With a new sense of confidence, honed by hours of exercising her own selfhood, she knew she had the stamina to get through it.

It had only been a few hours since her separation from Johnny but it felt more like a lifetime. She felt the blood pound in her veins, remembering those long, slow, burning kisses, the rapture of being in his arms, the way it felt being filled by him, whole for the first time in her life.

She knew she would never feel that way again.

"Flight 235 to Boston will be boarding soon. Please have your boarding pass and your identification ready."

The voice over the intercom reminded her of her destination.

Diana had done the impossible and had rented a place for Tish to practice just south of the city. It was the home of a friend of hers, complete with a baby grand, beach access, and available for as long as she needed it.

And she'd need a retreat where she could shore up the energy and strength for the battle ahead, one with her mother, one with her other demons. They had faded to a dull gray but were still too close to the surface. But she was determined to conquer them.

She turned from the window as people began to gather at the gate for boarding. A chill seeped into her bones. Once she took her seat on the airplane, the door to this chapter of her life would close. She hoped the house in Scituate would offer a new beginning, where music would fill her heart again, filling some of the space where Johnny had lived.

Johnny pinched his eyes.

They burned from exhaustion.

He was tired of dealing with this feeling, as if he were broken, smashed to bits, tired of pretending that what he had with Tish didn't matter, that she didn't.

Missing a step, he almost ripped when he noticed the conspicuous absence of the piano. He walked through the space it had occupied, just to the left of his platform, from where he could still watch fingers glide over keys, find himself captivated by the infinitesimal joy she transmitted to everyone around her.

Fear started to rise, from the bottom floor and he felt something inside him getting ready to set off an alarm.

His eyes darted around the stage, and hoped he was wrong, hoped he'd hear the sparkling laughter, see those witch-like eyes seeking him out. Thinking was becoming impossible, the fear now running rampant. He couldn't seem to see what was right in front of him. The thought registered that Tish probably wanted to be facing some other point. Especially after earlier this afternoon when he'd walked away from her.

He hadn't been able to stay in the bar, not with her looking so sad, not when he thought about the sex. Right. Sex.

Sex was empty, temporary lust. What they had shared was mind boggling fulfilling, out-of-the-ordinary and something he'd never have again.

Which was just the way he wanted it.

She was a complication he didn't need.

He couldn't do anything but leave her standing there, all but running to his room for some sanity.

But he had yet to banish her from his thoughts.

Tremors gripped every nerve and muscle in his body as he scanned the stage area. Her instrument wasn't here and his breath locked in his chest when he thought about what it could mean.

What was going on?

With an abrupt turn, he found someone who could help straighten this out.

"Chaps, are you running behind? It's getting pretty late."

He had stayed away for as long as he could and had arrived just in time for the sound check.

"For what Johnny?"

He should have caught the sarcasm but it went sailing over his head.

"The set-up."

"What set-up?'

"The piano?"

He should have sensed the act of surprise Chappy was putting on for his benefit.

"Are you playing tonight? No one told me."

When Chappy glared up, panic rushed him, the alarm blaring in his head. He had set up the one-two punch himself and he doubled over in pain as his body took the blow.

He was paralyzed, numb.

Because he knew.

Chappy didn't have to say another word.

She was gone.

"She left after talking to us in the bar."

"Why didn't anyone tell me?"

"*She* would have if you'd heard her out. But no, you had to be an ass. Like she would have come to you looking for sex. That would have been your move, not hers."

"But...I..."

"You told Tish you were finished in front of everyone on her bus. That you two were over. It's too bad. Most of us are going to miss her."

Johnny's bellow echoed in the empty space.

"Annie."

Her back was to him as he approached, her head directed up at the ceiling, her wall solid and unable to be breached.

"Where did she go?"

"I'm so not talking to you right now."

"Where did she go?"

Tim gave him a sad-puppy-dog look and said to his wife, "He's fighting a losing battle but he doesn't know enough to surrender. Yet."

Annie scoffed, "His problem, not mine."

"But you're his friend and you might be able to help him with his addiction."

Johnny snapped, "What addiction? What are you talking about?"

"Tish. You're love crazed. I can see it in your eyes."

With a caustic tone, Annie said, "Oh, so that must be why he dumped her. I'm not giving him the time of day."

"But he needs your help. He's hurting. Look at him, hon."

"Hurting my ass. She—"

Johnny's voice rose several decibels.

"I am not love crazed. I'm pissed. How could she have left the band like this? Doesn't she honor commitment?"

Tim guided them to a corner of the room. The scene was gaining rubberneckers.

"Seems she doesn't care much about contracts," Johnny said. "Maybe her mother's lawsuit is warranted."

Annie spun around, her eyes shooting daggers at him.

"You have one hell of a nerve. What kind of commitments do you honor? I'm certain it isn't friendship or family. You run like hell from responsibilities, when you might have to commit to something. To some of us, that's the important part of life. Being there for someone you care about. Oh, wait a minute. You never cared about her. It was a case of satisfying a sexual itch."

"Family doesn't have anything to do with this."

"Oh, really? Seems to me you ran away from your family at the first sign of conflict."

Stunned at her outburst, Johnny stared at Annie, who took a breath and added, "And Tish didn't run. She didn't have a contract with the band. You didn't even want her here. She's gone back to Boston to face her mother and to take back her life. I'd say that's quite the opposite of what you're implying."

Johnny's stomach churned.

He knew what that meant and he had seen how Tish's fears had almost crippled her.

Would she be all right?

His own fear howled through him, cramping his brain, prodding him to ask, "And if she can't? What'll she do then?"

The implication of what he was referring to stood between them like a concrete wall.

"She would never try to commit suicide again. That's not who she is. Her mother's been at her for years, trying to break her spirit, crush her creativity. Tish lost everything in the process. She's not in that place anymore."

He knew Annie was right. Tish had her music back and Johnny knew that could sustain her.

"I didn't mean that. I'm asking a real question, no inferences. What will she do if she can't break free?"

"I don't know. I'm hoping..."

Her eyes softened, as if she didn't know how to finish the thought.

She didn't have to. He knew what she meant.

"Me, too, Annie."

They all wanted Tish to overcome the obstacles and win.

Needing a few minutes alone before concert time, Johnny walked away in the direction of the stage. It was as if the weight on Tish's shoulders had been thrust onto his own, and he sagged at how heavy it was. He didn't like the thought of her facing her mother alone.

Annie believed Tish had only been a body to him, one used well and often.

She was wrong.

Tish had put a fucking spell on him and it was still at work.

Visions of her face, smiling, laughing, giggling as she led them around each and every town, grabbing on to whatever delight came her way, making them all so much more for just being with her. Her cheeks blushing with joy when she learned a new song and played it well. Her fingers finding the sound that would complement Reject's bass, tie in Terry's accompaniment, talk to Tim's guitar. Her eyes singed him with heat as she watched him, becoming one with each stroke of his drumsticks. Taking him under with each beat of their pummeling hearts.

The rush of emotion almost drowned him.

He needed to see her again. Now. Right this minute.

His eyes skimmed the stage, willing her back.

The empty spot where the piano sat every night glared at him and he closed his eyes against the charge, the zing of emotion he felt at Tish's absence.

Grounding the palms of his hands into his eyes, the excruciating emptiness taking over, he knew why he had walked away.

He knew if he'd offered to stay with her until this thing with her mother was over he wouldn't have been able to leave at all. He would have enfolded her in his arms, felt her vulnerability and it would have overwhelmed him again. It wouldn't have stopped with a word, a touch, but would have led to a kiss, a brush of his fingers against her hair, a tight fit inside her.

She was his weakness and he had wanted her gone.

He had gotten what he asked for, but he hadn't known just how much a part of him she'd become.

When the realization hit him, he almost moaned out loud.

Her music had given him a new strength. Her zest for life had given him a new lease on his own. He had watched her, savored her, enjoyed what she had given him to the point where he wasn't sure he could live without it. She'd rocked his soul with passion, played him with those fingers, those hands, her heart.

And those eyes. Those eyes could make him fall into the depths of the universe.

Johnny slapped his sticks against his leg as he tried to snap out of his confusion and headed for his platform. As he fine-tuned a couple of connections on his drums in anticipation of the opening song, it hit him.

Tish wasn't here to give their introduction. The piano was the lead in to "Almost There" and they'd have to scratch it. Along with some of their best, or else scramble to re-arrange the compositions and remove the instrument that had become so embedded in their sound. Thunder wouldn't be the same without her.

Reject leaned in.

"We're kicking off with 'After the Show'."

What the hell...

Johnny didn't want to do that song. It was old, usually well-received, but they hadn't played it in a couple of years and it wasn't who they were anymore, not on this tour anyway.

Johnny stomped across the stage to where Tim stood, waiting for the announcer to open the show.

"We agreed we wouldn't do that song anymore."

"Well, we gotta pull songs from somewhere. Tish doesn't have any prints on that one. What do you suggest?"

Every single one that flashed into his mind, Tish had put her mark on, like a brand.

"Let's try out the new material," Johnny suggested. "The stuff we wrote this week."

She had started sitting out the rehearsals, the implication clear that this day would come. Several of the last few songs they'd written didn't have a keyboard accompaniment.

"We haven't gotten them down yet."

Johnny's voice bristled.

"Every one of us can follow a lead."

He watched Tim think it through but he wasn't willing to have him think that long or hard.

"Let's try one. If it bombs...blame me...I won't be playing tonight if we can't do better than 'After the Show'."

Flashing him a cold smile, Tim said, "If you think you can threaten me, you don't know me as well as I thought you did."

Looking up into his friend's eyes, he admitted, "That's not what I'm trying to do. It's just that...look, I need to play tonight. Don't take that away from me."

In that moment, he was touched by what Tish had gone through. What the inability to play meant. His soul was connected to his sticks, his spirit tied to his music.

Without it? He wouldn't know who he was.

His eyes met Tim's and held.

Without anything left to say, Tim asked, "Which song?"

Johnny was lost in thoughts of Tish in pain, bleeding, lost, glowing, mischievous...his. It caused too much feeling but he was going to go with it anyway.

"Glinda."

Johnny had only written it in the last couple of days. About Tish, and the spell she'd woven around him. But then he'd felt ensnared, not free to choose where his life was going.

He wasn't sure the song was ready. Or that he could get through it. But he was so full of her that he needed to speak to her in some way and maybe...

"Okay. Tell the guys. Get us there."

And he did.

The intro was framed around the drums, the song building on the foundation of power, pummeling, thrashing power. Trying to exorcise the image of a blonde, green-eyed witch, eyes filled with unendurable pain, Johnny gave everything he had to her- his heart, his soul, his mind.

⌒

When Johnny mounted the steps to the bus, Tim was sitting in the first seat, talking to Ralph. He had a bag that hung heavily from his hand.

"What are you doing here?"

"Can I hang out with you guys...ride with you?"

"You know Annie and Marci's rules."

"Yeah, no women."

After making his way towards the bunk that used to be Tish's, the one he'd share on occasion, Johnny dropped his bag down as if to claim it.

"Not a problem. I seem to have given them up."

There was a tinge of horror when he made the statement as if he still couldn't believe he intended to stay monogamous. Even if the woman he was tied to was gone.

"Don't have a choice, do you, buddy?"

Tim had put his booted foot on the rail behind Ralph's seat and slid around to watch him settle on Tish's bed.

Johnny was ready to deny and defend himself but the look in Tim's eyes had him admitting the truth.

"No."

There was resignation in the one-word response.

Tim answered, regret in his voice.

"I know what that's like."

Exhaustion was wearing him down. Johnny was tired of fighting this issue.

"What do you mean?"

Tim leaned his elbows on the silver bar brace, his chin resting on his arms. "I wanted what you had so badly. You know, the freedom, a different woman every night, but I couldn't get beyond what I felt for Annie."

"You never did get into the swing of things, did you?"

"Afraid not."

Tim stood and walked down the aisle, taking a seat closer to Johnny.

"I wanted to, God, did I want to. It seemed such a waste to be single, popular, on the way to famous, mobbed and red-blooded and not be able to do anything with it."

"Yeah, a waste."

"When I stopped fighting what my heart was trying to tell me, I realized that I wasn't wasting my life away with Annie, I was wasting away without her. At least you got to enjoy some of the success."

Johnny's eyes came up to meet Tim's. "Are you saying that part of my life is over?"

"I can't speak for you, or how you feel. I only know that without Annie everything was empty. Nothing felt right, nothing felt whole. I hated it and it didn't seem to matter how long I put off the inevitable, it came anyway. All those women seemed to want was a piece of me. Annie wanted it all and gave back so much more."

Johnny's stare was vacant as he looked out the window.

He knew exactly what Tim meant.

It was the intimacy, the history, the knowing. Oh, the knowing was a big part of it. Knowing what was going to happen, how it was going to feel, unable to wait for it. The anticipation was almost as good as the sex. When she was under him, it went way beyond need or expectation.

"I don't like this, Tim."

"What? The loss of freedom or the ache because she's not around?"

"Both."

"Maybe you just need some time to get over her. What I have with Annie is a forever kind of thing. You never wanted that. Maybe you're just going through a let-down because Tish was so different."

Johnny admitted, "I don't know if I want to get over her."

He wanted his lonely arms to be filled with her while he was making up his mind.

Tim gave him a level look and advised, "You still have time to figure it out, to get over her. But if you decide to take advantage of the perks of being single, you'll have to do it from there."

His thumb was pointing in the direction of the other bus.

Johnny shook his head as if he didn't understand a thing anymore.

"It's kind of funny, but I never felt freer than I did with her. It's like I was in a box, and the sides were closing in. She lifted the cover and I was able to breathe again. Is that weird?"

"Not really. I think you were beginning to feel trapped by the success, the one-night stands."

"It was pretty boring. And I didn't even realize it, until Tish…"

Just saying her name had his heart lurching. It was reaching out for something he had refused to give it.

"Annie says she loves me for no reason at all. I don't have to be anyone special. I can just be me. I don't have to perform. It's nice."

"Yeah," Johnny said in return, "like my hair. She liked it I guess, but it was never who I was. And the sex…She wasn't in it to see how good I was. There was feeling."

So much feeling.

Johnny dug his fingers into his eyes again, but no matter how many times he tried to clear them, there was a grainy film that just wouldn't go away. Bending down to smooth out the lightweight blanket with his hand, he felt a lump and reached under to retrieve the ring he'd won for Tish at the amusement park.

The day came back to him in a rush, her in his arms on the roller coaster, the kiss that was devastating in its depth. She belonged to...

Fingering the ring as if it were a talisman of who they were together, disliking the fact that she'd left it behind, he jerked upright when Tim announced, "I'll have Ralph freshen up the bunk for you."

"No."

Tish's bunk would carry her scent, their combined scent, something he needed right now.

Johnny met Tim's eyes as if to confirm it, holding on to the ring for dear life.

Annie made her way up the steps, a coffee in her hand.

Johnny noticed her eyes stray to his bag, then land on him and the tee shirt he wore.

They widened as she said, "You didn't give it away."

He was wearing Tish's shirt, the one with the three monkeys on it that he had picked up off the floor one morning and never returned.

"No."

"Then why—"

"Did I want to keep it?"

"Why did you let me think you gave it away?"

"I never said that, Annie. You did."

"You told me you couldn't give it back. You implied that you didn't have it anymore."

"I told you the truth. I couldn't give it back."

She had asked him for it, per Tish's request, before...Tish left the tour. He might have walked away from the relationship but he needed a connection to her, and the shirt had been it.

Annie asked, "A souvenir?"

"No. Something to remember her by."

"That's what a souvenir is, Johnny."

He fingered the plastic ring that was still in his hands, a keepsake Tish had kept, at least for a time. Had she left it on purpose, no longer wanting it?

He had made it easy for her to hate him.

Annie took a step closer.

"Where did you find that? Tish looked everywhere for it before she left."

She extended her hand palm up. "She asked me to send it to Diana if I found it. Now give it over."

His relief was overwhelming. Tish had looked for it, wanted to take it with her. He wasn't giving it up as cavalierly as he had given her up.

"No."

He remembered the way it looked on her finger and his heart held at the thought of another type of ring there.

He dropped down on the bunk.

That thought had come out of nowhere.

And yet...it didn't surprise him as much as it should have.

Annie walked by him, without another word, and he lay down, Tish's pillow up against his nose, surrounding himself with her essence and he thought long and hard about what he should do.

He had run away from what he felt because it might hurt too much to stay. Tish was the woman who rocked his soul. Her eyes could make him fall into the depths of the universe. His wings had been clipped and he was now earthbound, no longer able to soar inside of her.

It was real.

And if he were honest, he'd have to admit he wanted all those things with her that he swore he'd never want. Love. Family. Children.

A wife.

With a connection so strong he became part of her.

Someone so precious to him that he'd cherish her every day of his life.

There was a flash of insight, a thought that he'd never examined before, his own anger clouding reality. It was how Paul treated his mother. With every look, smile, deed, he proved time and again that Celia was his everything. It had been there in plain sight but he'd refused to see it.

He'd been such an idiot.

Grabbing the phone from his back pocket, he poked in a number locked in his memory.

"Hey, Ma. How are you?"

"Surprised. It's not my birthday or Mother's Day but I love hearing your voice."

"I guess this is kinda out of the blue but I miss...talking to you. Like we used to when I was a kid."

They had been close, and he'd always gone to her for advice, to tell her what was going on his life, even when she didn't want to hear it.

She would have just the right words to counsel or comfort him.

He heard the sadness in her voice when she told him, "I've missed it, too, Johnny."

Hesitating, he asked, "Where are you?"

"At work but Lana can handle the set-up. Is everything all right?"

With the pillow still under his chin, his feelings still so scattered, he answered, "Yeah. No. I'm not sure."

"Johnny what's going on?"

"Um, I...might have met someone."

"Someone special?"

He heard the hope in her voice with those two words.

"Yeah. She's that."

"And you're calling to tell me?"

There was a rise in vocal pitch as if she was...happy.

Why had he put this off for so long? He had hurt not only her, but himself as well.

"I...think I screwed up, Ma."

"What do you mean?"

"I seem to have a habit of pushing people away."

There was a slight pause before his mother asked, "Does this mean..."

"If you'll let me back in...I'd like to be part of the family again."

He couldn't tell if she hiccupped or sobbed before she said, "There hasn't been a minute that you haven't been part of this family, Johnny. Not a second. You're the one who forgot that."

"I know, Ma. I'm so sorry. As soon as I get back I'll be by to see you."

"You might want to call Dennis and Tony. They've missed their big brother."

The big brother they used to look up to. He had lost their respect with his pig-headed decision to cut everyone out.

Other fences he'd have to mend.

"I will, I promise."

"So are we going to meet her?"

The quick shift in subject threw him off.

"I hope so, Ma. But like I said, I kind of screwed it up."

"You can't screw up love, Johnny. You can turn your back on it, but you can't stop it from being there. Does she love you?"

"She did, I think."

At least she made him feel loved with every word and touch, but her eyes spoke to his heart.

"Then she can't have stopped."

"I hurt her, Ma. I told her I couldn't commit. That I didn't want a family."

His mother was silent on the other end. He had hurt her the same way, with the same sentiment.

But he was ready to admit he needed them back in his life.

"I was wrong. I miss you guys. Even Paul. Especially Paul. He was so good to us when we were kids. I shouldn't have blamed him for enforcing your rules."

"They were mine. I didn't have many. But the ones I had were in stone. Coming home drunk was one of them."

"I know. I knew it then. I just missed Dad so much, I didn't know how to handle it. Taking it out on Paul was wrong. I hope he can forgive me."

"Of course, he will. Like I said, love doesn't disappear overnight. It sits in your heart just waiting to be...Oh, listen to me, sounding like some foolish old woman."

He heard the tears in her voice, and felt moisture pooling in his eyes. This is what he had needed, his mother's assurances that everything would be all right.

"I've got some work to do getting Tish back."

"Just tell her how you feel, Johnny."

"It's not that easy. She's not with me anymore."

"Then call her."

"I want to see her. Tell her in person."

"Then what's stopping you?"

"Um, the tour."

And the fact that he was scared shitless she'd reject him like he had her.

"You've got to have a free day coming up. If not, take some time, call her if you can't. Don't let it go too long, Johnny."

"Thanks, Ma. I'll call you as soon as I know what's going on. I think you're going to be very happy with who she is."

"If she loves you Johnny, I'll be happy."

Disconnecting, he reached for the baseball cap Tish had bought for him at the Baltimore Orioles game they'd gone to. She had one just like it, had it in her hands when she'd come into the bar to...say goodbye. Working the brim, he decided to get out in every city, collect memories to share with her. It would give him something to do while waiting for the right time to go after her.

It would have to be soon.

The separation was killing him and he couldn't go on much longer without her.

CHAPTER TWENTY-SEVEN

Tish had gone to bed early again. She didn't want to sit and think about what the guys were doing. Her separation anxiety wasn't just because of Johnny's absence but from his band mates as well. She had once been content with being alone, retreating to her room to get away from her mother's rants. But out on the road, she'd been surrounded by people who made her feel good, and she missed being a part of the whole.

Climbing beneath the covers of the duvet hadn't brought the relief she sought. Her mind had run rampant. Not only about the show but Johnny's activities for the night. Had he already extended an invitation to one of the women clamoring for his attention?

The green numerals on the alarm clock glowed in neon-11:33 p.m.

The band should be wrapping up the encore right about now.

What had they played? Had they rearranged the score to compensate for the missing piano?

She'd spoken to Annie a couple of times since she'd left the circuit and had been told the band was performing a lot of their newer material, the music she hadn't practiced with them. The cohesion was still strong. Johnny hadn't given up the role of leader when she left and he was pulling some powerful stuff out of them. The reviews were stellar.

She'd caught a few of the YouTube videos over the last few days and she agreed.

They'd be playing in Pittsburgh tonight, Buffalo tomorrow, two cities where she would have loved to sightsee.

With Johnny.

Rolling over onto her side, she pulled the pillows under her head. She was alone, in a strange house but she let the memories of shared adventures fill her with a sense of renewal, although it mixed with the melancholy of loss.

Her time with him and the band was a thing of the past.

She had to put it where it belonged. She just wished it didn't hurt so much.

After dragging herself out of bed the next morning she dressed for a meeting with Diana and her attorney. Diana had sent a car, which chauffeured her into Boston, in time for the mid- morning appointment. The office was in one of the professional buildings that almost touched the sky. The meeting didn't go much better than her flight back to Boston which had been turbulent.

Judith informed her that her mother had cause for the summons, that Tish had broken several clauses in the contract by performing with Thunder and they had to discuss how she wanted to proceed.

"I think it's in your best interest to counter-sue. Are you ready for that kind of fight?"

Tish had measured her anxiety level before answering.

"Yes, I am. I no longer want to be an unwelcome visitor in my own head."

"I haven't dealt with your mother, only her attorneys, but what they have to say is definitely hard-core. We're going on the offensive and I've already begun the siege. I want to make sure you can withstand the pressure."

It might have been contrary to who Tish was, once. But no longer.

She was willing to fight to the death for herself.

"I'm done defending myself, done trying to placate her. She can't love me and I want my life back and will do anything within reason to make that happen.

Judith gave her a pleased smile and said, "Okay then."

Sitting forward, her hands sifting through papers in a file, Judith began to outline her agenda.

"I'm deposing several people who can attest to your mother's abusive tendencies. Diana is a given. Arturo has agreed, as have Ned and Bruno. I've got a call in to the producer you worked with, the one who fought with your mother over control, to see if he's willing to make a statement. I've also reached out to your current record label to see where they stand. Your mother was convinced they would join her suit but it appears they know which side of their bread is buttered. The representative told me they're hopeful that when you get this resolved, you'll go right into production for a new CD. You make them lots of money. Your mother doesn't. We just have to get this to trial. You'll have your day in court and you can put this all behind you."

Tish's mind spun. So many people would be subpoenaed, so many lives interrupted.

What did her mother hope to achieve by dragging everyone through this?

Her compliance?

Her submission?

Why couldn't she believe it wasn't going to happen and just leave her in peace?

Her heart throbbed but it wasn't out of fear but out of anger. Madeleine was wasting everyone's time.

"How long might it take? And where do I stand on my upcoming concert series? Are the terms still in place? Does my mother still get all the proceeds?"

"The trust gets it all, minus Madeleine's expenses."

Then a thought slammed into her and her hands began to tremble. She fisted them, determined to fight off the potential threat.

"Can I get a restraining order? I don't want my mother attending any of my performances."

The thought of Madeleine sitting in the front row, her face a filter for what she thought, felt, and heard made Tish nauseous.

Judith smiled in a cunning way that made Tish feel more in control.

"That's actually a good idea. It'll prove you fear repercussions. I'm not sure it will be granted. Mental abuse can't be measured so the courts tend to disqualify it."

Diana was the one who asked, "How are we counteracting Tish's suicide attempt?"

Tish flinched at the words but settled herself, knowing that was a part of her life that she couldn't rewrite.

Judith answered in a calculated tone.

"I've talked to the attending doctor and the psychiatrist who saw Tish in the aftermath. They were both stunned that Tish attempted that. Neither could find anything in her aptitude tests that suggested those kinds of tendencies and noted that, in their opinion, it was a temporary lapse, not a personality flaw. They feel she is quite capable of taking care of herself, and thought her mother was the root of the problem, which will help our case."

Diana leaned forward. "I'm sure Madeleine will find someone to counter their opinion."

Judith's hands formed a steeple on the desk. "Not being the primary care-givers, they will have to reveal to the court they didn't treat Tish and are basing their evaluation on their own experience."

Becoming angrier by the minute at Madeleine's attempt to humiliate her in a new and improved way, Tish asked, "Will the judge require a mental com-petency test?"

Judith met her gaze head-on and made an honest assessment.

"It's possible. More than likely but I'll fight for a third party who can be objective and won't have a pre-existing bias."

Diana asked, "Could this go to mediation instead of trial?"

Judith sat back in her seat, her hands still touching at the fingertips, her voice tempered by professionalism.

"Madeleine seems adamant at taking it as far as she can. In fact, she's gone public, giving an interview that will appear in the next issue of *Classical Times*. It paints a disturbing picture of Tish's behavior."

Tish could feel Diana's eyes on her, then Diana was patting her arm.

"When this is over, she'll look like a fool."

Judith voiced her distaste of the situation.

"From talking to her attorney, it doesn't seem like Madeleine has a true understanding of what she's doing, how it looks to an outsider. She's moving full steam ahead without any thought to a potential loss, which her lawyers have told her is possible. In my opinion, it's more than possible. Once the judge reads the depositions, and the character references, once he or she goes over the financials, Madeleine will find out she doesn't have a leg to stand on."

Diana pointed out, "The absence of truth has never stopped Madeleine from believing what she wants. She probably thinks she can charm the judge into seeing her perspective. She expects everyone to bow to her superiority."

"Part of my strategy is to get her to attack, get under her skin, which I've heard is fairly easy to do. Defiance seems to bring out her dark side."

Tish had been listening, staring into space, the dark and gloomy adagio of Liszt's "Funeral Ceremonies", playing in her mind. War, lament, pain, suffer-ing, all the things Tish was facing expressed in forlorn chords and harmonic clashes.

"It's a good plan of attack. My mother's aggression is frightening."

Madeleine would come after Tish with teeth bared and the bite would be vicious.

What her mother wasn't counting on was her newfound confidence. She would make sure she gave as good as she got. Her mother wouldn't leave any confrontation without a few scars of her own.

Judith asked, "Would you be willing to give a rebuttal to the *Times* article?

Tish was tentative about airing so much dirty laundry but her mother had already put the quarrel out there for public viewing.

Judith explained her reasoning.

"It would signal to her, that you aren't going to let the attack against your character go undefended."

Most people didn't know how often she fought back, stood up to her mother. It was why she was punished so often.

You did not question Madeleine on anything. Period. End of story.

Or you paid.

This bill was going to be paid in full.

"You set it up, and I'll be more than happy to do it."

⌒

Johnny stomped across the stage, fuming, his sticks clutched in his hands.

Then he let them fly, flinging them at the back wall, and they clattered to the floor. Ron had just informed him they'd added another concert to the tour, which meant the free day he'd anticipated at the end of the week had been stolen from him.

He'd planned on flying to Boston to see Tish, had already purchased his plane ticket. Now he'd have to wait.

The anticipation had been building. There was a light at the end of the tunnel and he'd thought, just maybe, he would have been able to last that long.

Now...

Instead of waiting five days, he'd have to wait close to ten.

Not possible.

He'd have to break down and call her.

The need to hear her voice was strong, but paled in comparison to how much he needed to see her, read her eyes, see if she still cared about him.

Tell her he'd made a mistake.

Pulling his phone out, he stared at it.

What was he going to say?

What if she hung up on him, didn't answer?

He hated being this far away from her although every night, he played to her spirit which was still connected to him in as tight a bond as they'd shared when she was here in the flesh. His playing had gotten even better though he couldn't understand why. He was floundering, his focus was gone, yet when he picked up those sticks, it was like he had to prove to her he was all in. He would never relinquish his role again and if given the chance, he wouldn't relinquish her again either.

Hitting the direct dial key, he put the phone to his ear and listened to the ring, counting the times it purred in his ear, until her voice mail kicked in.

The automated voice stated its message, asking him to leave his name and number or press for more options.

Was there an option for time travel? Take him back to that moment he'd walked away from her.

The beep sounded and he cleared his throat before saying, "Hi, Tish. It's Johnny. Call me, please. I need to talk to you."

He hit the end call part of the screen.

Sliding it back in to his pocket, he groaned knowing she might not ever get the message. She'd never wanted to learn about the apps, how to retrieve missed calls, said it was crazy how people attached themselves to the devices.

He smiled for the first time in days when he thought about the trip to the Apple store. He'd been adamant about her having a means of communication. She went off too many times to be without one.

The salesperson had shown them the newest model and he had purchased it against her better judgment.

"Johnny, it's too expensive. You won't get your money's worth. All I need is something that allows me to call out if I'm stranded. Spending this kind of money is ridiculous."

"Babe, I'm sure you'll get used to it. After a while you won't know how you lived without one."

But she'd proved him wrong.

She very rarely had it on, and he was sure she wouldn't know how to retrieve her voice mails.

Trying to reach out to her this way was probably not going to work for him.

Which meant he was going to have to think long and hard about waiting ten days to see her. There had to be another option.

Three days later he still hadn't found it.

⌒

Tish spent the next week walking the beach, the water lapping her toes, the ancient rhythm coming in and going out, and it helped her satisfy her need for motion.

Sitting idle, her mother holding the strings for the moment while Tish's future hung in the balance, did not suit her mood. Playing had helped ease the ache. Her passion was back, and she was able to express it in a familiar way. Her fingers were nimble, covering the full spectrum of the keys, her cache of repertoire fully restored, and she could pick and choose from the inventory with ease. She had played Chopin's "Ocean Etude", the sweeping note sequence mimicking the surge of the sea. Her chest tingled at the depth of sound coming from her soul, as if the well she was drawing from had been expanded and enhanced.

There were still black moments when she'd remember Johnny. He was always there in some small way, hovering on the fringes of her mind, her heart.

She wished he'd given her a key to facing her fears. But there had been no words, other than "Look at me. Stay with me."

That didn't work anymore because he wasn't here with her. The ring had been symbolic of their time together, but she didn't have that with her, had been unable to find it before she left.

But his power had permeated her being and she felt stronger every day. It would have to be enough.

Then, one morning, she awoke to discover a new variable that had to be factored in. It gave her a new energy that fueled her for the battle ahead.

She was ready to face her mother.

She called Diana. "I want a face-to-face with Madeleine as soon as possible."

"What are you talking about? We're getting the chess pieces in place. Madeleine's going to be cornered soon. You're going to win this. Why would you want to waste all the pre-trial work we've done so far?"

"I want it done now. I don't want her in my life and she will insinuate herself as much and as often as she can. Her traveling to Europe for my concert series is out of the question. I just wanted to give you a heads up before I call Judith."

"Where has this come from? I thought you were willing to wait."

"I've had too much time to think. I don't want to think anymore. I want to act. And the interview brought it to a head. In answering her allegations, about my failures, my weaknesses, it became clear that I need to be free of her and her drama. Today."

Tish geared up for the disagreement during Diana's pause but was relieved when she didn't have to waste her energy.

"Do you want me there?"

"No. I don't want any distractions. She'll drag you in and you'll become a scape goat. I don't want to give Madeleine any other openings. If it's just me and her, I might be able to keep her on track."

Maybe.

Tish knew Madeleine would take everything she said and twist it to suit her purposes, take each point in so many directions they'd lose sight of where they were going. But if Tish set her agenda, decided what she would give up, what she'd keep, maybe, just maybe she could convince her mother to go away. And she was ready to give up what she needed to.

After setting the time and place for the stand-off, tomorrow at noon, she took off for a long walk along the beach, the Pokeman doll in her hand, and wished with all her heart she could feel Johnny's lips on her one more time before then. She could use a bit of his strength to see her through.

She stepped out onto the patio, and walked to the edge of the dunes and looked out at the ocean. The sea breeze pulled at her hair. The salty air filled her lungs with longing.

For a simpler time.

Her life had never been simple.

Even as a child, she'd felt the tension that was thick in the air between her mother and father, her mother scattered, overwhelmed, unhappy.

Worshiping at Madeleine's altar had ended when Tish's piano lessons had began. Oscar had spent less time at his daily devotions to his wife as his daughter's talent emerged. His time was then spent immersed in Tish's life, valuing her gift, validating her hard work with praise and affection. It hadn't suited Madeleine at all.

Madeleine had begun to hone her skill at sarcasm, her words cutting to the quick, dripping with derisiveness. She'd fly into a rage when father and daughter banded together in an argument with her, punish their perceived transgressions in subtle but effective ways.

Tish had hoped that as she became more proficient, her mother's behavior would change but the criticisms were never far from her mother's tongue. She'd cluck if she heard a mistake, sigh heavily if Tish tried to master a difficult piece.

Madeleine saw everything through her own magnifying glass. She was the center of her world and whatever happened could only be measured by what it meant to her wellbeing. She couldn't feel another's frustration or fear. Only saw it in terms of how it affected *her* life.

Diana had once commented that Madeleine was like a balloon with the incessant need to be inflated with hot air. The need to be puffed up a constant one.

Tish saw her in terms of a tornado, with the ability to destroy everything in her path and she was about to voluntarily put herself right in its violent center.

CHAPTER TWENTY-EIGHT

After packing a small bag, Tish called a taxi and made a reservation at one of the hotels in Boston, deciding to spend the night before the meeting in the city. She needed people, commotion, activity, not solitude and Boston would give her that. Intrepid now, she wandered the warm summer night, stopped at a bar for a glass of wine, intermingled with patrons and other pedestrians, if only with a smile.

Her time on tour had given her the courage to connect with others, self-confidence to connect with herself and although she didn't get a sound sleep that night, she didn't lie in bed fearing the worst.

When mid-day came around, she found herself at the conference table in Judith's well-appointed suite. The walls were lined with books, law reviews, tax codes, Supreme Court case logs. Eight chairs sat around the table. Judith sat in one next to her. Her fingers were clenched together, her breathing somewhat labored, but she inhaled a deep breath to steady herself.

Going over the document her lawyer had drawn up after their conversation yesterday, she saw the terms were exactly what she'd outlined. There had been a back-and-forth, Judith not pleased with her demands, reassuring Tish that if she waited she could have it all.

Tish didn't want it all. She wanted her freedom no matter what the cost.

"No. I want her out of my life."

"But Tish..."

But before she could finish, Madeleine swept in to the conference room, preceded by Judith's assistant, who was paving the way, followed by her attorney. It was a grand entrance and she had certainly dressed the part of diva.

She could have been Lana Turner in an old Hollywood movie, when elegance and haughtiness were inbred.

Tish steeled herself for some snide remark and was rewarded for her efforts.

"Letitia, you look terrible. Your hair is a mess and that dress... What have you done to yourself?"

Tish had donned one of the simple sundresses she'd purchased on the road, her hair was curled under and pinned, her make-up minimal. Her new look was not one her mother would be impressed with. It was a step she'd taken with intention.

"I kept telling people you'd fail without me. It looks like I was right."

Taking her seat at the table, her chin at an aggressive angle, Madeleine said, "I assume you're done with this foolishness and you'll be returning to the condo. You've wasted precious time with your childishness. It's about time you capitulate."

Steadying herself, knowing what kind of chaos would soon be released, Tish said in a determined voice, "But, Mother I'm not. That's not why we're here."

Madeleine's mouth slackened at the same moment there was a disturbance in the outer sanctum of the office.

Loud voices echoed through the walls and one familiar voice hit at Tish's core.

"Which room is Letitia Jones in?"

Expecting her mother to explode after the initial shock of her statement wore off, she wasn't prepared for another kind of significant threat.

A perfect storm was forming, the rare combination of elements. Madeleine and Johnny merging into a potential tempest that was about to hit her. She was armed for her mother, but Johnny's presence added a component she hadn't counted on.

She could hear footsteps, muffled by the plush carpet that adorned the floor and the deep, growly baritone of his voice. Clasping her hands together in her lap, she tensed, not knowing whether to jump for joy that he was here or bemoan the fact, knowing what it would cause.

The receptionist's alarm was evident in her tone as she tried to block Johnny's path.

"Sir, sir. You can't go in there. It's a private meeting."

"I'm not leaving until I talk to her."

"I'm sorry. That's not possible. I'll have to call security if you don't leave quietly."

"Then go for it. I'll be in there before they get here."

Footsteps continued to pound down the hallway and Tish sat with baited breath anticipating the hit of another hurricane as he reached the door and opened it.

His head peeked in, and when his inspection of the room and attendees was complete, he stepped through the door frame.

"Tish."

Her heart swelled at the sight of him, his hair back in a knot, totally out of place in his jeans and tee. What she wanted to do was fling herself into his arms, feel his lips on hers, but she couldn't give in to her need. It would give her mother too much of an advantage, create a shift in her own equilibrium.

So instead, she stayed glued to the seat and whispered, "Johnny, what are you doing here?"

He sauntered over to the table, crouched down and took her hand, linking their fingers.

"I'm not going to let you face this alone."

Tish didn't have time to let the flutter have its way down her body. Her mother stopped it cold.

"And who do we have here? One of your admirers? I shouldn't be surprised. He's a bit rough around the edges, don't you think?"

Tish watched her mother give Johnny a once over that was rife with condemnation.

She thought Johnny had let the insult sail over his head until he came back with, "Better than being bitter around the edges. I think it goes deeper than that, though. Doesn't it?"

Deigning that he was beneath her attention, Madeleine turned her contempt towards her daughter.

"I don't know who he thinks he is, Letitia, but he can't talk to me that way. You're my daughter and I expect you to do something."

Before she could answer, Johnny stood, glaring at the woman on the other side of the table.

"From what I hear, you don't have a daughter. You have a cash cow, related to you by blood that you tried to milk dry."

The head tilted in arrogance.

"I am trying to imagine what you'd be like with some taste, Letitia. I kept hoping one day you'd surprise me. Seems I should be used to the disappointment."

Judith slid her chair back as if to rise and take control but Tish held her in place with her hand.

She noticed her mother fingering the ring on her pinkie. Her mother had given it to her on her birthday one year but had taken it back. Punishment for transgressions came in subtle ways that were always effective. The ring had laid unused in a drawer for years. Madeleine wearing it today spoke volumes. If she didn't get Johnny out of here, her mother might call the whole meeting off in retribution. She couldn't afford for that to happen.

When her mother issued another scathing remark, she turned on her and said, "Mother. Shut up."

Madeleine's hands tightened in a prayer-like grip.

Tish looked around the table unable to miss the slight smirk on Judith's face.

"If you'll excuse us, please."

She slid out of her chair and stood, taking Johnny by the hand. "I need to talk to you in the hallway."

His eyes were lasers of rage, directed at the woman sitting across from them but he didn't utter a word.

She tugged on his sleeve.

"Johnny, now. Come with me."

He allowed her to lead him out as the roller coaster of her life made another winding turn.

Once they were out in the hall, she pulled him into the waiting area, and seethed, "I'm not going to ask you what you're doing here but I am telling you, you can't stay."

"Why?"

"I need to do this myself."

"Why?"

"Because..."

They were interrupted when Judith leaned her head out of the conference room doorway and said, "Tish, your mother's threatening to leave. You need to come back in."

She placed her hand on Johnny's chest and felt the power emanate out and she let it flow into her.

"Wait here."

Before she could turn to go, he clasped her fingers and slid on the plastic ring.

"You forgot this on the bus."

Taking her face into his hands, he bent down and brushed his lips against hers, the kiss light but enough to make her heart stutter.

Backing away, he said, "Go get her, babe."

Tish returned to the room filled with a cool confidence. She felt surprisingly calm and unemotional, even as her insides had taken a ferocious tumble with Johnny's out-of-the-blue appearance.

And she didn't waste time.

She rested her fingers against the table and leaned forward, choosing not to sit but to stand.

"I'm going to say this once, Mother. If you get up from the table, turn the offer that Judith's put together down, I will see you in court. I have proof that you've skimmed off my earnings, for your trip to the Bahamas with Steven, your river cruise down the Rhine with Eric, your neck tuck, your eyebrow work and your liposuction. I am prepared to offer you a settlement that should keep you in the style you've become accustomed to. But you will get nothing more."

Fiddling with the ring on her finger, Madeleine drew a breath.

"Letitia, dear. This is not like you at all. Has that barbarian talked you into turning on me?"

Tish gave her a slight smile of defiance.

"No, Mother, you did that all by yourself."

"I know you might think I was a bit...vigorous in my approach, but I was only trying to help you. You should be showing me gratitude, not this selfish attempt to cut me out of your life."

"This attempt to cut you out of my life as you call it, is actually my attempt at survival. Whether you take the offer or not is up to you. Any further interaction between us is over."

"You're bluffing. You don't have the nerve to take this all the way."

Looking Madeleine straight in the eye, Tish warned, "You are wrong. Don't underestimate me. You've taught me well."

"I don't understand any of this. Spending time with that…that…rock band is so beneath us. Is that boy who interrupted us part of the band?"

Tish knew her mother was intent on leading her down another path. She wasn't going to let her.

"You can try to divert attention elsewhere but it will not work. Johnny has nothing to do with this. This is between you and me. The offer is on the table. Take it or leave it."

Her mother's attorney began speaking in hushed tones, going over the legal papers Judith had drawn up at Tish's request. She had given out only the briefest of details. It was the core component that had drawn her mother in.

Sitting at the edge of her seat, Tish was not surprised at the way her mother's mouth twisted, her lips pinched in fury as she listened to the terms.

Her eyes were cold and flinty when she announced in her most imperious voice, "This is not acceptable. I can't possibly live the rest of my life on this amount. I need a percentage of your earnings."

When Tish was about to speak, Judith put her hand on her arm, preventing it, then set Madeleine straight.

"The terms are more than fair."

Madeleine flung the four-page offer across the table.

"Why should I walk away with less than I deserve? *Letitia* would not be where she is today without me."

Before Judith could counter that, Tish stated, "My talent, my success, my money."

As if taking another tack, Madeleine implored her, "I'm your mother, Letitia. Isn't that worth anything?"

Superficial charm that others found enchanting appeared on Madeleine's face. Tish read it with practiced expertise.

Fingering the ring that Johnny had slipped on her finger, Tish articulated what she was now able to admit.

It was a radical acceptance of sorts.

"It used to be, Mother. I tried so hard to please you, tried to be what you wanted, but you've done everything in your power to crush me. I've finally come to see that being my mother is only a means to an end for you. I don't need that kind of mother."

The shift in Madeleine's mood was expected. In a flash, the fake, sweet smile turned to a furious sneer.

"How dare you speak to me like that. Whether you like it or not, I am your mother. That will never change. You will never get rid of me."

"You are that. And it's a relationship that can't be changed. But I can sever it, cut you out of my life. Never speak to you again. That I can do. And your time is running out."

Madeleine's attorney attempted to bring her back to the offer on the table.

"I think you should reconsider your standing here. I advise you to take the deal."

Reaffirming what Tish had said about the inconsistencies of the financials, the real possibility she would be left with nothing was like talking to a very stubborn child.

Madeleine argued over the inconsequential, wanting a clothing allowance, her rent paid for, travel expenses but Tish was adamant that it was the trust fund or nothing. One payout.

"Not a dime more."

Getting up to leave, her face flushed, her eyes daggers, Madeleine attempted one final maneuver.

"I will smear you so badly your reputation will never recover. On the road with a rock band, sexual promiscuity with one of the members, the list could go on."

"Give it your best shot, Mother. You do your damage. And you'll end up broke, without one red cent."

They exchanged glares but Madeleine was the first to blink.

It was always about the money for her mother. It was her safe place and Tish knew she couldn't take the chance of losing it.

"You win you ungrateful little bitch."

After scrawling her name on the designated lines, Madeleine got up and walked out, her face pinched and pale.

Exhaling a deep breath, Tish felt her legs shaking, her heart racing.

Annie had been right.

Madeleine wouldn't fight anyone stronger than herself, and Tish's strength had been funded by a man she'd thought she'd lost.

A man who waited right outside the door.

Only now, with the mediation behind her, could she think about that and what it meant.

What did he want?

Why was he here?

Johnny had paced the waiting room, unable to sit still for any length of time. He missed his sticks, which he'd left in the rental and he had nothing to occupy his fingers, no way to relieve the turmoil of kinetic energy rushing through him.

He watched the receptionist watch him, as if attempting to keep him imprisoned in the waiting room. Her look was guarded and she had warned him several times that security was only a phone call away. He couldn't really blame her. He looked a sight. From the time he'd left Washington D.C, he'd hit traffic which had delayed his arrival. There had been no time to clean up after the ten hours on the road. Dressed in ripped jeans, and a tee shirt, he stuck out like a sore thumb in the exclusive surroundings.

Tish's mother had looked at him like he was a piece of refuse. Her sneer of condescension was mind-blowing and he'd gained insight into what Tish had lived with over the years.

His gaze shifted down the hall, agitation shifting in his gut.

What was going on?

How was Tish dealing with the face-to-face?

He'd have to trust that she could stand up for herself.

And once that victory was behind her, he could tell her all that was in his heart, what he was hoping their future looked like.

The initial anger, resentment and shock at his feelings for her had been replaced by a love so deep he was drowning in it.

The voices coming from down the hall told him the meeting was over. It sounded as if Tish had won from the malicious way Madeleine was talking about her.

"I'm not letting this go. She might think she won the war, but that was only the first volley. That little witch hadn't seen the last of me."

He couldn't make out what the attorney at her side said, because it was being whispered as they exited through the glass double doors.

He fidgeted as he waited for Tish to emerge.

What if her win signified that she didn't need anyone in her life? She had her music and control of her future in her hands. What if she had stayed with him for what he gave her? Maybe she didn't need it anymore. Maybe she didn't need him.

His worst fears were realized when she came out and faced him.

"Thank you for coming but I think it best if you returned to the tour."

He looked to her eyes. Her moods were always reflected there but there was nothing to read.

"We need to talk. I'm not going anywhere until we do."

"Johnny, it's over."

He deciphered her statement to mean her confrontation with her mother.

"I know. You won, didn't you? I saw Madeleine walk out and she didn't look pleased."

"I wasn't talking about that. I'm talking about us."

Dumbstruck, he watched her walk out of the suite with whom he assumed was her lawyer.

What the hell was he going to do now?

This was not the Tish who loved him.

Where had she gone?

Had he been wrong about her feelings?

Spurred on by the need to find out, he got Diana on the phone.

Without even a hello, he asked, "Where is she staying?"

"Who?"

"Tish. I need the address of the house you rented for her. She will be going back there, won't she?"

"I think so. She still has some practicing to do. The house is in Scituate."

"That much I know. The address, Diana."

"What's going on?"

"I have no idea. I waited for the mediation to end and then she just took off on me. Told me...I have to talk to her."

"What the hell are you doing there?"

"I drove out. Couldn't get a flight so I drove all night. I thought she might need me...but...I'm tired Diana and I need to see her."

"Judith just called. Told me Tish stood her ground and she won. Madeleine signed away future rights to Tish's earnings. I have to admit I didn't see that happening."

Johnny didn't inform her of Madeleine's last promise as she left the attorney's office. He only gave his opinion of the woman herself.

"She's a piece of work."

Diana gave him a bark of a laugh.

"You know that after how short a time in her presence?"

Rubbing his forehead, the biting words coming back to him he answered, "Let's just say the sarcasm gives it away."

Abruptly Diana asked, "Why are you in Boston? Who's playing drums for the band I represent?"

He was back to pacing now, scanning the area as if to get his bearings.

"Chappy. I'll fly back tomorrow. I just...The address Diana."

"What do you want it for? What are you going to do?"

"I want to talk to her. I have some things I...need to tell her. Please."

"I'm not sure I shouldn't talk to her first."

"Diana, please. You know I don't do things like this. This is a first for me. I need your help."

The sigh came over the line before she gave him the address.

"Is there a key?"

"On the back deck, under a potted plant."

He had barely gotten the thanks out before he'd hung up and was racing out towards the parking garage.

Flying down Route 3, he arrived to find the house deserted so with no recourse, he retrieved the key and entered the beach house that had light, expansive rooms.

He felt the ghost of Tish within..

Nothing stirred, but there were fleeting images that shot through his consciousness.

Her scent surrounded him, the soft aroma floating in the air. Her personal effects warmed him and gave him hope.

Thunder CDs were piled high on an iPod dock. So were her own and he selected one to play while he waited.

Powerful, masterful, brilliant.

His Tish was all those things.

Although she might not be his any longer.

She'd told him it was over, and he wasn't sure his heart was going to survive that direct hit.

Spending so many years running away from these kinds of feelings, he thought of how ironic it would be if she didn't want him.

The thought refused to stick. He was not going to let her slip out of his grasp.

Inspecting his surroundings, he fingered the sandals, sitting by the glass slider that led to the beach. A couple of bikinis hung in the downstairs bathroom. The stuffed brown bear he had bought for her at the Atlanta Zoo sat on the corner chair. Her baseball cap, the one she wore backwards to drive him crazy, lay on a shelf of the entertainment center, and the small plastic trophy he had won at the local fair in Greenville, South Carolina she had dragged them to sat atop the seven-foot grand piano that was the focal point of the living room. Classical sheet music was spread all over the top, and the selections ranged from Beethoven to Rachmaninoff. He recognized a few of the pieces and wanted nothing more than to hear the twinkling keys under her masterful fingers. Like he had the day her music had come flooding back.

He wanted to cradle her in his arms, telling her everything he found in his heart that was hers. She had filled it, leaving nothing exposed or empty, and the need to see her walk through that door was staggering. Fingers tapping in obsessive reflex, against his leg, against the window pane, against his chest.

He hadn't gone this long without his sticks since he'd started playing, taking over one of his younger brother's sets over fifteen years ago. Without them there was no place for the trapped energy to go, and he felt restless and edgy. His nerves were raw, his patience worn thin and his fear of what she meant with the words "*it's over*" growing by the minute.

Scratching the stubble that had collected on his face, he stood looking out the glass wall.

Where had she gone after leaving the attorney's office?

Shouldn't she be back by now?

Gazing out the slider, he didn't see a thing. He knew the view was panoramic, beige sand, dusky pink sky, white billowing clouds, pale blue water with white frothy foam rushing the shore. It was the perfect place for her. She'd have her walks, the sun, her peaceful surroundings. Maybe someday...

Without completing the thought, the dream, he turned to take in the rest of the room again, as if she'd slipped inside without him seeing her and she was hiding in plain sight. Once again he felt the emptiness in the pristine interior that was filled with chrome and glass, white walls adding to the starkness of the house. The piano sat on a carpeted platform, adding a regal bearing to the already majestic room. It made Tish's absence even more glaring.

Fingering the pages of the piece of music she had been working on, he squinted to read the basic notes and fiddled around with a one-finger rendition of Schumann's sonata and wished with everything in him he could hear Tish play it at least once. He liked the melody and wanted to sit back with his eyes closed and listen to what her fingers could do with the stationary notes that blackened the page. Magic.

She always created magic. With everything she touched.

Closing his eyes, he pleaded, "Please, Tish, come home to me."

The livery car pulled onto the dirt road that would lead her back to the piano. Loneliness swamped her at the sight of the gray shingled deck house. For as jubilant as she felt from the afternoon's success, Tish missed the constant activity she had found on tour with Raging Thunder. And she missed Annie. It was isolated here, although the house had been ideal as was the atmosphere. She had practiced for hours. It had felt more like an act of love as she immersed herself in the variations of sound. Seeing Johnny had been a dream come true but she knew there could be no future for them. Not even a shred of a chance.

Climbing out of the black Suburban and facing the house and all the promises she had made, she took her first step towards her new life and stopped short.

Whose car was parked on the gravel drive and at such an awkward angle?

Hurrying the last few feet to the door, she keyed the lock and opened it.

She saw his back before he spun around to face her.

"Johnny?"

The face that she loved, the lips so inviting, his eyebrows arched in question.

"Where have you been?"

Her breath held, knowing she was going to have to somehow convince him she didn't want him here, when what she wanted was to run into his arms and never leave.

"Why the hell didn't you talk to me at the attorney's?"

He seemed beyond angry.

Submerging her emotions, she took a page from her mother's book and gave him an imperious stare.

"There was really nothing to say."

"I came back to Boston because I thought you might need me. You know, like you used to."

She had survived the most painful thing in her life and she was still standing. Even the confrontation with her mother had paled in comparison to the moment Johnny had walked away from her. In retrospect, it had been a good thing. Better than taking care of her, he had helped her stand on her own two feet.

It felt good to be taking care of herself.

"I don't need you, Johnny. I've been fine. Am fine,"

That she wanted him beyond desperation was another thing altogether.

Not expecting the raised voice, the look of potent desire in his eyes, she took a step back when he blustered, "Well, what if I need you?"

Him need her? Her heart stammered but the question didn't change anything.

He might be more than willing to climb back into bed together, but what she needed from him now, he could never give her.

Trying to calm her racing heart, she said, "Johnny, we had a good time but it's over. I have mountains of work ahead of me, a five-week concert series coming up, a performance at Boston Symphony at the end of August. I've got to find a place to live, learn how to live on my own. I don't have time for this."

His eyes widened and his voice held a tinge of disbelief.

"What we had meant nothing to you?"

Her eyelids drifted shut.

"Tish?"

Her name was said in such a reverent way that her heart began to break and her unstable hormones played havoc on her emotions.

The tears she'd fought off all day had nowhere to go but out and down, until there was a steady stream coursing down her face. The way he had said her name had been so tender and raw she was almost tempted to tell him the truth.

Trust him with it.

She had counted on the memories she had banked, deposited in her mind, to help her deal with the work ahead but sometimes they worked to her disadvantage.

His words about family and kids came back in a rush.

"It meant something to me. You're the one who broke it off, remember? I didn't fit into your lifestyle."

"I know and it was the biggest mistake of my life. I'm here because I missed you. God, I missed you."

He took several steps forward so he was standing close.

Before she could think clearly, hand over the lie she was willing to tell, she was in his arms, his hand cupping her head, his thumb brushing away the moisture on her face.

She shook her head, fighting the lightheadedness. She had been dying a slow death, but she couldn't let him know.

Her face lay against the wet fabric of his shirt, the moisture of her tears bathing him.

His voice held on the tenderness and it only compounded her confusion.

"Babe, I was wrong. You're the best thing that ever happened to me."

Her attempt to pull away, to keep herself from melting into him, was obstructed as his arms wrapped around her even more securely.

Needing to convince him that she could not agree to what he offered, she said, "I'm sorry you came all the way out here. This won't work. I've...There are things that have changed."

"Everything's changed, babe."

She couldn't let him know just how much. He'd walk away without a backward glance. She'd rather it be on her terms.

"You're coming here made it worse."

She'd have to start missing him all over again, start from scratch, relive the last ten days with the loneliness and emptiness that came with it.

Extricating herself from his embrace, she spun around as if her feet were on fire and headed for the door, opened it as if inviting him to use it.

"I've got things to do Johnny. You can't stay. Can't you just leave me with my memories?"

His fingers closed around hers that gripped the doorknob and closed it.

"I don't want to be a memory, and I'm not going anywhere until you tell me what's going on."

There was a grim determination in his voice that had her second-guessing herself again.

The jumbled emotions and confusion were making her dizzy She stuttered out, "It's getting late and I have to get in a couple of hours of practice."

Not knowing where to put herself, not wanting to look at him any more than she had to, needing to get him out of here before she admitted something she'd regret, she snatched up her traveling case she had taken into the city last night and raced towards the grand staircase, the bag hanging from her hand.

He unnerved her when he said, "I was hoping to hear you play."

She paused before taking the first step, her legs unsteady.

"I'd rather be alone."

"Tish, didn't you hear what I said? I want us to be together. Don't you want that, too?"

She turned to face him and she saw a familiar expression, one she saw quite often in her own mirror but she couldn't imagine Johnny being afraid.

Of what?

Her saying yes? Or no?

His voice was ragged when he asked, "Don't you love me anymore?"

Clutching her fingers around the bag handle, she tried to clear the thick fog that clogged her throat. Dropping her eyes, she said, "I never said I did."

He took a step closer. She took a step up. His arms reached out and brought her to him, his voice intimate, his breath warm on her cheeks.

"You didn't have to say the words. I felt it every time we made love."

She felt gentle hands clasp her shoulders, and then felt his fingers tip up her chin, their eyes meeting.

"Are you still pregnant?"

A flash of curious panic streaked through her.

Was that why he'd waited for her to return?

To have it out?

"How did you find out?"

"While I was waiting for you to get back, I came up to see where you've been sleeping. The bathroom door was open, an empty test box on the counter."

"You went through my things?"

He dropped his hands to rest on his hips. His voice dropped to a hoarse whisper.

"Yeah. I checked the garbage to see if the test was positive. Sue me."

His tortured expression told her his feelings about family hadn't changed.

"What difference does it make? It doesn't concern you. I'll take care of it."

His voice cut through her.

"It concerns me...How dare you say it doesn't."

She was confused, his anger not directed at the pregnancy itself but at her attempt to keep it from him.

She didn't dare dwell on the inconsistency.

She shot back, "You told me often enough that you didn't want kids. Or a family. How was I supposed to know you'd want a say in this?"

He took a step up, and they were nose-to-nose, his eyes fierce and unflinching.

"You're not getting rid of it."

Caught off balance by what he said, a flash of illumination hit her.

"You think because of what I did in a moment of weakness, I wouldn't value this baby's life?"

His hands went to his hips.

"I don't know what I thought. You just told me you'd take care of it."

Her eyes narrowed. Her posture stiffened. "I'm not the one who didn't want a family, you are. You never saw the worth of that kind of connection while I spent my whole life wanting one. You don't know me at all if you think I could do that."

His words turned soft, were filled with hope.

"You want the baby?"

"Yes. But you don't have to have anything to do with her. I'll love her enough for both of us."

"I'm sure you could. But you won't have to. There's no way I'm missing out on this miracle."

Her eyes widened.

"What? But you said…"

He'd been so adamant about not wanting a family, kids.

"We're getting married."

Why was he looking at her if his heart was in his eyes?

She was sure he could read the panic in hers.

He leaned his forehead against hers and chuckled, "I thought it would be the other way around."

"No."

The word came out in a whispered rush.

He looked startled at her response.

Her breathing started coming in short, brief gasps.

She couldn't let him do this. It was one thing to allow him to initiate her in the art of making love, and encourage a relationship with their child. It was another thing altogether to allow him to give up his freedom. He'd end up hating her and she couldn't stand that thought.

She never wanted to see the look of pure disgust on his face.

She repeated her answer with emphasis, "No," then swirled around and ran up the wide, curving staircase and into her room, his pounding footsteps right behind her.

She threw her bag on the bed, unzipped it and started racing across the room as she put things away.

He was there, his magnetic presence making it hard for her to act in a rational way, his words making her want more than she had only an hour before.

"You're pregnant. It's my baby. We're getting married."

Her voice escalated into a wail.

"I can't let you do that."

She swiveled from one spot to another trying to remember where her shorts went.

"Sorry. You don't get a say."

His voice held a determined tone. But could she trust it to mean what she hoped?

At a complete loss, her mind blank yet whirling like a cyclone, she stopped in the middle of the room, threw her hands up in the air.

"You don't want to be tied down. It's the reason I wasn't going to tell you."

"You would have had to tell me sooner or later. It's not something you can hide. Annie would have told me."

Her voice crescendoed, panic coming in waves.

"I still don't understand what you're doing here."

"I thought I already made that clear."

She looked at him then, her voice more powerful than she realized. "I'm a lot of work. You should know that by now."

His voice gentled as he moved even closer, placing his palm against her cheek.

"All the work came after you were gone. It was so damn hard being without you."

Bringing his mouth to within a breath of her, he whispered, "I love you and I want to marry you."

The sight of her flushed cheeks, the look of disbelief on her face made him think he should explain things, discuss their future. He studied her eyes, brilliant green eyes that still bewitched him. They begged for an explanation. But he didn't have time for an explanation. That would have to come later.

Much, much later.

Nothing mattered but getting inside of her. That had to come first. He needed to feel whole again. His body had begun to demand it.

Taking her head in his hands, he brushed his lips over hers, and the fire burned out of control. Before he knew it, she was beneath him, and her body was pressed to his, her arms around his neck, the kiss deepening, tongues speaking another language, hands expressing what had been left unsaid.

She shivered under his touch, her need matching his, confirming that she still felt the same way, that she loved him still.

He could breathe again, so he moved at a slower pace, anticipating what was to come.

Leaning over her, undoing the small buttons on the sundress, his eyes drinking her in, he intoned, "Are you going to agree to marry me?"

He stripped them both and then his hand palmed her stomach in possession. He brushed his fingers against her belly, then lower, the strands of hair tickling the tips.

Her eyes closed and he heard her breathing stutter before she said, "You don't have to do this. I can take care of myself."

Kissing her neck, her shoulders, he whispered, "I want to take care of you. And the baby."

"I'd expect things you might not be able to give me."

He grabbed her hand, brought it to his mouth. Her skin felt like heaven, her fingers magical works of art.

"Do you love me, Tish?"

"Yes, Johnny. I love you. But that doesn't mean you have to give up your life."

Thinking it was because of his past, he was quick to reassure her, "I can be faithful, Tish. You wouldn't believe how faithful I can be."

Her tone had softened, her eyes assessing.

"Why would you want to do that? You'd be missing so much."

"I won't be missing anything if I have you."

"Think of all the women out there who want you. If we got married you'd have to settle on one woman satisfying you...and you've said..."

His words came back to him. *It's always good for me.*

He hadn't told her the truth. Not because he wanted to lie to her, but because he hadn't wanted to believe it.

Looking deep into those fathomless eyes, his voice somber and filled with emotion, he said, "Oh, babe. No one satisfied me until you. I never realized how empty I had become. You filled me with life again. I lied time and time again, not only to you but to myself as well."

Caressing her breast, his fingers stroking the nipple that puckered in anticipation of what was to come, he admitted, "There was a reason I had to be the first one to make love to you."

His teeth caught the protruding nub and he pulled.

"There was a reason I had to find you the morning after, a reason I made that promise to be monogamous."

His hands slid down her waist and he placed a kiss on her stomach.

"There was no one else for me but you from the first moment I saw you. I just couldn't admit it. I told you things that weren't true. That it was always good for me was one of them. What I found with you was something I had never felt before. Something I didn't know what to do with."

Kissing the column of her breastbone, he nudged her legs apart and nestled himself between them, drew her eyes up to his so that he could watch what happened to them when he entered her. Pressing the tip of himself into her, he felt his whole body tense. He saw the pupils of her bewitching eyes dilate, while his drowned in her.

"What do you feel?"

The whimper gave it away and he smiled.

"Tish, when I fill you what do you feel?"

His voice was low, his body insistent and he was halfway inside. Lingering, hovering, awaiting an answer.

"Strong. You give me strength and I feel like I can do anything."

He cupped her buttocks and filled her a little more. She writhed under him wanting more of him, but he held himself immobile.

"What else?"

His breath jerked out with the words and he found it almost impossible to keep himself in check and not to sink into her as deep as they both hungered for.

"Whole. I feel whole."

He slipped in another inch, every cell in his body shuddering in anticipation.

"That's what I feel, Tish. That we're separate halves of a whole."

She compressed her lips together to stifle a moan but she failed.

"Watch, Tish."

His eyes held hers, demanding she follow his lead and he prodded her in gentle tones.

"Watch me fill you. Watch us become part of each other."

She looked down as he'd asked, the penetration almost complete and then he became part of her, filling her with a need as strong as his own.

He exerted more pressure until he was up to the hilt, felt her grasping him, pulling him farther into her depths.

"Every time we did this, I was loving you. Every single time. I haven't touched another woman like this since the first night with you."

He felt her muscles cling to him, clenching in response to what she was seeing.

"Look at me now, Tish."

He waited while she did what he asked, until her eyes met his.

"You are mine. My life, my heart, my soul. There is no one who can satisfy me like you do."

Her eyes were filled with the kind of love he'd never dreamed he'd find, wasn't looking for, but he was grateful it had found him.

Moving, the friction building as it always did, the powerful surge of love driving him, they fell apart in each other.

He closed his eyes to savor the feelings rushing through him, then opened them so she could read what was there.

"You're the first woman I ever made love to. You are the only woman I want, now, forever. It's never been sex with you, it's, it's..."

He couldn't define it, couldn't describe it.

"It's you. I need you...I need you so much..."

He tasted her lips and never finished the sentence, his palm caressing her cheek and he let the feel of her soothe his senses.

His whisper was filled with awe.

"We made a baby."

Bringing her face up, he held his breath, then asked, "Do you want it as much as I do? You've just gained some freedom. Are you ready for this?"

Her eyes widened in shock at his question.

She answered in a solemn tone, "More, maybe. I've been alone for so long..."

Cradling her head in his hands, his thumb stroking the softness of her cheek, he gentled his voice, "You'll never be alone again."

He leaned his forehead against hers, not knowing what to say, or how to say it. All he knew for sure was he wanted to spend the rest of his life in the light and heat of her eyes.

He lifted his head.

"I am so sorry for the way I acted. You are everything to me. Tell me you love me, Tish. Say the words. I need to hear them. Tell me you love me as much as I love you."

As she brought her lips to his, a tingle of anticipation shot through him.

"I love you Johnny. More than I thought possible."

"Oh, babe. I forgot I had this much love inside of me."

He didn't give her the opportunity to say a word.

As soon as he said everything that needed to be said, he tucked her in the crook of his arm and they nestled into sleep together.

CHAPTER TWENTY-NINE

Tish scrambled for the phone, the insistent ringing of the landline disrupting her complacency.

She had been snuggled in Johnny's arms, content to stay there, but whoever was on the other end of the call wasn't going to let her.

"Hello."

She heard the sigh of relief before Diana said, "You're back. Johnny was supposed to have you call me. Is he still there?"

"Yes. We had some things to work out. I'm sorry I didn't call."

"Congratulations are in order. Judith said you were magnificent. Faced off against Madeleine like you've been doing it for years."

"I have, Diana. Faced off with her. I never had the opportunity to walk away when it was over."

Tish glanced over to see Johnny smiling at her, his fingers stroking her arm while she talked.

She rolled into him, his arm coming around her to secure her to his side. She nuzzled her face against his chest and kissed him.

His intake of breath surprised her.

He wanted her, still wanted her and even more potent was the fact the he loved her. The look in his eyes told her he was ready again.

Unable to look away from the love and tenderness written there, she let the conversation lag until Diana asked, "Well, how does it feel?"

Joy bubbled up in Tish's voice. "I am so happy to be alive."

"Where did you go after the meeting? Johnny wasn't the only one concerned it was taking you so long to get back to the house."

Tish's eyes were still on Johnny when she said, "I went to Daddy's grave. I haven't been there in a long time, and I guess...I just wanted to know if he was okay with how things turned out."

She had been thinking about Oscar a lot lately, maybe because she was pregnant. His burial site was in a cemetery just off the highway, on the route back to the rental house. The decision had been a spur-of-the moment one, one she was glad she'd made.

"And?"

"I felt some peace there. As if he approved."

"He'd be so proud of you, Tish."

"Thanks. That means a lot."

"I still don't understand why you chose to rush things with your mother, not that it didn't work out well."

"I woke up one morning and...well, things had changed. I needed to get my life in order. Madeleine was the first order of business."

Johnny's hand palmed her stomach as if he understood what she meant. She'd woken up one morning to find herself pregnant. It had given her the courage to face her mother and reclaim her life. He pulled her farther up and brace the phone between them so he could participate in the conversation.

"You never did tell me what you gave her."

"I knew the only thing that might satisfy her was my trust fund. And I was right."

"Tish, that was worth millions."

"You know I never cared about the money. It was the music that held everything for me. What good would it do me if I couldn't touch it? With the civil suit against me, my assets would have been frozen until the trial was over and who knows how long that would have taken. I'm sure Madeleine would have dragged her feet for as long as she could. I needed to start making money I could use if I wanted to support myself. So, I swapped the fund for earning rights."

Tish noted the narrowing of Johnny's eyes. He knew what she needed the money for- the baby and all it entailed. She brushed her lips against his and gave him a smile, telling him without words she was happy it had turned out the way it had.

"So you'll get to keep what you earn on tour?"

"Every single penny. And the recording sales, past, present and future."

"I knew you had it in you. Battling with Johnny did you some good."

Tish felt the hurumph in Johnny's chest and grinned.

"I'm sure that helped, but the fact is I didn't feel like I had to please her anymore."

"Does this mean you'll be ready for the tour?"

"I will."

"Okay. I'll let you two get back to what you were doing. Talk to you later."

"Bye."

She placed the receiver back on the stand and cuddled up close to the man who was giving her a strange look.

"Where are you going on this tour?"

"Europe."

He bolted upright.

"And how long will you be gone?"

"Five weeks."

Before she could satisfy her craving for him that she thought went both ways, Johnny grabbed his cell.

"What are you doing?"

"Calling Diana back. Shit. It's dead."

As he reached over her for the landline, Tish fell off his chest and onto the mattress. Trying to regain her balance, she pulled herself up on her elbow and asked, "Can't this wait?"

"No. It can't."

She laughed when he pulled up the comforter to cover her exposed breasts as he fumbled to punch in Diana's number for the third time.

"I have to make sure I'm on that plane with you."

"What plane?"

"If you think I'm letting you go to Europe for five weeks without me, you better start making some mental adjustments."

Within seconds, he barked into the phone, "Make sure I'm included in the arrangements for Tish's tour."

"You're going with us?"

"Yeah. We should be married by then and there's no way I'm going to be separated from her for that long."

"You're getting married? You?"

"Yeah...she's...um, we'll explain everything next time we see you."

Tish was tucked into his shoulder, his hand lying on her still-flat stomach, his fingers stroking it.

"There's more?"

"Yeah. My body seems to have beaten my brain by a month or so. We're getting married as soon as I can arrange it. Where are we going?"

"Paris, Athens, Prague, London, Istanbul and Vienna."

"Shit. Some honeymoon."

"How can you take so much time away? Don't you have to finish up the CD?"

"The guys will just have to deal. We can start on the album when I get back. Or maybe we can put together a live recording somewhere on the road. Our stuff has been well received."

"I'm pleased to say I've heard."

"Oh, and I'm taking Tish back on the road with me. I don't want her alone here. We still have the baby grand she used, and I'll make sure she practices."

He slipped the receiver back, and she felt his arms move down her body as if everything was settled.

Pushing him off her, she glowered and said, "Um, did you just set my whole life up for the next few months without even discussing it with me?"

He gave her a look of disbelief.

"You didn't want me to come with you?"

Pulling the covers with her, she sat up against the backboard, her knees tucked under her chin.

"That's not the point. I just extricated myself from someone who tried to control me. I'm not about to step back into that place, even for you."

Disbelief shifted into astonishment as if he had no idea what she was talking about.

"I'm not trying to control you."

Irritated by his lack of awareness, she pointed out, "You just gave Diana a list of instructions for how my life will unfold under your care. How do you know I want to go back on tour with you or that I want to practice on the road and not here in peace and quiet? The only detail you had any right to lay out was the one regarding Thunder's live album."

He had gotten out of bed and began pacing, his vexation evident in the way he moved.

"I thought...You couldn't possibly...I can't believe this."

He spun to face her, his arms akimbo, his voice incredulous as he asked, "You don't want to be with me?"

A shiver of love slid through her, his naked, physical presence so arousing.

Removing herself from the protective layer of sheet and blanket, she scrambled out of the bed to go to him.

Her hands cupped his face, and she met his still-angry eyes.

"I love you and of course I want to be with you. But I'm not invisible and I have a voice. All the suggestions you made I would have agreed with, but I should have been consulted first. Do you hear me, Johnny?"

She felt his hand brush the back of her neck, his thumb caressing her ear.

"I do. I'm sorry, I wasn't thinking..."

She brushed her lips against his before saying, "I've earned the right to make my own decisions. They will be made in concert with you, not in deference."

Softly his breath fanned her face.

"You have. I promise I won't make that mistake again."

Her arms were around his neck when she asked, "I'm giving a concert in Boston before the tour. Accompanied by the symphony orchestra. Will you come? I might need you."

Nuzzling her neck, he said, "I hope you always need me. And I'll always be there for you. Do you think you could get tickets for that concert for my mother and Paul? I know she'd love to see you perform."

He gave her a smile. "If that's okay with you."

"Your mother?"

"Yeah. When you left, I realized what a mess I'd made of my life. I called her and...well let's just say I have my family back. I can't wait for you to meet her."

Kissing him again, she announced, "I can't wait, either, and there should be plenty of tickets available. Some of the ticket holders reneged when Georg pulled out and asked for a refund when they heard I'd be replacing him so we can probably get as many as you want. Seems there's not a lot of trust out there in my ability to show up."

"I bet the rest of the band will want to attend. And the ones who asked for refunds? Dumb asses in my book."

"My mother's article did nothing to add to my already floundering reputation. I can't blame them for—"

"They will regret their decision. I have a feeling this will be one of your shining moments."

"Will you stay with me backstage? Until I go on?"

Gathering her up in his arms, he assured her, "Anything you want, Glinda."

"You might want to rethink that promise. Some of the European concerts will require you to wear a tux."

"Fine. I'll buy one while you're practicing."

"No argument?"

"None. Whatever I have to do to be with you, I'll do. Would you be willing to come to my mother's birthday party with me? I'm going to be a little nervous. This will be the first time I plan on talking to *everyone*."

"You're going to apologize to Paul?"

"I am. I think I've been an idiot for long enough."

"Does your mother know about me?"

"She does and she can't wait to meet you, the woman I fell in love with. It's not going to hurt that you're one of her favorite classical pianists."

Her body was tingling from the contact with the hard planes of his and she rubbed herself against him like a cat wanting to be petted.

"You have to practice, babe. Isn't that what you told me?"

She felt the chuckle as he held her tight.

"Yes, I guess I did."

Sweeping her up in his arms, he carried her to the bed, pressing his need home. Her slumberous eyes left him breathless, light feather strokes along his back accelerated his heartbeat, her scent swirled around him, and he was lost as never before.

"I love you, Tish."

"I need—"

Before she could tell him what that was, he crushed his lips to hers and fulfilled every one.

EPILOGUE

Tish peeked out from the backstage curtain, the butterflies not yet flying in formation. Symphony Hall was packed with patrons and she couldn't see an empty seat in the house no matter how far or wide she looked. For as many ticketholders that had asked for refunds, there were many more who'd purchased tickets for her return performance and her insides were jiggling like Jell-O.

She had practiced endless hours for this, all across the country, as Raging Thunder toured. Johnny had made good on his promise to have the piano set up every afternoon and before each concert she'd had hours of uninterrupted rehearsal time. Afterwards, she'd sit in the audience or stand backstage to enjoy the raucous sound of the band, then return to the hotel and make love with a man who had given her his heart.

When the tour had ended, she'd taken up residence in Johnny's house on Commonwealth Avenue. The minute she'd walked in, she'd felt the same affinity for the place as he did. A grand piano graced the interior of the rotunda room, just as Johnny had said he'd envisioned it, and she'd made it her sanctuary. It was her sacred space where she'd steal to in the early-morning hours, the sun not yet streaming through the floor-to-ceiling windows. She'd miss it while they were gone.

They'd be leaving for Europe in another week, and tonight would give her a good indication as to whether she was ready.

"Hey, babe, are you okay?"

She turned to see Johnny hovering close, his eyes filled with concern.

"A little nervous but still standing."

Taking her hand in his, he said, "You look beautiful."

Dressed in a sleek mauve-colored gown, the bodice outfitted with beads and sequins, her feet encased in strappy sandals, she could say she at least looked the part of classical pianist. She had shopped on her own for a new wardrobe, a first since leaving her mother behind and she felt cool and confident. At least on the outside.

"Thank you."

Straightening his tie, she said, "So do you."

She glanced up to look in his eyes.

"Do you mind too much? Wearing the suit?"

"Nah. It's good. Besides, if you're going to look this good, I better keep up. I want those eyes on me, not someone else."

Johnny continued to offer words of encouragement, and she fingered a different kind of ring as she waited, a band of diamonds that Johnny had slid on her finger a couple of days after the tour ended.

A man with a clip board came over to where they stood.

"Ms. Jones, the orchestra is assembled on stage. Please get ready for your entrance."

Licking her lips, she said, "Thanks, Gaston, I'm on my way."

She bent her head and studied her hands. "I guess this is it. Wish me luck."

"Do you want me to stay back here?"

"No. I need you sitting out front so I have a focal point."

Placing her hands on his chest, she felt his heartbeat, steady and strong. His hands cupped her shoulders and he dipped his head for a brief brush of his lips on hers.

"Go get 'em Glinda. I love you."

"I love you, too."

Watching his back as he left behind the curtain, she walked to the edge of the stage and was given her cue. Squaring her shoulders, she took a deep breath, fingered the ring on her left hand and stepped out into the spotlight. The sound of her name being announced and the thunderous applause that came with it, as she walked across the stage, gave the butterflies free rein.

Reaching her bench, she ran her hands beneath her gown before sitting and settled onto it.

Her foot found the pedal, her fingers hovered over the keys, and she shifted a bit before she found her comfort zone.

Directing her attention to the conductor, she took another deep breath and gave a nod.

When the clapper smacked, her fingers flew over the keys, strains of Ravel filling the air, strings, woodwinds, percussion coming together in a familiar sequence. Ravel had scribbled his thoughts on paper and the tempo matched the furious scrawl with idioms and harmonies, the rhythm rich, influenced by the jazz movement the composer had experienced on a visit to the Deep South. She had chosen it because there was no down time between clacker and piano. She was able to plunge right in rather than wait for the orchestra to carry the piece to her cue. Sometimes the orchestral introduction could take four or five minutes before signaling her entry, and she didn't want time for nervous worry.

She was rewarded for her insight. The concerto flowed masterfully through her fingers, the butterflies now flying free but in tight formation. The pace of the Schumann selection was slower, balancing the tempo and the finale was Rachmaninoff's Piano Concerto.

As soon as she raised her fingers, the sign that applause could begin, she was stunned by the audience reaction. Everyone was on their feet, shouting *bravura*.

There was no higher praise. It signified that she had performed with virtuosic technique, skill and courage. For her, the reward was the joy she felt as soon as her fingers touched the keys.

She rose from the bench, and walked towards center stage, looking out at the patrons, her eyes lighting on Johnny, his smile radiant, and took her bow.

The conductor presented her with a huge bouquet of flowers that filled her arms as she continued to face the standing ovation.

When she exited, she walked straight into Johnny's arms, not quite knowing how he'd made it here in time. Kissing her, beaming with pride at what she'd accomplished, he said, "You were magnificent."

Camera's flashed, reporters asked questions about her sabbatical, her return, her future plans, and when she had answered them all, she lead Johnny in a new direction.

After guiding him to an older man, gray hair an unruly mass on his head, she let Johnny's hand go and stepped into arms reaching out to her.

The hug was warm and welcoming, her smile even broader than before.

"I can't believe you're here."

"Do you really think I would have missed this?"

Then tilting her head around, she made the introductions.

"Johnny, this is Arturo. My teacher."

Arturo corrected her.

"I think, actually, I was the student."

He praised her tonality and technique, reaffirming his opinion that she was his best student by far.

"Arturo, this is my...husband, Johnny Scalera."

The term was still so new that she stumbled over it.

"It is nice to meet you. If you had anything to do with her performance tonight I say she better keep you. She has matured to a level I have rarely seen."

Feeling Johnny's arm go around her, she beamed "I intend to keep him, trust me."

Arturo offered, "If you ever need me, for advice, to learn something new, please call on me. I am forever at your service."

Tish hugged the gruff old man again, "I'm taking you up on that. After the tour, I'll be in the studio working on a new CD. I'd love you to be there with me. I've missed you and value your judgment."

Tears in his eyes, Arturo said, "I am so sorry I had to leave you that way."

Patting his hand, Tish replied, "Everything that happened got me here so I am grateful to everyone who had an impact on my life. You were one of the most important."

"Call me when you get back."

"I will."

As several people started pushing forward, all talking at once, Arturo stepped to the side. Johnny's family surrounded her, showering her with praise. She had met them a week ago when she'd attended Johnny's mother's birthday party, which had turned into a wedding reception as well. They had welcomed her with open arms, especially Celia who couldn't believe her favorite musician had become part of the family.

Paul had the good grace to fawn less, but his welcome had been just as warm. She'd been introduced to siblings, aunts, uncles, cousins, friends, basking in the familial affection she had hungered for, for so long.

Acknowledgments

After writing for over two decades, the pen being picked up and put down year after year, I'd like to thank those who brought me back to the table. This novel is a result of their encouragement.

A shout out to Kathy, who on my retirement told me to get back to the page. She read my first attempt when I was as green as they come and still thought I had a story to tell.

To Bunny, who read several versions, bless her heart, and insisted I do something with it.

To Aunt Carol who sent me a personal note, by mail, to tell me she that she'd buy anything I published.

To my kids, Justin and Kait, who always made me feel that I could do anything.

To Caroline Tollcy, my editor, who versed me on POV, point of view, and taught me how to use all the senses to describe my scenes. My first draft must have given her nightmares.

To Amy Knupp who corrected all my grammatical mistakes. Dangling participles will always my Achilles' heel.

To Jaycee de Lorenzo at Sweet 'N Spicy Designs for my cover, she did an amazing job.

To my dogs, who behaved well enough throughout the hours of rewrites, but never did get the hang of sitting patiently at my feet.

To my husband, who always let me go in the direction I needed to go.

About Faith

Faith O'Shea is a contemporary women's literature writer who loves writing about strong women and the friendships they build. She throws in a little magic, a little romance, and develops unique personalities, and what you get are characters who come alive on the page. She's found that strong women need more than a happily ever after.

Faith lives in a small town in Massachusetts with her husband Jeff, dogs Cooper and Molly, and Isis, the Egyptian feline queen. Her children live close and are a big part of her life. In her spare time, she reads, walks Coop, dabbles in all kinds of cooking, and takes time to play with her grandchildren.

You can visit her on Facebook and Twitter or find her through her website at www.faithoshea.com.

Edge of Forever

Rissa Scalera was sick of getting dumped.

She couldn't seem to tell the good from the bad and the ugly, so love might not be in the cards for her. When she agrees to tour with Raging Thunder as her niece's nanny, she swears she'll stay away from bad boy bassist Luca "Reject" Caroli. He's exactly what she doesn't need. But as she gets to know him, peeling away layer after layer of the melancholy, she begins to sense he's not what he appears. Problem is he's otherwise engaged. If not with one of his lusty fans then with a woman from his past who's reached out.

Luca shouldn't be following his urges.

He's got a future to think about. The first woman he ever loved is meeting him at one of the upcoming concerts and he's got to see if they can go back. But with each touch and every kiss, Rissa awakens parts of him that he thought he'd buried. Their combustible chemistry isn't making it easy. She knows the score but she's made it clear she won't hang around as second choice. As he wrestles with his troubled past, and the stars begin to align, he sees where the edge of forever lies. Will he too late to claim it?

CHAPTER ONE

Marissa Scalera was reeling as she tried to grasp what had just happened. It had been so sudden it had cut the legs right out from under her. Nausea curdled in her stomach, and a frightening sense of disorientation only added to the crippling sensation. Her breathing was erratic, coming in shallow spurts, so she put her hand on the kitchen counter to keep her legs from buckling. The retching convulsions began and she stumbled to the toilet just in time. She wiped her mouth and leaned her head against the cool ceramic bowl, trying to regain her bearings.

This isn't working. I want you to cancel the wedding.

She should have seen this coming, but the disquieting sense of alarm came too late to make a difference. It was over.

You need to be gone by the time I get home. Leave the keys to the condo and the car on the counter before you leave.

Did he expect her to eliminate every trace of herself from his life?

Wipe her prints from every surface, eliminate any telltale sign that she had ever lived here?

Not that there was much to pack. He had stripped her life down to a few inconsequentials so most everything of value was already at her mother's.

It was final this time. He wouldn't change his mind. He'd found someone else.

She hadn't even noticed.

With the bile settling, and as feeling came back into her fingers, her mind cleared and she finally swallowed a dose of anger. She scrambled up from the marble tiles, ran into the kitchen and flung open a cabinet. The box of green garbage bags sat on the shelf, the thick plastic peeking out from the slit and she ripped two of them out. With jerky movements, she stripped the closet clean of her meager possessions, and stuffed them in. Then into the bathroom, removing toiletries, feminine products, shower cap, towels. With two bags filled, every shred of what she owned cleared out, she wrestled the diamond off her finger and flung it on the quartz counter, along with both sets of keys. Finally, she stood in front of her most prized possession, the Monet print her parents had framed and given her for Christmas, and gently lifted it up off the hook, carefully wrapping it in another bag. The last scan of the room alerted her to the picture of her family resting on a table in the stark and sterile living room. She swept that into her backpack, shrugged into her coat and went out to the front stoop to wait for her step-father Paul to arrive. The snow was falling lightly, the air chilly, typical for March in New England and drifts of snow enveloped her feet.

Her head dipped as one of her...former neighbors passed her, and she could feel the inquisitive eyes take in the small pile around her before she disappeared behind her door. The shame covered her more thickly than the accumulation of snow.

She was alone again, staring out into the distance.

What the hell was she going to do now?

Before long, a car pulled up along the sidewalk, the headlights illuminating the white powder, but she was frozen in place and couldn't move.

She felt the warmth of her step-father's body as he wrapped his arms around her, helping her to her feet. The anger emanating from his sold form seeped through her as well.

She felt bedraggled. Or maybe it was shell shocked.

"Come on sweetheart. I've got your bags."

Paul supported her weight by taking her by the arm as she let him lead her to the back door of his car, his partner from the homicide unit in the passenger seat, a captive audience to her humiliation.

Making sure the seat belt was secure, he offered her soft assurances.

"It's going to be alright Rissa. I'm going to take you home."

Her arms snaked around her middle to keep herself from spilling out.

Once he was back behind the wheel and pulling out from where he double-parked, she said in a raw voice.

"I'm sorry. I called Ma but she didn't answer."

She could have called one of her brothers but it was Paul's calm demeanor she needed right now.

"I'm glad you called me, Rissa. I've always told you I'd be there if you needed me."

She had given him only a brief rundown of what had happened when she'd called him but even with as little as he knew, he looked like he wanted to pummel her ex-fiancé, his eyes dark and dangerous. She might only be his stepdaughter but he'd always made her feel loved, even as a baby. Her father's partner for over twenty years, Paul Catalano had taken over full responsibility for her family not long after her father's death. And he'd worn the mantle of protector better than his predecessor although she'd never said that out loud.

She heard the jab as he punched the button that controlled the heat, the full thrust of hot air reaching her in the back. When she noticed his eyes in the rearview mirror as if to check on her, she asked so softly he must have read her lips to understand her question.

"How could he have done this?"

She didn't mean the break-up but the callous way he'd gone about it. To drop in, drop his bombshell and then leave was the height of cruelty.

Paul's expression was tight, his answer held a bite.

"Jude is a certified asshole. That's why. It has nothing to do with you. And if I hadn't sworn to protect and defend there'd be a bloody murder on my hands."

Choking back the sob that threatened, she sat silently until they pulled up to her childhood home where her mother came racing out to meet them.

Celia Scalera Catalano brushed away the clinging snow off Rissa's head. "I'm sorry I didn't get your call. I always have my phone off while we're serving.

Celia was catering a wedding reception that night, something Rissa had forgotten, her brain too numb to process thought.

Paul got the bags out of his trunk along with a large rectangular package and deposited them in the front hall before kissing both women goodbye.

Rissa leaned on her mother as she helped her out of her coat and threw it over the banister.

"You go on up. I'm going to heat up some soup. That will make you feel better."

She felt like a decrepit old woman as she struggled up the stairs, her grip on the wooden bannister taut, her shoulders curling in.

After taking a few steps along the landing, Rissa came to a stop at the threshold of her old room, the twin beds on either side of the window like they always were. The walls had been repainted a pale, soft blue but she could still see the bright pink walls of her youth, the coverlets white eyelet, hers covered with her softball uniform that had never made it to the wash after her last game, a pair of sneakers peeking out from under the duster ruffle skirt, her muddy cleats sitting on the mat her mother insisted she use. A pitcher's glove sat on the floor, along with her roller blades. Athletic apparel was strewn around the room, and on the table against the wall were her brushes, small canvases and tubes of paint.

Lana's side was more girlie than hers, stacks of cooking magazines on her nightstand, a glass mirror tray on the bureau where she stored earrings, bangles and necklaces, a picture of whatever current boyfriend she had in view. It changed every month.

They had always been so different. Today it was more glaring than ever.

Lana was living in an apartment, totally self-supported. Although she didn't have the kitchen of her dreams, she could go home at the end of her working day to her own personal space. No one could kick her out, no one could tell her what she could leave out and what had to be hidden. Her cookbooks were all over the place, taking up a good portion of the little counter area she had and they sprouted little tabs where she could easily find her favorite recipes, spiral notebooks filled with a list of ingredients for the new cooking experiments. She had a steady boyfriend but she refused to be bogged down with restraints of any kind.

While Lana didn't mind living alone, it scared her to death. No matter how hard she tried to escape her feelings of loneliness, they always found her.

Would everyone she loved, abandon her?

Rissa crossed over the threshold into her old life, sank onto the new duvet, dropping her head into her hands wanting to cry but her nervous system and all her senses had shut down leaving her numb.

Her body swiveled to take in the woman standing at the doorway, a bowl of soup in her hand. Her mother was petite and round, with curly brown hair and an apron around her waist, she felt her mother's love wash over her. Love in Italian meant food so she knew she'd be coddled and fed for as long as it took for her to get back on her feet. If she ever did.

The anger had seeped out and the tears were finally ready to fall.

"Oh, Ma. How could he have done this to me?"

Rissa looked to her mother for an answer, the tears falling in big, fat drops.

Celia took a step into the room and gently placed the oversized cup on the nightstand before she plopped down beside her daughter.

"I don't like the way he did this any more than you do. But it was the best thing to happen. You know this."

"What I know is that I wasted three years of my life. How can I be back here with you and Paul?"

"We love having you, you know that. I miss the noise, the life you kids brought to this house. It will be nice having you here for a time."

She patted her daughter's hand.

"I'm going to have Paul clear out the back landing so you can paint again. The light is good there and I think it's the best spot."

It's where she used to paint when she was younger, the space small but adequate for her needs. And the light spilled in from the double window. She found it difficult to see herself at the spattered table again.

"I haven't painted in ages. I'm not sure..."

"You gave up who you were for him. I never liked that."

Celia's lips curled and her voice held hostility, something Rissa rarely heard from her.

Her eyes shot up to meet her mother's.

"You never said anything."

"It was your mistake to make. I just prayed...a lot."

She thumbed the moisture off her face and a weak laugh broke free.

"It seems your prayers were answered."

"I had always hoped it would be you who broke it off, not him."

Celia clasped her hands and squeezed.

"Marriage today is different than it was when I was your age. Back then, women stayed home, had kids, smothered their own needs. Today women have choices. Jude took them away from you."

"But I wanted kids..."

She pulled Rissa close with an arm around her shoulder, she admitted, "I know. I did, too."

"You know I loved your father."

Rissa went on alert. She nodded and said, "Of course."

Celia hesitated, glanced up, before going on.

"Well, there was a time I resented my life. Five kids in seven years is a lot to take on. Don't doubt that I always loved you with my heart and soul. You know that, right?"

Rissa sat up. What was her mother trying to tell her?

"Your father expected me to live his life. Be home when he got here, have supper waiting, cook, clean, take care of him. I lost myself. It's hard to remember who you are when you're someone's wife and someone's mother. I got restless. I needed something that was mine. But he never encouraged it. I had to fight him when I opened the catering business. And then he was killed and it was up to me to support you all. So, in the end my decision was a good one."

"You're so good at what you do. Cooking is your life."

"No, Rissa. Cooking is a part of who I am. It is not my life. No one single thing should be. I have a good one and it includes you kids, Paul, the Italian Club, my movie nights with my friends."

Rissa stared at her mother. Understanding was beginning to dawn.

"Paul never made you give any of that up."

"No. He wanted me to find those things that made me feel good about myself, and do them without guilt or consequence. It was one of the reasons it was so easy for me to fall in love with him."

Her eyes grew wide and she stammered, "Were you and Paul..."

"Absolutely not. We didn't even look at each other that way for over a year after your father died."

As if to make sure Rissa believed her Celia measured her facial expression before going on. "From where I'm standing today, I know it's important to find a man who values your passions as much as you do. One who doesn't want to mold you into someone you're not but gives you the freedom to be exactly who you are. Jude was not that man, my love."

She let her mother's words permeate her mind, and took them to heart.

"I guess I was trying so hard to be who Jude wanted that I forgot what I wanted, that I was important, too."

"And you are. Very important to a lot of us. I say good riddance to someone who was never right for you. Now you can start being you again."

She hugged her mother tightly, like she had when she was younger.

"Thank you for sharing that. I would never have guessed that you had a hard time with Dad. You kept it hidden well."

"I fell in love with your father when I was sixteen years old. What does a person know at that age? And it was right for me at the time. All I wanted was a family, lots of kids, like my own mother and your father gave me that. Ten years later, I wanted more. I was the one that changed."

"Do you think you would have gotten a divorce if he hadn't died?"

With a measured response, her mother assured her, "No. I would have muddled through, fighting him more often than I'd want but doing what was important to me in spite of it."

She gave her mother a knowing look.

"It takes so much energy to fight all the time."

"When you try to be someone you're not, you waste a lot of energy. Don't hide who you are my love. Let it spill out."

Rissa embraced the woman who had always seemed so wise. "I love you Ma."

"I love you, too, Rissa."

As panic came back to assault her, she asked, in almost a wail, "What am I going to do now?"

"You're going to go to work tomorrow as you always do, putting one foot in front of the other."

"But it's so embarrassing."

"There would have been more shame in marrying the wrong man."

She studied her mother, thought maybe she was right. But it would still be hard going work and telling everyone that the wedding was off, only one-month shy of the event.

She should have called his bluff when he'd postponed it the first time.

Or gotten the message that it was doomed.

Celia placed her hands on either side of Rissa's face and looked her straight in the eye.

"This will always be your home. Take some time to heal and to remember who you are."

"I got a little lost. I'm just not sure how to find myself again."

"I think that will be easy enough. The hard part will be growing into who you can be. And finding someone who can encourage you to get there. And that isn't Jude."

Celia got up to leave.

"I'll be in the kitchen if you need me. Lana will be here when she's finished up with the event."

"I'm sorry you had to leave because of me."

"I'm not. My children have grown and they don't need me as much, which is the way I wanted to raise you. But it's nice every once in a while, to truly be a mother again. You have your family behind you and we'll be there for you, Rissa, whenever you need us."

When she exited the room, Rissa lay down on the narrow bed, curled into a ball, sobbing until there was nothing left except exhausted sleep.